THE
EDGE
OF
ALWAYS

D0964247

THE EDGE OF ALWAYS

J. A. REDMERSKI

FOREVER

NEW YORK   BOSTON

Copyright © 2013 by Jessica Redmerski
Excerpt from *The Edge of Never* copyright © 2012 by Jessica Redmerski

Forever
Hachette Book Group
237 Park Avenue
New York, NY 10017

www.HachetteBookGroup.com

Printed in the United States of America

RRD-C

Originally published as an ebook
First trade paperback edition: January 2014
10 9 8 7 6 5 4 3 2 1

Forever is an imprint of Grand Central Publishing.
The Forever name and logo are trademarks of Hachette Book Group, Inc.

The Hachette Speakers Bureau provides a wide range of authors for speaking events. To find out more, go to www.hachettespeakersbureau.com or call (866) 376-6591.

The publisher is not responsible for websites (or their content) that are not owned by the publisher.

Library of Congress Cataloging-in-Publication Data

Redmerski, J. A.
    The edge of always / J.A. Redmerski. — First trade edition.
        pages   cm
    ISBN 978-1-4555-4900-9 (pbk.) — ISBN 978-1-4789-2643-6 (audiobook) — ISBN 978-1-4789-7935-7 (audio download)
    I. Title.
    PS3618.E4344E34 2014
    813'.6—dc23
                                                              2013030544

For anyone who has ever had a moment of weakness.
It won't be painful forever, so don't let it get the best of you.

Andrew

ONE

$\mathcal{A}$ few months ago, when I was laid up in that hospital bed, I didn't think I'd be alive today much less be expecting a baby and engaged to an angel with a dirty mouth. But here I am. Here *we* are, Camryn and me, taking on the world...in a different way. Things didn't quite turn out how we planned them, but then again, things rarely do. And neither of us would change the way they turned out even if we could.

I love this chair. It was my dad's favorite chair, and the one thing he left behind that I wanted. Sure, I inherited a fat check that will set Camryn and me up for a while, and of course I got the Chevelle, but the chair was equally sentimental to me. She hates it, but she won't say so out loud, because it was my dad's. I can't blame her; it's old, it stinks, and there's a hole in the cushion from my dad's cigarette smoking days. I promised her I'd get someone in here to clean it, at least. And I will. As soon as she figures out whether we're going to stay in Galveston or move to North Carolina. I'm fine with either, but something tells me she's holding back on what she really wants, because of me.

I hear the water from the shower shut off, and seconds later a loud *bang* vibrates through the wall. I jump up from the chair, letting the remote control hit the floor as I rush toward the bathroom. The edge of the coffee table clips the shit outta my shin as I pass.

I swing open the bathroom door. "What happened?"

Camryn shakes her head at me and smiles as she leans over to pick the hair dryer up from the floor beside the toilet.

I breathe a sigh of relief.

"You're more paranoid than I am," she laughs.

She glances down at my leg as I rub it with my fingertips. She sets the hair dryer back on the counter, comes up to me, and kisses the side of my mouth. "Looks like I'm not the one of us who needs to worry about being accident-prone." She smiles.

My hands cup her shoulders and I pull her closer, letting one hand fall down to touch her little rounded belly. I can barely tell she's pregnant. At four months I thought she'd at least be emulating a baby hippo, but what do I know about this stuff?

"Maybe so," I say, trying to hide the red in my face. "You probably did that on purpose just to see how fast I could get in here."

She kisses the other side of my mouth and then goes in for the kill, kissing me fully and deeply while pressing her wet, naked body against mine. I moan against her mouth, wrapping my arms around her.

But then I pull away before I fall into her devious trap. "Dammit, woman, you've gotta stop that."

She grins back at me. "You *really* want me to stop?" she asks with that up-to-no-good smile of hers.

It scares the shit out of me when she does that. Once after a conversation laced with that smile, she stopped having sex with me for three whole days. Worst three days of my life.

"Well, no," I say nervously. "I just mean right now. We have exactly thirty minutes before we have to be at the doctor's office."

I just hope she's this horny throughout her entire pregnancy. I've heard horror stories about how some women go from wanting it all the time until they get really big and then if you touch them they turn into fire-breathing banshees.

Thirty minutes. Damn. I could bend her over the counter real quick…

Camryn smiles sweetly and jerks the towel from the shower curtain rod and starts drying off. "I'll be ready in ten," she says as she waves me out. "Don't forget to water Georgia. Did you find your phone?"

"Not yet," I say as I start to ease my way out the door, but then I stop and add with a sexually suggestive grin, "Ummm, we could—"

She shuts the door in my face. I just walk off laughing.

I rush around the apartment, searching under cushions and in odd places for my keys and finally find them hiding underneath a stack of junk mail on the kitchen counter. I stop for a moment and take a particular piece of mail into my fingers. Camryn won't let me throw it away, because it was the one she looked at when giving the 911 operator my address the morning I had that seizure in front of her. I guess she feels like that piece of paper helped save my life, but really what it did was help her eventually understand what was going on with me. The seizure was harmless. I've had several. Hell, I had one when we were staying in the hotel in New Orleans before we started sharing a room. When I finally told her about that later, needless to say, she was not happy with me.

She worries all the time that the tumor will come back. I think she worries about it more than I do.

If it does, it does. We'll get through it together. We'll always get through everything together.

"Time to go, babe!" I yell from the living room.

She comes out of our room dressed in a rather tight pair of jeans and an equally tight T-shirt. And heels. *Really? Heels?*

"You're going to squeeze her little head in those jeans," I say.

"No, I'm not going to squeeze her *or his* head," she counters as she grabs her purse from the couch and shoulders it. "You're so sure of yourself, but we'll see." She takes my hand and I walk her out the door, flipping the lock on the knob before I close it hard behind us.

"I know it's a girl," I say confidently.

"Care to wager?" She looks over at me and grins.

We step out into the mild November air, and I open the car door for her, gesturing inside with my palm up. "What kind of bet?" I ask. "You know I'm all for betting."

Camryn slides onto the seat, and I jog around to my side and get in. Resting my wrists on the top of the steering wheel, I look over at her and wait.

She smiles and chews gently on the inside of her bottom lip in thought for a moment. Her long blonde hair tumbles down over both shoulders, and her blue eyes shine with excitement.

"You're the one who seems so sure," she finally says. "So, you name the bet and I'll either agree to it or I won't." She stops abruptly and points her finger sternly at me. "But nothing sexual. I think you pretty much have that area covered. Think of something…" she whirls her hand around in front of her "…I don't know…daring or meaningful."

Hmmm. I'm officially stumped. I slide the key in the ignition, but pause before turning it.

"OK, if it's a girl, then I get to name her," I say with a soft, proud smile.

Her eyebrows twitch a little and she turns her chin at an angle.

"I don't like that bet. That's something both of us should take part in, don't you think?"

"Well, yeah, but don't you trust me?"

She hesitates. "Yes…I trust you, but—"

"—but not with a baby name." I raise an eyebrow interrogatively at her, but really I'm just messing with her head.

She can't look me in the eyes anymore, and she appears uncomfortable.

"Well?" I urge her.

Camryn crosses her arms and says, "What name did you have in mind, exactly?"

"What makes you think I already have one picked out?" I turn the key and the Chevelle purrs to life.

She smirks at me, cocking her head to one side. "Oh, please. You obviously have one picked out already, or you wouldn't be so sure it's a girl and making bets with me when we have an ultrasound to get to."

I look away, grinning, and put the car into reverse.

"Lily," I say and just barely catch Camryn's eye as we back out of the parking space. "Lily Marybeth Parrish."

A little smile tugs the corners of her lips.

"I actually like that," she says, and her smile gets bigger and bigger. "I admit, I was slightly worried—why Lily?"

"No reason. I just like it."

She doesn't seem convinced. She playfully narrows her eyes at me.

"I'm serious!" I say, laughing gently. "I've been going over names in my head since the day after you told me."

Camryn's smile warms, and if I wasn't such a guy, I'd cave to the moment and allow myself to blush like an idiot.

"You've been thinking of names all this time?" She seems happily surprised.

OK, so I blush anyway.

"Yeah," I admit. "Haven't thought of a good boy name yet, but we've got several months to think about it."

Camryn is just looking at me, beaming. I don't know what's going on inside her head, but I realize my face is getting redder the longer she stares at me like that.

"*What?*" I ask and let out a laugh.

She leans across the seat and raises her hand to my face, her fingertips pulling my chin to the side. And then she kisses me.

"God, I love you," she whispers.

It takes a second to realize I'm grinning so big my face feels stretched out. "I love you, too. Now get your seat belt on." I point to it.

She slides back over onto her side and clicks the seat belt buckle into place.

As we ride toward the doctor's office we both keep glancing at the clock in the dashboard. Eight more minutes. Five. Three. I think it hits her as hard as it does me when we pull into the building's parking lot. In no time at all we may meet our son or daughter for the very first time.

Yeah, a few months ago, I didn't think I'd be alive…

———

"The wait is killing me," Camryn leans over and whispers to me.

This is so strange. Sitting in this doctor's waiting room with pregnant chicks on all sides of us. I'm kind of scared to make eye contact. Some of them look pissed. All of the magazines for guys seem to have a man on the cover in a boat holding up a fish with his thumb in its mouth. I pretend to read an article.

"We've only been sitting here for about ten minutes," I whisper back and run the palm of my hand across her thigh, letting the magazine rest on my lap.

"I know, I'm just nervous."

As I take her hand, a nurse in pink scrubs steps out from a side door and calls Camryn's name, and we follow her back.

I sit against the wall while Camryn undresses and then puts on one of those hospital gowns. I tease her about her butt being on display and she pretends to be offended, but the blush gives her away. And we sit here and wait. And wait some more until another nurse comes in and has our full attention. She washes her hands in the nearby sink.

"Did you drink enough water an hour before your appointment?" the nurse asks after the hellos.

"Yes ma'am," Camryn says.

I can tell she's afraid something might be wrong with the baby and the ultrasound will show it. I've tried to tell her that everything will be fine, but it doesn't keep her from worrying.

She looks across the room at me, and I can't help but get up and move over to her side. The nurse asks a series of questions and snaps on a pair of latex gloves. I help answer the questions that I can, because Camryn seems increasingly more worried every second that goes by and she doesn't talk much. I squeeze her hand, trying to ease her mind.

After the nurse squirts that gel stuff on her belly, Camryn takes a deep breath.

"Wow, that's some tattoo you've got there," the nurse says. "It must've been pretty special to sit through one as large as that on the ribs."

"Yeah, it's definitely special," Camryn says and smiles up at me. "It's of Orpheus. Andrew has the other half. Eurydice. But it's a long story."

I proudly raise my shirt over my ribs to show the nurse my half.

"Stunning," the nurse says, looking at both of our tattoos in turns. "You don't see that in here every day."

The nurse leaves it at that and moves the probe through the gel pointing out the baby's head and elbow and other various parts. And I feel Camryn's grip on my hand slowly ease the more the nurse talks and smiles while explaining how "everything is lookin' good." I watch Camryn's face go from nervous and stiff to relieved and happy, and it makes me smile.

"So are you sure there's nothing to worry about?" Camryn asks. "Are you *positive*?"

The nurse nods and glances at me briefly. "Yes. So far I don't see anything of concern. Development is right where we want it to be. Movement and heartbeat are normal. I think you can relax."

Camryn looks up at me, and I have a feeling we're thinking the same thing.

She confirms it when the nurse says, "So, I understand you're curious about the gender?" And the two of us just pause, looking at one another. She's so damn beautiful. I can't believe she's mine. I can't believe she's carrying my baby.

"I'll take that bet," Camryn finally agrees, catching me off guard. She smiles brightly and tugs on my hand, and we both look at the nurse.

"Yes," Camryn answers. "If that's possible now."

The nurse moves the probe back to a specific area and appears to be giving her findings one last check before she announces it.

"Well, it's still kind of early, but...looks like a girl to me so far," the nurse finally says. "At about twenty weeks during your next ultrasound, we'll be able to determine the sex officially."

Camryn

TWO

I honestly don't think I've ever seen Andrew smile like that before. Maybe that night I sang with him the first time in New Orleans and he was so proud of me, but even still I'm not so sure anything can match his face right now. My heart is pounding against my ribs with excitement, especially over Andrew's reaction. I can tell how much he wanted a little girl, and I swear he's doing everything in his power to keep from tearing up in front of the nurse. Or me, for that matter.

It never mattered to me whether it was a boy or girl. I'm like just about every other expecting mom out there who just wants it to be healthy. Not that our baby's health doesn't take precedence over gender in Andrew's mind, though. I know better than that.

He leans over and kisses me lightly on the lips, his bright green eyes lit up with everything good.

"Lily it is," I say with complete agreement, and I kiss him once more before he pulls away, running my fingers through his short brown hair.

"Pretty name," the nurse says. "But keep a boy name handy, too, just in case." She pulls the probe back and gives us a moment.

Andrew says to the nurse suddenly, "Well, if you don't see a little package of junk already on my kid, it's definitely a girl."

I choke out a small laugh and vaguely roll my eyes as I look at the nurse. What's even funnier is that Andrew was being serious. He cocks his head to one side when he notices the amused look on my face.

We spend the rest of the day shopping. Neither of us could resist it. We've spent some time looking at baby stuff before but never bought much, because we didn't know if it should be pink or blue and we didn't want to end up with a room full of yellow. And even though there's still a chance it could be a boy, I think Andrew is more convinced than before that it's a girl, so I go along with it and let myself believe it, too. But he still won't let me buy much!

"Just wait," he insists when I go for the next girlie outfit in the newborn section. "You know my mom's planning a baby shower, right?"

"Yeah, but we can get a few more things now." I put the outfit in the cart anyway.

Andrew looks into the cart and then back at me with his lips pursed in contemplation. "I think you've surpassed a *few*, babe."

He's right. I've tossed about ninety dollars' worth of clothes in the basket already. Oh well, if anything, if it turns out to be a boy I can exchange it all later.

And that's how the rest of the day goes until we stop by his mother's house to give her the news.

"Oh, that's wonderful!" Marna says, pulling me into a hug. "I thought for sure it'd be a boy!"

My hands slide away from Marna's arms, and I sit at the kitchen table with Andrew while Marna heads to the fridge. She pulls out a tea pitcher and starts preparing us a glass.

"Baby shower will be in February," Marna says from the bar.

"I've already got everything planned out. All you have to do is show up." She beams at me and puts the tea pitcher away.

"Thank you," I say.

She sets a glass down in front of each of us and then pulls out the empty chair.

I really do miss home. But I love it here, too, and Marna is like another mom to me. I haven't been able to bring myself to tell Andrew yet about how much I miss *my* mom and Natalie, just having a friend to talk to. You can be in love with the greatest guy on the planet—and in fact, I am—but it doesn't mean it won't be somewhat difficult not having other friends. I've met one girl my age here, Alana, who lives upstairs with her husband, but I just haven't been able to click with her on any kind of level. I think if I'm already making up lies to keep from going somewhere with her when she calls, then clicking with her at all might never happen.

But I really think my secret sadness and missing home and all that is because of the pregnancy. My hormones are all out of whack. And I think it also has a lot to do with worrying. I worry about everything now. I mean, I did a lot of that before I met Andrew, but now that I'm pregnant, my worries have multiplied: Will the baby be healthy? Will I be a good mother? Did I screw up my life by... I'm doing it again. Fuck. I'm a horrible person. Every time that thought crosses my mind it makes me feel so guilty. I love our baby and I wouldn't change the way things are if I could, but I can't help but wonder if I... if *we* messed up by getting pregnant too soon.

"Camryn?" I hear Andrew's voice and I snap out of my deep thoughts. "Are you all right?"

I force a believable smile. "Yeah, I'm good. Was just daydreaming—y'know, I prefer purple over pink."

"I got to name her," Andrew says, "so you can choose whatever colors you want." He encloses my hand underneath his on the table. It makes me smile just to know that he cares about any of this stuff at all.

Marna pulls her glass away from her lips and sets it on the table in front of her.

"Oh?" she asks intrigued. "You've already picked out a name?"

Andrew nods. "Lily Marybeth. Camryn's middle name is Marybeth. She should be named after her mom."

Oh my God, he just melted my heart. I don't deserve him.

Marna smiles over at me, her face full of happiness and every other emotion imaginable that someone like Andrew's mother could possess. Not only did her son beat his illness and come back strong from the brink of death, but now she has a granddaughter on the way.

"Well, it's a beautiful name," she says. "I thought Aidan and Michelle would be first, but life's full of surprises." Something about the way she said that seemed to have a hidden meaning and Andrew notices.

"Something going on with Aidan and Michelle?" Andrew asks, taking a quick sip of his tea.

"Just part of being married," she answers. "I've never seen a marriage without *some* kind of struggles, and they've been together for a long time."

"How long?" I ask.

"Married only five years," Marna says. "But they've been together for about nine, I believe." She nods as she thinks about it further, satisfied with her memory.

"It's probably just Aidan," Andrew says. "I wouldn't wanna be married to him." He laughs.

"Yeah, that would be weird," I say, wrinkling my nose at him.

"Well, Michelle won't be able to make the baby shower," Marna says. "She has a few conferences she has to attend, and it just doesn't fit with her schedule, especially since she's so far away. But she'll probably send the best gifts out of everyone." She smiles sweetly over at me.

I acknowledge her and take another sip, but my mind is wandering again and I can't stop it. All I can think about is what she said a few comments back, about never knowing of a marriage without struggles. And I slip right back into worry mode.

"Your birthday is December the eighth, right, Camryn?"

I blink back into the moment. "Oh...yes. The big twenty-one."

"Well, looks like I have a birthday party to plan, too, then."

"Oh, no, you don't need to do that."

She waves away my plea as if it's ridiculous, and Andrew just sits back with that dopey grin on his face.

I give in because I know with Marna there's no use trying.

We head home after an hour, and it's already dark out. I'm so tired from running around all day and from the Lily excitement.

Lily. I can't believe I'm going to be a mom. A smile spreads across my face as I step into the living room. I drop my purse on the coffee table and plop down on the center cushion of the couch, kicking my shoes off. But before too long, Andrew is sitting down next to me with that knowing look on his beautiful face.

I could fool Marna, but I should've known better than to think I could fool him.

Andrew

THREE

I lift Camryn into my arms and pull her onto my lap. We sit here together, my arms wrapped around her and my chin nestled into the crook of her neck. I know something's bothering her. I can feel it, but a part of me is afraid to ask.

"What is it?" I ask anyway and hold my breath.

She turns to look me in the eyes, and they're consumed with worry. "I'm just afraid."

"What are you afraid of?"

She pauses, letting her gaze fall about the room until resting directly out in front of her. "Everything," she says.

I reach up and turn her chin back toward me. "You can tell me anything, Camryn. You know that, right?"

Her blue eyes fill with tears, but she doesn't let them fall.

"I...well I don't want us to end up like...well like a lot of people."

Oh, I know where this is going. I grab her by the waist and turn her body around so that she's facing me, straddling my lap.

"Look at me," I say, taking both of her hands. "We're not going to end up like everybody else. You want to know how I know?"

She doesn't respond, but she doesn't need to. I know she wants me to go on. A tear escapes one eye, and I reach up and wipe it away with the pad of my thumb.

"We won't because we're both conscious of it," I begin. "Because it was fate that we met on that bus in Kansas, and because we both know what we want out of life. We may not have the details mapped out—and we don't need to—but we both know which direction we *don't* want to go."

I stop and then say, "We can still travel the world. We just have to put it off for a while longer. And in the meantime, we live our lives the way we want to. None of that daily monotonous bullshit."

I get a tiny smile out of her.

"Well, how do we avoid that exactly?" she asks, crossing her arms and smirking down at me.

Now there's the playful smartass Camryn I know and love.

I rub my hands up and down her thighs briskly and then say, "If you want to work, you can work. I don't care if you want to flip burgers or shovel shit at the zoo, do whatever you want. But the second you get tired of it or feel like it's becoming your life, walk the fuck away. And if you'd rather sit back and do nothing, you can do that too, like I've told you before. You know I'll take care of you no matter what."

I know what's coming next, so I brace for it. And sure enough Camryn snarls at me and argues, "No way in hell will I sit back on my ass and let you take care of me."

She's so hot when she's bein' all independent.

"Well that's fine. Whatever," I say, raising my hands up in surrender. "But I want you to understand that I don't care what you do as long as you're happy doing it."

"And what about you, Andrew? You can't just tell me not to

worry about 'the monotony of life' while you take it on headfirst just because we have a baby to support. That's not fair."

"That's sort of what you said that first night I buried my head between your thighs. Did I have a problem with it then?"

She blushes hard. Even after all this time and all that we've been through together, I still manage to make her blush.

I lean up and cup her face within my hands and pull her into a kiss.

"As long as I have you, Lily, and my music, I don't need anything else."

Another tear streams down her soft cheek, but this time she's smiling underneath it. "You promise?" she asks.

"Yes, I promise," I say with determination, squeezing her hands within mine. I let the seriousness fade from my face and smile at her again.

"I'm sorry," she says, letting out a defeated breath. "I don't know what's wrong with me lately. One day I'm all smiles and perfectly fine and then it's like, out of nowhere, I'm doom-and-gloom pathetic."

I laugh a little under my breath. "Bitch-slapped by mood swings. Get used to it."

Her mouth falls open slightly, and she laughs too. "Well, I guess that's one way of putting it."

She stops abruptly. "Do you hear that?" Her eyes narrow as she pushes her ear toward the source of the sound that I hear, but pretend not to.

"Oh great," I say. "Don't tell me that pregnancy causes schizophrenia, too."

She smacks me gently on the chest and climbs off my lap. "No, it's your cell phone," she says, walking around to the back of the couch. "I thought the battery was dead."

No . . . I just turned the ringer off and hid it to make you think that. At least I thought I turned it off.

"I think you're sitting on your phone," she says.

I stand up and play stupid, rummaging around underneath the cushion. Finally, I pull it out to see Natalie's picture (technically, it's a picture of a hyena that I thought represented her best) looking back at us from the screen. Dammit. This is going to be awkward.

Camryn reaches out for it when she notices Natalie's name.

"Since when did Natalie start calling you?" she asks, snatching it from my hand.

Yes, definitely awkward because she doesn't look the slightest bit jealous. She's grinning!

I reach up and nervously scratch the back of my head, avoiding eye contact, but then I try to take it back from her.

"Oh, no way in hell," she laughs, stepping away from the couch. "Come on, give me the phone."

She taunts me with it as I leap over the back of the couch to go after her.

She thrusts her empty hand out at me. "Be careful! I'm pregnant and you might hurt me!" She smirks.

Oh now she plays the I'm-too-fragile card. So evil.

She runs her finger over the Answer bar and puts the phone to her ear, grinning the whole time.

I just give up. I suck at this stuff.

"Well, hello Natalie," Camryn says, her playful gaze never moving from me. "Have you been seeing my man behind my back?"

She shakes her head at whatever Natalie's answer is. It's obvious

Camryn knows what's going on, or at least has a pretty good idea, because she knows I'd never cheat on her, especially not with her best friend. The girl is pretty but, yeah, she's like a reality TV train wreck.

Camryn puts her on speakerphone. "Out with it, both of you," she demands.

"Ummm...uhhh...," Natalie manages on the other end.

"For the first time ever, Natalie has nothing to say. I'm shocked!" Camryn looks to me for the answers.

"Sorry, Andrew!" Natalie shouts.

"Not your fault," I say. "I left the ringer on."

Camryn clears her throat impatiently.

"It was going to be a surprise," I say, frowning.

"Yeah! I swear he's not doing me!"

I outwardly cringe at Natalie's comment and Camryn tries her damnedest to hold back her laughter. But being Camryn, she won't pass up any opportunity to torture those she loves, though with the most innocent of intentions.

"I don't believe you, Nat," she says gravelly.

"Huh?" Natalie sounds completely stunned.

"How long has it been going on?" Camryn continues, putting on a convincing show. She walks around and sets the phone down on the coffee table and then crosses her arms.

"Cam...I swear to *God* it's nothing like that. Oh my God, I would never, ever, *ever* do something like that to you. I mean Andrew is smokin' hot, yeah, I totally admit that, and I would probably be on him like sexy on Joseph Morgan if you two weren't together, but—"

"I get it, Nat." Camryn stops her—thankfully—before she goes off on what Camryn calls a Natalie Tangent.

"You do?" Natalie asks carefully, still confused, which doesn't surprise me.

Camryn picks the phone up again and holds the screen up to me and mouths the words: *Seriously?* Apparently about the picture of the hyena.

I shrug.

"So, what's really going on?" Camryn says to both of us, setting the jokes aside.

"Camryn," I say, walking toward her, "I know you're missing home. I've known for a while, so a couple weeks ago I got Natalie's number from your phone and decided to give her a call."

Camryn narrows her eyes. I guide her to sit back down on the couch with me.

"Yeah, he called me up and told me your ultrasound date and thought I might want to..." Natalie's voices trails, waiting on me to be the one to spill the surprise.

"I figured she would want to organize a baby shower for you when we found out if it was a boy or a girl—I tried calling your mom first, but she must've still been in Cozumel."

Camryn nods. "Yeah, she likely was around that time."

"But your mom is totally onboard now," Natalie's voice streams through the tiny speaker. "She and I were kind of planning it together behind your back. I couldn't wait any longer for your boy toy to call me with the news today, so I called him and now you know everything and the surprise is ruined!"

"No, no, Nat, it's not ruined at all," Camryn says, picking the phone up and holding it closer to her mouth as she leans her back into the couch. "It's actually better that I know now, because I can be excited from now until then knowing I'm heading back to North Carolina soon."

"Well you won't have to wait long," I say beside her, "because we're leaving Friday afternoon."

Camryn's eyes widen and so does her smile.

I think this is just what she needed. It's like a happy girl just crawled her way to the surface of a homesick one in two seconds flat. I love to see her like this. I should've done it sooner.

"Four months is kind of early for a baby shower, though," Camryn says. "*Not* that I'm complaining!"

"Maybe so," Natalie says. "But who cares? You're coming home!"

I say, "Yeah, we figured why not knock out two birds with one stone?"

"Well, I'm excited. Thank you both," Camryn says, beaming.

"So . . . what's the big news?" Natalie asks.

Camryn holds it in for a few long, torturous seconds, knowing it's driving Natalie batshit, and then she says, "It's a girl!"

Natalie squeals so loud through the phone I wince and recoil.

"I knew it!" she shrieks.

Normally this would be reason enough for me to remove myself from the slumber party atmosphere and go make a sandwich or take a shower or something, but I can't get myself off the hook so soon on this one. I was part of the "big secret," and so I guess I should stick out the rest of the conversation.

"I'm so excited, Cam. Really, you have no idea."

"Actually, uhh, yeah she has a pretty good idea," I say.

Camryn looks at me warningly.

"Thank you, Nat. I'm excited, too. And we've already decided on a name. Well, technically Andrew chose the name."

"What?" Natalie says in a deadpanned tone. "You mean like he actually . . . picked it out?" She says this as if it's something very dangerous.

What, do all women think guys suck at names, or some shit?

"Lily Marybeth Parrish," Camryn says proudly.

It makes me feel that much better that my girl really seems to love the name as much as I do and isn't just pretending to keep from hurting my feelings.

"Oh my God, I actually like that, Cam. Andrew, you did good!"

Not that I needed the Natalie stamp of approval, but it still makes me grin like a little boy that even *she* likes it.

Camryn

FOUR

*Y*esterday was an exhausting day. In a good way. Good news seemed to come from everywhere, and I'm still reeling about it all. It'll only make tonight at our favorite bar in Houston that much more exciting.

Andrew and I started playing a few bars here and there a little over a month ago, and I love it. Before Andrew, I never in my life imagined playing live in bars. Playing live anywhere, for that matter. It's not something that crossed my mind even once. But the taste I got for it back in New Orleans opened up a new world to me. Of course, Andrew being there with me played a huge part in my enjoyment of it and that still holds true today. I doubt I could keep doing this if it weren't for him.

Performing isn't what I enjoy the most; performing with *him* is what makes me love it.

I talk to my mom for a while about coming home in a couple of days, and she's so excited to see me. She and Roger got hitched in Mexico! It kind of ticked me off because I didn't get to be there, but now that I think about it more it doesn't bother me. They were being spontaneous. They did what they felt they wanted to do in their hearts and just went for it. I've learned during my time with Andrew that being spontaneous and breaking free from the mold is often a good thing. After all, we wouldn't be together today if I myself didn't have some firsthand experience with being spontaneous.

As far as our own wedding date, well, we haven't set one. We talked about it one night and agreed that we will get married when and wherever it feels right. No dates. No planning. No five-thousand-dollar dress that I'll only wear once. No matching the flowers with the décor. No best man or maids of honor. All of that stuff stresses both of us out just thinking about it.

We'll get married when we're ready, and we both know that the wait has nothing to do with not being sure. It's what we both want, there's no mistaking that.

I hear Andrew rustling the keys in the apartment door and I meet him there. I jump up, wrapping my legs tight around his waist, and kiss him fully on the mouth. He slams the door shut with his foot and wraps his arms around me, keeping his lips locked with mine.

"What was that for?" he asks, pulling away.

"I'm just excited."

His dimples deepen.

I hold on to him with my arms draped around his neck as he carries me through the living room and into the kitchen.

"I wish I would've taken you home sooner," he says, setting me on top of the bar. He stands between my suspended legs and tosses his keys on the counter.

"None of that guilty stuff," I say, pecking him once on the lips. "I'll miss Texas if I stay in North Carolina too long, I'm sure."

He smiles but doesn't seem convinced of that.

"You don't have to make a decision now," he says, "but I do want you to decide where we're going to live, and I don't want you picking Texas because of me. I love my mom, but I won't be as homesick as you."

"What makes you think that?"

"Because I've lived on my own for a while," he says. "You never got the chance to do that before you left Raleigh."

He grins, stepping back subtly, and adds, "Besides, you're all hormonal and crazy and shit, so I'll gladly do whatever you say and you won't get any arguments from me."

I playfully kick my leg out at him, but miss him on purpose.

He leans in between my legs, lifts the end of my shirt, and then presses his warm lips against my belly.

"What about Billy Frank?" I ask as he lifts upright. "If you leave him again he might never hire you back."

Andrew laughs and makes his way around the bar and toward the cabinets. I swing around on the top of the bar to face him, hanging my legs over the opposite side.

"Billy Frank has been my boss off and on since I was sixteen," he says, taking down a box of cereal. "We're more like family, so it's not your average mechanic job. I need him more than he needs me."

"Why do you still do it?" I ask.

"What, work under a hood?"

I nod.

He pours milk over the cereal he just made and puts it back in the fridge. "I like working on cars," he says and then takes a monstrous bite. With his mouth full, he goes on, "Kind of like a hobby, I guess. And besides, I like to keep the money flowing in the bank."

I feel a little small, not having a job yet. He senses it, like he seems to sense just about everything. He swallows the food and points his spoon at me. "Don't do that."

I just look at him curiously, pretending not to know about how easily he caught on.

He sits on the bar stool next to me, propping his shoes on the spindles below.

"You do realize you work, right?" he asks, looking at me in a sidelong manner. "Last week we raked in four hundred bucks the night we played at Levy's. Four hundred in one night ain't too shabby."

"I know," I say. "It just doesn't feel like a job."

He laughs lightly, shaking his head. "It doesn't feel like a job because you happen to enjoy it. And because you're not punching a clock."

He has a point, but I wasn't quite finished explaining. "If we were constantly on the road, didn't have rent and utilities and a baby on the way, it would be different." I take a sharp breath and just get to the point. "I want to get a hobby job. Like you."

He nods. "Awesome," he says and takes another bite, all the while sitting casually with his arms resting on the bar around his bowl. "What would you like to do?" He points at me. "Note the important keyword in that question: *like*."

I think on it a moment, pursing my lips in contemplation.

"Well, I like to clean, so maybe I could get a job at a hotel," I begin. "Or it might be nice to work at Starbucks or something."

He shakes his head. "I doubt you'll like cleaning rooms," he says. "My mom used to do that before my dad started his business. People leave nasty shit in those rooms."

I cringe. "Well, I'll figure something out. As soon as we get to Raleigh, I'll look for a job."

Andrew's spoon pauses just above his bowl. "So your decision is to move back home, then?"

Andrew

FIVE

I didn't mean to cause her face to go all stiff like that. I move my bowl out of the way and pull her toward me, sliding her across the bar top. I rest my arms across the tops of her bare legs and look at her with the most sincere smile.

"I'm really OK with it, babe."

"Are you sure?"

"Yes. Definitely." I lean over and kiss the top of her left thigh and then the other. "We'll go for the baby shower this weekend, come back here and start packing."

She grabs my hands. "But after we move, we'll definitely have to come back here in February for the shower your mom is planning."

My smile widens. "Sounds like a plan," I say, not surprised, though, that she's taking my mom's feelings into consideration, too. "So then it's settled. Raleigh will be our new home. At least until we get tired of it."

Camryn, happier now than she was when she first greeted me at the door, reaches out and grabs me around the neck. I stand up and lift her back into my arms, her cute butt propped in my hands.

"Sorry about the cereal," she says.

"Huh?"

She lowers her eyes, embarrassed. "I bet when you dreamed

about being married you pictured your wife cooking man-meals that'd make Gordon Ramsay's toes curl."

I throw my head back and laugh.

"No, I never really thought about stuff like that," I say, our faces just inches apart. "Now the toe-curling stuff, trust me, you've got that down pat."

She squeezes her thighs around my waist, her face getting redder. I kiss her on the nose and then look into her beautiful blue eyes. I close my eyes and feel the minty warmth of her breath close in on me. Her tongue gently touches my bottom lip, urging my mouth to part for hers. I give in so easily, touching the edge of her tongue to mine before I kiss her forcefully, squeezing her body in my arms. I carry her off to our bedroom, never breaking the kiss, and I have my way with her for the next hour before we head out to Houston to play.

———

We arrive at the airport in North Carolina midday Friday, and already I see the spark in Camryn's eyes. It's only her second time back here in four months. We get our bags and head outside in the sunshine to find Natalie and Blake waiting to pick us up. And just like the first time I met her, I brace myself to stand face-to-face with Camryn's hyena of a best friend.

"I missed you so much, Cam!" Natalie engulfs her in a hug.

Blake—I might start calling him Blondie for the hell of it— stands tall behind Natalie with his hands buried deep in his pockets, his shoulders slumped over, and a big goofy smile on his tanned face. I can tell which one of those two is the master of their domain. That guy is whipped hardcore. I laugh it off inside. More power to him. Hell, I can't say anything...

"Andrew!" Natalie moves toward me next, and I put up my invisible crazy shield as I return her unsolicited hug.

OK, the truth is I don't like Natalie much. I don't hate her, but she's the kind of girl I wouldn't think twice about talking to without Camryn being in the mix. And what she did to Camryn before Camryn got on that bus left a bad fucking taste in my mouth. I'm all for forgiveness, but just that Natalie could do something like that to begin with is cause for caution around her all of the time. It was hard for me to take it upon myself to call her up that day two weeks ago and tell her about Camryn's ultrasound date and all that. But I was doing it for Camryn, and that's all that matters to me.

"Good to see you again, Blake," Camryn says, pulling him into a friendly hug.

I know everything about Blake, too, about how he was interested in Camryn first before later hooking up with Natalie. And regardless of his attraction to Camryn before we met, he's all right in my book.

He and I shake hands.

"Oh my God, let me see!" Natalie says. She lifts up Camryn's shirt, places both hands carefully over her stomach, and beams up at her. A tiny squeal-like sound reverberates through Natalie's throat, and I find myself wondering how a human body can make such noises.

"I can be Aunt Natalie, or Godmother Natalie!"

Ummm, how about no?

Camryn's smiling head nods rapidly, and I just make sure I'm not putting off any negative energy that she can detect. The last thing I want to do is ruin this homecoming for her by letting her know I tolerate her best friend only for her sake.

Camryn

SIX

The baby shower my mom and Natalie threw turned out great. I ended up with a brand-new baby bed, a walker, a swing, a high chair, two baby bathtubs—one pink and one blue, just in case—about 984 diapers—well, it seems like a lot of diapers—multiple bottles of baby shampoo and powder, and something called Anti Monkey Butt and Butt Paste, which is really disturbing, and...I can't remember all of this stuff and some of it I have absolutely no idea what it is.

After a while of sitting in the room surrounded by everyone, I start to feel overwhelmed, but I'm ready to tone this get-together down and soak in a long, hot bath.

Two more hours drag by and everyone has left except for Natalie, who finds me soaking in that much-needed bath, surrounded by frothy bubbles.

"Cam?" I hear Natalie's voice on the other side of the bathroom door. She knocks softly a few times.

"Come on in," I say.

The door creeps open and Natalie peeks around the side. Wouldn't be the first time she saw me naked.

She sits on the closed toilet lid.

"Well, it's official," she says, grinning down at me, "pregnancy does make the boobs bigger."

As always, she's exaggerating.

I raise my hand from the water and flick droplets at her.

"Are you feeling all right?" she asks, toning down the jokes. "You look exhausted."

"I'm pregnant," I say flatly.

"True, but Cam, you look like shit."

"Thanks." I reach back, readjust the clip I put in my hair to keep it from getting wet, then relax my arm along the side of the tub.

"Well, aren't you supposed to be glowing? That's what they say pregnant women do."

I shrug and shake my head against the back of the tub.

A dull wave of pain moves through my lower back and passes as quickly as it came. I grimace and readjust my body.

"Are you sure you're all right?" She looks more concerned than she needs to.

"Aches and pains. Nothing to worry about. It's only going to get worse from here on out, I imagine. Aches and pains, that is." I don't know why I felt compelled to clear that last part up, except that I wanted to make sure she knew I didn't mean it any other way.

"Still no morning sickness?" she asks. "I'd take a little back pain over puking my guts up, any day."

"Nope," I say. "But let's not jinx it, Nat."

I admit, if it were actually a choice, I'd choose pain over puke, too. And so far it looks like that's what I'm getting. I guess I've been one of the lucky ones who the morning sickness passes right over. And I don't have any weird cravings, either. So, either I'm a freak of nature, or all that talk about pickles and ice cream is just a load of crap.

I get out of the tub and wrap a towel around my body before hugging Natalie good-bye.

Then I lie across my bed, remembering how comfortable it was. But I don't miss this room so much, or feel any sense of longing to get back into my old life. No. The "old life" I still want to avoid, and this is the number one reason I've been so divided about whether to come home or not. I've missed my mom and Natalie, and I admit that I've just missed North Carolina in general. But I don't miss it in the way that makes me want to end right back up here doing the same things I was doing before. I ran away from that lifestyle for a reason, and I'm not about to run right back to it.

Instead of going out with Natalie and Blake later in the evening, I decide to stay here and go to bed early. I feel overly exhausted, as if my body is being drained of energy faster than normal, and the back pain hasn't really subsided at all, either. It has been coming and going for the past few hours.

Andrew crawls into the bed with me and lies on his side, his head propped on his knuckles. "I feel like I'm doing something I shouldn't, being up here in your childhood room with you like this." He grins.

I smile slimly and bury my body deeper underneath the blanket. It's only a little chilly outside, but I'm freezing. I pull the blanket up to my chin, curling my fingers tight around the fuzzy fabric.

"If my dad was here," I say, chuckling, "you'd be in Cole's room."

He moves closer to me and drapes his arm over my waist. At first it seems like he's about to take full advantage of the fact that we're finally alone, but his expression hardens and he moves his arm from my waist and runs his fingers through the top of my hair.

"OK, you're starting to worry me," he says. "You've been acting strange since I got back here with Blake. What's going on?"

I pull my body closer toward his and say, "You and Natalie both, I swear." I gaze at him across the few inches of space between our faces.

"Oh, so then she noticed, too?" he asks.

I nod. "Just some back pain and generally feeling like shit, but you two fail to remember my predicament."

He barely smiles back at me. "Maybe you should go to the doctor and get checked out."

I shake my head gently. "I'm not going to be one of those paranoid people who run to the hospital for every little thing. I was at the doctor's office just last week. Everything's fine. Even she said so." I lean toward him and kiss him softly on the lips and smile a little more, hoping to ease his mind.

He smiles back and moves the blanket from around my body so he can curl up next to me. I lift up and lie on my other side so that my back is facing him, and he presses his warm body against mine, wrapping his arm around me from behind. He's so warm that I melt into him, knowing it'll only be minutes before I'm fast asleep. I feel his breath on my neck as he kisses me there. I close my eyes and take him in, his natural scent that I always crave, the hardness of his arms and legs, the heat coming from his skin. I honestly doubt I'll ever be able to fall asleep without him next to me again.

"If it gets worse," he says in a quiet voice behind me, "you better tell me. I don't want you to also be one of those stubborn people who doesn't get checked out when they know something could be wrong."

I turn my head slightly in his direction, looking faintly amused.

"Oh, you mean like someone I know who refused to see a doctor for eight months because he was so sure his brain tumor was inoperable?"

He sighs and I feel the heat from his breath on my shoulder. My intention was to get a laugh out of him, but apparently he doesn't find it funny.

"Just promise me," he says and squeezes me gently with his arm. "Any more pain or anything weird, you'll tell me and we'll go to the hospital."

I give in, not because I want to appease him but because he's right. I've never been pregnant before, so I know as much about what is normal and what isn't as any other first-time mom-to-be.

SEVEN

*I*t's Sunday afternoon, and I think all I needed yesterday was a good sleep. I feel a little better today, and the back pain is gone. I get dressed and go ahead and pack my things so everything will be ready when Andrew and I leave later tonight to catch our plane back to Texas. But before we head back, I have a girl's day out to spend with Natalie, and I'm looking forward to it.

"Are you sure you don't mind hanging out with Blake?" I ask as Andrew slips a navy T-shirt down over his abs. He's standing in front of the mirror fixing his hair, if you can call running his fingers through it once fixing it. He never has cared much what it looks like as long as it's not sticking up in places it shouldn't be.

He turns around to face me. "I don't mind. Blake's a pretty cool guy. We're going to head over to some pool hall and shoot a few games for a while." He wraps his arms around my waist. "Don't worry about me. Just have a good time with Natalie."

I laugh lightly. "Y'know, if she finds out about that picture you used for her on your phone, she's going to kill you."

Andrew's grin deepens. "You're very brave, Camryn Bennett." He cups my shoulders within his hands and shakes his head at me dramatically. "I would die under the weight of that girl's personality if I had to spend more than an hour in the same room with her.

Either that or I'd jab my eardrums with a pencil, whichever came first."

I choke out a laugh and press my hands hard against his chest. "You're so mean!"

"Why yes, yes, I am," he says, grinning hugely.

He leans in and presses his lips against my forehead. I do one better and gently grab the front of his shirt and pull him toward me, locking lips with his.

"It's not too late to get it on in here, just so you know." His hooded green eyes scan my face and then my lips before he kisses me again, tugging my bottom lip with his teeth.

"Oh hell yeah it is," I hear Natalie say from the door of my room.

The kiss breaks and we both turn around at the same time to see her standing there with her arms crossed and wearing a lopsided smirk. Her long, dark hair rests over both shoulders. First thing I do is wonder just how much she overheard.

Andrew covertly rolls his eyes at the intrusion. Poor guy. The things he does for me.

Natalie saunters into the room and plops down on the end of my bed. Obviously she didn't hear anything incriminating or else we'd know it by now. She slaps her hands together sharply and says, "Chop! Chop! We're going to get pedicures and manicures and all kinds of cures today."

By the look on Andrew's face, I know he wants so damn bad to call her on that foot-in-her-mouth moment. I glare at him sharply to warn him not to say a word and he just smiles, zipped lips and all.

"Feelin' any better today?" Natalie asks.

I slip my feet down into my Rocket Dog loafers—or as Andrew

calls them, the ugliest shoes he's ever seen—and then start brushing out my hair.

"Yeah, actually I do feel better," I say, looking at her through the reflection in the mirror. "Still a little off, but better than yesterday."

"Do me a favor and keep an eye on her," Andrew says to Natalie. "If she starts complaining of pains or whatever, give me a call, all right?"

Natalie nods. "Sure thing. I mean it wouldn't be the first time the girl ignored a health problem. Last year she lay around for two days moaning and groaning about a toothache—it was *so* annoying—before she finally went to the dentist."

"I'm standing right here," I say, pausing with the brush against my hair.

Natalie waves me off and goes back to Andrew. "I'll call you if she sneezes more than four times in a row."

"Good," Andrew says and then turns back around to me. "You hear that?" he asks sternly. "I've got backup now."

Since when did Andrew become part of the Natalie clique? Just a few seconds ago he was one hundred percent anti-Natalie. I shake my head and go back to my hair, twirling it through my fingers into a braid and snapping a rubber band on the end.

Andrew kisses me and Lily good-bye and heads out to wherever with Blake. And I'm heading out the door with Natalie shortly after, hoping I can get through this day without back pains or anything else that might trigger Natalie to call Andrew and haul my ass off to the nearest emergency room.

We spend some time in our usual Starbucks first and then hit the mall to swing by Bath and Body Works, where Natalie has been working for a month. She introduces me to her manager and the two girls who work with her. I forget their names right after they tell me. Her manager is nice, even told me to come back and fill out an application if I wanted. Natalie jumped right in to explain that I would be heading back to Texas soon, and when I didn't confirm her statement fast enough, Natalie knew I was holding something in and she could hardly stand it. I smiled and thanked her manager, and the next thing I know, Natalie is practically dragging me out of the store and is in my face.

"Spill it!" she says, her eyes bugged out of her head.

I step over to the balcony railing and lean against it. She follows, dropping her purse and one store bag on the floor next to her feet.

I contemplate my answer, because really I'm not sure what to say. I can't say that yes, I'm moving back to Raleigh, because to Natalie that will translate as: *I'm moving back here and everything is going to be exactly the way it was before.* What it really means is that I miss Natalie and my mom, and because Texas and I just weren't right for each other.

The truth suddenly dawns on me as I stare out intently across the mall. All those days I lay around in bed staring up at the ceiling while Andrew was working at the shop with Billy Frank, I kept trying to figure out what the hell was wrong with me, why I've been feeling so homesick yet at the same time not really wanting to come back home. I remember when I first arrived in Texas with Andrew. Hell, I remember while we were on the road together shortly *before* we drove over the Texas state line. I didn't want to go there. I was afraid that everything would end in Texas, that the exciting life I was living with Andrew on the road would become nothing more than a memory once we made it to our final destination.

And in a way…it has…

I swallow a huge lump in my throat and mentally catch my breath.

It's not because of Lily. I love her so much and could never blame her. Because the truth is that life doesn't end with a pregnancy. A lot of people seem to think that, but I believe in my heart that it's all in the way you choose to live it. Sure, having a baby is one of the most difficult things to do, but it's not the end of the world. It doesn't have to be the shattering of a person's dreams. What Andrew and I have been slowly doing without realizing it is what shatters dreams: we've been getting too comfortable. The kind of comfortable that sneaks up on you years later, hits you in the back of the head, and says: *Hey dumbass! Do you realize you've been doing this shit every day for the past ten years?*

I keep my eyes trained out ahead. "I'm not sure what we're doing, Nat," I say and then finally look over at her. "I mean, yes, I'm moving back home, but…"

Her dark eyebrows draw inward with a questioning look. "But what?"

I look away, and when I don't answer her fast enough she says, "Oh, no, don't tell me Andrew's not coming with you. Girl, is something going on with you two?"

I swing back around. "No, Nat, it's nothing like that, and yes, he's definitely coming with me—I don't know. It's just hard to explain."

She purses her lips, lifting one side of her mouth, and takes a hold of my elbow. "We've got all afternoon for you to figure it out, so let's get to the salon and you can be thinking really hard about it on the way." She bends over and takes up her purse and bag, dangling them on her free wrist while walking with me toward the closest mall exit.

We're at the salon in minutes and it's a packed house, which is exactly how I remembered it being on weekends. Natalie and I are perched high in the pedicure chairs with two girls tending to our bare feet. It's been a long time since my last pedicure, so I hope my toes aren't too hideous.

"You know, Cam, you never did tell me why you left." Natalie looks over at me. "Please tell me it wasn't my fault."

"It wasn't anyone's fault in particular," I say. "I just needed to get away for a while. I couldn't breathe."

"Well, I'd never do something *that* reckless, but I admit, the way things turned out was nothing short of amazing."

That makes me smile. "They did, didn't they?"

"Absolutely," she says beaming, her brown eyes lit up. "You ended up with sex on legs"—the girl doing her pedicure glances up briefly—"an engagement ring, and a cute-ass baby on the way." Natalie laughs. "I'm fuckin' jealous!"

I laugh too, though not as loud. "First off, why be jealous of me when you've got Blake? And second, how do you know what our baby will look like?"

Natalie purses her lips and looks over at me like I'm stupid. "Seriously? The two of you couldn't produce an ugly baby." The girl doing my toes rolls her eyes at the other girl. "And I'm not jealous of you because of Andrew, I'm jealous because I'll probably end up like my mom, never seeing much outside of North Carolina. I'm OK with that. I'm not like Miss Greyhound and feel claustrophobic when someone breathes on me too closely, but in a way I do envy you."

I think to myself about what she said, but I don't elaborate on it.

My back is starting to hurt again, and I try readjusting myself on the seat without being able to move my feet much. My side hurts a little, too, but I'm sure it's from all of the walking around today.

"So have you figured it out?" Natalie asks.

"What?"

She blinks, surprised at how easily it seems I forgot our conversation at the mall. I didn't forget at all; I've just been trying to avoid it.

"The truth is," I begin, looking away from her and picturing Andrew in my mind, "I don't want to move back home *or* stay in Texas. I mean I do want to be here, but I'm terrified I'll end up like your mom, too." I never would've used her mom as an example, but it really was the easiest way to make Natalie understand, especially since she just used the same comparison moments ago, so it was a no-brainer.

"Yeah, I totally get you," Natalie says, nodding. "But what else would you do? There's really not much you can do otherwise, especially with a baby on the way."

God, why did she have to say that? I sigh quietly and try not to look at her so she doesn't see the disappointment in my face. Natalie is my best friend, but I've always known she'll be one of those people who live out their entire lives in a colorless bubble and only wake up to regret it when it's too late to change it. She just proved it with her comment about how having a baby pretty much means the end of the line as far as a fun, fulfilling kind of life is concerned. And because she'll never understand, I don't respond to that, either.

"Cam? You sure you're OK?"

I catch my breath and look over at her. Another sharp pain moves through my side and suddenly I feel like I'm starting to break out in a mild sweat. Without regard to the girl doing my pedicure, I pull my foot away from her hands and grab the arms of the chair to lift myself out of it.

"I need to go to the restroom."

"Camryn?"

"I'm alright, Nat," I say, stepping down from the chair. "Sorry," I say to the girl, and I make my way past her and head toward the short hallway underneath the restroom sign. I try not to look like I'm in pain on the way because I don't want Natalie following me, but knowing her she will, anyway.

Placing my hand on the stall door, I swing it open and lock myself inside, finally able to show my true level of discomfort. Tiny beads of sweat cover my forehead and the area underneath my nostrils. Something's definitely not right. This may be my first time ever experiencing a pregnancy, but I can still tell that what I'm feeling right now isn't normal. I use the restroom quickly, head out of the tiny stall that's only adding to the discomfort, and move over to the elongated sink.

This can't be happening…

My hands are shaking uncontrollably. No, my whole body is shaking. I raise my hand to the automatic soap dispenser and wash my hands but I never get the chance to dry them off before what is going on hits me full force. I break down in a blubbering mess, pressing my hands against the edge of the counter. The physical pain is gone for now, but…maybe I'm just being paranoid. Yeah, that's all it is. Paranoia. The pain is gone, so surely I'm all right.

I take a deep breath and then several more before raising my head from between my slouching shoulders and look at myself in the mirror. I lift one wet hand and wipe the sweat from my face and the leftover tears from my cheeks. I even feel better long enough to be grossed out when I realize I'm standing in a public restroom with bare feet.

The entrance door swings open and Natalie marches inside.

"Seriously, are you OK? No, I take that back, obviously you're not, so what's going on? I'm calling Andrew. Right now." She starts to leave the restroom and go back into the front where her phone is, but I stop her.

"Nat, no, just wait."

"Screw that," she says. "I'm calling him in exactly sixty seconds, so you have less than that now to explain."

I give in because as much as I wanted to let myself believe I'm OK, deep down I know I'm not. Especially after what I saw before I left the stall.

"I've been having back and side pain and I'm spotting."

"Spotting?" She makes a slight disgusted face, but masks it well and is clearly more worried than disgusted. "You mean like... blood?" She looks at me in a suspicious sidelong glance and then holds it there until I answer.

"Yes."

Without another word, the bathroom door swings shut behind her and she's gone.

Now, there comes a time in a person's life when you have to face something so horrible that you feel like you'll never be the same person again. It's like something dark swoops down from somewhere above and steals every shred of happiness you have ever felt and all you can do is watch it, *feel* it go, knowing that no matter what you do in your life that you'll never be able to get it back. Everybody goes through this at least once. No one is immune. But what I fail to understand is how one person can go through it enough for five people and in such a short time.

———

I'm lying in an emergency room hospital bed curled up within a blanket. Natalie sits on the chair to my left. I can't speak. I'm too scared.

"What the fuck is taking them so long?" Natalie says about the doctors. She stands up and begins to pace the room, her tall heels clicking softly against the bright white tile floor.

Then she changes her tune.

She stops and looks at me and says with a hopeful face, "Maybe since they're taking their sweet time about checking you out, they don't think it's anything to worry about."

I don't believe that, but I can't bring myself to say it out loud. This is only the second time I've ever been to an ER. My first time, when I nearly drowned after jumping off bluffs into the lake, it seemed I was in there for six hours. And that was mostly just to stitch up the gash I got on my hip from when I hit the rocks.

I roll over and lie on my side and stare at the wall. Just seconds after, the sliding glass door opens. I think it's finally a doctor, but my heart skips a few beats when Andrew comes into the room. He and Natalie exchange a few low words that I pretend not to hear.

"They haven't even been in here yet except to ask her a few questions and to give her a blanket."

Andrew's eyes fall on mine briefly, and I see the worry in his face even though he's trying really hard not to be so obvious. He knows what's happening as much as I do, but also like me, he's not going to say it or let himself believe it until a doctor confirms it first.

They talk for a few seconds more and then Natalie comes over to the side of the bed and leans over to hug me.

"Only one person allowed in here with you at a time," she says as she pulls away. "I'm going to sit out in the waiting area with Blake." She forces a smile at me. "You'll be alright. And if they don't hurry up and do something, I'm going to raise some hell up in this bitch."

I smile a little, too, thankful for Natalie's ability to make that happen even in my darkest hour.

She stops at the door and whispers to Andrew, "Please let me know as soon as you do," and then she slips out of the room, closing the glass door behind her.

My heart sinks when Andrew looks at me again, because this time I have his full attention. He pulls the empty chair over and sets it down next to my bed. He takes my hand and squeezes it gently.

"I know you feel like shit," he says, "so I'm not going to ask."

I try to smile, but I can't.

We just look at each other for a while. It's like we know what the doctor will say. Neither one of us are allowing ourselves to believe that maybe, just maybe, things will be OK. Because they won't be. But Andrew, doing everything he can to comfort me, won't allow himself to cry or to appear too concerned. But I know that he's wearing a mask for my sake. I know his heart is hurting.

Before long, a doctor comes in with a nurse and in some strange, dreamlike state I eventually hear him say that there is no heartbeat. I think the world has come out from underneath me, but I'm not sure. I see Andrew's eyes, glazed over by a thin layer of moisture as he stares at the doctor while the doctor speaks words that have faded into the background of my mind.

Lily's heart is no longer beating.

And I think … yeah, neither is mine …

Andrew

EIGHT

We've been in Raleigh for two weeks now. I won't even go into all the shit we—*Camryn*—has gone through in that time. I refuse to talk about the details. Lily is gone, and Camryn and I are devastated. There's nothing I can do to bring her back, and I'm trying to cope any way I can, but Camryn hasn't been herself since that day and I'm starting to wonder if she ever will be again. She won't talk to anyone. Not to me or her mom or Natalie. She talks, just not about what happened. I can't stand to see her this way because it's obvious, under that I'm-perfectly-fine façade, that she's in so much pain. And I feel powerless to help her.

Camryn has been in the shower for a long time while I've lain here in her bedroom staring up at the ceiling. My phone rings next to me on the nightstand.

"Hello?" I ask.

It's Natalie. "I need to talk to you. Are you alone?"

Caught off guard, it takes me a second to reply. "What for? And yes, Camryn's in the shower."

I glance toward the door to make sure no one is listening. The water is still running in the shower, so I know Camryn is still in there.

"Has her mom said anything to you about…anything?" Natalie asks suspiciously, and I get the strangest feeling from it.

"You need to elaborate a little more than that," I say. Already this conversation is annoying the piss out of me.

She sighs heavily into the phone and I'm growing impatient.

"OK, listen; Cam is obviously not herself," she begins (*yeah, no shit*), "and you need to try to talk her into going back to her psychiatrist. Soon."

Her psychiatrist?

I hear the water shut off, and I glance toward the closed door again.

"What are you talking about, her *psychiatrist?*" I ask in a lowered voice.

"Yeah, she used to see one and—"

"Wait," I whisper harshly.

The bathroom door opens, and I hear Camryn shuffling back toward the room.

"She's coming back," I say really fast. "I'll call you back in a few."

I hang up and set the phone on the nightstand seconds before Camryn opens the door wearing a pink bathrobe and a towel wrapped around her head.

"Hey," I say as I pull my hands behind the back of my head and lock my fingers.

All I really want to do is call Natalie back and find out everything she was going to tell me, but instead I do one better and just go to the source. Besides, I'm not about keeping secrets from her. Been there, done that once, and I won't do it again.

She smiles across the room at me, then tosses her hair over and works the towel in it with her hands.

"Can I ask you something?"

"Of course," she says, rising back up and letting her wet blonde hair fall behind her.

"Did you used to see a psychiatrist?"

The smile disappears from her face and is instantly replaced by a deadpanned expression. She walks over to the closet and opens it. "Why do you ask?"

"Because Natalie just called and suggested that I try to get you to go back."

She shakes her head with her back to me and starts sifting through the clothes hanging in front of her. "Leave it to Natalie to make me out to be a crazy person."

Still in my boxers, I get out of the bed, letting the sheet fall away from my body and I walk over to her, placing my hands on her hips from behind.

"Seeing a psychiatrist doesn't make anyone crazy," I say. "Maybe you should go. Just to talk to someone."

It does bother me that I can't be that someone, but that's not the important issue.

"Andrew, I'll be fine." She turns around and smiles sweetly at me, placing her fingertips on the edge of my jawline. Then she kisses my lips. "I promise. I know you and Nat and my mom are really worried about me and I don't fault you for that, but I'm not going to a psychiatrist. It's ridiculous." She turns back around and pulls a shirt from a hanger. "Besides, what those people really want to do is write a prescription and send me on my way. I'm not taking any mental drugs."

"Well, you don't have to take any 'mental' drugs, but I think if you had someone else to talk to it would help make what happened easier."

She stops with her back still turned to me and lets her arm drop to her side, the shirt clenched in her hand. She sighs, and her shoulders finally relax amid the silence. Then she turns around and looks me dead in the eyes.

"The best way for me to cope with what happened is to forget it," she says, and it tears a gash in my heart. "I'll be OK as long as I'm not forced to be reminded of it every day. The more you all try to get me to 'talk about it'"—she quotes with her fingers—"and the longer you all keep looking at me with those quiet, sad expressions every time I walk into the room, the longer it's going to take me to forget."

This isn't something you can't just forget, but I don't have the heart to say this to her.

"OK, so…" I step away and move absently back toward the bed "…how long are we staying here? Not that I'm eager to get back." It's only one of several questions I want to ask her, but I'm equally leery about all of them. I've felt like I've been walking on eggshells around her with everything I've said in the past two weeks.

"I'm not going back to Texas," she says casually and goes to slip on a pair of jeans.

Eggshells. They're everydamnwhere.

I reach up and rub my palm over the back of my head.

"That's fine," I say. "I'll go back by myself and pack and if you want to, while I'm gone you can go out with Natalie and look at apartments for us. Your pick. Whatever you want." I smile carefully across the room at her. I want her to be happy, and I'll do anything I can to make that happen.

Her face lights up, and I think I'm genuinely tricked by it. Either that or she's genuinely smiling. At this point, I can't tell much anymore.

She walks over to me and backs me up toward the foot of her bed, pressing her palms against my chest. Then she pushes me down against it. I look up at her. Normally I would be on her by now, but it feels wrong. I know she wants it. At least, I think she does...but I'm scared to touch her and have been since the miscarriage.

She sits on me, straddling my waist, and despite being afraid to touch her it's instinct to press myself against her. She drapes her hands over my shoulders and gazes down into my eyes. I bite down on the inside of my mouth and shut my eyes when she leans in to kiss me. I kiss her back, tasting the sweetness of her lips and taking her breath deep into my lungs. But then I pull away and hold her by the waist to keep her from trying to force herself on me.

"Babe, I don't think..."

She looks stunned, cocking her head to one side.

"You don't think what?"

I'm not sure how to word this, but I just say the first version that comes to mind.

"It's only been two weeks. Aren't you still—"

"—bleeding?" she asks. "No. Sore? No. I told you, I'm fine."

She's anything but fine. But I have a feeling that if I try to convince her, it'll backfire on me somehow.

Damn...maybe I *do* need to brave the wild and talk to Natalie, after all.

Camryn slides off my lap, but I stand up with her and wrap my arms around her back, pulling her into my bare chest. I press the side of my face against the top of her wet hair.

"You're right," she says, pulling away to see my eyes. "I should, ummm...get back on my birth control pills. We'd be stupid to risk this again."

She walks away from me.

That's not exactly what I was getting at. Sure, it's probably for the better that we were more careful this time around because of what she just went through. But to be completely honest, I would lay her down right now with the sole intention of getting her pregnant again if that was what she wanted. If she asked me to. I don't regret the first time at all and would do it all over again. But it would need to be what she wants, and I'm afraid if I was ever the one to bring it up that she might take it as *my* suggestion, that she might feel guilty about losing *my* Lily, and she'll want to get pregnant again because she thinks it's what *I* need to feel better.

Camryn takes the robe off and tosses it on the end of the bed and then starts to get dressed.

"If that's what you want to do," I say about the birth control pills, "then I'm with you on that."

"Is that what *you* want?" she asks, pausing to look me in the eyes.

Feels like a trick question. Be careful, Andrew.

I nod slowly. "I want whatever you want. And right now I think for your sake, it's the best thing to do."

There's absolutely no readable emotion in her eyes, and it's making me nervous.

Finally she nods, too, and her gaze falls away from mine. She slips on her jeans and then rummages through her dresser drawer for a pair of socks.

"I'll go to my doctor today if they can squeeze me in."

"All right," I say.

And as if we didn't just have a somewhat depressing, serious conversation, Camryn comes over and smiles at me just before pecking me on the lips.

"And then you can be yourself again," she says.

"What do you mean?"

"Oh come on," she says, "you've not tried to have sex with me once since this happened." She grins and then her eyes scan my naked chest slowly. "I have to say, I miss my sex-crazed Andrew Parrish. For the past three days, I've been taking care of myself a lot." She leans in toward my lips and then moves toward my ear, tugging my earlobe carefully with her teeth, and whispers, "I did it in the shower just minutes ago. You should've been there."

Shivers run down my back and all the way into my feet. Shit, why didn't she just ask me to get her off? I'd happily do it for her. Surely she knows *that* by now.

I grab her face and kiss her hard while she grabs a handful of my cock. The next thing I know, I'm lying across her bed and she's crawling on top of me. Her fingers linger around the elastic of my boxers while she looks across my body with devilishly hooded eyes.

Oh God, if she's about to put me in her mouth . . .

I didn't even realize my eyes had shut until I feel her fingers wedge between my boxers and my skin. Then she starts to slip them off, and all I see is the back of my eyelids.

My conscience rears its ugly head and I stop her, lifting halfway from the bed, my upper body held up by my elbows. "Baby, not right now."

She pouts. She actually pouts, and it's the perfect equivalent of puppy-dog eyes, and I sort of want to give in to her because it absolutely melts me.

"I want you to. Trust me . . . I *really* want you to." I laugh a little with those words. "But let's wait. Your mom will be back anytime, and I—"

She cocks her head to the side and beams at me. "It's OK," she says and kisses me one more time before hopping off the bed.

"You're right. The last thing I want is my mom to catch me giving you a blow job."

Did I just refuse a blow job? This girl really has no idea how firmly she has my nuts in a sling. I better not tell her or she might abuse her power. Hell, what am I saying? I *want* her to abuse it. I fucking love her.

Camryn leaves with her mom later in the morning after they managed to get a last-minute appointment with her gynecologist. I had this urge to pull her mom off to the side at some point to ask about the things Natalie tried to tell me, but I never got the opportunity. They had to leave within the hour to make that appointment, and it would've been weird if I slipped into a room with her mom. She'd know right away that we were talking about her.

NINE

*C*amryn left me with her car. I briefly asked her why she didn't just drive her car instead of taking the bus that day last July, and she responded with: "Why didn't you take yours?" It took everything in me to put myself in the driver's seat of a little red Toyota Prius, but I sucked it up and drove to Starbucks, where I agreed to meet Natalie.

Everything about this feels dangerous and dirty. And I don't mean dirty in a good way. I mean that I will want to shower with Lava soap once this is over with. Natalie walks in without Blake and moves her way through the room toward me, her long, dark hair pulled into a ponytail. I made sure to get a table farthest away from the tall glass windows for fear of someone seeing me with her. It doesn't matter that no one around here knows me; that's beside the point. I tried to get her to just tell me whatever it was she needed to tell me, over the phone, but she insisted we meet.

She sits down on the empty chair, and her purse hits the table-top at the same time.

"I don't bite," she says, smirking.

Maybe not, but I bet your—

"You don't have to pretend to like me," she interrupts my thoughts. "Cam's not here. And I'm not as dense as you think I am."

I admit she surprised me. I really thought she had no clue about my dislike of her. She may be my fiancée's best friend, but she really hurt Camryn when she shut Camryn out months ago and didn't believe her when Natalie's ex, Damon, confessed that he had fallen for her. That's bullshit.

I lean away from the table and cross my arms over my chest. "Well, since we're being honest, tell me, what the hell is your problem?"

That caught her off guard. Her eyes grow wide with surprise and then narrow. It looks like she's chewing on the inside of her mouth out of frustration.

"What do you mean by that?" She crosses her arms now and cocks her head to one side, her ponytail falling to one side.

"I think you know what I mean," I say. "And if not, then maybe you *are* as dense as I thought."

I can't help being such an asshole toward her. I could've gone on forever just tolerating her and never saying a negative word to her, but she was the one who put it all out on the table when she sat down. It's her own damn fault.

A little lightbulb just flickered in her head and the glint in her brown eyes darkens with comprehension. She knows exactly what I'm referring to.

"I know, I deserve that," she says and looks away from me. "I'll regret what I did to Camryn probably forever, but she forgave me, so I don't know why you have to be such an ass about it. You didn't even know me then. You *still* don't know me."

No, I don't, I'll give her that much, but I know enough and that's all I need. At least I can confront Natalie. Damon, or whatever the hell his name is, is another story. I sure would like to have him sitting in front of me instead of her. I'd like nothing more than to bury his lip between his front teeth.

"But this isn't about me," she says, again with that smirk of hers, "so let me just get on with why I asked you to meet me here."

I nod and leave it at that.

"Cam and I have been best friends for a really long time. I was there for her when her Grandma died, when Ian died, when her brother Cole killed that man and went to prison. Not to mention when her dad cheated on her mom and they got divorced." She leans over the small table. "All of that happened just within the last three years." She shakes her head and presses her back against the seat and crosses her arms again. "And those were just the major things to turn her life upside down, Andrew. Honestly, I think that girl was dealt a really shitty hand." She raises her hands up in front of her and says dramatically, "Oooh, but no way can I tell Cam that. She bit my head off the last time I tried to give her some credit. I'm tellin' yah, she doesn't like pity. She hates it. She has this screwed-up mind-set where no matter what bad falls in her lap that there are too many people out there who have it worse." She rolls her eyes.

I know exactly what Natalie is referring to. Camryn tried to avoid her problems while on the road with me, so I know firsthand, but what Natalie doesn't know is that I helped pull Camryn out of that shell somewhat. It makes me smile inside to know that I could succeed in under two weeks where Natalie, her so-called best friend, couldn't in the years they've known each other.

"So, she just accepts it," she goes on. "She always has. I'm telling you, she has a lot of pent-up hurt and anger and disappointment—you name it—that she's never been able to properly deal with. And now with what happened with the baby…" she swallows and her brown eyes grow heavy with unease "... I'm really afraid for her, Andrew."

I did not expect that my meeting with Natalie would result in the deep worry over Camryn's health and state of mind that it has. I was worried about her before, but the more she talks, the worse it gets.

"Tell me about this psychiatrist thing," I say. "I asked her about it earlier, but she wouldn't really go into it with me."

Natalie crosses one leg over the other and sighs heavily. "Well, her dad talked her into seeing one shortly after Ian died. Cam went every week, and she seemed to be getting something out of it, but I think she had us all fooled. You don't leave without telling anyone and board a bus like she did, if you're 'getting better.'"

"Her dad was the one who talked her into it?"

Natalie nods. "Yep. She's always been closer to her dad than her mom—Nancy's great, but she's kind of ditzy sometimes. When her dad packed up after the divorce and moved to New York with his new girlfriend, I think that messed her up even more. But of course, she would never admit it."

I take a deep breath and run both hands over the top of my head. I feel guilty hearing all of this from Natalie of all people, but I'll take it where I can get it, because apparently Camryn wasn't ever going to tell me any of it herself.

"She mentioned something about pills," I say. "Said she wasn't going to go to any psychiatrist because they just—"

Natalie nods and interrupts, "Yeah, she was put on some anti-depressants, took them for a while. Next thing I know, she's admitting to being off of them for a few months. I had no idea."

Finally, I just cut to the chase. "So what exactly did you bring me here for?" I ask. "Hopefully it wasn't just to tell me all of her secrets." I do appreciate knowing this information, but I have to wonder if Natalie is only telling me because she gets off on it. Probably not. I think she genuinely cares about Camryn, but Natalie is Natalie, after all, and that's just not something I can overlook.

"I think you need to watch her," she says and has my full attention again. "She really did fall into some depression after Ian died. I mean it was like I didn't know her for a long time. She didn't cry or act like I expect depressed people are supposed to act, no, Cam was..." She looks up in thought and then back at me again. "She was stoic, if that's even the right word. She stopped going out with me. She stopped caring about school. Refused to go to college. We had our college plans all mapped out in our freshman year, but when she fell into that depression stuff, college was the last thing on her mind."

"What *was* on her mind?"

Natalie shakes her head subtly. "Can't really say, because she rarely talked about it. But she did talk sometimes about deep, weird shit: backpacking across the world, stuff like that. I don't remember, exactly, but she definitely wasn't on Cloud Reality, that's for sure. Oh, and she did mention on occasion how she wished she could feel emotions again. Weird to me how anyone can *not* feel any emotions, but whatever." She waves her hands in front of her dismissively. Then she smiles at me, and I'm not sure what to make of it until she speaks. "But then you came along and she was herself again. Except like a hundred times better. I could tell that night I talked to her while in New Orleans with you, that something had changed. Honestly, I've never seen her the way she is with you." She pauses and says, "I think you're the best thing ever to happen to Cam. Don't shoot me for bringing it up, but if you would've died..."

I wait impatiently for her to go on, but she doesn't. She looks away from my eyes and seems to be ready to retract everything she was about to say.

"If I would've died, *what?*"

"I don't know," she says, and I don't believe her. "I just think you need to watch her. I'm sure I don't need to tell you that she needs you now more than ever."

No, she didn't need to tell me that, but with everything else she's told me, I can't help but feel like I need to be with Camryn *right now* and every minute of every day. I almost hate Natalie for telling me all of this stuff, but at the same time, I needed to know.

I stand up from the table and toss my arms inside my black jacket, then push my chair in.

"So, you're leaving just like that?"

I stop and look down at her. "Yeah, I am," I say, and she stands up. "I think I know enough."

"Please don't tell—"

I put up my hand. "Look, don't get me wrong, I appreciate you telling me all of this, but if Camryn asks, I will tell her that I met you here privately and that you told me everything that I know. So don't expect me to keep any of it from her."

Her cheeks deflate with air. "Fair enough," she says and grabs her purse from the table. "But I was only saying that because I'm worried how she might feel if she knew I came to you, not because I'm worried she'll be pissed at me for doing it."

I nod. I admit, I believe her this time.

———

I'm hanging out in the den watching TV when Camryn and her mom come home from the birth control appointment. I find myself sitting up straighter, feeling awkward being in her mom's house and all. I set the TV remote down on the oak coffee table and get up to meet Camryn halfway.

"So, how'd everything go?" Awkward posture. Awkward filler questions. Awkward everything. I hate awkward. We need to get our own place soon. Or a hotel room.

Camryn's eyes soften as she comes up to me.

"It went fine," she answers and pecks me on the cheek. "I got what I needed. What did *you* do today? I bet you looked all sexy driving around in that New Age chick car all day, huh?" The left side of her mouth lifts into a grin.

My face feels a little flush.

Her mom smiles faintly at me behind Camryn's back as she passes and heads into the kitchen area. It's the same kind of "quiet smile" Camryn was talking about this morning, the one that screams *She's so fragile* and *I feel so bad for both of you*. I'm starting to understand why Camryn hates it so much.

"Well, I didn't do much, but I did endure a fifteen minute face-to-face conversation with Shenzi at Starbucks."

"Shenzi?"

I shake my head, smiling and say, "Never mind. Natalie. She wanted to meet me to talk about you. She's just really worried."

Camryn, annoyed, starts to walk toward the hallway leading to her bedroom. I follow.

"I can only imagine what she told you," she says as she rounds the corner into her room. She sets her purse and a shopping bag on her bed. "And it pisses me off she'd call you behind my back."

"I probably shouldn't have met up with her," I say, standing near the doorway. "But she was persistent and, honestly, I wanted to hear what she had to say."

She turns to face me. "And what did you get out of it?"

The faint trace of discontent lacing her tone stings me a little.

"Just that you've been through a lot and—"

Camryn puts up her hand and shakes her head scoldingly at me. "Andrew, seriously. Listen to me, OK?" She steps right up and takes my hands into hers. "Right now, the only thing that's causing me any added misery is everybody worrying about me all the time. Think about it—we basically had this conversation just this morning. Now look at me."

I look at her, not that I wasn't already.

"Am I moping around?" *No, you're not.* "How many times have you seen me smile in the past week?" *Many times, actually.* "Have you once heard me say anything to indicate I'm hurting more than I'm letting on?" *No, not really, I guess.*

She tilts her beautiful blonde head gently to the side and reaches up, brushing the side of my face with her soft fingertips. "I want you to promise me something."

Normally I'd say "anything" without hesitation, but this time I hesitate.

She tilts her head to the other side, and her hand falls away from my face.

Finally, I say with reluctance, "It depends on what it is."

She doesn't fight it, but I see the disappointment in her expression.

"Promise me we'll get back to normal. That's all I ask, Andrew. I miss the way we were before. I miss our crazy times together and our crazy sex and your crazy dimples and your crazy, vibrant, life-loving attitude."

"Do you miss the road?" I ask, and the light snaps out of her face as if I've said something horribly wrong.

Her eyes stray from mine and she seems lost in some deep, dark moment.

"Camryn...*do you* miss the road?" I need the answer to this question now more than I did seconds ago, because of her unexpected reaction to it.

After a long, silent moment she looks at me again and I feel lost in her eyes, though in an uncomfortable way.

She doesn't answer. It's like...she can't.

Not knowing what's going on inside of her head and eager to find out, I finally say, "We can do it now." I place my hands on her upper arms. "Maybe that's exactly what you...I mean, *we* need." As the idea comes together on my tongue, I get more excited by the second just thinking about it. Camryn and me. On the open road. Living free and in the moment like we had planned to do. I realize I'm smiling hugely, my face lit up with excitement. Holy shit! Yes, this is what we need to do. Why didn't I think of this before?

"No," she says flatly, and her answer snaps me right out of that blissful, dreamlike state.

"No?" I can hardly believe it, or understand it.

"No."

"But...why not?" I ask and she walks away from me casually. "There's no reason we have to wait anymore."

I understand in this very second the reason behind her answer. But I don't have to be the one to bring it up because she does it for me.

"Andrew," she says, her expression soft with regret, "if we did that it would always linger in the back of my mind that it was something we were putting off because of the baby. It wouldn't feel right to do it now. Not for a while. A long while."

"OK," I say and step up to her. I nod and smile warmly, hoping to make her understand that no matter what she wants to do, or not do, I'm behind her all the way.

"So, what level of bipolar did Natalie make me out to be today?" She laughs under her breath and goes over to the shopping bag she brought with her and reaches inside.

I laugh too and lie horizontally across her bed, my legs hanging over one side, bent at the knees.

"Level yellow," I say. "Lowest level possible. But she made herself out to be a level red." I tilt my head sideways to see her. "But I'm sure you already knew that."

She smiles back at me and pulls a stack of panties out of the bag and starts peeling the sticker labels from the fabric.

"Well, I'm sure she filled your head full of stuff about how I went through a depression phase and all about the 'shitty hand'"—she quotes with her fingers—"I was dealt." She points at me, squinting one eye. "But that's just it. It was a phase. I got over it. And besides, who *doesn't* go through deaths in the family, divorces, and bad breakups? It's ridiculous that—"

"Babe, what did I tell you before? Back in New Orleans?"

"You told me a lot of things." She tosses the sticker labels into the nearby wastebasket.

"About how pain isn't a damn competition."

"Yes, I remember," she says. She starts to take the panties from the bed, but I reach over and snatch a few pairs off the top before she gets the chance. I hold up a pink lacy pair in front of me and set the other two pairs on my chest.

"Damn, I like these," I say, and she snatches them from my fingers.

"Anyway," she goes on, while I pick up the next two pairs and do the same thing, "I don't want to talk about this stuff anymore, alright?" Then she snatches the last two pairs from my hands and makes her way to her top dresser drawer and stuffs them all inside.

She walks back over to me and crawls onto my lap, her knees buried in the blanket that covers the bed. I rub my hands back and forth over her thighs, on either side of me.

"I want to go out tonight," she says. "What do you think?"

I curl my bottom lip between my teeth in thought and make a sucking sound just before I say, "Sounds like a plan. Where do you want to go?"

She smiles sweetly down at me as if she has been giving this plan a lot of thought today already. I love to see her smile like that. And it's totally fucking real, so maybe Natalie is overreacting, after all.

"Well, I thought we could go to the Underground with Natalie and Blake."

"Wait, isn't that the place that douchebag kissed you on the roof?"

"Yeah," she says in a singsong voice. Damn, if she doesn't stop moving around on my lap like that... "but that 'douchebag' is in jail for a year. And Natalie really wants us to go. She texted me about it just before I got here."

"Sure she's not trying to suck up to you because she's got a guilty conscience?"

Camryn shrugs. "Maybe so, but it'll be fun to go, regardless. And it'll be nice to watch live bands play rather than be on the stage for a change."

She lies across my chest, and I reach down and fit her perfectly shaped ass in the palms of my hands and squeeze. She kisses me, and I move my hands up and wrap my arms tight around her body.

"All right," I say softly when the kiss breaks and her lips linger an inch from mine. I run my fingers through her hair and then hold her head in place with her cheeks in my hands. "The Underground it is. And then tomorrow I'm going to fly back to Texas and start packing."

"I hope you're OK with me not going," she says.

"Yeah, I'm fine with it." I kiss her forehead. "Y'know, you never did say whether or not you were going to have Natalie go with you to look for an apartment."

She lifts up, straightening her back and then grabs my hands, interlocking our fingers.

"I'll get around to it," she says with a smile. "One step at a time, and right now the next step is getting ready to go out tonight."

I nod, smiling back at her, and then I squeeze her hands and pull her down toward me again.

"You're the world to me," I whisper onto her lips. "I hope you never forget that."

"I'll never forget," she whispers back and moves her hips very subtly on my lap. Then she nudges my lips with her own and says just before kissing me, "But if I ever do, for whatever reason, I hope you'll always find a way to remind me."

I study her mouth and then her cheeks resting underneath the pads of my thumbs.

"Always," I say and kiss her ravenously.

TEN

*I*t's been a while since the last time I partied at a club like the Underground before. Hell, I'm only twenty-five, and that place made me feel old. I guess spending most of my bar and club nights in more laid-back places like Old Point made me forget that heavy metal exists. Hey, I like heavy metal, but give me the old stuff any day. Camryn and I spent the night with Blake and Natalie, listening to some band who calls themselves Sixty-Nine—how original—screech out fuck-up note after fuck-up note on the guitar while the lead singer growled into the mic like a moose during mating season.

But the crowd seemed to like it. Or maybe it was because most of them were drunk or high. Probably both.

I should be drunk, but I agreed to be the designated driver for the night. And I'm OK with that. I wanted Camryn to party her ass off and have a good time. She needed this. And I'm proud of her for trying, because I halfway expected her to refuse to do anything for a very long time. I'm hurting over the loss of Lily, too, but Camryn is still here and she's what matters right now.

The cold November night air feels good after being cooped up inside that warm, smoky warehouse for the past three hours.

"Are you all right to walk?" I ask Camryn, walking alongside her with my arm firmly around her waist.

She lays her head on me and buries her hands inside her coat sleeves.

"I'm good," she says. "You cut me off at the right hour this time, so you don't have to worry about carrying me the rest of the way like you did that night back in New Orleans." I feel her head shift to gaze up at me, and I glance down at her briefly, trying also to watch our steps along the dark sidewalk. "You remember that night, don't you?"

"Of course I remember." I squeeze my arm tighter around her waist. "It wasn't that long ago and besides, even if it was, I could never forget that night, or any night with you, for that matter."

She smiles up at me and then watches out ahead, too.

"You're very unforgettable," I add, grinning at her briefly.

"I woke up once that night," she says, burrowing her head into the warmth of my arm. "I saw the toilet on one side of me and wondered how I got there. Then I felt your body behind me, your arm over my waist, and I didn't want to get up. Not because I was still half drunk and my head felt like it had been run through a shredder, but because you were with me."

"Yeah, I remember…" I lose myself in that memory for a moment.

We walk huddled together through the cold for ten minutes until we make it to the gas station where the car is parked in an abandoned lot nearby. I turn the heat on full blast and drive the chick car back to Camryn's mom's house, wishing we had just stayed in a hotel all this time when we pull into the driveway and I see her mom's car parked out front. I like Nancy, but I also like being able to walk around the house in my boxers, or naked, without worrying about an audience.

I help Camryn out of the car and take her inside, my arm still around her waist just in case any of the liquor hasn't caught up to her yet. But she's fine. Buzzed pretty good, but fine. I lock the door behind us, and Camryn immediately slips out of her coat and tosses it on the coat rack in the corner of the foyer. I do the same.

The house is dead quiet, and the only lights are the dim orange glow from the nightlight plugged in the nearby hallway and the one over the kitchen counter, illuminating the bar.

Camryn surprises me when her hands slither up my chest and she presses hard with her fingers on my abs, pushing me against the foyer wall. She slips her tongue into my mouth and I kiss her. Her right hand moves down to the button on my jeans and she pops it right out with ease, sliding the zipper down afterward. I kiss her harder and groan against her mouth when she slides her hand into my boxers and grabs me.

God, it's been so fucking long…

She presses harder against me, shoving my back against the wall.

I break the kiss just for seconds long enough to get out, "I want you so fucking bad, but let's at least get to your room first."

Her kiss turns more ravenous and then she says with her lips still on mine, "My mom's not here." She bites down hard on my lip, enough to make it sting, but it drives me absolutely mad for her. "She took Roger's car to work tonight."

I crush my mouth against hers and lift her into my arms to carry her through the hallway toward her room. We can't get there fast enough, and she's already got my shirt off before I carry her through the door and throw her back against the mattress. I strip the rest of her clothes off, leaving just her panties. She sits up on the edge of the bed and takes my jeans and boxers down the rest of the way. I crawl on top of her, holding the weight of my body up with one fist ground into the mattress on her side while I tease her with the other hand, rubbing my finger between her wet lips over the fabric of her panties. She squirms beneath me, shutting her eyes and tilting her head back on the mattress so that her breasts rise a little higher in front of me.

I move off the bed and slip her panties off with my middle fingers. I kiss her inner thighs and can't stop myself from falling in between her legs so fast because I haven't been able to do this for her in what feels like forever. I don't tease her anymore. I don't because I'm making myself crazy in the process.

I lick her furiously, and she tries to crawl her way across the bed and away from my mouth. She grips the sheets above her head until her head is hanging off the bed on the other side. I hold her firmly in place with my hands around her thighs, my fingers digging into her skin. I suck on her clit even harder until she can't stand it anymore and her thighs try to close around my head.

I can tell she's about to come when suddenly she grips my hair and forces my mouth away.

I look across the smooth geography of her body from between her legs to see her gazing down at me. She works her fingers through my hair. I wait, wondering what she's thinking, wondering why she made me stop.

It's like she's waiting for something, but I'm not sure what. All I can think about right now is forcing myself on her. It takes everyfuckingthing in me to hold back, to keep from rolling her over and forcing her on her hands and knees, from gripping her hair so hard that it hurts her, from...

She cocks her head to one side and watches me, studies me as if she's contemplating my next move. I'm mesmerized by her face. There's something enigmatic and frail in it that I've never seen before. Then she guides me up away from the edge of the bed and on instinct I lay down on my back. She crawls across my body, kissing my stomach and my ribs and my chest as she makes her way up, positioning herself on top of me. A low moan rumbles uncontrolled through my chest just feeling the warmth and wetness of her. She smiles down at me, sweet, innocent, though I know it's anything but. And then takes me into her hand, and I feel my eyes roll into the back of my fucking head when she places me inside of her and slides down on me so slowly that it's torturous.

I let her fuck me for as long as she wants, but it takes everything in me to keep from getting off before she does. And in that last second, something happens that I never anticipated, and I'm panicking inside, hoping she doesn't sense it when I have to make that vital split-second decision whether to pull out of her or not.

Camryn

My heart is beating so fast. I'm out of breath and sweat is beading off my forehead even amid the cool air lingering within the room. As I start to come, Andrew, in a confused panic of some sort, pulls out. It surprises me a little, but I don't let him know that. Instead, I lean forward, just barely touching my chest to his and I slide him up and down within my hand.

Afterward I collapse on top of him fully, my cheek pressed against his chest, my knees still bent at his sides as I straddle his lap. I hear his heart beating rapidly in my ear. He splays his arms out on both sides across the bed and catches his breath before enveloping me within them. I feel his lips press against my hair.

I just lay here, thinking. I think about what just happened and what didn't. I think about how good he smells and how warm his skin is against mine. I think about how tame he has become. All because he's worried he'll hurt me, physically, emotionally, probably even spiritually, if that were possible. And I love him for it. I love him for how much he loves me back, but I hope he doesn't stay this protective of me forever.

For now, I'll leave him alone about it. I guess I have to prove that I'm myself first before he can let his guard down from around me. And I respect that.

I lift my cheek from his chest and smile into his eyes.

I wonder if he'll try to explain himself, tell me why he pulled out, maybe say he just wasn't sure if he should, or not. But he never does. Maybe he's waiting on me. But I never say anything about it, either.

To stir the silence between us and cut some of the uncertainty in the room, I playfully wriggle my hips on top of him and laugh a little.

"You gotta let me recuperate first, babe." He smiles back at me and smacks my ass with both hands.

I let out an exaggerated yelp, pretending that it actually stung and then I wriggle on him some more.

"You better stop," he warns me, his dimples deepening in his cheeks.

I do it again.

"You think I'm playin'? Do it again and you'll regret it."

Of course, I do it again and brace myself mentally for whatever he plans to do to teach me a lesson.

He reaches between us and grabs both of my nipples in his fingers and squeezes them just enough to make me freeze for fear of moving too abruptly and risk them getting ripped off.

"Oooowww!" I let out a peal of laughter and grab his hands, but he pinches a little harder when I try to pry them away.

"I told you." He shakes his head at me, putting on such a serious face that I'm impressed at how convincing it actually is. "Should've listened."

"Please, please, *please*, let gooooo!"

He licks the dryness from his lips and says so casually, "Are you going to be good?"

I nod fast about ten times.

He narrows those devilish green eyes at me, stringing me along. "You swear?"

"I swear on the grave of my long-lost dog, Beebop!"

He pinches my nipples one last time, making me wince and grit my teeth, before letting go. And then he raises himself upright on the bed and wraps my legs around his waist. He leans inward and traces each of my breasts lightly with the tip of his tongue, kissing them afterward.

"All better?" he asks, staring into my eyes.

"All better," I whisper. Then he kisses my lips and makes love to me gently before we fall asleep, curled up with each other, sometime after three in the morning.

ELEVEN

I thought I'd have a much worse hangover than I do this morning. Last night was the first time I've had a drink in months, but I'm not complaining. I roll over on my side, and when I see the clock next to my face reading an hour and a half past the time Andrew was supposed to be at the airport, my eyes pop open and I shoot upright on the bed.

"Andrew!" I say, shaking him awake.

He groans and rolls over, barely opening his eyes a crack. He reaches out his arm and tries to bury me underneath it so he can go back to sleep, but I push it away.

"Get up. Missed your plane."

The only part of his body that moves are his eyes popping open much like mine did, and when reality sinks in, the rest of his body follows suit.

"Shit! Shit! Shit!" He gets out of the bed and stands in the center of the room, naked.

I never get tired of looking at him—naked or clothed, it doesn't matter. How I ended up with him still defies my comprehension to this day. He raises both hands to his face and runs them over the top of his hair, resting them on the back of his head, his arms hardened with well-defined muscles. And then a long, defeated sigh deflates his chest.

"I'll have to catch a later flight."

I climb out of the bed and grab my robe from the floor so I can get in the shower.

"Not that I mind staying here with you for a few more hours," he says, coming up behind me.

"I don't know, Andrew." I slip the robe around my body and tie it at the front. "I was kind of looking forward to getting rid of you." I'm totally smiling with my back facing him.

Silence bathes the room.

"Are you serious?"

His stunned voice makes it impossible not to laugh. I whirl around and kiss his lips.

"Hell no, I'm not serious. Maybe *I* was the one who turned the alarm off last night. Maybe *I* planned this all along."

His smile widens and he kisses me back and then walks around to the side of the bed to find his boxers.

"*Did* you?" he asks, stepping into them.

"No, I didn't. But it's a good idea. I'll remember it for next time. Want to shower with me?"

At that second, there's a knock at my bedroom door. Knowing it's probably my mom, Andrew's posture stiffens a little and he sits down on the bed to cover his lower half with the blanket.

I open the door to see my mom in all her bleached-blonde glory standing there. She's wearing a light pink button-up top and soft pink blush in her cheeks to match it.

"Are you up?" she asks.

No, Mom, I'm sleepwalking. She's funny sometimes.

I notice her glance at Andrew once. She has already expressed her worry about me getting pregnant again, but surely she can't expect us not to have sex. It's what she wants, but yeah, not gonna happen.

She smiles weakly at me and asks, "Do you want to go with me to Brenda's today?"

Definitely not. Love my aunt Brenda, but not so much being choked to death by her cigarette-smoke-filled house.

"No, I've got plans with Natalie."

Really, I don't have any plans at all, but whatever.

"Oh, all right. Well…" She glances at Andrew again and then back at me. "Thought he was going to Texas this morning?"

I tighten the rope around my robe and cross my arms.

"Yeah, well we overslept, but he's going to take a later flight out."

My mom nods and looks across the room at him one more time. She smiles slimly and he does the same. Awkward. She really likes Andrew, but she's definitely not used to a guy sleeping with me in my room, even if he's been here with me for two weeks. If I wasn't almost twenty-one and engaged to him, he definitely wouldn't be in here at all. At the same time, she knows we love each other and after what happened with the baby, she wants him here for me. But it's still awkward. For all of us. Yeah, Andrew and I are seriously gonna have to get a place of our own.

A place of our own…here in Raleigh. My chest feels like there's something heavy sitting on top of it all of a sudden.

My mom finally leaves us, and I gaze over at Andrew, who looks all uncomfortable with the sheet draped over his lap and a sort of nervous frown.

"Shower with me?" I ask again, but I can tell he's not up for it anymore.

He flinches. "I think I'll get one after you."

I chuckle at his boyish awkwardness and then soften my face. "I'll look for a place this weekend. I promise."

He stands up. "If you want me to look with you, just tell me. I only suggested Natalie in case you wanted something to do while I'm gone. Y'know, get that girl opinion on drapes and color palettes 'n' shit."

I laugh out loud.

"I won't be picking out any drapes," I say. "Curtains maybe, but drapes are for interior designers and rich cougars."

He shakes his head at me as I leave the room and head to the bathroom down the hall.

I feel like Jekyll and Hyde. All the time. When in front of Andrew I put on my happy face, but not as if I'm faking it. I *am* happy. I think. But the second I'm alone again, it's like I become someone else. I feel like someone invisible is always standing behind me, flipping a fucking switch inside my brain. Off. On. Off. On. O—no, On.

I sit in the bottom of the tub with my knees drawn up against my chest, and I let the hot water stream down on me forever. I think about the inevitable apartment I'm bound to find, the good time I had at the Underground last night, the load of laundry I need to start, and how that logo is starting to fade from the top of the soap bar. When the water begins to cool, the change in temperature wakes me up enough from my strange daydreaming to take notice of how long I've actually been in here. I don't even shave before I shut the water off and get out, purposely avoiding the bath rug because I hate the way it feels underneath my feet. I throw a clean towel over it and then I just stand here, gazing at myself in the mirror. Absently I begin to count the flecks of toothpaste staining the glass. I stop at fourteen.

Pulling open the medicine cabinet, I sift through the bottles and tubes of stuff in search of Advil. Thankfully, my so-called hangover only requires a couple of headache pills. When I find it, I go to pluck the bottle from behind a few brown-orange prescription bottles, and then I pause. I take down one of the prescription bottles instead and read the label. *Percocet 7.5—Take one tablet every six hours as needed for pain—Nancy Lillard.* No idea why my mom has a bottle of pain pills, which she obviously hasn't taken, but she's had back problems for a while, so maybe she finally saw a doctor about it. Or, maybe my mom, being an RN, is turning into a criminal on me and taking advantage of her easier-than-the-average-citizen's access to prescription drugs.

Nah. That's not likely, considering this bottle was purchased a month ago and is still full. She's the same old mom I've known all my life who's never been fond of taking anything for pain beyond the harmless over-the-counter stuff.

I start to put it back when I find myself stopping just before the bottle touches the tiny shelf. I guess it can't hurt. I do have a headache and that qualifies as pain, right? Right. I push down and turn to twist the childproof cap off and shuffle a pill into my hand. I swallow it down with a handful of water from the sink, dry my body off, and wrap my hair in the towel afterwards. Slipping back inside my robe, I tie it closed and go back into my room to get dressed. I hear Andrew talking in the kitchen, but his laid-back tone tells me it's not my mom he's talking to. He's probably on the phone. When I hear him mention his brother Asher's name, I'm satisfied that my assumption was right, and I get dressed.

I was going to have to tear Natalie a new one if it had been her again. She's got to stop with that worrying stuff and plotting against me behind my back with Andrew.

After combing out my wet hair, I head toward the kitchen to join him.

"I know, bro, but I don't think it's a good idea right now," I hear Andrew say, and I fall back a little so I don't intrude too soon. "Yeah. Yeah. No, she's doing better. She's definitely not as messed up as she was after the first week. Umm-hmm." I look around the corner to see him standing at the bar with his cell phone pressed to one ear and his other hand resting on the bar top. He nods here and there, listening to whoever is on the other end, which I get the feeling is Aidan. I'm right again when he says, "Tell Michelle I said thanks for the offer. Maybe we'll visit in a month or two after Camryn's had time to—No, maybe in the spring. Chicago is way too fucking cold for my blood in the winter." Andrew laughs and says, "Hell no, bro, why do you think I prefer Texas?" He laughs again. Finally I round the corner completely, and he sees me.

"I would like to go," I announce.

Andrew just stares at me for a moment and then cuts Aidan off. "Hold up a second." He covers the mic part of the phone with the palm of his hand. "You want to go to Chicago?" He seems mildly surprised.

"Sure," I say, smiling. "I think it would be fun."

At first, he seems to be working through something in his head. Maybe he doesn't believe me, or maybe he's just considering the idea and all he can see is wind and snow. But then his face lights up and slowly he begins to nod. "OK," he says, hesitates, and puts the phone back against his ear. "Aidan, let me call you back in a few, all right? Yeah. OK. Talk to you soon. Later."

He runs his finger over the phone and hangs up. Then he looks across the room at me again. "Are you sure? I thought you'd want to stay here for a while."

I walk into the kitchen and get a bottle of orange juice from the fridge. "No, I'm sure," I say, taking a sip. "Sounds like it was Michelle's idea."

He nods once. "Yeah, Aidan said she's been worried about you. She offered to put us up for a few days if we wanted to visit."

I take another sip and set the bottle on the bar top. "Worried about me? Well, that's nice of her and all, but I hope we don't go up there and I find myself in the same situation as I'm in with Natalie here."

Andrew shakes his head. "Nah, Michelle's not like that." He backtracks that comment to put more emphasis on just how true it is. "Michelle is *nothing* like Natalie."

"That's not what I meant, Andrew."

"I know, I know," he says, "but really, she's all right."

Knowing Michelle enough myself, I know he's right.

Then that pill hits me out of nowhere, and suddenly my head feels like it's sort of loose on my shoulders. My whole body from my toes to the center of the top of my head is tingling, and it takes me a second to straighten my vision. My hand comes down on the edge of the bar instinctively to hold myself up.

"Whoa." I swallow and blink my eyes a few times forcefully.

Andrew looks at me curiously. "You OK?"

A smile stretches so far across my face I feel the air from the room hit my teeth. "Yeah, I'm totally fine."

He tilts his head to one side. "Well, I haven't seen you grin like that since I slid that ring on your finger." He's vaguely smiling, too, but his curiosity dominates it.

I bring my finger up into view and admire my engagement ring, which cost under one hundred bucks and probably isn't considered an engagement ring by brides-to-be all over the country. I saw it in a little shop in Texas one day and just briefly mentioned how pretty it was:

"I love this," I said, holding it up to the sunlight at just the right angle. "It's simple and there's something special about it."

I handed it back to the woman behind the makeshift booth, and she placed it back in the glass case between us.

"What, you're not a diamonds-are-a-girl's-best-friend type of girl?" Andrew asked. "No wedding rock so big you have to carry your ring hand around in a wheelbarrow?"

"No way," I said and laughed. "Nothing meaningful about a ring like that. It's usually about the price tag." We walked out of the jewelry shop and along the sidewalk. "You said so yourself once, remember?"

"What did I say?"

I smiled and slipped my hand into his as we came to the street corner and took a left toward the café. "Simple is sexy." I leaned my head against his shoulder. "That day in your dad's house when you were preachin' about why I shouldn't spend an hour on makeup and hair, or whatever."

I looked up to see him smiling, lost in the memory of that day, and then he pulled me closer.

"Yeah, I did say that, didn't I? 'Simple is sexy.' Well, it is."

"It's also beautiful," I said.

The day after that, Andrew came home with that same ring and held it out to me. Then in proper Andrew style, he got down on one knee and old-schooled it, except a little more dramatic than how it usually goes:

"Will you, Camryn Marybeth Bennett, the most beautiful woman on the planet Earth and the mother of my baby, do me the honor of being my wife?"

I grinned and looked at him in a suspicious, sidelong glance and replied, "Just planet Earth?"

He blinked and said, "Well, I haven't seen the chicks from other planets yet."

Neither of us could resist a laugh. But then he became very serious, and his mood shifting like that only made mine do the same.

"Will you marry me?" he asked.

The tears streaming down my face, and the long, deep kiss I gave him, which caused us both to fall over onto the carpet, said yes a million times over.

Sure, he had asked me to marry him that day I told him I was pregnant, but on this day he did it right, and I'll never forget it for as long as I live.

"Are you alive in there?"

Andrew waves his hand in front of my face.

I snap out of the past and wake up back in the present, high as a fucking kite from that pill. And I realize immediately how fast I need to gather my composure so he doesn't know what's going on.

Andrew

TWELVE

J guess the mood swings hang around even after... well, after pregnancy for a while. Camryn flip-flopped from average to frolicking in La La Land in under an hour. But she's happy, it seems, and who am I to judge her on how she chooses to express it?

But the fact that she suddenly wants to leave Raleigh and go somewhere entirely different, even just for a weekend, is strange to me, and I just have to ask, "Why so soon? I mean I'm all for going if you want to, but I thought you wanted to be here, find an apartment and all that?"

"Well, I do...," she says unconvincingly. She's still vaguely smiling, which is so damn odd to me. "I just think we should go visit while we have the chance, because once I get a job here, finding free time on a weekend will be hit or miss."

She brings her hands up near her stomach and folds them together, her fingers moving over the tops of her knuckles like she's fidgeting.

"Are you—" I stop myself. I'm not going to do exactly what she said she wanted all of us to *stop* doing: worrying constantly about her and asking if she's all right all the damn time. I smile instead and say, "I'll call Aidan back and tell him and Michelle that we'll be there this weekend."

I wait for her to agree to the time frame, or not, and when she doesn't say anything, I add, "So this means there's no point in me going back to Texas for our stuff until after we get back from Chicago." It was really more like a question. I have to admit, all of this uncertainty about where we're going to be the next day is starting to make my head spin. It's different from when we were on the road, living in the moment and defining the word *spontaneous*. At least then it was our goal to not know what the next day would bring. Right now, I'm not sure what's going on.

She nods and pulls out a kitchen chair, where she never sits unless she's eating breakfast. It just seemed like she needed to sit down.

"Wait," I say suddenly. "Are you OK with getting an apartment? We can get a little house somewhere." I guess this is my way of probing for answers as to what might be wrong with her without actually saying: *What's wrong with you?*

She shakes her head. "No, Andrew, I don't mind an apartment at all. That has nothing to do with anything. Besides, I'm not gonna let you spend your inheritance on a house in a state not of your choosing."

I pull out the chair next to her and sit with my arms across the table in front of me. I look at her in that you-know-better-than-that way. "I go where you go. You know this. As long as you don't want to buy an igloo in the Arctic or move to Detroit, I don't care. And I'll do what I want with my inheritance. What else would I do with it anyway, besides buy a house? That's what people do. They buy the big stuff with the big stuff."

We're sitting on $550,000 that I inherited from my father when he died. My brothers got the same. That's a lot of money, and I'm a simple guy. What the hell else would I do with money like that? If Camryn wasn't in my life, I'd be living in a modest one-bedroom house somewhere in Galveston by myself, eating ramen noodles and TV dinners. The small bills I have would stay paid, and I'd still work for Billy Frank because I happen to like the smell of an engine. Camryn is a lot like me in this frugal sense, and that makes our relationship kind of perfect. But it does bug me sometimes how she just can't seem to accept the fact that my money is her money, too. She wouldn't even let me pay off the credit card she used on her bus trip when we met. Six hundred dollars on a card her dad gave her for emergencies. But she insisted—very stubbornly—that she pay it off herself. And she did with her half of our earnings from performing at Levy's.

If anything at all bothers me about her, it's this one issue. Taking care of her is what I'm gonna fucking do whether she likes it or not. And she's gonna have to get over it.

"Let's just enjoy a few days in Chicago, and when we get back, we're going house shopping. Together."

I stand up and push my chair in as if to say *This isn't up for debate*.

She looks surprised, but not in a good way, and the weird smile has dropped from her face.

"No, if we're going to buy a house then I'm going to save—"

I slash the air in front of me with both hands.

"Stop being so damn stubborn," I say. "If you're so worried about 'your half' of the money, you can always pay me back with sex and a striptease every now and then."

Her mouth falls open and her eyes grow wide.

"What the hell?!" She laughs beneath her failed attempt at

being offended. "I'm not a hooker!" She stands up and gently slaps the palm of her hand on the table, but I think it's more to keep her balance than to protest.

I grin and start to walk away. "Hey, you brought that one on yourself." I make it to the den entrance, and I glance back briefly over my shoulder to see that she hasn't budged, probably still in shock. "And you're whatever I *want* you to be!" I shout as I get farther away. "Nothing wrong with being *my* hooker!"

I catch a glimpse of her running toward me. I take off through the den, leaping over the back of the sofa like a goddamn ninja, and then out the back door of the house while she chases after me. Her shrill voice and laughter carries on the air as she tries to catch up.

———

Our plane lands at O'Hare late Friday afternoon. Thank God there's not a mountain of snow on the ground. I take back one thing I said to Camryn, about moving to any place she wants to. I would definitely argue my case if she ever decided she wanted to live anywhere where snow and bitter cold is the norm in the winter. I hate it. With a passion. And I'm as freakishly giddy as Camryn seemed to be on Tuesday when I see a snowless landscape and feel the fifty-three-degree temperature on my face. A little warm for this time of year in Chicago, but I'm not complaining. Global warming? Hey, it's not entirely a bad thing.

Aidan meets us in the terminal.

"Long time, bro," I say, gripping his hand and hugging him. He pats my back a few times and looks to Camryn.

"Good to see you," he says.

She hugs him tight. "You too," she says, pulling away. "Thanks for inviting us up."

"Well, you have to give that credit to my persistent wife," he says and then raises a brow. "Not that I didn't want you to come, of course." He winks at her.

Camryn blushes, and I take her hand into mine.

Michelle has a late lunch made for us by the time we get to their house. The woman can cook. And she's like Aidan and me when it comes to food, so it doesn't surprise me that she made fat cheeseburgers with cheese dip on the side. And beer. I'm in food heaven right about now.

The four of us eat in the living room watching a movie on Aidan's sixty-inch television and we talk during the boring parts about this and that. When we first got here, a small part of me was worried about Aidan or Michelle bringing up anything remotely close to the off-limits topic of Camryn's miscarriage. But the bigger part of me knew they wouldn't go there. I can't even tell by looking at them that it's on their minds at all. Aidan, probably not so much. He stays away from deep topics like that. And Michelle's playing her cards right, making Camryn feel completely comfortable and not giving her any reason to have to think about what she wants to forget.

And I've never seen Camryn around Natalie the way she is right now with Michelle, so this is nice. Looks like this unexpected trip is turning out to be more beneficial than I imagined.

During one of our conversations, Aidan throws his head back and laughs. I'll never fucking live that moment down with either one of my brothers.

"Yeah, Andrew was drunk out of his mind," Aidan explains

to Camryn to the constant rolling of my eyes, "when the modeling scout came up to him in my bar that night."

Oh, here it comes, Aidan's overly dramatic replay of that event. Camryn's smiling from ear to ear and no doubt getting a kick out of watching me squirm next to her.

"The guy sat down beside Andrew on the barstool and said something about him having 'the look.'" Aidan stops long enough to shake his head. "And before the guy could finish, Andrew turned to him and said with a crazy Charles Manson expression, 'Dude, did you eat my fuckin' peanuts?' The look on that guy's face was priceless. He was scared, even backed up like he thought Andrew was about to hit him."

Camryn and Michelle laugh.

"Then the guy pulled a business card from his wallet and said, 'Ever thought of modeling?' and handed the card out to him. Andrew just looked at it, but didn't take it."

"I did take it," I say.

Aidan smirks over at me. "Yeah, but not until after you so *eloquently* explained how you could never be a model because it's for 'guys without nutsacks' and—"

"Yeah, all right, Aidan," I interrupt and take a quick sip of my beer.

"Why have *I* never seen you that drunk before?" Camryn asks. She can't wipe the grin off her face, loving every minute of this, and it makes me smile and give up the act. I reach out and skim her golden braid with the tops of my fingers.

"Well," I begin, "you've never seen me that drunk because I've grown up since then."

Michelle chokes out a laugh.

"Hey," I say, pointing at her, "you're one to talk, 'Chelle. I do recall the last time I was here, you dancing like a drunk stripper at the bar after a few too many drinks."

Her mouth falls open. "I did not strip, Andrew!"

Aidan laughs and takes a swig of his beer. "I don't know, if I hadn't been there that night we might be divorced."

Michelle whaps him across the face with the couch pillow she had been leaning against.

"I never would've stripped off my clothes." She laughs. Aidan, unfazed by the attack, can't stop smiling.

Neither can Camryn. I get lost in Camryn's smile for a minute, glad to see she's having such a good time.

Michelle adds, "You two are awful when you get together."

"Hey, because you're married to the dickhead," I say, "it makes you fair game."

"Yeah," Aidan says. "Just be glad Asher's not here, too, because he's not as innocent as you think he is."

Damn right he's not. That little shit can be devious when he wants to be.

Michelle unfolds her legs from the cushion and stands up to clear away the plates and stuff from the coffee table. Camryn gets up, too.

"Well, I think I've been a Parrish long enough to know. Trust me." She stacks the plates while Camryn helps her clear away the napkins and a few empty beer bottles.

"Why so quiet, Camryn?" Aidan says from the couch. "You may not be married to my brother yet, but you might as well be, and that makes you fair game, too." He raises his beer toward her as if to toast and then takes another drink, grinning mischievously.

Smart brother I have. If he wasn't so ugly, I'd kiss him on the mouth for that. Last thing I want is for Camryn to feel left out.

She smirks at him, balancing the stuff in her arms. "I guess it's a good thing you have nuthin' on me yet."

"*Yet,*" he says, nodding once as if to underline the inevitable in that word. "Guess you have a lot of uncomfortable hazing to look forward to then, huh?"

Camryn wrinkles her cute nose at him and follows Michelle into the kitchen.

Camryn

THIRTEEN

I'm really glad you invited us here," I say behind Michelle as I toss the empty beer bottles into the trash.

Michelle sets the small stack of plates on the counter and starts to rinse them off in the sink before loading them into the dishwasher. "Hey, no problem," she says, smiling at me. "I needed some company, to be honest. It's been pretty stressful around here." She places another plate into the dishwasher rack below.

I move closer and lean against the counter, crossing my arms. Is she giving me permission to probe by saying that? I'm not sure, but I'm comfortable with her enough that I go ahead and do it anyway.

"Your job taking a lot out of you?" What I really wanted to ask was: *Everything OK between you and Aidan?* remembering what Marna said about she and Aidan having some marriage troubles, but I think that's probing a little too much too soon.

She smiles warmly and rinses off the last plate. "No, I think being at the clinic is therapy, if anything."

I stay quiet, but attentive.

"That bar is taking a lot out of Aidan lately," she goes on, "but he's doing it to himself. He has more than enough employees to handle things, but he spends a lot of time there dealing with the things he's paying everyone else to do."

I look at her curiously. "Why?"

She shuts the dishwasher and glances toward the arched entry-way that leads into the living room where Aidan and Andrew are talking and laughing and saying "Shit, bro" a lot. Then she turns back to me and says in a lowered voice, "He's just upset with me." She looks away and dries her hands off on a dishrag hanging from the cabinet knob above the counter.

That's it? I keep quiet a few seconds just in case she's the really-long-pause type, but she doesn't go on. It frustrates me a little. Then suddenly she says, "I shouldn't be bringing things like this up. Not after what you and Andrew went through. I'm really sorry."

"No, Michelle," I say, hoping to ease her mind. "Hey, I'm here to listen."

For some strange reason, Michelle bringing up what Andrew and I "went through" doesn't bother me like it always did when everybody else would do it. Maybe it's because I know she's not try-ing to force me to talk about it, or is afraid to be normal around me. Right now, it's all about Michelle, and I want to be here for her.

She hesitates, glancing once more toward the living room, and sighs. "He wants children," she says and I feel my heart tighten, but I don't let it show in my face. "And I do, too—just not right now."

"Oh, I see." I nod and think about it for a second. "Well, it could be worse. At least it has nothing to do with an affair or that he has suddenly started cooking meth in the basement."

Michelle laughs lightly and hangs the dishrag back on the cabinet.

"You're right," she says, her brown eyes lit up with her smile. "I never thought of it like that. I just wish he'd give me three more years at least. I'm around children all day, being a pediatrician. I love them. You have to, to do the kind of work I do, but I have a deeper level of insight when it comes to the responsibility of raising one. Aidan's insight stops at Little League and camping trips, you know what I mean?"

I laugh gently. "Yeah."

A very small part of me wonders if Michelle is saying this to me as her way of trying to ease my own pain, by telling me that raising a baby is hard. Maybe she is, but at the same time, I think it's just me. Telling me what's going on between her and Aidan and considering the issue, it would be hard not to say something like that.

"So, how is Andrew's physical therapy going?"

The mood instantly shifts within the room, like we can both breathe a little easier now that we've gotten through the risky subject matter.

"He had some muscle weakness for a while, but he's been doing great. Doesn't really go to physical therapy much at all anymore."

Michelle nods and pulls out a chair, too. "Well that's good," she says and there's an awkward bout of silence.

Aidan and Andrew break that awkward moment when they both come into the kitchen with us. Aidan heads straight for the fridge while Andrew sits his heavy ass right on top of my lap.

"*An-drew!*" I whine and laugh at the same time, trying to push him off. "Lose a few pounds! Damn, baby, you're squishing me!"

He turns on my lap, facing sideways long enough to squish my face in both of his hands and kiss me between the eyes.

"Get. Off!" I shout and finally he does. "You've got a bony ass." I rub my hands across my legs to work out the muscles. Of course, his ass is nowhere near bony, but the look on his face was worth the dramatic lie.

"Like little boys," Michelle says from the sink now.

I didn't even notice her get up.

Aidan shuts the fridge with another bottle of beer in his hand and sits down in the chair Michelle just left. Andrew lifts me up as if I'm weightless and steals my chair, putting me on his lap afterward.

"Much better," I say.

He wraps his arms around my waist. "So, Aidan and I were talkin'."

Uh-oh, I don't know if I like the sound of that.

"Yeah?" I ask warily, looking more at Aidan since I can't really see Andrew behind me.

"This should be interesting," Michelle jokes from the sink, facing us all with her hip propped against the counter's edge.

Aidan sets his beer on the table and says, "Would you be interested in playing at my bar tomorrow night? Busiest night of the week. The stuff you two play will fit right in with the customers."

The only time I've ever really felt this nervous playing in any bar or club was the first time I performed with Andrew at Old Point in New Orleans. I think it just makes me really nervous to sing in front of his family. In front of people I don't know and will likely never see again. It's not so nerve-wracking, but this, I have to say, is causing my stomach to twist into knots.

"I don't know…"

Andrew squeezes me gently from behind. "Oh come on," he says, trying to encourage me without being too pushy.

Be pushy, Andrew! Stop being so cautious! Be like you used to be when you told me to get on the roof of your car in the rain, or when you forced me to help change that stupid tire!

"Come on," Aidan says with the quick backward tilt of his head. "Andrew says you're quite the singer."

I blush and wince at the same time. "Well, Andrew is also biased, so you can't really take his word for it."

"I think it's a wonderful idea," Michelle adds and takes her own seat on Aidan's lap. He playfully smacks her thighs with both hands, and it reminds me of how Andrew tends to do that same thing to me a lot. Aidan doesn't look as much like Andrew as Asher does, but as far as everything else they share, you can definitely tell they're brothers.

I think on it a moment and turn at an angle to see Andrew behind me, draping my arms around his neck and interlocking my fingers. He's grinning from ear to ear. How can I say no to that?

"All right," I agree. "I'll do it. But I get to pick the music."

Aidan nods his acceptance.

"Whatever you want," Andrew says.

"How long would we play?" I ask.

"However long you choose," Aidan says. "As little as one song if you want. It's up to you."

Andrew and I go to bed late after playing a few competitive games of Spades with Aidan and Michelle. And even though we're in the spare room right across the hall from theirs, it's not as awkward being here as it is at my mom's. Only there isn't any noise coming from their room like I know there was from ours during the past half hour. I tried to keep my moans and whimpers at a low volume, but, well, that's not an easy thing to do when Andrew's having his way with me.

I think I've been laying here for three hours since Andrew fell asleep. I hear the noise from the street outside and Andrew breathing softly next to me. Every now and then the light from a car will move across one section of the wall and blink out seconds later.

I can't sleep. I've had a hard time falling and staying asleep since . . . well, for a couple of weeks. I try not to toss and turn too much so I don't wake Andrew up. He looks so peaceful lying there.

Finally, I crawl quietly out of the bed and rummage inside my purse for one of those pills. They've been helping me sleep. And I like the way they make me feel. Because they make me feel something other than pain. But I'm being careful. I don't have an addictive personality, and I've never taken any kind of drugs ever in my life. Though I did try pot a few times my senior year, but everyone did.

Though I admit I think a lot about what I'm going to do when I run out of these...

I shuffle one into my hand and look at it for a moment. Maybe I should take two tonight so I can get some deep sleep. I want to be refreshed and ready to perform tomorrow night at Aidan's bar. Yeah, that's a good enough reason to take one extra.

I swallow the pills down with the bottled water I left next to the bed, and I lie down next to Andrew, just gazing up at the ceiling and waiting for the effect to kick in. Andrew, feeling my movement, rolls over instinctively and lays his arm over my waist. I curl up next to him, carefully tracing the outline of Eurydice down his side. I do this until finally my head feels as light as air, and my eyes are filled with hundreds of tiny butterflies tickling the back of my eyelids and around my temples.

And I...

Andrew

Camryn slept way past lunch. When I finally got her to wake up, she did so with a migraine and a bitchy attitude. Cute, but bitchy. She barely had two beers last night but you'd think she drank a fifth of rotgut the way she's lying in the bed with her face buried underneath the pillow.

"I brought you some Advil," I say sitting down next to her. "Maybe you have a brain tumor."

She knees me in the thigh. "Not funny, Andrew," she says with a little moan in her voice.

I thought it was funny.

"Well, take these," I say, removing the pillow from her head. She protests for a second before giving in.

She raises enough from the bed to wash them down with water and then collapses back onto the mattress, squeezing her eyes closed and rubbing her temples with her fingertips. I give her the pillow back, and she hides underneath it.

"Y'know, people usually get accustomed to drinking the more they do it, not the other way around."

"I only had two beers," she says, her voice muffled by the pillow. "It's just a headache, probably has nothing to do with the beer at all."

I lean over and kiss her on the stomach, briefly recalling the last time I actually did that, when she was pregnant. It makes me sad for a second, but like I've been doing since it happened, I force that shit down and suck it up.

"I can stay here with you if you want," I say.

"No, I'll be all right," she says, and her hand emerges from the confines of the pillow. She blindly places it on my crotch until she realizes what that is and moves it quickly to my knee instead. I would mess with her about it, but I'll let her slide this time.

"Alright, I'll be with Aidan for a couple of hours," I say and stand up from the bed. "Hopefully you'll be better before tonight. I really want us to play."

"I do, too," she says and reaches out her hand to me.

I grab it and lean over, kissing her knuckles before leaving to ride around with my brother while he takes care of some business.

By early evening, Camryn is dressed and her headache seems to be gone, so the four of us head to Aidan's fine establishment of beer, peanuts, and live music.

———

Business at Aidan's bar has been thriving, according to him, and when we walk in through the front door at barely seven o'clock, I see he wasn't exaggerating. I've never seen it this packed before, and I've spent my fair share of Friday and Saturday nights here over the six years he's owned it. Music funnels through the numerous speakers in the ceiling and walls, something folksy rock, much like Camryn and I have inadvertently made our trademark style. A couple of years ago, if someone were to ask me what kind of music I'd play if I ever had my own band, I never would've thought folksy rock. I've sung and performed classic rock like the Stones and Zeppelin in bars and clubs for a long time, but since meeting Camryn that has changed somewhat. We've adopted the Civil Wars' style for the most part, just because it came so natural to us as a duo, but we still play a few classic rock greats when we perform, too.

One of our favorites: "Hotel California" by the Eagles, technically the very first song we ever sang together. It may have been in the car while on the road and all just for fun, but it stuck with us. And we've done "Laugh, I Nearly Died" by the Rolling Stones, which Camryn insisted on learning.

But Camryn still loves the newer stuff and The Civil Wars more than anything and so that's usually what we play.

Tonight will be no different.

I kind of had a feeling she'd pick "Tip of My Tongue" and "Birds of a Feather," because those are the two songs she has the most fun with. I love watching her perform them next to me up on stage because she becomes so vibrant and playful and sexy as hell. Not that she isn't all of those things already, but it's like another more daring and flirty side of her comes out when she's singing. And she doesn't just sing—she puts on a show. I think it's that little actress she's always had buried somewhere in herself. She told me she performed in plays at school, and I can definitely see she has the knack for it.

But singing alongside me also seems to make her happy, and that's why tonight is so important. It's the first time we'll be performing together since she lost the baby, and I'm hoping it'll be therapeutic.

We weave our way through the thick crowd of people and head to the stage where we take our time setting up. Not much to set up really with just a guitar—unfortunately not one of mine—and two microphones, but we're not going on for another fifteen minutes.

"I'm so nervous," Camryn says next to my ear, having to speak loudly over the music.

I make a *pffft* sound with my lips. "Oh, please. Since when do you get nervous anymore? We've done this dozens of times."

"I know, but I'm singing in front of Aidan and Michelle this time."

"He can't sing for shit, so his opinion is hardly valid."

She smiles. "Well, I'm not nervous to the point that I don't want to do it. I guess it's actually kind of exciting."

"That's my girl," I say and lean in to kiss her lips.

"Those two girls," Camryn yells to me without looking in their direction, "front table to your left, they're having sex with you in their heads right now, I swear to God."

I laugh lightly and shake my head.

"And that guy standing next to the woman in the purple shirt,"

I say, nodding subtly in his direction, "has had your thighs wrapped around his head since you walked on this stage."

"So it'll be them tonight then, huh?" she asks.

I nod and say, "Uh-huh."

"Make sure you give it to them good, baby," she says, grinning wickedly at me.

"Oh, I will," I say with the same amount of wicked on my face.

We started this back on our second night at Levy's: we each pick a guy and a girl from the crowd who give off that I'd-love-to-fuck-you vibe and we make them feel "extra special" during one of our songs. But we always start giving our targets small bits of attention long before we go in for the kill. Just one look, a three-second-long meeting of the eyes to let her, or him in Camryn's case, know that we've noticed them a little more than anyone else in the room. Camryn's already working her magic. The guy has a dopey-ass grin plastered on his face now. She glances at me and winks. Slipping my guitar strap over my shoulder, I slowly look over at the two girls. They're pretty hot, I have to say. I make eye contact with the brunette first, hold it for a few seconds, and then look at her friend for the same amount of time. The second I look away, I notice them giggling and talking to each other behind their hands. I just smile and move my fingers across the guitar strings to test out the tuning. Camryn taps her thumb on her mic and then walks over to the side to drag the two stools that we'll end up only sitting on for maybe one song. She hops onto hers and crosses her legs; those sexy black mile-high heels are enough by themselves to make her look like she knows what she's doing in this business. Little silver studs decorate them. God damn, some of the things she wears make me crazy.

An announcer, young guy, comes out on the stage and introduces us. Many of the voices carrying through the vast space quiet down and then even more when I start to play the guitar. And when Camryn leads the first song, her voice is so sultry that she pretty much gets everyone else's attention in no time.

We go through four songs to an awesome welcoming crowd who are dancing, getting drunk, and trying to sing along. The vibe in the bar is explosive, and I love it.

Camryn walks down the three steps from the stage with her mic in hand and makes her way toward her victim. Before the song is over he's dancing with her, having one helluva time. When his hands get too close to parts only I'm allowed to touch, Camryn, like a professional, smiles and continues to sing to him while pushing him away.

Then we take a short break.

Camryn pulls me off toward the back of the stage as the voices rise up all around us again.

"I've gotta go to the bathroom," she says.

I pull the guitar strap over my head and set the guitar against the back wall.

"You go and I'll get us a drink," I say. "Do you want anything?"

She smiles, nodding. "Yeah, just get me whatever, I don't care."

"Alcoholic?" I ask.

She nods again and kisses me, pretty eager to break away quickly probably so she doesn't pee on herself.

"Oh, and why don't you do the next song solo tonight?" she suggests.

"Really? Why?"

She comes up closer and rests her hands on my chest. "You do that song better by yourself, and I think I'm done for the night. I'd like to watch you." She pecks my lips. She's so much taller in those shoes that she's looking me straight in the eyes.

If that's what she wants, I'm good with it. I don't want to push her.

"All right, I'll sing it alone," I say. "It'll make it easier to seduce my two girls out there, anyway."

She smiles and says with a little laughter in her voice, "Don't overdo it, Andrew. Remember what happened the last time."

"I know, I know," I say, waving her on.

She turns around, and I smack her on the butt as she scurries off toward the restrooms.

Camryn

FOURTEEN

When I make it into the restroom, there's a line of women waiting for empty stalls. The air is thick with liquor breath, perfume, and cigarette-smoke-laden clothes. A stall door will open and shut with an obnoxious bang every few seconds as people come and go. I go to wash my hands first, having to cram myself in between two drunk girls sitting on top of the counters on either side of me. Thankfully they're the overly nice kind of drunk, because I can't deal with a fight-ready rude one tonight. They apologize for being in the way and move over to give me some space.

"Thanks," I say and reach out to turn on the water.

"Hey, you're the singer chick," the girl on my left says, pointing her finger at me and smiling. She glances at her friend on the other side and then back at me.

"Yeah, that'd be me, I guess."

I'm so not in the mood for bathroom conversation. The longer I linger in public restrooms, the grosser I feel.

"You two are great," she says, beaming.

"Yeah, seriously," her friend says. "What the hell are you doing singing in bars, anyway?"

I just shrug and squirt more soap from the dispenser into my hand and try to avoid them as kindly as possible.

"Yeah, really," the one on my left adds. "I'd pay to see you play."

OK, so I'm not entirely immune to compliments. I smile and thank her again.

When two more stalls become free, they jump at the opportunity and shut themselves inside. Soon after, they wave good-bye and wish me good luck with my "music career." When I'm almost the only one left, I turn to the mirror, but I don't look at myself. Instead, I reach into my pocket and take a pill, washing it down with water from the sink.

It's just to take the edge off.

Then I look at myself, pushing the pill and the guilty feeling I get every time I take one, far into the back of my mind. I make up excuses to justify taking them, and I almost fool myself. But I know that the guilt I always feel is there for a reason.

In less than eleven minutes, I don't care about the guilt, the excuses, or the edge anymore, because that part of my brain has been numbed.

I run my fingertips underneath my eyes to wipe away any smudged mascara, then blot the oil from my face with toilet paper. I have to look good when I go back out there. I feel great, but I have to look as good as I feel.

Pushing myself through the crowd, I find Aidan and Michelle standing behind the enormous bar and join them. I then remember Andrew was getting me a drink, but I'm not walking back through all of those people just to get it.

"You two are fantastic!" Michelle shouts over the noisy crowd. She hugs me, and I return it, feeling my pill-induced smile stretching hugely across my face.

I turn to Aidan. "What did you think?"

"I agree with Michelle!" he says. "You should write your own music and play here more often. I get all kinds of talent scouts in here. And celebrities." He points to the back wall, where a series of autographed photos of various musicians and movie stars hang in an even line. "Get a head start with your own material," he goes on. "I bet you two would easily land a music contract within a year."

I'm so high right now that he could tell me he thinks we suck and have no future in music at all, and I'd still smile like this, letting his words go through me like air.

I look out across the length of the room to see Andrew up on the stage with his guitar and the house band getting ready to sing his trademark song, "Laugh, I Nearly Died." He likely can't see me through the crowd, but he knows I'm watching. I love to watch him onstage, in his element. I know that as good as we are together musically, he'll always own it more when he performs alone. Maybe it's just me, but I like to think of him the way he was the first time I saw him perform. Because on that night in New Orleans he was singing *for* me, and I felt like the luckiest girl in the world.

I'd do anything to feel like that again. Anything…

Seconds into the song, Andrew, like always, has the attention of everyone in the room. The two girls at the table are standing up now, dancing with each other provocatively, but I know it's all for Andrew. I've seen it before. They want him, and he lets them believe, just for one night, that he wants them, too. Perfectly harmless. Andrew and I both look at it as making other people feel good about themselves. A little flirting here and there, making some lucky girl or guy the center of attention just long enough to make them blush and smile. You never know what's going on in people's lives behind closed doors, and a little flirty, positive energy can never be a bad thing.

When we get back to Aidan and Michelle's just after midnight,

I head to bed before everyone else. I lay here for an hour, listening to their voices filter down the hallway and into the room. Andrew was going to come to bed with me, but I insisted he hang out with his brother. He worries about me way too much these days. We'll be going back to Raleigh tomorrow, and I want him to spend as much time with Aidan as he can.

Another hour passes and I'm still awake.

Frustrated, I thrust my hand inside my purse, fishing for the bottle. Without even realizing it, I am now down to my last few pills.

I pass out on three this time.

Andrew

FIFTEEN

*C*amryn? Baby, please wake up." I shake her back and forth, my hand gripping her shoulder.

My dominant emotion right now is worry. My secondary emotions are anger and hurt. But strangely enough, the feeling of uncertainty is keeping all of the others at bay.

I shake her again. "Get up."

I have no idea how many of these fucking pills she took, but judging by the nearly empty bottle, the prospect of it being enough to overdose sends a panic through my entire body. But she's breathing steadily and her heartbeat seems normal. If she doesn't wake up—

Her eyes creep open, and I suck in a fast breath of relieved air. "Camryn. Look at me."

Finally she focuses enough to look me in the eyes. "What?" she moans softly and tries to shut her eyes again, but I grab her by both shoulders and force her to sit up.

"I said wake up. Keep your eyes open."

She sits up sloppily, but it's nothing too out of the ordinary from having been forced awake and upright like that.

"How many did you take?"

Michelle stands in the doorway behind me. "Do you want me to call an ambulance?"

Suddenly, Camryn becomes completely coherent. I don't know if my question has finally caught up with her, or if the mention of an ambulance is what did it, but she looks at me with wide, frightened eyes.

"How many of these goddamn pills did you *take*?"

Her gaze drops from mine, and she looks over to see the prescription bottle on the nightstand. When I decided that sleeping past two in the afternoon was not at all like her and came in here to check on her, I found the bottle on the floor

"Camryn?" I shake her again and get her attention back.

She just looks at me. I see so much in her eyes right now that I can't choose between humiliation, regret, hurt, anger, or surrender. And then her eyes begin to fill with tears. I feel her body shaking underneath the weight of my grip on her arms. She bursts into tears, falling into my arms, sobbing uncontrollably, and it rips me in half.

"Andrew?" Michelle says from the door.

Without looking back at her, I say, "No, she'll be all right." And I swallow down my own tears and anger, feeling my chest constrict.

The door shuts quietly behind me as Michelle leaves the room.

I hold Camryn for a long time, letting her cry into my shirt. I don't say a word. Not yet. Partly because I know she needs this, just to be able to cry and get it all out. But the rest of me is so fucking pissed off and hurt that I feel like I need to take a step back and gather my composure so I don't say the wrong things. I hold her tight, wrapping my arms around her trembling body. I kiss her hair and try not to cry myself. The pissed-off part of me helps with that.

"I'm so sorry!" she cries out, and in that fraction of a second when I hear the pain in her voice, it almost completely erases the angry part of me and I grip her even tighter.

"You're apologizing to *me*?" I ask with disbelief. I pull her away with my hands firmly around her upper arms. Shaking my head furiously at her, I go back to a few minutes ago. "No, first I need you to tell me how many you took." I look her dead in the eyes.

"Last night," she says. "Only three."

"How many were in this bottle originally?"

"I don't know. Twenty, maybe."

"Then how long have you been taking them?"

She pauses and answers, "Just since Tuesday. They're my mom's. I took one when I had a headache, but then I started taking them..." Her eyes well up with moisture again.

I reach out and wipe the tears from her face. "God damn it, Camryn," I say, pulling her into my chest again for a brief moment. "What the hell were you thinking?!"

"I wasn't!" she cries. "I don't know what's wrong with me!"

I grab her cheeks in the palms of my hands. "You *know* what's wrong. You're fucked up over losing Lily, and you don't know how to deal with it. I just wish you would've talked to me."

With her face still in my hands, her eyes stray from mine. The eerie silence between us strikes me in the strangest way.

"Camryn?" I try to get her to look at me again, but she won't. "Talk to me. You have to talk to me. Listen, there's nothing you did wrong, or could've done to prevent what happened. You have to know that. You have to under—"

Her head jerks away from my hands, her eyes boring into mine full of pain and . . . something else.

"It *is* my fault!" she says, backing away from me on the bed.

She stands up from the bed on the other side and crosses her arms, her back facing me.

"It's not your fault, Camryn." I walk toward her, but the second she feels me getting too close, she whirls around at me.

"No, it *is* my fault, Andrew!" she says with tears barreling from her eyes. "I couldn't stop thinking about how being pregnant was going to mess everything up! I hated it that we were still living in Galveston after four months! I wondered how we were ever going to do the things we wanted to do with a baby! So yes, it's my fault that we lost her and I fucking *hate* myself for it!" She buries her face in her hands.

I rush the short distance over to her, wrapping her up within my arms again. "God, Camryn, it *wasn't your fault!*" I don't think I've ever said anything to anyone with that much emotion before. My chest shudders uncontrollably against her.

"Look at me!" I say, pulling her away again. "That shit is so normal. And if you're guilty, then so am I. I thought about things like that every now and then, but also like you, I wouldn't have given her up willingly if I could have."

She doesn't really have to confirm that statement out loud because I know she wouldn't have either. But she confirms it anyway:

"I didn't regret her at all," she says. "And I . . . I want her back!"

"I know. I know." I hug her tight and walk her to the foot of the bed, guiding her to sit down. I crouch between her legs, propping my arms on her thighs and taking both of her hands into mine. I look up at her and say one more time, "It wasn't your fault."

She wipes away a few tears, and we just sit here like this for what feels like forever. I think she believes me—either that or she's just avoiding it. Then she looks toward the wall behind my head and says in a quiet voice, "Does this make me a drug addict?"

I want to laugh, but I don't. Instead, I just shake my head and smile softly up at her, pressing my fingertips around her hands gently.

"It was a moment of weakness, and even the strongest person isn't immune to weakness, Camryn. Four days and one bottle of painkillers doesn't make you a drug addict. Bad judgment call, but not an addict."

She looks back down at me. "Michelle and Aidan are going to think so."

I shake my head. "No, they won't. And no one else will, either." I stand up and sit down beside her. "Besides, it's nobody's fucking business. This is something only you and I have to know about and deal with."

"I've never done anything like that before," she says, looking out ahead of her. "I can't believe—"

"You weren't yourself," I say. "You haven't been since Lily died."

The room gets strangely quiet again. I look at her from the side, but I give her this moment. She appears lost in deep thought.

And then she says, "Andrew, maybe we shouldn't be together," and her words hit me so fast and so hard that I feel like the air has been sucked out of my lungs.

I'm so stunned that it's like her words have completely stolen all of mine. My heart is racing.

Finally, when she doesn't elaborate, I manage to get out, "Why would you say that?" And I'm scared of her answer.

She continues to stare out ahead of her, tears rolling slowly down her cheeks. And then she does look at me and I see the same intense pain in her eyes that I know she sees in mine.

"Because everybody that I love tends to leave me, or die."

Relief courses through me, but it's overshadowed by her pain.

It's in this very moment that I realize this is the first time Camryn has opened up about any of this to me, or to anyone else. I think about the things Natalie told me, and about the conversations that Camryn and I had while on the road, and I know that right now Camryn is admitting the depth of her pain not only to someone else, but more important, to herself.

"I feel so selfish saying it," she goes on, and I absolutely let her without interruption. "My dad left us. My mom changed. My grandma, the only person that was the same and was always there when I needed her, died. Ian died. Cole went to prison. Natalie stabbed me in the back. Lily..." She looks at me finally, the pain intensified in her face. "And you."

"*Me?*" I crouch in front of her again. "But I'm here, Camryn. I'll *always* be here." I take her hands into mine. "I don't care what you do, or what happens between us. I'll never leave you. I'll always be with you." I wrench her hands. "Remember when I said you were the world to me? You asked me to remind you if you ever forgot. Well, I'm reminding you now."

Sobs shudder through her body.

"But you could've died," she says, tears straining her voice. "Every single day I was at that hospital, I thought it was going to be your last. And then when it wasn't and you pulled through, I still found myself reading your letter weeks, *months* later, because a part of me felt like I needed to get used to the idea of you being gone. Someday. Because I just *knew* you were going to leave in one way or another. Just like everybody else."

"But I *didn't*," I say with desperation and smile a little with it. I sit on the floor and pull her down with me. "I didn't die. I didn't because I knew you were there with me the whole time. Because I knew we were meant to be together, and that if you were going to be alive then so was I."

"But what if you do?" she asks.

I didn't anticipate that.

"What if the tumor comes back?"

"It won't," I say. "And even if it does, I'll beat it again. Hell, I went eight months without going to the doctor once and I *still* beat it. With you in my life, whipping my ass to make me go regularly for checkups, there's no way it could kill me later."

She doesn't seem fully convinced of that, but I see a tiny ray of hope in her face and that's what I wanted to see.

"I really am sorry," she says, but instead of telling her not to be, I let her have this moment, too, because it feels more like allowing herself some closure. "I bet you never bargained for this kind of crazy baggage." She wipes her fingers underneath her eyes.

Trying to lighten the mood some, I rub my hands across her bare knees and say, "I'd still love you if you were one of those chicks who runs to the bathroom to gag themselves after they eat, or if you had a secret clown sex fetish."

She laughs lightly through her tears, and it makes me smile.

I raise her chin with the edge of my finger and get serious again, looking deep into her beautiful watery-blue eyes.

"Camryn," I say, "Lily just wasn't ready. I don't know why, but you can't blame yourself for her, or for anyone else. And you have to understand that we're in it together. All of it. Do you believe that?"

She nods. "Yes."

I lean in and kiss her first on the forehead and then on the lips.

Silence ensues and the atmosphere in the room feels different. Brighter. I know that Camryn isn't going to be one hundred percent overnight, but I can see that she's better already. I can tell just by looking at her that she feels less burdened now that she got a lot of that shit off her mind. She needed this. She needed someone to straighten her out. Not someone indifferent, or someone who will only give her the cookie-cutter answers to everything.

She needed *me*.

I stand up and take her hand. "Come here."

She follows. I pick up the pill bottle from the table beside the bed and then pull her along with me to the bathroom inside the room. I lift the toilet lid and hand her the bottle. And before I even get a word out, Camryn turns the bottle upside down without hesitation and dumps the remaining four or so pills into the toilet.

"I still can't believe I was that weak." She stares at the water as the pills circle it and are sucked into the pipes. She looks over at me. "Andrew, I could've easily become addicted to them. I can't imagine—"

"But you didn't," I interrupt before she drills it any further into her head. "And you're entitled to a moment of weakness. Enough said."

I walk out of the bathroom and pace the bedroom floor. She follows me out and stands in the center of the room, watching me.

"Andrew?"

I stop and turn to face her and say, "Give me one week."

She looks slightly confused.

"One week for what?"

I smile faintly. "Just agree to it. Stay here with me for one week."

Growing more confused by the second, she says, "Ummm, all right. I'll stay here with you for one week," though it's clear in her face that she really has no idea what she's agreeing to.

But she trusts me and that means everything to me. I'm going to give us what we both need, whether she wants it or not.

Camryn

SIXTEEN

Day Three

$\mathscr{I}$ never thought for a minute that I could've done what I did. Andrew calls it a moment of weakness and maybe he's right, but it will take a long damn time for me to forgive myself for it.

Michelle has made it clear that she isn't judging me, and although it does make me feel better, I feel a sense of humiliation whenever I'm in the same room as her or Aidan. Maybe that's why it feels so bad, because they're so understanding.

One week. No idea what Andrew meant by that, but I owe it to him not to ask questions and to let him do whatever it is he plans to do. He's been very secretive the past few days, often taking his phone calls into other rooms so that I can't hear. I only tried to listen in once, just by becoming extra quiet on the couch when he stepped into the kitchen to talk to Asher. But then the eavesdropping made me feel guilty, so I turned the TV up so that I couldn't hear.

And I may have only been taking the pills for a week, but apparently it was long enough to still feel messed up three days after the last few I popped. I feel off, unable to sleep even worse than before I started taking them, but the mild headaches are finally starting to wear off, at least. I can't imagine being addicted to them for months or years. I feel sorry for people who are...

Day Four

Aidan walks in with a small stack of mail in his hand, sifting through each piece as he walks through the living room.

He looks at one white envelope awkwardly for a moment and holds it up, glancing at me first until Andrew walks into the room.

"Looks like this is yours?" He glances at me again, but hands the envelope to Andrew.

I get the strangest feeling from it, so instinctively I get up from the recliner and walk up next to Andrew to check it out.

Just before Andrew moves it out of my view and lets his hand drop to his side with the envelope clasped within it, I see Natalie's name scrawled across the front.

He knows I saw it, too.

"No," he says, shaking his head. "I'll let you see it some other time." And then he slips the envelope into the back pocket of his jeans.

I totally trust him, but I'm human and a small part of me is nervous about this whole situation. Why would Natalie be sending Andrew letters? Trust or not, the first thing that always comes to mind, no matter who you are, is wondering if something might really be going on between them. But that's absurd, and I push that thought out of my head as fast as it came.

They're plotting against me.

I just wish I knew what was going on.

Day Five

I talk to Natalie, my mom, and then to Marna on the phone today. Marna tries to act as if nothing ever happened with the baby, and she does as good a job as Michelle did my first day in Chicago. She's so kind and careful. My mom, on the other hand, can't seem to talk about much other than mine and Andrew's relationship. She hounds me every chance she gets about when we're getting married, and she has it set in stone that we're doing it the same way everybody else does. I try to tell her that I don't want a fancy dress or a chapel or thousands of dollars' worth of flowers that are going to die the week after, but it's as if she doesn't even hear me. She just wants us married. Maybe that'll make her feel better about him sleeping in my room. I have no idea what goes on inside my mom's head, and half the time I don't think she does, either.

Andrew goes to a doctor today here in Chicago for a checkup. And like every time he goes to one, I'm sick to my stomach until it's over. Thankfully, he came back with good news.

Day Six

I talk to Natalie again on the phone, but I still don't bring up anything about the envelope. She's not acting herself much, either. It's obvious she's trying really hard not to spill any of Andrew's secrets, which only makes for conversations full of awkward, silent moments. I want to laugh at her for sucking at acting normal when all she wants to do is tell me everything and get it over with.

Day Seven

This One Week has been one of the longest weeks of my life. I hang around in bed because it's starting to get colder, but I'm also nervous and just can't bring myself to do anything else. Andrew was up an hour ago, and I've only seen him come back into the room once, and that was to find his shoes. He kissed me and smiled down at me like he was secretly excited and then walked back out without saying a word.

I roll over onto my side, curled up within the blanket, and stare out the window. The sun is shining bright today, and the sky is blue and cloudless.

I hear the three of them stirring in the house.

Andrew's shoes squeak down the hardwood floor outside our room. He opens the bedroom door and stands in the doorway, looking across at me.

"Get up and get dressed," he says with his hand still on the knob.

I just look at him for a second, thinking maybe he's going to explain what for, but he just points at my shoes on the floor as if to say to *put them on*, then closes the door and leaves me here.

I do exactly as he says. I get up and put on my favorite jeans and a long-sleeved, oversized knit sweater, then a pair of socks and my loafers. When I head out of the room and into the den, Michelle is curled up in the corner of the couch with a blanket over her legs watching TV. She turns her head to see me, and she's smiling warmly as if she knows something I don't. And surely she does.

"He's outside with Aidan," she says, nodding in the direction of the front door.

Growing more nervous, I walk slowly to the door and open it.

Stepping out onto the rock front porch, I see Andrew and Aidan standing on the side of the road in front of the house with Asher, and they're all leaning against the side of the Chevelle.

For a moment, I'm thinking, *All right, so Asher visiting is what this is all about?* Not that I'm not happy to see Asher, but face it, that's not something I would think would warrant this hush-hush thing Andrew has been planning.

It's the car, I realize, but that's about all I put together on my own. I have a theory as to why he's here with it, but at this point I'm just going to try my best not to think about that.

I walk quickly down the rock steps and give Asher a big hug.

"You're lookin' great, girl," he says with those nearly identical Andrew dimples and bright green eyes. Then he squeezes me tight and lifts me a little off my feet.

"It's great to see you," I say, beaming.

I keep glancing between him and Andrew, who's smiling so hugely that I doubt he'll be able to hold in whatever it is for much longer.

I look at the Chevelle and then at Asher. I do it again.

"So, you drove all the way from..." OK, so this is a little more confusing than I anticipated at first. The car was in Texas, and as far as I know, Asher was in Wyoming. Finally, I continue, "What's going on?"

Asher looks at Andrew, and Andrew steps out front and center. "I had Asher drive the car here," he says.

"But why?"

Asher crosses his arms and leans against the back door of the car. "Because he's crazy," he says, laughing lightly. "And because he didn't trust a delivery service to ship it here for him."

I turn to Andrew again, waiting for him to spit it out. A cold breeze rushes through my knitted sweater, and I hide my hands inside the sleeves.

"You have five minutes to throw all of your stuff in your bag," he says, and my heart is beating erratically before he finishes the sentence. He taps his wrist where there is no watch. "Not a second more."

"Andrew—"

"This isn't up for debate," he says. "Go get your stuff."

I just look at him, face blank.

My theory was right, but I didn't want it to be. I don't want to go on the road...I mean, I *do*...but it's not right. It's just not right.

"You have four minutes now," Asher says.

"But we can't just leave like this," I argue. "It would be rude." I point at Asher. "And Asher just got here. Don't you want to visit with—"

"I can visit my big brother anytime," Asher counters. "Right now, I think you better do what he says or you might end up on the road wearing the same panties for a week."

A few more seconds pass and I still haven't moved. I'm in a state of mild shock, I guess.

"Three minutes, babe," Andrew says and is looking at me with a serious face. "I'm not kidding. Get up there, throw your shit in your bag, and get in the damn car."

Oh hell, he's back to his old self again...

When I start to argue again, Andrew's eyes get all feral-looking, and he says, "Hurry up. Time's running out!" and he points to the house.

Finally, letting down my guard and going with the moment as much as I can allow myself, I glare at him and say, "Fine." I'm only agreeing to it because I know he's trying to make things better. But I feel guilty as hell.

Disregarding his playful five-minute demand, I turn on my heels and walk very slowly back toward the house, purposely taking my time, partly my way of silently arguing the situation.

"You knew about this, Michelle?" I ask as I walk past her and down the hall.

"Sure did!" she yells back at me. I can hear the smile in her voice.

I push open the bedroom door, set my bag on the bed, and start stuffing everything inside of it. Then I go into the bathroom and grab our toothbrushes and various bathroom necessities. I yank our phone chargers from the wall and then my phone from the nightstand and chuck it all into my purse. I make my way around the room, hoping that I'm not missing anything.

Looks like Andrew already packed his stuff at some point and I never noticed.

Then I just stand here, scanning every inch of the place around me but not really seeing any of it. I don't want to do this, but maybe it's the right thing.

I hear the horn honk three times, and it snaps me out of my thoughts. Grabbing my bag, I swing it over my shoulder and grab my purse from the bed.

"See you around!" Michelle says from the couch.

I stop just before I go past her, and I lean over the back of the couch to give her an awkward hug, hindered by the bags on my shoulders.

"Have a great time," she adds.

"Thank you for inviting us," I say.

With a big smile, Michelle waves me on, and I head out the front door.

When I make it down the steps, Andrew pops the trunk on the Chevelle, and I toss my bag inside. It's long past the five minutes he gave me, but I dare him to say anything to me about it.

"Are you ready?" Andrew asks, shutting the trunk.

I inhale a deep breath, look at Asher and Aidan and before I answer, I go over to hug them both.

"Glad you came up," Aidan says.

"Keep my brother in line," Asher says.

I smile at them both and hop in the front passenger's seat and Andrew shuts the door for me.

They say their good-byes. A minute later Andrew slides into the driver's seat, and a wisp of cold air escapes into the car behind him.

He looks over at me. "So this is how it's gonna go," he says, resting his wrists on the steering wheel. "We head southeast, toward the coast—"

"Wait," I interrupt him, "you planned it out?" That's so against his style. It makes me wonder.

Andrew grins softly and says, "Some of it. But it's necessary."

"What part is necessary?"

He looks at me as if to say, *Will you let me finish?*

I get quiet and let him continue while he reaches over me and pops the glove box. "We're going to head southeast and stay on the coast through the winter," he says, and now all I can think about is just how long he plans to be on the road. Through the winter? I can't wrap my head around what the hell he's thinking. He pulls out a map and unfolds it on the steering wheel. I look at him warily. "I hate the frickin' cold. If we stay on the coast and head farther south, time it just right, we can avoid snow and shit for the most part."

OK, good plan, I admit. I can't stand cold weather, either, so yeah, this is definitely necessary. I nod and let him go on.

Andrew points at the giant map and starts to run the tip of his finger along our route. "We'll start on the Virginia coast and go south from there, making our way through your home state—but no stopping to visit." He points at me. "We're just passing through, all right?" He waits for me to answer.

I nod again and say, "All right," because surely there's a method to his madness, and I feel like I need to go along with it.

He looks back at the map and his finger starts to trail along it again. "Then South Carolina, down to Georgia, and then we'll make the trip around the entire length of Florida's coastline from Fernandina Beach"—his finger makes a long, wide sweep over the paper—"and all the way around to Pensacola."

"How long will all of this take?"

He smiles and shakes his head at me. "Does it matter?" Then he sloppily folds the map into an uneven stack of paper and tosses it on the seat between us. "I'm calling the shots as far as direction, this time. Mainly because I don't want to freeze my ass off. But—" he turns back around and faces the front, looking away from me "—well, it's just the way it needs to be."

"Why are you doing this, Andrew?"

His eyes fall on me again. "Because it's right," he says with such a deep gaze. "Because you're in the car."

His words confuse me. "Because I'm in the car?"

He nods subtly. "Yeah."

"But…what does that even mean?"

His green eyes soften with his smile, and he leans across the seat and takes my chin into his hand. He kisses my lips and says, "You could've fought me tooth and nail over this. You could've told me to go fuck myself when I said to get your stuff. But you didn't." He kisses me softly one more time, and the mint from his breath lingers on my lips. "You didn't run in that house because I told you to, you did it because it's what you wanted. You've never done anything just because I told you to, Camryn. I'm just the kick in your ass, is all."

I try to hide the smile sneaking up on my face, but I can't. He leans over, presses his lips to my forehead, and straightens in his seat. The engine purrs aggressively for a moment when his foot taps the gas pedal.

He's right. Anything he's ever told me to do, even if I complained about it, I never would've done if a part of me didn't want to. It amazes me how he always knows things about me before I do.

Andrew

SEVENTEEN

I think yesterday in Chicago was the first time I couldn't pre-
dict Camryn's reaction to one of my demanding ideas. My
girl was broken. It was scarin' the shit outta me more every day,
the person she was becoming. I took a risk calling Asher up that
night and asking him to drive the Chevelle all the way to Chicago.
I didn't know what Camryn might do, and truthfully, I was worried she'd refuse to go. Because of the guilt. Hey, I hate it that we
lost our Lily. I would cut off an arm or a leg to have her back. But
what's done is done, and sitting back drowning in our sorrows and
refusing to do what makes us happy for *any* reason is total fucking bullshit. That's how you kill yourself. A slow, painful suicide. If
Camryn would've refused, I would've carried her over my shoulder,
kicking and screaming, and shoved her in the backseat of the car.
Because this is our life. We met on the road; we grew to know and
to love each other on the road. It's where we were meant to be for
however long, and it's what we're going to do until it becomes clear
that we were meant to do something else.

The first fourteen long hours of our road trip are uneventful
and quiet. I drive the whole way from Chicago to Virginia Beach
listening mostly to the radio or my CD's when I can't find a decent
station. Camryn, although smiling and talking about the sights as

we drive past, still isn't herself, but she'll get there. It might take her a few days, but she'll start to come around.

The beaches are different on the East Coast than they are in Texas. They're cleaner, and the ocean water over here looks like ocean water is supposed to and not the muddy, murky Gulf water of Galveston.

It's late in the evening. We watched the sun set over the horizon just as we entered Virginia Beach, and it was the first time I've seen that spark in Camryn's eyes since before the miscarriage. If I'd known that a sunset could do that, I would've taken her to watch one a long time ago.

"So, are we getting separate rooms?" she asks as we get out of the car in the parking lot of our first hotel.

I can tell she's joking, but I bet she doesn't expect me to call her on it.

"That's exactly what we're doing." I pop the trunk and shoulder both of our bags.

"Are you serious?" She's shocked, and it's funny.

I just play it off the best I can. I never intended to get separate rooms, but now that she brought it up, it's not such a bad idea.

I close the trunk, and we head into the hotel lobby.

"Andrew, I think we're past this."

"Two nonsmoking king rooms side by side, please, if you've got 'em."

The front desk clerk taps the stuff in on her computer. I ignore Camryn for the most part, fumbling in my wallet for my credit card.

"Andrew?"

"I don't have two side by side," the woman says, "but I do have two directly across the hall from each other."

"That'll work," I say.

Camryn whispers, "I can't believe you're going to spend money on two rooms when clearly we've had tons of sex already..." Camryn just goes on and on while the clerk looks covertly at us like we're nuts. I love that look on people's faces, that dumbfounded I-can't-believe-you-just-said-that look.

"Please just shut up," I say, turning to Camryn. "I'll come over to your room and do you for a little while, don't worry. So stop making a scene."

Camryn's eyes grow as wide as the clerk's.

I take Camryn's hand and pull her along toward the lobby exit.

"I hope you enjoy your stay," the clerk says in a bewildered manner as we round the corner toward the elevator.

Camryn bursts out laughing the second the elevator doors close. "What was *that*?!" she asks, unable to contain herself. "I feel like we're two immature sixteen-year-olds!"

"But you're laughing," I point out. "So it's totally worth the immaturity."

The elevator stops on the second floor and we step out into the hall.

"But really, Andrew, why separate rooms?"

Proving further that spontaneity really does serve a purpose, I think about the mail I had Natalie send me in Chicago as we walk the length of the hall together. We stop in the center of the hall in front of our rooms, and I drop the bags on the green-speckled carpeted floor.

"Just for tonight," I say, reaching into my bag in search of that envelope.

Camryn stands over me, watching quietly. I can tell she wants to say something but she isn't sure at this point what it could be.

I stand up straight with the envelope in my hand. She glances down at it, but isn't sure what my intentions are.

"Tonight you'll stay alone in your room," I say and hold the envelope out to her.

She stopped smiling when I first pulled the envelope out of the bag. All she can do now is look at me in confusion and wonder.

Carefully, she reaches out and takes the envelope, still unsure of everything, maybe even whether or not she *wants* to know what's inside.

I slide her card key into her room door and open it, carrying her bag inside. She follows several steps behind, wordless and suspicious, the envelope clasped in her reluctant fingers. I set her bag on the long TV stand and check out her room like I always did before. I flip the lights on and test the heater before pulling back the sheets to make sure they're clean. Remembering Camryn's hotel comforter phobia, I strip it completely off the bed and toss it on the floor in a corner of the room.

She stands at the foot of the bed, unmoving.

I move over to stand in front of her. I look into her eyes and just watch the way hers look back at me. I move my index finger along the edge of her eyebrow and then down the side of her face and feel her skin heat under my touch. I want her. When her eyes lowered to look at my lips, it triggered something predatory in me. But I hold my needs back for her sake. Tonight, hopefully, will be about closure.

"Cam went to the funeral," Natalie said to me on the phone the day I called her from Aidan's house. "But she arrived late, sat in the very back near the exit and left before the service was over. She refused to walk up to the casket."

"Did she ever talk to you about it at all?" I asked.

"Never," Natalie said. "And whenever I tried to bring it up, the funeral, the accident, anything about it, she shut me down."

Tonight will be hard for Camryn, but if she doesn't go through with it, she'll never get better.

"You know where I'm at," I whisper softly, letting my hands slide away from her arms. "I'll be up all night. Started writing another song yesterday, and I really want to work on it while it's fresh in my mind."

Camryn nods and smiles weakly underneath that look of concern on her face, concern over what's lurking inside that envelope.

"What if I don't want to stay in this room by myself?" she asks.

"I'm asking you to," I say earnestly. "Just for tonight."

I don't want to say any more than that, but I hope the sincerity in my face does what words might otherwise do.

"OK," she agrees.

I peck her on the lips once and leave her alone in the room.

I just hope this doesn't backfire on me.

Camryn

Andrew leaves me in the room. Alone. I don't like it, but I've learned to listen to him over the short five months we've been together. *Five months.* That amazes me every time I think about it because it feels more like we've been together five *years*, all of the stuff we've gone through. I sometimes think about my ex Christian, my cheating rebound boyfriend after Ian, who I was with for four months. We barely knew each other at all. Now that I think about it, I can't even remember his birthday or his sister's name, who lived two streets over from where he did.

A whole other world with Andrew.

In five months I *found* myself with him, fell in total, unconditional crazy love, truly learned how to live, met practically his entire family and quickly felt like a part of them, went through a life-and-death journey with Andrew, got pregnant and engaged. All in five months' time. And now here we are facing another hardship. And he's still with me every step of the way. I was stupid and weak and took pills and he's still here. I wonder if there's ever anything I could actually do that would be so awful that he'd ever leave me. Something in my heart tells me that, no, there isn't anything. Nothing at all.

I will never understand for as long as I live, how I was lucky enough to be with him.

In my moment of reflection, I notice that my eyes never left the door after he walked out. Finally, I look down at the envelope in my hand, and I don't know why but it scares me to think about what's inside. I've contemplated it over and over for the past week. A letter? If so, what could it possibly be about? And who would it be for and from? Why would Natalie write me a letter? Why would she write Andrew a letter?

None of it makes any sense.

I sit on the end of the bed, letting my purse drop on the floor next to me, and I run my fingers over the contours of whatever is inside the envelope. But I've done that a few times in the past week, too, and I'm still coming to the same conclusions: it's paper, sort of thick, folded two or three times. There's nothing bumpy or uneven or textured inside. It's just paper.

I sigh and start to set it down, but I just hold it. I don't know why I don't just open the damn thing. It's driven me sort of crazy for a week and here I am, finally able to put the secret to rest once and for all by opening it, but I'm too afraid.

I set the envelope down on the bed and I get up, crossing my arms and watching it from the corner of my eye as I start to pace the room. I'm wary of it, like it's going to jump out at me and claw me in my leg as I walk by. Like that bitch of a cat my aunt Brenda has. I even start to dig in my purse for my cell phone to call Andrew and have him just tell me what this is all about, until I realize how stupid that would be.

Finally, I pick up the envelope, and after a long pause, feeling the light weight of it in my hand, I slide the tip of my finger underneath the sealed flap to loosen it. After breaking the seal and failing to open it carefully, I say screw it and I rip the hell out of it the rest of the way. I toss the tattered envelope on the bed and unfold the Hallmark-looking stationery to see that most of it is blank. It had been used merely to conceal the picture inside. With the back of the picture facing me, at first I refuse to turn it over to see what's on the other side. Instead, I read Natalie's handwriting in the center of the last piece of stationery:

> This is the best one I found.
> I hope it helps with whatever it is you're trying to do.
>
> > Sincerely,
> > Natalie

I turn the picture over and my heart sinks like a stone when I see Ian's smiling, vibrant face looking back at me. My cheek is pressed against his as we stare into the camera. The colored lights from the rides at the North Carolina State Fair illuminating the night in the background behind us. As if I've fallen into a freezing cold lake, the sight of his face shocks the breath out of my lungs. Tears instantly spring up from my eyes, and I let the picture fall from my fingers and onto the bed. Both hands come up to my face where my fingers cover my quivering lips.

How could I let myself cry over him?! Why is this happening?!

I got rid of all of Ian's photos for a reason. Everything. I deleted every single file with digital photos of us, removed his name from my cell phone. I even threw out my nightstand that I'd had since I was a little girl because Ian had etched IAN LOVES CAMRYN into the wood on the underside of it. I removed all reminders of him from my life the best I could because it hurt too much to know that all I had left of him were material things. I couldn't do much about the memories, but I did my best to forget about those, too.

Why would Andrew do this to me? Bring all of that pain back into my life not just so soon after losing Lily, but at all?

A part of me wants to scream at Andrew, to march through that door and across the hall to his room and tell him how much this hurts. But my reason catches up to me too fast. I know why he did it. I know why he put me in this room alone with this photograph. Because he loves me so much that he's willing to give me back to Ian for just one night so that I can maybe come to terms with losing him in the first place.

But I can't look at that damn picture! I just can't do it!

With tears streaming down my face, I grab my thick sweater from my bag and slam my arms into the sleeves roughly. And then I storm out of the room and head for the elevator.

Seconds later, I'm sitting in the cold sand on the beach looking out at the endless ocean.

Andrew

EIGHTEEN

I wonder if she'll open it. Shit, I wonder if she'll hate me for doing this to her, but if it'll help her I'll take the trade.

I press the power button on the remote control and an old *Seinfeld* rerun fills the quiet in my room. I kick off my shoes and hit the shower, letting the hot water beat down on me until it begins to run lukewarm. All I can think about is what Camryn is doing alone in her room, if she's staring at that photo of her dead ex-boyfriend, and if she's handling it. I want to go over there and be there for her, but I know this is something she needs to do on her own. Something she should've done a long time ago, long before we met.

After drying off I wrap the towel around my waist and rummage through my bag on the bed for a pair of boxers. I sit down, stare at the TV, then the wall, and then back at the TV again until I realize I'm just looking to do anything to take my mind off of Camryn.

I let my MP3 player run about five random songs through my ears before I decide that I at least need to check on her. I try her cell first but she doesn't answer. Then I pick up the hotel phone and try her room. Still no answer. Maybe she's just taking a shower.

I try to force myself to believe that until my instincts get the best of me. I slip on my jeans and a long-sleeved shirt and head across the hall to her room. I put my ear to the door to see if I can hear the shower running. Nothing. So I slip the extra card key into the door to unlock it.

She's not here. My heart picks up as I walk farther into the room. The first thing I notice is the photograph, which I haven't actually seen myself until right now, lying on the bed. I pick it up and study it for a second. Camryn looks so happy. That's the Camryn I used to know, the one with a beautiful, energetic smile. I remember that smile. I saw it dozens of times when we were on the road together.

Panicking inside, I look away from the photo and then go toward the window. I gaze out at the black ocean and see a few people walking along the boardwalk. With the photo still in my hand, I walk quickly back to my room and slip on my shoes, leaving them untied as I head outside toward the beach. The chill in the air isn't unbearable, but it's enough to make me glad I at least have long sleeves on. I search for any sign of her, looking up and down along the boardwalk and in the beach chairs near the hotel building, but she's nowhere to be found. Slipping the photo into my back pocket, I break out in a mild jog and head toward the beach.

I find her sitting in the sand not too far away.

"God damn it, babe, you scared me."

I sit down beside her, wrapping one arm around her body.

She stares out at the ocean, the chilly wind whipping gently through her blonde hair. She doesn't look at me.

"I'm sorry," I say. "I just wanted to—"

"I love you, Andrew," she interrupts, but keeps her gaze fixed out ahead. "I don't know how a girl can be both so lucky and so *un*lucky at the same time."

Unsure where she's going with this, I'm afraid to say anything because I don't want to say the *wrong* thing. I squeeze my arm around her to share our warmth. And I don't say a word.

"I'm not mad at you," she says. "I was at first, but I want you to know that I'm not anymore."

"Tell me what's on your mind," I say softly.

She still hasn't shifted her gaze from the blackness out ahead. The waves just barely lick the shore several yards out. A tiny white dot, the light from a boat, moves along the horizon.

Suddenly, I feel Camryn's gaze on me and I look over to meet it. There's just enough light from the buildings behind us, and from the moon to see her soft features, wisps of her hair blow across her cold cheeks. I reach out a hand and pull a few strands away from her lips. Her eyes soften as she looks at me and says, "I did love Ian, very much. But I don't want you to think—"

I shake my head. "Camryn, don't do that. This isn't about me, all right?" I tuck my finger behind another strand of her hair and pull it away from her mouth. "Don't make it about me."

She pauses for a moment, and I feel her hand move into my lap and my fingers link with hers.

She looks back out at the ocean.

"I didn't want to go to Ian's funeral," she says. "I didn't want the last time I saw him to be like that." She glances over at me. "Do you remember that day in your apartment when I walked in on your phone conversation with Aidan, when he was trying to get you to go to your father's funeral?"

I nod. "Yeah, I remember."

"Something you said to him, about how the last time you see someone you'd rather it be of them alive, not lying dead in a box. Well, that's how I felt about Ian's funeral. I never wanted to go. It's also why I didn't want to see Lily. It's why I chose cremation."

"But you *did* go. To Ian's funeral." I steer clear of the Lily subject for now. She's a more painful topic. For both of us. I saw her. She was so small she would've been able to fit in the palm of my hand. But Camryn refused to look.

She shakes her head. "Not really," she says about Ian's funeral. "I was there, but I wasn't. My way of letting him go was shutting him out of my mind, every word he ever said to me, his face, anything I could shut out, I did. I only went because it's what everybody expected of me. If I wasn't so worried about what everyone else would think, I would've stayed home that day."

"But that's not closure," I say carefully. "That's the same thing as sweeping the dirt underneath the rug. It's still there. You know it's there. And it'll bug the shit out of you until you do it right."

"I know," she says.

After a few long seconds of silence, I reach into my back pocket and pull out the photo.

"Y'know, if he was still alive, I'd be a little jealous. He's kind of hot, for a guy."

Camryn smiles over at me and I notice her eyes just barely skirt the photo.

I set it down on the sand next to our knees. Then I get serious again. "Camryn, what's going on with you—the pills you took, all of it—isn't just about losing Lily. You know that, don't you?"

She doesn't answer, but I can sense that she's thinking hard about what I said.

"You shut everything out. Ian. Lily. According to Natalie, even your grandma and Cole and the fact that your dad left and seems to care more for his new girlfriend than he does for you." I say it like it is because that's exactly how it needs to be said. "Instead of dealing with it, grieving, whatever, you just shut that shit out and expect it to go away on its own. You've been doing that long before we met. You've got to know that it just piles up, and one day you'll snap and go off the deep end."

"I know. You're right as usual," she says dejectedly.

"Do you believe that, or are you just agreeing with me to get me to shut up?" I grin over at her, hoping to get a smile out of her.

And it works.

She smiles and says, "No, I do believe it. I just wish I would've believed it sooner."

"Why do you believe it now?"

"Because you're like a philosopher with tattoos." She laughs and it sends a shot of warmth through my blood.

I can't believe she's laughing. At first, I thought it was going to take a long time for Camryn to come to terms with all of this, but she surprises me every day.

"A *philosopher*?" I say. "Hardly. But I'll take the credit."

Camryn turns sideways and lays her head on my lap. She looks up at me with those doelike blue eyes of hers, and I can't help but reach down and touch the softness of her face.

"Do you want to know the truth?" she asks.

"Of course," I say, but I'm feeling a little anxious all of a sudden.

"It's like I told you back at Aidan's," she says. "If I ever lost you, of all people, that would do it for me. When I miscarried, it triggered all of my fears again. About losing you. It was like, in that second of tragedy I was reminded about death all over again and how fast it sneaks up on a person. If God or Nature or whoever or whatever the hell it is out there controlling all of this could be so cruel and heartless to kill my baby, then It wouldn't have any second thoughts about killing you, too. It scares me, Andrew. The thought of ever losing you kills me inside. And because I almost lost you once, it makes the fear that much worse."

"But I told you before—"

She lifts away from my lap and sits directly in front of me, her knees burrowed into the sand.

"I know what you told me," she says. "But it doesn't matter what you believe, or that you know all the right things to say to make it better. You don't know for sure what will happen, Andrew. The tumor could very easily come back and despite everything we do, all of the precautions we take, it could kill you."

I start to argue, but she's so intent on saying these things to me that I know I have to let her.

"You're the best thing that's ever happened to me," she goes on, "and I can look you in the eyes right now and say that as much as it hurts, I can accept Ian's death. I can accept Lily's death. I can accept anyone else's death even though whoever it is, it will be unbearably hard. But yours..." She pauses and doesn't even blink as she looks deeply into my eyes. "I could never accept yours. *Never.*"

The silence between us only amplifies the sound of the ocean. I want to take her into my arms, to crush my lips over hers, but I just sit here, staring at her because the words she just spoke to me are the most powerful words I've ever heard or felt or understood.

Finally, I reach out both arms and lift her onto my lap. I wrap my arms around her back and look into her eyes and say, "I believe you and I feel the same way."

She cocks her head gently to one side. "Really?"

"Yeah. Camryn, I can't live without you. I could try, but it would be a miserable existence. It isn't just about me; you could die tomorrow just as easily as I could. Neither one of us are immune to it."

She doesn't object, but she looks away for a brief moment.

I cup her cheeks within my hands, forcing her gaze. Her skin is cold.

"We have to live in the moment, remember?" I say and instantly get her attention again. "We need to make a pact, you and me, right now. Will you make a pact with me?" I move my hands back a little to warm her cold ears.

She nods. "OK," she says, and I'm glad she trusts me enough with this not to ask questions before agreeing.

Moving one hand away from her ear, I trace the tips of my fingers across her forehead and down the sides of her cheeks. "We can't control death," I say. "There's nothing either of us can do to avoid it or to hold it off. All we *can* control is how we live our lives before it comes for us. So, let's promise each other things that we can hold true to no matter what."

Camryn nods and smiles slimly. "What kinds of things?" she asks.

"Anything. Whatever we want from each other. Like…" I stand up from the sand and bury my hands in my pockets. I gaze out at the ocean, sifting through my mind for the best promise to start with. I can think of only one thing at the moment, so I turn back to her and point my index finger upward and say, "This has nothing to do with the tumor or anything specific, but I want you to promise me that if I'm ever put on life support for any reason and you feel in your heart that I'm not going to pull through, you feel like I'm suffering, that you'll take me off of it."

Her smile fades, and she just looks up at me like I ruined the moment. I reach down to her and take her by the hand, bringing her to her feet with me.

"I'm not trying to be morbid. This is just something that's always bothered me, y'know? You see it on TV and in movies. Some guy is hooked up to every machine known to man trying to keep him alive because the family has hope, or whatever. Nothing wrong with hope, but damn, that shit terrifies me." I gently wrap my hands around her arms. "Never let me live like a vegetable. Promise me that. You know me better than anyone, and I trust you to know when I've had enough. So promise me."

Slowly, she starts to come around. It takes her a second, but she begins to nod. "Promise me the same," she says.

I smile and say, "You got it."

She takes a step back and hides her hands in her sleeves. Wrapping her sweater tight around her body, she begins to pace.

She stops and looks at me. "Promise me that if I ever get Alzheimer's or dementia, and I don't remember anyone that you'll visit me every day and read to me like Noah read to Allie."

"Who?" I ask, but then it hits me. "Oooh, I see." I laugh and shake my head at her.

Her eyes and her smile get bigger and she yells, "*Andrew!* It's not funny! I'm being serious!" She laughs and I grab her, pulling her into my arms.

"All right, all right!" I say, squeezing her wriggling body against me.

"It was your idea," she says, "so don't make a joke out of it."

"I know. You're right, but...*really*? You have to go all Sparks on me?"

I feel her elbow dig into my gut, and I double over a little and overdramatize the pain it caused, my face strained with agony and laughter. To add insult to injury, Camryn gives me a push and knocks me over into the sand. Then she stands directly over me with one foot on each side of my waist, hands propped on her hips all authoritativelike. I keep one hand on my gut, laughing and straining to keep my face straight, though I know damn well I'm not really fooling her.

"Leave it to you to make fun of a very serious moment." She says this so seriously that it just makes me laugh harder, mainly because it's so hard for her to keep a straight face.

She starts to sit on me, and she'll probably try to beat me with her flimsy little hands, but I reach out just before she does and I grab her between the legs and squeeze really hard.

"*Owww!*" she moans and starts to fall over but I hold her still in the position. "What is it with you grabbing my *paarrr—shit*, Andrew!—grabbing my parts?!"

I apply more pressure and slowly raise my back from the sand, guiding her backwards. She falls to her knees at eye level with me.

"Because I like it," I whisper onto her lips. "Now be still."

The mood between us shifts in a matter of seconds. Her cold skin becomes warmer, her eyes become rapt, her body compliant.

"There's people out here...," she tries to say softly, but my hand tightening between her legs steals her voice away.

"I don't care," I say, scanning her eyes first and then the plump, wetness of her lips. "They're far enough away."

"But... what are you doing..."

"Just be still. Be quiet." I trace my tongue over her bottom lip and gently suck on it. I feel her try to kiss me, but I don't let her.

I move my hand from the outside of her pants and slide it behind the loose-fitting fabric to find her warmth. God damn, she's already wet. Leaning into the crook of her neck, I shut my eyes and inhale the scent of her skin. She stays very still, but I can feel her body quivering and her pulse beating fast under my touch. I want to fuck her so bad. But I won't yet, because I like to torture myself. I fucking love it.

My free hand drops from around her waist, and I move it to her thighs, forcing her to spread her legs farther apart. "Open them," I say with my lips barely touching hers, and she does exactly what I tell her, moving her knees outward against the sand. She tenses up a little when I sense a man walking by not too far away, but I squeeze her again, slipping two fingers inside of her and forcing her to look only at me. She gasps and I shudder quietly, feeling the inside of her tightening around my fingers. I look into her eyes, sometimes mine straying to study the curvature of her mouth. "Don't look away from me," I say. "I don't care if you feel like you need to shut your eyes. Don't. Keep your eyes on mine."

She nods subtly as if she's afraid I'll stop if she does it wrong.

I move my fingers in and out of her slowly at first, pulling them out and using her wetness to keep her clit wet, rubbing my middle finger over it in a circular motion. Every time I touch it her eyes start to close, but I stop the second I notice and she regains control of her gaze. I move my fingers inside her again, a little faster and with my thumb apply more pressure to her clit each time. Tiny moans escape from her parted lips, sucking in the chilled air around us and my warm breath as I breathe harder onto her mouth. But she never takes her eyes off of mine and she doesn't speak, even though I know she wants to do both.

"Admit it," I whisper leaning in to her ear, "at this point, you wouldn't care if anyone was watching. Would you? You'd let me fuck you right here in front of everybody and worry about the shame only after it was over."

I feel her head nod next to mine.

"What else would you let me do?" I ask and keep my lips near her ear. I keep my fingers moving.

"Anything you wanted," she says with a gasp in her voice.

"*Anything* I wanted?" I rub my thumb firmer against her clit.

"Yes...," she says and her breath sputters softly. "*Anyfuckingthing* you wanted..."

Her words, her voice laced with need, make me insanely hot for her, and I'm so fucking hard I can hardly stand it. My fingers move harder and faster. Her body begins to tremble, her thighs shake trying to hold herself up. I pull away from her ear and look into her eyes again. She keeps hers trained on mine the best she can, her lids are getting heavier, her breath uneven and wispy. But her eyes widen and freeze when I hit that special spot, and I make sure not to break the rhythm.

"Don't look away," I say and continue to stare fiercely into her eyes.

As she starts to come, my gaze only strengthens, piercing hers in a moment of hungry lust. It's like I can see the pleasure emanating from around her irises, feel the heat of her orgasm coming off the sensitive skin on her lips, which want to kiss mine so savagely, but I still won't let her. And as her quivering body begins to calm, I push my two fingers deeper inside, feeling her constrict around them all the while keeping pressure on her clit with the pad of my thumb.

She collapses onto my chest.

I wrap her trembling body up in my arms and kiss the top of her head.

"What the fuck are you doing to me?" she says.

I laugh lightly and hold her tighter. "Whatever the hell I want," I answer cunningly.

Tilting her head back away from my chest, she gazes up at me. "Well, I don't care what you say, you're not going to get me off this time without me returning the favor."

"Oh, is that right?"

"Yes, that's exactly right, so don't even try it."

"What are you going to do to me then?" I feel my grin deepening.

"Whatever the hell I want," she says with a grin even more wicked than mine.

Then she rises to her feet and taking a hold of my hand brings me up with her.

"But not out here," she says. "It's getting too cold."

"You're the boss," I say and let her start to pull me along.

I would never bring it up, but I do notice as we walk away from the beach, Camryn looks back once at the photo of her and Ian lying on the sand. Her hand squeezes firmly around mine, and she looks over at me smiling softly as we cross the boardwalk.

I know I really had little to do with her finally finding her closure. Yeah, I forced it on her, but it was Camryn who in that moment faced one of her biggest fears. She stared into the face of someone she loved and lost, and finally accepted it. I admit, it was strange how it all happened, and I never went out there with any sexual intentions, especially in a moment like that. But Camryn, in the time she spent alone on that beach thinking about Ian, long before I joined her, she had already figured it all out.

I can't say for sure how she did it, or how much I had to do with it, but by the time she left the beach with me that night, she was starting to become herself again.

Camryn was coming back, and I was living in the clouds with her.

Camryn

NINETEEN

December 8—my twenty-first birthday

As it started getting colder, Andrew and I started heading farther south. We spent only one night in Virginia Beach, and from there we traveled North Carolina's coastline, staying a few days in Myrtle Beach, South Carolina, where I got my first road-trip job. Housekeeping. Definitely not my first pick, especially after Andrew reminded me that day about the gross things guests tend to leave behind in the rooms. But it was a job, and I didn't mind it so much, except when they expected me to wash out wastebaskets with disgusting hockers stuck to the bottom. Sorry, but just thinking about that makes me gag. I called Andrew and begged him to come do it for me. Of course, I totally bribed him with promises of mind-altering blow jobs in random places in exchange for his services. Fucking yay. Nah, who am I kidding? I enjoy the hell out of doing it for him. I only pretend to hate it sometimes, but I think he likes it when I pretend because he likes to hear me whine.

Anyway, apparently, housekeeping jobs are like revolving doors, employees come and go so fast you might as well not even officially add them to the payroll. I thought to myself how this could really work in my favor while on the road. So, in exchange for half of the rent of the room we were staying in and because the hotel staff was shorthanded, I asked if I could help out and they hired me on the spot.

But the job was only temporary, as Andrew and I needed to get out of Myrtle Beach and head to our next destination, wherever that might be. We never plan destinations in advance. The only rule we're going by is staying on the coast. At least until the spring. But it'll be a few months before spring gets here, and right now, we're happily set up in a cottage-style hotel right on the beach in beautiful Savannah, Georgia.

And today, I turn twenty-one.

Andrew wakes me from a deep sleep by opening the curtains on our giant room window and letting the sun fill the room.

"Get up, birthday girl," he announces from somewhere near the foot of the bed. I hear him slap the tabletop by the window with the palm of his hand repeatedly.

I moan and roll over onto my side, putting my back toward the bright sun and then burrow underneath the sheets. A gust of cold air hits me when Andrew snatches the sheets off me.

"Oh *come on*!" I moan, drawing my knees toward my chest and pulling the pillow over my head. "I should be able to sleep in on my birthday."

Suddenly my body is being dragged off the bed and my arms come up wildly, trying to hold on to the edge of the mattress. Andrew's hand is wrapped firmly around my ankle. I kick and flail, trying to get away, but he drags me across the bed so fast and without much effort that I just give up. My butt hits the floor and the sheets tumble down and around me.

"You are such an ass!" I laugh.

"But you love me. Now get up."

With my hair all tangled around my head, I look up at him and pout. He smiles at me and reaches out his hand. I take it, and he pulls me into a stand.

"Happy birthday, babe," he says and pecks me on the lips.

I flinch a little, because I know I have morning breath, and I'm already so used to him never passing up the opportunity to tease me about it.

Without looking at me, Andrew reaches inside his coat pocket and pulls out a little black velvet box. Obviously, he's already been out and about today, but I'm more interested in the box he's putting in my hand. I look at him warily, ready to chew him out if he went behind my back and spent a lot of money on a piece of jewelry.

"Andrew?" I say suspiciously.

"Just open it," he says. "I was good. I promise." He puts up both hands in surrender.

Still totally wary of his apparent sincerity, I lift the lid on the box to see a diamond pendant necklace inside, and I gasp a little. Then I narrow my eyes at him. "Andrew, I swear." I glance down at it again, feeling guilty for even holding it. "There's no way this wasn't—"

"I promise," he says with a charming smile. "It wasn't expensive."

Chewing on the inside of my lip skeptically, I ask, "Then how much did it cost?"

"Ah, just around one twenty-five. No more than that. Cross my heart." He makes a crossing motion over his heart with his finger.

Then he reaches out and takes the necklace from the box, letting it dangle on his hand. "Do you like it?" he asks as he moves around behind me.

Instinctively, I reach up and move my disheveled hair away as he slips the necklace around my neck. "It's perfect, Andrew. I more than like it. I *love* it." I look down once he clasps it in place and hold the shiny silver pendant in my fingers.

I turn around to face him and push up on my bare toes to kiss him deeply.

I just can't see how something like this didn't cost a boatload, but he's telling the truth. I think . . .

"Thank you, baby," I say, beaming.

Suddenly, he smacks me on the butt and says, "We've gotta get out of here today. I'm sick of hiding out in these rooms. Sick of this cold weather. I wish we could hibernate."

"You and me both. What exactly are we going to do?" I grab a clean outfit from my bag by the TV.

"I don't know. Anything," he says. "Just dress warm."

He didn't need to tell me that, really. Not even being on the coast and farther south has done a lot to keep us warm the past several days. We both dream of spring and summer, so much so that it has gotten to where it's all we talk about anymore. I complain a lot about not being able to hang my bare feet out the car window without freezing us out, and he complains that we still have yet to accomplish sleeping in that field under the stars. Of course, I won't say it out loud because it'll just make him want to do it even more, but I'm really not looking forward to sleeping under the stars. Ever. Not after what happened the first time we tried. No. I think I'm content with the hotel beds. No snakes in those.

Winter is depressing. I think it's why the suicide rate is so high in Alaska. Beautiful state, but give me the sweltering heat of a southern desert state any day.

I dress extra warm for my birthday: thick coat, scarf, gloves, you name it I'm wearin' it. And I'm *still* frickin' cold.

———

Andrew, he kinda makes winter hot. I've always thought guys with beanies are sexy, but the way he looks in his black designer jacket and knit beanie, dark gray sweater, dark jeans, and Doc Marten boots is really all the birthday present that I need. I smile to myself as we walk hand in hand through a small crowd of people, all shuffling into the lighthouse and out of the cold when three girls, probably tourists like us, gape at Andrew as we walk by. That happens a lot, and I should be used to it by now. I gloat privately, but who wouldn't in my situation? He's the sexiest thing I've ever seen. No wonder he was a model at one time. He hates talking about it, so naturally I often bring it up just to see him squirm. He's been shaving less, too; he's got that whole sexy stubble thing goin' on.

We climb the spiral stairs up into the lighthouse overlooking the ocean and we gaze out at the view together. Because it's something to do. We've just been playing it by ear—driving around town and picking something as we see it. Though, in the cold months, even that is a hit or miss. We hang our arms over the railing and move closer to each other to keep warm. The cold wind batters us, being so high off the ground, and I know my nose and cheeks are probably red.

It takes us all of five minutes to say "Screw this," and we practically run back to the car.

"Maybe we should just go to a movie," he says in the driver's seat. "Or . . . OK, I say we just hibernate."

We sit here for a long time just trying to figure out something to do.

"Let's just drive around some more," I say, coming up short.

"Maybe we should just leave."

I shrug. "If you want to." Then I see a sign that reads Fleas & Tiques Flea Market & Antique Store.

"Let's go shopping," I suggest.

Andrew doesn't look enthused. "Shopping?"

I nod and point to the sign. "Not the mall or anything," I say. "You can find some great stuff in flea markets."

His expression is still flat, but I guess he realizes it sure as hell beats walking around outside in the cold, or sitting in this car doing nothing at all.

Giving in because, face it, he really doesn't have much of a choice, he backs out of the parking space, and we follow the signs to the flea market. We find a bit of everything: stupid-looking hats, old-timey dental tools, handmade quilts, VHS tapes, and records. Andrew didn't care for much until the wooden box of records came into view.

"I haven't seen an actual Led Zeppelin record in years," he says, holding one in his hands. The cover is so beat up and faded it looks like it's been sitting in an attic for thirty years, but he holds it so carefully you'd think it was in mint condition.

"You're not planning on buying that, are you?"

"Why not?" he asks, not looking at me.

He turns it over in his hands to look at the back side.

"Because it's a *record*?"

"Yeah, but it's a *Led Zeppelin* record," he counters, glancing at me briefly.

"Yeah, *and*?"

He doesn't answer.

I go on, "Andrew, what would you play it on?"

Finally, he gives me his full attention. "I wouldn't play it."

"Then why would you buy it?" I ask, and then answer for him

sarcastically, "Oh, it's a collectible. I get it. You could mount it some-where in the backseat of the car." I smirk at him.

"Or, I could put *you* in the backseat and mount it in the front."

My mouth falls open slightly.

Andrew grins and slides the record back in the box.

"I'm not going to buy it," he says, taking my hand.

Minutes later, we come to another booth chock-full of vintage-style clothing. As I'm meticulously combing through everything on the racks, Andrew falls back into the booth next to me where a wall of hundreds of DVDs and Blu-rays are displayed. He stands there in front of it with his arms crossed, practically unmoving as he scans each and every title. I can see the back of his head through the wooden mesh barrier that separates his booth from mine. I go back to the clothes, feeling a sense of urgency and need with just about each piece I touch. I frickin' *love* vintage clothing. Not that I actu-ally wear it, or ever really have, but it's one of those things you can't help but look at with admiration and imagine yourself in.

I push the thin metal hangers back, one by one, out of the way so I can see everything. Shirts with poet's sleeves and leather laces, corsets, dresses with long, flowing sleeves and draping ruffles, Victorian-style boots—

What is *this*?

My heart stops for a second when I slide one hanger away and see the dress. An ivory vintage Gunne Sax with short flutter sleeves. I take the hanger from the rack and hold the dress against me and turn to the mirror. The length just barely drags the floor. With one hand holding the dress at level with my height, I reach down with the other and pull the fabric out with my fingers. Then I twirl around.

"God, I love this dress," I say out loud to myself. "I have to have it."

"I uhhh, have to say," Andrew says from behind, startling me, "that's a sweet dress."

A little embarrassed that he likely saw me admiring myself in it, and talking to myself no doubt, I don't look right at him. Instead, I peek inside to check out the size on the tag. It's my size! Of course, I have to buy it now, no questions asked. It was meant to be!

Crushing the dress against me, I whirl around to face Andrew standing there.

"Do you really like it?" I ask guiltily, my way of begging him not to throw that old record conversation up in my face.

"I think you should get it," he says with a big, dimpled smile. "I can picture you in it already. Beautiful. Naturally."

I blush hard and look down at it again. "You think so?" I can't stop smiling.

"Definitely," he says. "And it would give me easier access."

Leave it to him!

I let his perverted comment slide, mainly because I'm just way too in love with this dress. Then I realize suddenly that I haven't looked at the price tag yet. Already familiar with Gunne Sax dresses, I know they aren't expensive. But when it comes to some random person who thinks they can fool a buyer into paying three times what it's worth, there's no telling what that tag says. I hold my breath and look down. Twenty bucks! Perfect.

I look back at Andrew, and I feel like a bitch all of a sudden.

"Why don't you go ahead and get that Led Zeppelin record," I say timidly.

Andrew shakes his head, smiling. "Nah, an old record really has no use. But a dress like that, it has uses." He crosses his arms and looks me up and down.

I'm thinking he's just being a pervert again, and I start to call him on it this time when he adds, "Like getting married to me in it."

His green eyes seem to flit across my blue ones.

My smile softens and I say, "It's a perfect wedding dress."

"Then it's settled," he says, taking my hand. "Whenever we get married, at least you have the dress taken care of."

"That's all we need, really," I say, walking with him out of the booth with the dress draped over my forearm.

He glances over at me. "Rings," he says with a curious look hidden within his eyes.

"I have a ring," I say, holding out my hand in case he somehow forgot about the one he bought me in Texas.

"That's an engagement ring."

"Yeah, but it's enough."

"Well, I need one, too," he says. "Or did you forget about me? It takes two, y'know."

I chuckle lightly as we make it to the short line at the register. "OK, you're right, but I'm fine with the ring I have. Besides, I know you spent a lot of money on this necklace. You can't be doing that."

"Are we back to that already?" he asks playfully, pulling his wallet from his pocket. "I didn't lie to you about what I paid for the necklace."

Maybe he really is telling the truth.

"I believe you," I finally say.

He smiles and leaves it at that.

Andrew

TWENTY

*Y*es, I'm a damn liar. That necklace cost a little over six hundred bucks, but I know better than to tell her that. She thinks that expensive things are always all about how many zeroes are behind the decimal, but it's not always about that. Really, I think it's usually the girl that makes it all about the price. Shit, I've seen chicks bitch and moan about how their guy didn't spend enough. I wonder if they even realize that they make it hard on us when they get together with their friends and compare rocks like we might compare inches. We don't *really* do that, by the way. At least, I've never known a guy who wanted to whip his shit out and compete with me.

I wanted to buy something really nice for Camryn for her birthday. It just so happens that the one thing I liked out of everything I looked at happened to be expensive.

Deal with it, baby.

She might faint if she ever finds out how much I spent on our wedding rings, which I bought while we were in Chicago. It's been hard keeping Camryn from seeing them. But I managed to tuck the little box I keep them in safely into a hidden compartment in my duffel bag.

We spend the entire day doing what we always do, hanging out together and making the most of the cold weather. When we arrive back at our hotel, I grab my guitar and play for her a song I wrote and have been working on for a week. I hoped to have it done by her birthday because it is part of her birthday present. I wrote it just for her. I call it "The Tulip on the Hill," a song inspired by the first day we spent together when I got out of the hospital after my surgery:

"I just think you should take it easy," Camryn said that day. "No burying your head underneath Billy Frank's hoods for a while, or bungee jumping or drag-racing."

I laughed lightly, letting my head fall to the side to see her. I was laying longways across the top of a stone picnic table. Camryn sat on the bench near my head.

"So your definition of taking it easy is to do absolutely nothing?" I asked, smiling at her with my head propped in my hands behind me.

"What's wrong with a quiet day in the park?" she asked and reached out to trace my brow with her fingertips.

"Nothing," I said and kissed her fingers when her hand made it to my mouth. "I like being alone with you."

She tilted her head gently to one side and her expression softened. Then she looked out at the park. The trees were full, and the grass was thick and green. It really was a nice day. I wondered why we seemed like the only two outside enjoying it.

"I think tulips are pretty," she said distantly, staring toward the small, grassy hill on the other side of me.

I looked, too, and saw a single tulip perched on the top of that hill, all alone.

I'm not sure why, but ever since that day, whenever I see a tulip anywhere, I think of her.

I'll never forget the smile on her face as I play and sing the song to her. It's so warm and bright and endearing, the kind of smile that says *I Love You More Than Anything In This World* without having to say the words.

TWENTY-ONE

January 21—my twenty-sixth birthday

I'm having a sweet dream that involves me skydiving (for some odd reason, with actor Christopher Lee) and the sky is as blue as...well, the sky. Christopher Lee, with red goggles plastered over his eyes, gives me a thumbs-up just before the wind whisks him away into the blue ether. Then suddenly my heart stops, and I suck in a sharp, frigid breath. My eyes pop open to the real world. My body jerks upward from the bed so fast that my arm swings out beside me, and I hit the lamp mounted on the wall.

"*Ho-ly-shit!*" I yell out.

It takes me a second to realize what happened. Between seeing Camryn at the foot of the bed holding an ice bucket and me frantically tossing the cold, wet sheets to the side, I'm still trying to catch my breath.

Camryn cackles loudly. "Happy birthday, baby! Get up!"

I guess I deserved that after what I did to her on the morning of her birthday last month. But the devious little shit really got me good, much worse than I did her. I guess paybacks really are a bitch.

Unable to keep from smiling, I just go with it and slowly ease my naked ass off the bed. Already she's got that *uh-oh* look on her face as she begins to back away from me and move toward the door. Knowing it's her only way out, I watch as she gauges the situation.

"I'm sorry!" she says with a terrified smile, her hand bent behind her feeling her way for the door.

"Uh-huh, I'm sure you are, babe."

I walk very slowly toward her, my hooded eyes watching her as if I'm a predator toying with its prey.

She cackles again. "Andrew! You better not!" She's just two feet from the door now. But I take my time, letting her think she might actually make it that far, my grin deepening to the point that I know I must look like a sadistic madman by now.

Suddenly, Camryn squeals, unable to contain it any longer and dashes to the door thrusting it open. *"Nooo! Please!"* she yells and laughs at the same time as the door swings wide open, smashing into the wall. She runs out into the hallway.

When I come running out after her, the shocked look on her face and the hilarious fact that she actually stopped, is a dead giveaway that she didn't expect me to go this far with no clothes.

"Oh my God! Andrew, no!" she screams out as she starts running full throttle down the length of the brightly lit hall.

I just keep on running after her, everything I have hanging in the breeze. That girl has a lot to learn if she actually thought I'd be too embarrassed to run out after her, butt naked *and* with shrinkage. I don't care. She's going to regret that bucket of ice.

We run past room 321 just as an elderly couple is stepping out. The man pulls his wide-eyed wife back as the crazy naked man zooms past.

"Oh dear God...," I hear a voice far behind me say.

Finally, when Camryn makes it to the very end of the long hallway, she stops and faces me, her back arched over, both hands out in front of her as if to put up a shield. Tears are streaming from her eyes from laughing so hard.

"I give up! I give up! Oh my God, you're *naked*!" She can't stop laughing. I laugh too when I hear her snort once.

"You're really in for it," I say as I grab her and hoist her over my shoulder.

She doesn't even try kicking and screaming and flailing this time. One, she still can't stop laughing long enough to gain that kind of control over her body. And two, she knows better. I just hope she doesn't pee on me.

I carry her all the way back down the hallway toward our room, and when we come to room 321 I say "Sorry you had to see that. You have a good day now" with a nod as I pass. The couple just stares, the husband shaking his head at me with a revolted look.

I close the door behind us and throw Camryn down on the bed amid the chunks of ice and freezing water. She's still laughing.

I stand between her legs and take off her shorts and panties at the same time, staring down at her without muttering a word. I'm hard in seconds. Her playful mood shifts in an instant, and she bites down on her bottom lip, looking up at me with those sweetly seductive blue eyes that always bring out the primal in me.

Without any real warning, I lower myself on top of her and bury myself inside her.

"Are you really sorry?" I whisper, moving in and out of her slowly. My chest pressed hard against hers, our tattoos touching, Orpheus and Eurydice becoming whole again as we become one with each other.

"Yes...," she says, the word shuddering from her lips.

I thrust inside of her a little deeper, pushing one of her thighs up with my hand.

Her eyelids become heavy and she tilts her head back.

I crush my mouth over hers, and her moans reverberate through my throat as I start to fuck her harder.

Then something inside of me grows dark, predatory. I climb onto the bed and grab both of her thighs, digging my fingers into her flesh as I drag her across the bed toward me so fast she doesn't get a chance to move. Seizing both of her arms, I flip her body over and pin her wrists behind her back and force her on her knees. With my free hand, I touch the soft contours of her ass as it's raised up in front of me, squeezing each cheek in my hand tight before I smack them so hard her body jerks forward. She whimpers. Then I press my hand against the back of her neck, pushing the side of her face harder against the mattress. I feel the heat coming off her flesh from where my hand has already left red marks.

She whimpers again, and I twist her wrists tighter in my hand. Reaching down with the other, I put two fingers in her mouth and hook her cheek with them while pushing my cock inside of her from behind.

She cries a little, her thighs beginning to shake, but I don't stop. I know she really doesn't want me to.

After I come and my heartbeat slows, I pull her naked body next to mine, her sweating head nestled in the crook of my arm. She kisses my chest and walks her index and middle fingers over my bicep and toward my mouth. I take her hand and kiss her fingers.

"I'm so glad that you're you again," she says softly.

"That I'm me?" I ask, and she tilts her head back so she can see my eyes. "Haven't I always been?"

"No, not always."

"When have I not been?" I'm truly confused, but I find her coyness over whatever she's getting at adorable.

"After we lost Lily," she says, and the playful smile that had been growing at my lips fades. "I don't blame you for it, but after Lily you treated me like a porcelain doll, afraid you'd break me if you handled me too roughly."

I squeeze my arm around her a little tighter and her cheek falls back against my chest.

"Well, I didn't want to hurt you," I say, brushing my thumb back and forth over her arm. "I still feel like that sometimes."

"Well don't," she whispers and kisses my chest again. "Never hold back with me, Andrew. I always want you to be yourself."

I grin and squeeze her arm again. "You know you're giving me permission to ravage you whenever I want, right?"

"Yeah, I'm fully aware of that," she says, and I hear a matching grin in her voice.

I kiss her on the top of her head and pull her over on top of me.

"Happy birthday," she says again and slips her tongue into my mouth.

———

Thank God for Florida in the winter. After my very surprising—and satisfying, I might add—birthday this morning, Camryn and I spend the day practicing our new song. Well, it's not technically ours, but to mix things up a bit we've adopted Stevie Nicks's kickass hit "Edge of Seventeen." Camryn is getting frustrated with the way the lyrics blend so fast into each other, but she's determined to get it right. This is her song, the one she wants to sing on her own. That's a huge step for her, because we've always done songs together.

And I admire her for it.

She looks so frustrated, but underneath it, all I see is my Camryn coming back to me more every day. Her soul seems lighter, the light in her eyes brighter, and every time she smiles it reminds me of when we first met.

"You can do this," I say sitting on the windowsill with my electric guitar resting against my chest. "Don't try so hard, baby, just own it."

She sighs and throws her head back, plopping on the chair by the small round table next to me. "I know all the words, but I always get tripped up on those last few verses. I don't know why."

"I just told you," I say. "You're thinking about it too hard, because you start the song already expecting to mess up when you get to that part. Don't think about it. Now try again."

She takes another deep, aggravated breath and stands up.

We practice for another hour before we head to the nearest steak house for a late afternoon lunch.

"You'll get it right. Don't worry about it," I say, as the waitress brings us our steaks.

"I know. It's just frustrating." She starts to cut her steak, knife in one hand, fork in the other.

"It took me a little while to get 'Laugh, I Nearly Died' down," I say and bite a huge chunk of steak off the end of my fork. I chew a little bit and then say, with my mouth still full, "My next must-learn song is 'Ain't No Sunshine' by Bill Withers. I've always wanted to learn that song, and I think it's about time I retire the Stones."

She seems surprised. She points her fork at me and swallows and says, "Oooh! Nice choice!"

"You *know* that song?" I'm a little surprised too, considering she wasn't much of a classic rock or blues buff when we met.

She nods and takes a quick bite of mashed potatoes. "I love that song. My dad had it on a playlist he liked to listen to when he drove out of state on business. That Withers guy can sing."

I let out a ripple of laughter.

"What's so funny?" she asks, looking at me confused.

"You sounded so country just now." I take a swig of my beer and laugh a little more, shaking my head.

"What? Sayin' I sounded like a hick?" Her eyes are all wide, but her smile couldn't be any more obvious.

"More like a country bumpkin. That Withers guy can sang! *Ooooh-weee!*" I mock her, throwing my head back.

She laughs with me, though trying her damndest to hide her red face. "Well, I'm definitely with you on that," she says, taking a swig of her own beer. She sets the glass back down on the table and adds, with narrowed eyes, "The song choice, not the country bumpkin thing."

"Of course," I say with a grin and finish up my steak.

The first steak we ever had together was just like she promised, a few days after I got out of the hospital after my surgery. And like that day and every steak she's had since, she only manages to eat half. Just means more for me. When I see her give off signs of being so stuffed she's getting nauseous, I reach across the table and slide her plate toward me.

She keeps glancing at her phone, and at one point she starts texting a reply to someone.

"Natalie on you again about coming home?"

"Yeah, she's relentless." She puts the phone away in her purse.

Camryn is a horrible liar. Horrible. She couldn't lie to save her life, and right now, the way she keeps gazing off at the log-cabin-style wall, she's definitely lying. I pick my teeth clean with a toothpick and study her.

"Are you ready to go?" I ask.

She smiles weakly at me, obviously hiding something, and then

I notice the screen on her phone illuminate inside her purse. She checks the text message and suddenly she's more eager to leave. Her smile gets bigger, and she stands up quickly from the table.

"Wait, I have to pay." I wave the waitress over to us, and Camryn sits back down in the booth impatiently.

"Why so in a hurry all of a sudden?" I tease her as the waitress places the bill on the table, but before she walks away I pull my credit card from my wallet.

"No reason," Camryn says.

I just grin. "OK," I say and lean back against the seat, stretching my arms over the top and making myself comfortable. It's a ploy. The more comfortable that I look the more impatient she becomes.

Minutes later the waitress returns with my credit card and the receipt. I jot down her tip on the store receipt and very slowly get up, put on my coat, stretch my arms high in the air above me, fake-yawn—

"Dammit, will you hurry *up*!"

I knew she couldn't stand it much longer. I laugh, grab her by the hand, and leave the restaurant.

When we make it back to the hotel, Camryn stops in the lobby, "You go ahead. I'll be up in a second."

It's obvious she's up to something, but it being my birthday I just play along with her game, kiss her cheek, and hop inside the elevator. But once I'm inside the room, I'm the one getting impatient.

I don't have to wait long before she's entering the room holding a new guitar.

I stand up the second I see it. "Wow . . ."

Her smile is sweet and tender, bashful even. It's as though a tiny part of her is worried I won't like it.

I walk straight over to her.

"Happy Birthday, Andrew," she says, holding it out for me.

I place one hand around the neck, the other at the body and I admire it with the biggest smile. Sleek. Beautiful. Perfect. As I turn it around in my hands to check out the backside, I notice a line of silver cursive writing along the back of the neck that reads:

He drew iron tears down Pluto's cheek,
and made Hell grant what Love did seek.

A line from one of several stories told of Orpheus and Eurydice. I honestly don't know what to say.

"Do you like it?"

I look up at her. "I love it. It's perfect."

She looks away from my eyes with a blush in her face. "Well, I don't know anything about guitars. I hope it's not a sucky brand or anything like that. The guy at the guitar shop helped me pick it out. Then I had to wait a few days to have the script put on it, which I never thought would happen because of this and that and—"

"Camryn," I say, stopping her nervous rambling. "I've never had a better birthday gift." I close the empty space between us and kiss her lips softly.

Camryn

TWENTY-TWO

Somewhere on Interstate 75—May

We've been on the road for months. By March, we had already grown so used to it that living in and out of hotels had become second nature. A new room every week, a new city, a new beach, a new everything. But no matter how new it all is, each time we go in it's as if we're stepping through the front door of a house where we've lived for years. I never would've imagined calling a hotel room "home," or that life on the road would be as easy to adjust to as it has been for us. Sometimes it's been hard, but everything is an experience and I wouldn't change any of it.

But I wonder if the long winter got to me. I wonder, because I've caught myself daydreaming about being in a house somewhere, living the home life with Andrew.

Yeah, I'm pretty sure it was just the winter.

It's two o'clock in the morning, and we're broke down somewhere in southwest Florida on a long stretch of desolate highway. And it's pouring down rain. Buckets of rain. We called for a tow truck an hour ago, but for some reason it still hasn't showed.

"Is there an umbrella in the car anywhere?" I ask over the rain pounding loudly on the roof. "Maybe I can hold it over you while you fix the car!"

"It's pitch-black out there, Camryn," he says, his voice raised as high as mine. "Even with a flashlight I doubt I could do it. I'd have to figure out what's even wrong with it, first."

I slump down further into the front seat and prop my feet on the dash, my knees bent toward me. "At least it's not cold," I say.

"We'll manage out here tonight," he says. "Wouldn't be the first time we slept in the car. Maybe the tow truck will show up before daylight, and if not, I'll fix it when I can see."

We sit together in silence for a moment, listening to rain beat on the car, the thunder rumbling like a wave through the clouds. Eventually, we get so tired that we crawl into the backseat, curl up on it together, and try to get some sleep. After a short while, when it's obvious we're both uncomfortable and there's not enough room for us to sleep like this, Andrew crawls over into the front. But we still can't fall asleep. I feel him shifting for a while and then he asks, "Where do you see yourself in the next ten years?"

"I'm not sure," I say, staring up at the roof of the car. "But I do know that I want to be doing whatever it is with you."

"Me too," he says from the front, laying the same way that I am now, on his back looking upward.

"Have you thought about anything specific?" I ask, quietly wondering where he's going with this. I switch my left arm for my right, tucking it underneath the back of my head.

"Yeah," he says. "I want to settle down somewhere warm and peaceful. Sometimes I picture you on the beach, barefoot in the sand with the breeze blowing through your hair. I'm sitting under a tree not too far away, playing around with my guitar—"

"The one I bought you?"

"Of course."

I smile and continue to listen, picturing the scene in my mind.

"And you're holding her hand."

"Whose hand?"

Andrew falls silent for a moment. "Our little girl," he says distantly as if his mind is a little further away than mine is.

I swallow and feel a knot grow in my throat. "I like that visual," I say. "So, you want to settle down?"

"Eventually," he says. "But only when it feels right. Not a day before."

A gust of wind hits the side of the car, and a loud clap of thunder shakes the ground.

"Andrew?" I ask.

"Yeah?"

"Number three, to add to our list of promises. If we make it to old age and our bones hurt and we can't sleep in the same bed anymore, promise me we'll never sleep in separate rooms."

"It's a promise," he answers with a smile in his voice.

"Good night," I say.

"Good night."

And when I fall asleep minutes later, I dream about that warm beach and Andrew watching me walk along the sand with a little hand clasped in mine.

————

The tow truck never came. We wake up the next morning stiff and in pain, regardless of each of us having a seat to ourselves.

"I'm going to kick the shit out of that tow truck guy if I ever see him," Andrew growls underneath the hood.

He's busy twisting a wrench around... I'm not even going to

pretend that I know what that thing is. He's fixing the car. That's all I know. And he's in a seriously foul mood. I just hang around to help him with whatever he needs, and I don't play the dumb-blonde card by asking him what this doohickey is or what that thingamajig does. Truth is, I really don't care. And besides, it'd just aggravate him more if he had to explain it.

But the sun is out. And it's hot! I feel like I've died and gone to heaven!

I splash around in the puddles from last night's rain, soaking my flip-flops. I don't know what's gotten into me other than simply the weather, but I raise my arms high in the air above me and look up at the sky, twirling around and around in the middle of the road.

"Will you get over here and help me?" Andrew grumbles.

I skip over to him and pinch his sides playfully because I'm in such a great mood, and I just can't help it. But then *bang*, Andrew's reaction to it causes his head to dart up and hit the underside of the hood. I wince and my hand flies over my mouth.

"Shit, baby! I'm sorry!" I reach out to a pissed-off Andrew, green eyes swirling, but then he shuts them as his cheeks fill up with air and wheeze out slowly.

I grab his head, rub it, and then kiss him on the nose. I still can't stop smiling, but I'm not laughing at him, just trying to work the puppy-dog eyes.

"You're forgiven," he says and points underneath the hood. "I need you to hold this piece still right here for a second." I go around to that side, peer underneath the hood, and stick my hand into the area, feeling for his fingers to guide me.

"Yeah, right there," he says. "Now just hold it."

"For how long?"

"Until I say," he says, and I see the grin sneak up at the corner of his mouth. "If you let go, the oil pan will fall out and we'll be stuck here for a long time."

"Well, hurry up then," I say, already feeling a crick in my neck beginning to form.

He walks around to the trunk and gets a bottle of water. Slowly he twists off the lid. Takes a sip. Looks around at the fields. Takes another sip.

"Andrew, are you screwing with me?" I peek around the raised hood the best I can to see him.

He just smiles. And takes another sip.

Dammit, he is screwing with me! I think . . .

"Don't let go. I mean it."

"Bullshit," I say and start to move my fingers, but decide not to. "Are you telling me the truth? Seriously?"

"Yeah, sure I am. The oil pan will fall right out and it'll probably splash all over you too. Hard to get that shit off your skin."

"My back is starting to hurt," I say.

He takes his sweet time, and just when I'm about to let go, he moves around behind me and grabs me by the waist, pulling me away from the hood. One hand comes up and he smears black gook all over my cheek. I shriek at him and push him away.

"Gah! Shit, Andrew! What if I can't get this stuff off?" I'm seriously pissed, but a small part of me can't resist that smile of his.

"It'll come off fine," he says, leaning back underneath the hood. "Now just get in the car and turn the key when I tell you to."

I snarl at him once before doing what he asked, and in no time the Chevelle is running again and we're on our way to St. Petersburg, just an hour away.

Today feels a lot like summer, and we can't get enough of it. After we get to our hotel room and take a much-needed shower, we head to the nearest department store to buy him a pair of swimming trunks and me a bikini, intent on heading to the ocean for a swim.

He insists on the tiny black bikini with little silver stars, but he isn't the one who'll have to keep pulling that butt floss from between my cheeks every five seconds. So I settle for the cute red one with a tab bit more coverage.

"Probably better you picked that one, anyway," he says, as we hop inside the car in the parking lot of the store.

"Why's that?" I ask, grinning, as I kick off my flip-flops.

"Because I might end up busting a few jaws." He puts the car into reverse and we back out.

"Just for looking?" I ask with a hint of disbelief and laughter.

His head falls to the side to look at me. "Nah, I guess not. I kind of get off on it when other guys look at you."

"Ewww!" I scrunch up my nose.

"Not like that!" he says. "Geez!" He shakes his head as if to say *UNbelievable*, and we pull out of the parking lot and onto the street, which is busy with tourist traffic. "It just makes me feel good, y'know, having you on my arm. Does wonders for a guy's ego."

"Oh, so I'm just an arm trophy to you?" I cross my arms and smirk over at him.

"Yeah, babe, that's all I keep you around for. I thought you knew that already."

"Well, I guess then it's no secret that I keep you around for the same reason."

"Oh, really?" he asks, glancing over before staring at the road in front of him.

"Yep," I say and lean my head back on the seat. "I just keep you around to make bitches jealous. But at night, I'm dreaming about the love of my life."

"Who might that be?"

I purse my lips and look all around me, then back at him playfully. "Well, I won't tell you his name because I don't want you to go after him and see you get your ass kicked. But I can tell you that he's got medium-brown hair, gorgeous green eyes, and a few tattoos. Oh, and he's a musician."

"Really? Well, he sounds awesome, so why use *me* as your arm trophy then?"

I shrug, because I can't really think of a good line.

"Come on, you can tell me," he says. "It's not like he and I talk."

"Sorry," I say, glancing over, "but I don't talk about him behind his back."

"Fair enough," he says with a smile. "You know what?"

"What?"

Andrew grins mischievously, and I don't like it one bit.

"I remember a couple of things on our first road trip that you never got around to doing."

Uh-oh...

"I have no idea what you're talking about," I lie.

He drops his right hand from the steering wheel and rests it on his leg. That daring look in his eyes is gaining momentum, and I try not to make my growing nervousness so obvious.

"Yeah, I think you owe me a bare ass in the window, and I still need to bear witness to your bug meal. What will it be? Grasshopper? Cricket? Earthworm? Or, maybe a granddaddy long leg. I wonder if they have granddaddy long legs in Florida..."

My skin is crawling. "Give it up, Andrew," I say, shaking my head. I prop my foot on the door and twirl my braid between my fingers, trying to mask my worry. "I'm not doing it. And besides, that was the first road trip and you can't just carry stuff over like that. Should've made me do it when you had the chance."

He's still grinning like the devious shithead he is.

"No," I say again, flatly.

I glance over. "No!" I say one last time, and it leaves him laughing.

"All right," he says, putting his right hand back on the steering wheel. "It was worth a try, though. Can't blame me for tryin'."

"I guess not."

Andrew

We spend the entire day swimming and laying out on the beach. We watch the sun set over the horizon and eventually the stars, as they come alive in the darkness. Just an hour after nightfall we're met by a group of people our age. They've been on the beach not far from us for a while, hanging out.

"From around here?" the tall guy with a full-sleeved tattoo down his right arm asks.

One of the couples sits down in the sand near us. Camryn, sitting between my legs, leans away from my chest attentively.

"No, we're from Galveston," I answer.

"And Raleigh," Camryn adds.

"We're in from Indiana," the black-haired girl sitting down says. She points at the others she came with who are still standing. "They live here, though."

One of the other guys wraps his girlfriend up in his arms. "I'm Tate, this is Jen." He indicates his girlfriend, then points to the others standing nearby. "Johanna. Grace. And that's my brother, Caleb."

The three of them nod and smile down at us.

"I'm Bray," the black-haired girl sitting by Camryn says. "And this is my fiancé, Elias."

Camryn sits up fully and dusts the sand away from her hands by brushing them together. "Cool to meet you," she says. "I'm Camryn and this is my fiancé, Andrew."

Elias reaches out to shake my hand.

Tate, the guy with the tattoo says, "We're heading to a private spot on a beach about thirty minutes from here. It's a great party spot. Pretty secluded. You're both welcome to join us."

Camryn twists her body a little at the waist to see me behind her. We talk to each other with our eyes for a moment. At first, I'm not really up to it, but she seems to want to go. I stand up, helping her up with me.

I turn to Tate. "Sure. We can follow you out."

"Kick ass," Tate says.

Camryn and I grab our beach towels and the bag we brought packed with beef jerky, bottled water, and sunscreen, and we follow Tate and his friends off the beach and to the parking lot.

And now we're back in the car being spontaneous again. I'm not so sure about this shit, maybe because it's been so long since I've partied with anyone other than Camryn, but they seem harmless enough.

The so-called thirty-minute drive ends up being more like forty-five.

"I have no idea where the hell we are anymore."

We've been on a dark highway and off the main freeway for the past twenty minutes at least, their Jeep Sahara coasting over the road in front of us at seventy-five miles an hour. I've got no problem keeping up, but I don't usually speed like this in unfamiliar territory at night where I can't spot the cops hiding on the side of road out ahead. If I get a ticket it'll be my own damn fault, but I might still bust that Tate guy's head for it just on principle.

"At least we have a full tank of gas," she says. Then she laughs and hangs her foot out the window and says, "Maybe they're leading us to a creepy cabin in the woods somewhere and plan to kill us."

"Hey, that thought did cross my mind," I laugh back at her.

"Well, I trust you to keep me safe," she jokes. "Don't let any of them cut me up into little pieces or force me to watch Honey Boo Boo."

"You got it," I say. "Which brings to mind number four on our list of promises: if I'm ever lost or missing, promise you'll never stop looking for me until it's been exactly three hundred sixty-five days. On day three sixty-six, accept that if I was alive I would've already found my way back to you, and that I'm long dead. I want you to go on with your life."

She lifts away from the seat, bringing her foot back inside the car. "I don't like that. Some people go missing and are found years later, alive and well."

"Yeah, but that won't be me," I say. "Trust me, if it's been a year, I'm dead."

"OK, fine," she says, slipping out of her seat belt and scooting over next to me. She lays her head on my shoulder. "Only if you agree to do the same for me. One year. Not a day more."

"I promise," I say, though I'm lying through my teeth. I would look for her until the day I died.

Camryn

TWENTY-THREE

*I*t's OK to lie about some things. This "promise" just happens to be one of them. There's no way I could stop looking for him after one year. Truthfully, I'd never stop looking for him. This pact full of promises that we swore to keep is important to both of us, but I guess when it comes to some things, I'll just have to openly agree and deal with things however I want if it ever comes to that.

Besides, I get the feeling he's lying, too.

Andrew doesn't know it, but that black-haired girl, Bray, I saw a couple of hours earlier in the restrooms not far from the beach. She ended up using my stall after me. We didn't actually talk to one another, just passed each other with a friendly smile and that was it. I'm guessing that's what motivated her to have her friends invite us to party with them.

I think it'll be fun. Andrew and I spend one hundred percent of our time alone with each other, and I think it'll be good for both of us to step out for a while and associate with others more. And he didn't have any objections, so I'm guessing he probably thinks it couldn't hurt, either.

The drive to this "private" spot feels more like an hour.

Their Jeep turns left onto a partially paved road and the farther we follow, the bumpier the drive. Their headlights bounce through the darkness in front of us until finally the tree-enveloped road opens up into a wide area of rocks and sand. Andrew pulls up beside them and shuts off the engine.

"Well, it's definitely secluded," I say as I get out of the car.

Andrew comes up next to me, gazing out at the deserted beach. He takes my hand. "We can turn back now, there's still time," he taunts me. "Once they get us away from the car, it might be the last time we ever see each other." He squeezes my hand and pulls me closer to him playfully.

"I think we'll manage," I say just as the last of them pile out of the Jeep and meet us at the back of the vehicles.

Tate opens the back of the Jeep and lifts out a giant ice chest and drops it in the sand. "We've got plenty of beer," he says, lifting the lid and reaching inside.

He tosses a bottle of Corona to Andrew. Not Andrew's first choice of beer, I know, but he won't turn one down, either.

Bray and her fiancé, I can't even remember his name, step up together beside me while Tate pops the cap on another bottle of Corona and hands it out to me.

I take it. "Thanks."

Andrew pops the cap on his with the bottle opener he keeps on his key ring.

"If you've got any blankets to lie on, might want to bring one," Tate says. His girlfriend joins him, passing me a smile as she walks in between us wearing her skimpy white bikini. "And I've got a kickass system in this baby," he adds, patting the back of the Jeep with his hand, "so I've also got the music covered."

Andrew pops the trunk and grabs the blanket he always keeps back there, the same one we used the night we tried to sleep in that field last July. Only now, thanks to me, it has been washed and doesn't stink like oil and car funk.

"Where are my shorts?" I ask, rummaging around in the backseat.

"They're right here," Andrew says from the trunk. When I lean out of the car, he throws them toward me, and I catch them in midair.

"I don't plan on swimming in that abyss at night," I say, slipping them on over my red bikini bottoms.

Overhearing, Bray says, "I'm glad I'm not the only one!"

I smile over the roof of the Chevelle at her and then shut the door. "Have you been out here before with them?"

Tate and the others are walking toward the beach now carrying the ice chest, beach bags, and other random items. They leave the doors open on the Jeep with the speakers blasting rock music.

"We did last night," Bray says, "but Elias got drunk way too early and started puking up his insides, so I drove us back to our hotel pretty early."

Elias, yeah, that's her fiancé's name. He shakes his head and gives her the sarcastic yeah-thanks-for-telling-everybody look.

Andrew and I walk alongside Bray and Elias, hand in hand toward everybody else already setting up camp not too far out, closer to the water. As we step up and lay our blanket out on the sand, Tate lights a match and tosses it onto a pile of tree branches. The flame ignites the lighter fluid he had already squirted all over the pile. A tall, searing rod of fire curls up over the top of the pile and illuminates the darkness all around us with a dancing orange glow. Already the heat from the flames is making me hot, so I slide our blanket a few feet farther away from the bonfire before Andrew and I sit down on it. Bray and Elias follow suit with two giant beach towels. Tate, his brother, and the other three girls all share a large quilt. I dig the bottom of my beer bottle into the sand beside me so that it sits upright.

Tate makes me think of those really blond, tanned California surfers. Like every guy here, including Andrew, Tate sits with his knees bent upward and his arms propped on them at the wrists. And as I'm quietly checking everybody else out, I catch something briefly in the corner of my eye that instantly puts me into territorial mode. The blonde sitting next to Tate's brother, who I doubt is his girlfriend because they don't act like they're together, is watching Andrew with hungry eyes. I don't just mean the innocent look-but-won't-touch kind. No, this girl would try to sleep with him the second I walked away.

When she notices me watching her, she looks away and starts talking to the other girl beside her.

I don't have anything to worry about where Andrew is concerned, but if she disrespected me knowing he's my fiancé, I would not think twice about kicking her ass.

I wonder if Andrew noticed.

Andrew

I hope Camryn didn't notice the look that chick was giving me just now. Five seconds alone with that one anywhere out here, and she'd try to get me to fuck her. No way in hell would I ever entertain that, but this bonfire party just got a bit more interesting.

I'd bet my left nut she has slept with Tate and his brother already. Probably not Elias—he seems like the loyal type—but she'd do him, too, if he was up for it.

Shit, she just looked at me again.

I glance over at Camryn to keep from meeting the chick's gaze and sure enough, Camryn's got that telling smile on her face. Yeah, she definitely saw it.

I reach out, pick Camryn up, and set her between my legs.

"Don't worry, baby," I whisper into her ear, and then I kiss her neck to make sure the chick sees it.

"I'm *not* worried," Camryn says, lying back against my chest.

She's not worried about me, sure, but I can feel the territorial tension coming off her body. Damn, the thought of her throwin' down on that girl over me...OK, I shouldn't think about that. Fuck. Too late.

"Those are some wicked fuckin' tattoos," Tate points out.

Everyone is eyeing mine and Camryn's ink now. Camryn lifts away from my chest to give them a better look.

"Yeah, no doubt," Bray says, enthralled. She crawls across the sand closer toward us. "I've been curious about them."

The blonde chick eyeing me moments ago sneers at Camryn, though Camryn doesn't notice, as she's too busy showing the tattoo to Bray.

I use this opportunity to my advantage. "Turn around here, babe, and show them how it fits." I lift Camryn around on my lap and then lay my back against the sand, bringing her body down on top of mine.

The group watches closely, the blonde chick's face turning faintly bitter when I look right at her while at the same time pressing my body against Camryn's. We line up our tattoos to form a seamless picture of Orpheus and Eurydice; my Eurydice wearing a long, flowing see-through white gown pushed against her body by the wind, wisps of flowing fabric blowing behind her as she reaches out her arms to Orpheus inked along Camryn's ribs. Bray gawks down at the detail, her dark eyes wide with awe. She glances back at Elias and now he looks nervous, as though he's worried Bray is going to drag him to the closest tattoo parlor after tonight.

"That. Is. Awesome," Bray says. "Who are they?"

"Orpheus and Eurydice," I answer. "From the Greek legend."

"A tragic tale of true love," Camryn adds.

I squeeze my arms around her.

"Well, nothing seems tragic about the two of you," Tate says.

I squeeze Camryn even tighter, both of us sharing private thoughts that are better kept to ourselves. I kiss the top of her hair.

Bray leans away, still sitting with her knees in front of her pressed into the sand. "I think it's beautiful. And I guess it better be because I know that had to hurt like hell."

"Yeah, it definitely hurt," Camryn says. "But it was worth every hour of pain."

Sometime later, Camryn and I have both gone through at least three Coronas each, but she's the only one of us who shows it. She's a little buzzed, but just enough that it's making her more talkative.

"I know!" she says to the black-haired Bray. "I saw them in concert with my best friend, Nat, and they were amazing! Not too many bands who sound almost just like they do on their album."

"Yeah, that's the truth," Bray says and finishes off her beer. "Did you say you're from North Carolina?"

Camryn lifts her back from my chest and sits Indian style on the sand.

"Yeah, but Andrew and I don't really live there now."

"Where do you live?" Tate asks. He takes a long pull from his cigarette and holds the smoke in his lungs while he goes on. "Texas?"

Everyone turns to look at me when I answer, "No, we sort of ... travel."

"Travel?" Bray asks. "What, like driving around in an RV?"

"Not exactly," Camryn says. "We just have the car."

The blonde-haired girl who has been eyeing me all night speaks up: "Why do you travel?"

I notice the look in her eye right away, the one where she's trying her hardest to get my attention, but I ignore it and answer, looking back over at Bray next to us, "We play music together."

"What, you're like in a band?" the blonde girl asks.

I look right at her this time. "Sort of," I say, but that's all I give her, and I turn my attention back to Bray.

"What kind of music do you play?" Tate's brother, Caleb, asks. He's been getting comfortable with the other girl since we got here. They're probably not together, either, but he's definitely getting laid tonight.

"Classic rock, blues, and folk rock, stuff like that," I answer and take a swig of my beer.

"You'll have to play for us!" Bray says excitedly.

Clearly, she's about as buzzed as Camryn, and the two of them seem to get along good.

Camryn swings around on the sand to see me, her eyes wide and enthusiastic. "You could. You've got the acoustic in the backseat."

I shake my head. "Nah, I'm not up to it right now."

"Oh come on, baby, why not?"

There are those puppy-dog eyes and Camryn's trademark whine, which never fail to make me do whatever she wants. But I play around with it for a moment longer, hoping maybe she'll give in and say *never mind*.

Of course, she doesn't.

"Yeah, man, if you've got a guitar with you and know how to play, that'd be awesome," Tate says.

By now, everyone is looking right at me—even Camryn, who is really the only one of them I'm going to do it for.

Giving in, I get up, head back to the car, and return carrying the guitar. "You're going to sing with me," I say to Camryn as I sit back down beside her.

"Nooo! I'm too buzzed!" She kisses me on the mouth and then moves over to sit next to Bray and Elias, I guess to give me some space.

"All right, what do you want me to sing?"

The question was for Camryn, but Tate answers, "Hey, whatever you feel like, man."

I run a few different songs through my head for a minute and finally choose this one because it's so short. I mess around with the strings a few times, tune it real quick, and then start to play "Ain't No Sunshine." I began not really giving a shit about how good it was, but like always, once I start, I become someone else and put everything I've got into it. My eyes stay closed through most of the song, but I can always feel the energy of those around me, whether they're getting into it or not.

All of them are.

By the second chorus, I lock eyes with Camryn as I strum the strings. She sits in the sand on her knees, her body swaying side to side. The other girls are doing the same, getting into the music heavily. I belt out the last chorus, and that one song is all it takes for me to want to play more. Bray can hardly contain herself, telling me how great it was and being very attentive to Camryn, which makes her all right in my book. Unlike the blonde who has her eyes on me a little more than before.

"Man, you weren't fuckin' playing' around," Tate says.

He lights up a joint.

"Play another one," Bray says, lying against Elias again, as he wraps his arms around her from behind.

Tate passes the joint to Camryn first. She just looks at it for a second, unsure about whether or not she should. I see a trace of pain flash over her face; I know she was recalling her moment of weakness with the painkillers. She shakes her head. "No thanks, I think I'll just stick to liquor tonight."

I smile inwardly, proud of her decision. And when Tate offers it to me next, I follow suit, not because I wouldn't mind a hit or two, but because I can't bring myself to enjoy it when Camryn won't.

I've never been much of a pot smoker, but it's all right every once in a while. Right now isn't one of those times.

I play a few more songs by the bonfire. Camryn finally does sing one with me, and then I just want to kick back with my girl and enjoy the night. I set my guitar down beside us on the blanket and pull Camryn onto my lap again.

Tate's brother has been sucking face with that girl and feeling her up for a while. They don't talk much, for obvious reasons. The blonde who had been eyeing me earlier has finally taken the hint, I think. Either that or she's too stoned out of her mind to care about me anymore.

The music from Tate's Jeep gets loud again, and he walks away from it carrying a bottle of Seagram's 7, a two-liter of Sprite, and a stack of plastic cups. His girlfriend starts mixing the drinks and passing cups around.

"Have at it, man," Tate urges us. "Don't worry about having to drive anywhere tonight. Cops don't even know about this place."

"Yeah, sure I'll have a cup," I say.

I look to Camryn, recalling the look on her face when Tate passed her the joint earlier. "I won't if you don't want to," I say.

Aside from not wanting her to feel like she's betraying herself by getting too drunk, I don't want her getting so messed up she's miserable in the morning, either.

"No, I'm good, baby. I'll just have one cup, all right?"

She smiles sweetly up at me like she's waiting on me to give her permission, which I find extremely fucking cute.

"All right," I give in, not wanting to hurt her feelings, and she takes the cup from Tate's girlfriend.

We all sit back, drink, and talk about all kinds of random shit for the longest time. Camryn is laughing and smiling and carrying on with Bray about tampons, which I have no idea how that topic came up, nor do I want to know, but we're having a great time. Music by bands I've never heard of before carry loudly through the speakers not far away, and I find myself intrigued by the last few songs that have played, which I'm sure are the same singer.

"Who is that?" I ask Tate.

He looks up from his girlfriend, who is lying with her head in his lap. "Who? The band?"

"Yeah," I say. "They're pretty awesome."

"That, my friend, is Dax Riggs. Solo now. He started out in Acid Bath, I think—" He looks up in thought, as though unsure. "Well he's been in a few different bands. Acid Bath and Agents of Oblivion are the best known."

"Y'know, I think I've heard of Acid Bath before," I say and take another drink of my gin and Sprite.

"Wouldn't be surprised," Tate adds.

"I'll have to check out his stuff. Is he underground?"

Camryn, breaking free from her tampon conversation with Bray, moves back over next to me and lays her head on my shoulder.

"Yeah, he never went mainstream," Tate says. "Good thing, though, 'cause mainstream is bullshit. It pisses me off to see great bands sell out by doing toothpaste commercials 'n' shit."

I laugh lightly. "Yeah, definitely. I'd never sign a contract with a record label, if I'm ever offered one."

"I hear ya, man," Tate says. "Once you do that, you're their bitch. Your music is no longer yours, and you're bending over for the jackoffs that sign your checks."

I'm starting to kind of like this guy. Just a little.

"Andrew, I need to pee," Camryn says.

I look over at her. Taking her cup from her hand, I set it on the sand. "I need to take a piss, too," I say to her and Tate both.

Tate points to the left with another cigarette between his fingers and says, "Go around that way. There's no glass and shit to step on over there."

I set my cup down beside Camryn's and help her up. We walk with her through the sand toward a dark patch of trees and rocks until we're far enough away that no one can see us.

"We're gonna have to sleep out here tonight. No way I can drive us home."

She squats down while I piss a few feet over from her. "I know," she says. "I guess we'll finally get to sleep under the stars, huh?"

I'm laughing inside at her. My baby's so damn drunk she's slurring a little.

"Yeah, I guess so," I say. "Though you should know it doesn't really count because you'll barely remember it in the morning."

"Yes I will."

"*Naaah*, you won't."

She almost falls over when she's done and pushes herself back into a stand. I grab ahold of her arm and slip mine around her waist from behind. Then I kiss her on the top of the head. "I love you so much."

I don't know why I felt so compelled to say that in this moment, but just having her next to me and knowing that she's in no condition to take care of herself tonight, I needed to say it. The words were there in the back of my throat and, I admit it, they were starting to choke me up. I would blame it on the alcohol, but no, even completely sober I love her just as fucking much.

She wraps both arms around my waist, nestles her head against my chest as we start to head back, and squeezes me. "I love you, too."

TWENTY-FOUR

As the night wears on, things happening in our small group begin to shift. People are talking less and making out more. Bray and Elias are lying down next to each other on one side of the bonfire. Tate and his girlfriend might as well be fucking already; only thing left to do is take off their clothes. Thankfully, the shady blonde chick is over me and is helping her friend feel Caleb up about eight feet away from Camryn and me.

Yeah, I'm pretty sure I have a feeling I know where this is heading. No big deal. It's not like I've never been in a situation like this before, but this time my main focus isn't trying to please two chicks at once. I just need to keep Camryn away from their shit.

Just as I start to roll over onto my side to talk to Camryn lying next to me, the whole fucking world comes out from under me. I try to lift my head. I think. My eyes feel like fairies are dancing on top of them. With them open.

"Oh shit . . . ," I say out loud, but then, maybe I didn't. Maybe it was all in my head.

I raise my hand in front of my face and it looks like the moon is sitting between my thumb and index finger. I try to shake it off, but it's too damn heavy and it weighs my arm down. I feel my elbow hit the sand like an eighty-pound weight.

My head is spinning. The color of the fire is blue and yellow and dark red. The sound of the ocean is tripled in my ears, blending with the crackling of the wood on the fire and someone moaning.

"Camryn? Where are you?"

"Andrew? I...I'm right here. I think."

I can't even tell if that was really her voice.

I squint my eyes tightly and reopen them again, trying to focus, but I realize I don't want to focus. I'm smiling. My face feels so stretched out that I'm afraid for a second that it's not gonna stop stretching and it's going to rip my face in half. But then it's OK.

Oh my fucking God...I'm trippin'. What. The. Fuck. Did they give to me?

I try to stand up, but when I think I'm standing I look down and see that I haven't moved at all. I try again with the same result.

Why can I not stand up?!

"Holy fuck, Tate," I hear a voice say but I can't even make out if it's male or female. "This is some good shit. Ho-ly fuck. I'm seeing rainbows and shit. It's the Reading Fucking Rainbow..."

Then whoever just said that starts singing the *Reading Rainbow* song.

I feel like I'm in Crazy Town, but I don't really wanna leave.

Finally, I lay flat on my back and double-check my position by patting the sand on either side of me with the palms of my heavy hands. Then I look up at the star-filled sky and watch the stars move back and forth across the blackness in a poetic pattern.

Camryn's face appears on my chest like a ghost out of mist.

"Baby?" I ask. "Are you all right?"

I'm worried about her, but I can't stop smiling.

"Yeah. I'm goooood. I'm good."

"Lay by me," I tell her.

I shut my eyes when I feel her head on my chest, and I smell the shampoo she always uses, but it's so much stronger than before. Everything is stronger. Every sound. The feel of the wind on my face. Dax Riggs singing "Night Is the Notion" in the background somewhere that my mind tells me is far away, but it's so goddamn loud it's like the Jeep is right next to my head. I can almost smell the rubber from the tires.

And I can't help it. I start singing "Night Is the Notion" as loud as I can. I don't know how I know all the words already, but I know them. I fucking know them. And it feels like the song is going on for hours and I don't care. Eventually, I stop singing along and just close my eyes and feel the music move through me. And I don't care about anything right now except the moment. And I'm horny as fuck. It takes me a second—I think—to realize that my dick feels the same breeze that my face feels. And it feels good.

"Camryn? What? Yes."

I don't even know what I'm saying, or if I'm really saying anything at all. My mind tells me that I need to make sure she's not so messed up that she's giving me a blow job in front of these people, but at the same time I don't want her to stop.

My breath catches and my head falls over to one side. I see Caleb on top of one of those chicks, her naked thighs crushed around his thrusting body. I look away. I stare back up at the sky. Traces of light move back and forth as the stars move. I shudder when I feel my dick hit the back of her throat.

I look down. I see blonde hair. I reach out to touch it, part of me wanting to pull her away, the other part wanting to force her to take it deeper. I end up doing the latter, but when I throw my head back and see Camryn's face lying next to mine, I snap upward from the shoulders.

"Get *off* me, bitch!" I manage to get out.

I kick her off of me and the high does a one eighty. I'm not enjoying it anymore.

I force myself to sit upright. I try smacking myself in the head with both hands hoping to jar myself sober, but it does jack shit. I manage to get my dick back in my shorts, and I look across the sand through the fire to see that slutty bitch already passed out next to Caleb. I don't know how much time has gone by, but everybody is passed out but me.

I'm panicking. I can't fucking breathe. What the fuck just happened?

I roll over onto my side and grab Camryn, forcing her next to me, and I don't let her go.

And that's the last thing I remember.

Camryn

I feel sick. God, I've never, *ever*, had a hangover like this before. The early morning sun and the breeze coming off the ocean wake me up. At first I just lay here because I'm afraid if I move I'm going to throw up. My head is pounding, the tips of my fingers are numb, the rest of my body a nauseous, trembling mess. I moan and open my eyes the rest of the way, pressing one arm horizontally across my stomach. I know there's no way I'm getting off this beach without puking for a good five minutes first, but I try to hold it back as long as I can.

My cheek is pressed into the sand beneath me. I feel grains sticking to my skin. Very carefully, I reach up a finger and shuffle it away before it gets inside my eye.

I hear a *thwap* followed by a cracking noise and shouting.

Against the argument from my stomach, I roll over onto my other side facing the ocean.

"Get off of him!" I hear a girl scream.

That wakes me up even more, and for a split second I realize just how out of it I really was. But I'm wide awake now. I raise my head from the sand to see Andrew pummeling Tate with his fists.

"Andrew!" I try to shout, but my throat is sore and my voice is hoarse, so I only manage to croak out his name instead. "Andrew!" I say again, gaining more control over my voice.

"What the fuck is wrong with you, man?!" Tate yells.

He's trying to back away from Andrew, but Andrew just keeps coming. He punches him again and again, this time knocking Tate on his ass in the sand.

Then Tate's brother joins in and spears Andrew from the side. They both fall off of Tate and roll several feet. Andrew grabs Caleb by the throat and lifts him over his body, throwing him hard against the sand, and is on top of him in seconds. He punches Caleb three times before Tate is behind him, pulling him backward and away.

"Chill the fuck out, man!" Tate screams.

But Andrew rounds on him catching his chin with an upper-cut, and I hear another stomach-turning *crunch*. Tate stumbles backward, holding his hand over his jaw.

"You drugged us! I'll fucking *kill* you!" Andrew roars.

I finally manage to get to my feet, though I stumble once before I make it over to him. Just as I go to grab his arm to try pulling him away, I'm pushed hard on my ass from behind. I don't even know what happened, but for a second it knocks the breath from my lungs. I look up to see Caleb on top of Andrew. I must've been caught in the crossfire of Caleb's attack on Andrew from behind.

I raise my body back out of the sand and see Elias coming our way.

In a panic, I look to both sides of me and back at Elias seemingly in slow motion. Are all three of them about to gang up on Andrew? Oh no way in hell! I start to grab Tate while he and Caleb are punching Andrew, but I'm pushed out of the way by Elias.

"Move!" he growls at me.

Andrew manages to hold his own well against Tate and Caleb, he's still on his feet and he's still returning punches with both of them, but if Elias joins in, I don't think he'll be able to fight all three of them.

Elias jumps in, and I can't tell who's hitting who when a pair of hands grab me underneath the arms from behind.

"Stay back here with me, girl," Bray says.

Amid my confusion and dread, I see Elias punching Caleb and relief washes over my body, though it's short-lived.

Andrew's mouth is bleeding. But then all four of them are bleeding somewhere. I think the fight is going to go on forever, and with each blow Andrew gives and receives, I wince and shut my eyes, just wanting to block it all out of my head. I'm sitting in the sand with Bray's arms wrapped around me from behind, because she still thinks I'll try jumping into the fight myself. But I'm right back to feeling like I'm going to puke, and I can hardly move. Sweat is beading off my forehead. The back of my neck feels clammy. The sky is starting to spin.

"Oh no. Bray . . . I think I'm—"

I lose it right there. I feel my body heave violently out of her grasp and my hands come down in front of me, digging into the sand. My back arches and falls, arches and falls, as I vomit over and over and over again. *Oh God, please make it stop. I'll never drink again! Please just make it stop!* But it seems like I *never* stop. The more I vomit, the more my body reacts to the smell of it, the sound of it, the taste of it, and it just makes me vomit that much more. I can barely hear the fighting in the background anymore over my own noises and the dry heaving when there's nothing left in my stomach to come up. Finally, I fall over onto my side. I can't move. My body is shaking uncontrollably, my skin is both cold and hot and now clammy all over. I feel Bray sitting next to me.

"You'll be all right," I hear her say. "Wow, that stuff really messed you up."

"What was it?" I ask, and right when I do, pieces of my memory from last night start to come back to me.

I don't even hear if she answered my question, or not.

I remember that everything was fine, just a normal kind of drunk, until shortly after we started drinking the gin. And then out of nowhere, I couldn't see anything directly in front of me because it was way too close. I kept focusing my eyes at things farther out, the ocean and the stars and the light from the boats moving across the water in the distance. I remember thinking that a ship was coming toward us and that it was going to crash onto the beach. But I didn't care. I thought it was…beautiful. It was going to kill us all, but it was beautiful. And I remember hearing Andrew singing this sexy song. I laid my head on his chest and listened to him sing. I wanted to crawl on top of him and get naked, and I would have if I could've moved.

And I remember…

Wait.

That blonde bitch. She asked me…wait.

I raise my body from the sand.

"I think you need to lay still for a bit," Bray says.

My fingertips come up to my forehead.

I remember her sitting next to me and Bray. She was as messed up as the rest of us, but I didn't feel jealous of her anymore. She talked to us for a while, and I didn't mind.

As it's all coming back to me, my body is starting to shake more.

She tried to kiss me. I think I kissed her back...

I think I'm going to be sick again.

I draw my knees up and rest my elbows on top of them, burying my face in my hands. I'm still so dizzy. I still feel like I'm not done puking. I don't have that great feeling of relief after vomiting. No, the need to be sick just intensified, this time brought on by my nerves.

The rest is coming back to me and even though I want to force it out of my mind, I don't.

She asked me if she could sleep with me and Andrew. Yeah, I remember now. But...oh God...I thought she really meant to *sleep*, but I realize now that I was so high I didn't know she meant it sexually.

I told her I didn't care.

Then I remember her...

My breath catches. My hand flies to my mouth, my eyes are wide and stinging from the breeze.

I remember her giving Andrew a blow job.

Trying to push myself to my feet, I feel Bray's hand on my back.

"Girl, come on," she says, pulling me back down on the sand with her. "Don't go over there. You'll just get hurt."

I jerk my wrist from her hand and try to get up again, but the sudden movements mixed with the frayed nerves just send me back into a dry-heaving episode.

Then I hear Andrew above me.

"Shit," he says to Bray. "Will you run to my car and get a bottle of water out of the ice chest in the back?"

Bray takes off to do it.

Andrew rolls me over onto his legs just as I stop dry-heaving. He brushes my hair away from my eyes and my mouth.

"They fucking drugged us, baby," he says.

My eyes open a crack to see him above me, his palms resting on my cheeks.

"I'm going to kill that bitch. I swear to God, Andrew."

The look in his eyes is that of a person being stunned. He probably didn't know that I knew. "She's still passed out. Baby, I'm..."

The guilt in his face cuts through me. "Andrew, I know what happened," I say. "I know you thought she was me. I saw what you did."

"It doesn't matter," he says, gritting his teeth. Moisture is forming around his eyes. "I should've known it wasn't you. I'm so fucking sorry. I should've known." His hands tighten a little around my face.

I'm about to tell him to stop blaming himself when Elias comes over to us.

"I'm sorry, man, we didn't know. I swear."

"I believe you," Andrew says.

Bray comes back with the water, and I'm already regaining some of my strength. I lift myself up and sit upright, lying against Andrew's bare chest. He wraps his arms around me and squeezes me so hard, like he's afraid I'm going to get up and run away.

Then he reaches out and takes the bottle from Bray. He twists off the top and pours some in his hand and wipes it across my forehead and mouth. The coolness of it instantly soothes me.

"Look man, I'm sorry," Tate says, coming up behind us. "We thought you wouldn't care. We just dropped some in everybody's drinks. Being generous. We didn't bring you out here with any fucked-up intentions."

Andrew manages to carefully move away from me, though still so fast I barely felt his absence and he punches Tate again. A nauseating *crunch* echoes through the space around us.

"Please, Andrew!" I shout.

Elias grabs Andrew and Caleb grabs Tate, holding them off of each other.

Andrew lets Elias hold him back, but then he shakes him off and turns back to me, helping me up from the ground.

"Let's go," he says. He starts to carry me, but I shake my head at him, letting him know that I'm OK to walk on my own.

He grabs his guitar and I grab our blanket, and we head toward the Chevelle.

"Maybe we should give Bray and Elias a ride back," I say.

Andrew tosses the guitar in the trunk and takes the blanket from me, throwing it back there with it. Then he walks over to his side of the car, lays his arms across the roof and then his head in between them. He takes a deep breath and then slams his fist down on the metal. "*God damn it!*" he shouts and hits it again.

Instead of trying to talk some sense into him, I decide to let him cool down on his own. I look at him with a kind expression from the other side of the car. And then I get inside and close the door. He stays there for a minute longer until I hear him say, "I'll give you two a ride back if you want."

Elias and Bray, carrying their stuff, approach the car and get in the backseat.

Andrew

TWENTY-FIVE

I don't even know how I find our way back so easily. I think at one point, I didn't care much if we got lost. But I get us back without a wrong turn or having to pull over and ask for directions. Not much is said between the four of us. And the little that was spoken, I don't remember any of it.

We pull into the parking lot of the hotel and part ways with Elias and Bray. Maybe I would've thanked Elias or wished them luck on the rest of their trip, or maybe even invited them with us somewhere tonight, but given the circumstances all I can do is nod when they thank us for the ride.

I pull away and drive around to our side of the hotel.

Camryn seems uncertain about talking to me yet. Not afraid, just uncertain. I can't even look at her. I feel like fucking shit for what happened, and I'll never forgive myself for it.

Camryn grabs my hand and we head straight up to our room. I swing open the door and start tossing our stuff in our bags.

"It wasn't your—"

I stop her. "Don't. Please. Just...give me a minute..."

She looks at me so dejectedly, but nods and gives in.

Soon, we're on the road again, heading north up the coast. Destination: Anywhere But Florida.

After driving for an hour, I recall what happened last night in my head over and over again, trying to make some kind of sense out of it. I pull off the highway and the car crawls to a stop on the side of the road. It's so quiet. I stare down at my lap and then up through the windshield. I realize that I'm white-knuckling the steering wheel. Finally, I swing open the door and get out.

I walk fast over the gravel and dirt and then down through the slope in the ditch, coming up the other side and head straight for the first tree.

"Andrew, stop!" I hear Camryn calling out to me.

But I keep going and when I face that goddamn tree, I hit it as hard as I hit Tate and Caleb. The skin over two of my knuckles splits open and blood runs over the top of my hand and in between my fingers, but I don't stop.

I only stop when Camryn steps around in front of me and pushes me so hard in the chest with the palms of both hands that I almost fall backward. Tears are streaming from her eyes. "Stop it! Please! Just stop it!"

I let myself fall onto the grass into a sitting position, my knees bent, my bloodied hands dangling at the wrists. My body slumps over forward, my head hanging there. All I can see is the ground beneath me.

Camryn sits down in front of me. I feel her hands on the sides of my face, trying to raise my head, but I don't let her.

"You can't do this to me," she says, her voice shuddering. She tries to force my gaze, and finally I let her because it hurts like hell to hear her cry. I look her in the eyes, my own eyes brimmed with angry tears that I'm trying to contain. "Baby, it wasn't your fault. You were *drugged*. Anybody could have made that mistake as messed up as you were." Her fingers tighten against both sides of my face. "It. Wasn't. Your. Fault. Do you understand me?"

I try to look away, but she moves my hands out of the way and sits between my legs on her knees, facing me. Instinctively, I put my arms around her.

"I should've known still," I say, looking down. "And it's not just about that, Camryn, I was supposed to keep you safe. You never should've been drugged in the first place." Just thinking about it causes the anger and hatred toward myself to rise up again. "I was supposed to keep you *safe*!"

She wraps her arms around me and forces my head onto her chest.

She pulls away. "Andrew, look at me. Please."

I do. I see pain and compassion in her eyes. Her gentle fingers cup my unshaven face. She kisses my lips slowly and says, "It was a moment of weakness," as if to remind me of what I said to her several months ago about the pills. "It's my fault as much as it was yours. I'm not stupid. I should've known too not to leave our drinks alone with them even for a second. It's *not* your fault."

My eyes stray downward, and then I look back at her again. I don't know how I can make her understand that because of how and who I am, I feel an intense sense of responsibility for her. A responsibility that I take pride in, that I've felt since the day I met her. It kills me . . . it *kills* me to know that in my "moment of weakness" I couldn't protect her, that because I let my guard down she could've been hurt, raped, killed. How can I make her understand that it doesn't matter if she doesn't fault me for it, that her opinion, although I don't take it for granted, doesn't excuse my moment of failure? She's entitled to a moment of weakness. I'm not. Mine is just failure.

"And I would never, *ever* hold that against you," she adds.

I just look at her, searching her face for meaning and then she goes on:

"What that girl did," she clarifies. "I'd never bring it up. Because you did nothing wrong." I feel her fingertips press into the sides of my face. "Do you believe me?"

I nod slowly. "Yeah. I do believe you."

She sighs and says, "It might've been partially my fault, anyway." She looks away from my eyes.

"How so?"

"Well," she says, but hesitates with a distant look of regret on her features, "I think I may have accidently given her permission."

That certainly takes me by surprise.

"I remember her asking about sleeping with us, and I think I told her that yes, she could. I-I didn't know she meant it…sexually. If I had been sober I definitely would've caught onto that. Andrew, I am so sorry. I'm sorry I let that crazy bitch violate you."

I shake my head. "It's neither one of our faults, so don't feel like putting any of the blame on yourself, all right?"

When I don't see that smile I was fishing for fast enough I reach out and grab both sides of her waist. She squeals as I start tickling her. She laughs and squirms so hard that she falls backward onto the grass, and I sit on top of her waist, holding my weight up by my knees on either side so I don't crush her.

"Stop it! No! Andrew, I fucking swear! Stooooop!" She laughs hard, and I bury my fingertips around her ribs some more.

Then I hear the warning siren from a cop car sound once and go dead as it pulls up behind my car.

"Oh shit," I say, looking down at Camryn. Her hair is matted with dried grass sticking out in various spots.

I jump off her and reach out my bloody hand to help her up.

She takes it and rises to her feet, dusting herself off. We head back to the car just as the cop is getting out of his.

"Do you normally leave your door wide open on the highway like this?" the cop asks.

I glance at my door and back at him.

"No, sir," I say. "I had to throw up and just didn't think about it at the time."

"License, insurance, and registration."

I pull my license from my wallet and hand it to him and then go around to the passenger's side to fish for my insurance and registration from the glove box. Camryn leans against the back of the car with her arms crossed nervously over her chest. The cop goes back to his car—after taking notice of the blood on my hands—and sits inside to run my name.

"I hope you've not been hiding any robberies or murders or anything from me," Camryn says, as I lean against the hood next to her.

"Nah, my serial-killing days are over," I say. "He's got nothin' on me." I elbow her gently in the side.

A few unnerving minutes later the cop joins us at the back of the car and hands my stuff back to me.

"What happened to your hand?" he asks.

I look down at it, for the first time feeling the throbbing pain now that he's brought it to my attention. Then I point to the tree not too far away. "I sort of hit the tree."

"You *sort of* hit the tree?" he asks suspiciously, and I notice him glancing at Camryn every few seconds. Great, he probably thinks I beat her or some shit, and considering she does look pretty rough after last night's incident and our recent scuffle in the grass, it probably helps confirm his assumption.

"OK, I hit a tree."

He looks right at Camryn now. "Is that what happened?" he asks her.

Camryn, nervous as hell and likely knowing what the cop is thinking *really* happened as much as I do, suddenly has a Natalie moment.

"Yes, sir," she says, gesturing her hands. "He got mad because some assholes—" she winces "—sorry, took advantage of us last night, and he was beating himself up over it all morning to the point of ultimately taking it out on that tree! I ran out there to stop him before he hurt himself and we talked about it and the reason I look like hammered shit—sorry—is because of the screwed-up night we had. But I promise we aren't bad people. We don't do drugs and he's not a serial killer or anything, so please just let us go. You can even search the car if you want."

Face. Palm. Moment.

I laugh it off inside. We don't have anything to worry about if he searches the car. Unless…our temporary friends, Elias and Bray, just happened to drop a bag of weed or any kind of incriminating stuff somewhere in my backseat, by accident.

Oh shit…please don't let this turn out like it does on television.

I glance over at Camryn and subtly shake my head at her.

Her eyes widen. "What'd I say?"

I just smile, still shaking my head, because it's all I really can do.

The cop sniffles and then gnaws on the inside of his mouth. He looks back and forth between Camryn and me several times without a word, which only increases the tension we're feeling.

"Next time don't leave the door wide open like that," the cop says, his expression as unmoving as it has been this whole time. "It'd be a shame to see a passing vehicle knock the door off a 1969 Chevelle in that good a condition."

A slim smile brightens my face. "Absolutely."

The cop pulls out ahead of us and leaves while we stay parked inside the car for a moment.

"'You can search the car if you want'?" I repeat.

"I know!" She laughs and throws her head back against the seat momentarily. "I didn't mean to say that. It just came out."

I laugh, too. "Well, looks like your innocent rambling, which by the way scares me a little; I think that bipolar best friend of yours has rubbed off on you, but it charmed us out of that one."

I rest my hands on the steering wheel.

She was smiling and probably about to comment on my Natalie joke, until she sees my bloody knuckles again. Then she moves over next to me and takes my hand carefully into hers.

"We need to clean this before it gets infected," she says. She leans closer and carefully starts picking tiny pieces of grass and dirt from around and inside the open gash. "That's pretty bad, Andrew."

"It's not too bad," I say. "I don't need stitches."

"No, you just need to be slapped. Don't ever do something like that again. I mean it." She picks out one last bit of debris and then leans over the back of the seat, reaching for the small ice chest in the back.

I turn my head to the right, and all I see is her ass hanging out of those shorts. I reach up with my bloodied hand and slip my finger underneath her bikini bottom elastic and snap it back against her skin. It doesn't faze her, but she rolls her eyes at me when she emerges from the backseat and sits down with a water bottle.

"Rinse it out," she demands, holding the bottle out to me.

I open my door and take it from her, holding my hand out and pouring water over the wound.

As she's rummaging through her purse for something she says,

"The next time you get that pissed off and feel the need to take out your anger on inanimate objects, I'm officially going to jot your name down on my Psychotic List." She holds out a tube of Neosporin to me.

I just shake my head and take it. Guess I can't argue with her on that one.

She points at the Neosporin in my hand and tells me to hurry and put it on. I laugh and say, "You sure are a demanding little heifer."

She play-punches me in the arm (which actually hurts her) and accuses me of calling her fat. It's all in good fun, and I think it's her way of helping take my mind off what happened. Within minutes we're lost in conversations about music and what kinds of bars or clubs we might play in along the way to New Orleans.

Yes, we decided at one point that no matter where we stop on the way or how long we stay that eventually we'll visit our favorite place along the Mississippi, no matter what.

———

That was two days ago. Today, we're laid up in a decent hotel in the great state of Alabama.

Camryn

TWENTY-SIX

*A*re you excited about tonight, or do you need a paper bag to blow in?" Andrew asks, coming out of the bathroom with a towel around his waist.

"Both," I say. I set the remote control down on the nightstand and sit up in the bed. "I know the song, but it's my first solo. So yes, I'm freaking out a little."

He digs around inside his bag by the TV and finds a pair of clean boxers. The towel drops to the floor. I tilt my head to one side, watching his sexy naked ass from the bed. He steps into his boxers and snaps them around his waist.

"You're going to kick ass," he says, turning to face me. "You've had plenty of practice and you've nailed it already. Besides, if I thought you weren't ready, I'd tell you."

"I know you would."

"Well, are you ready for work?" he asks, slipping on the rest of his clothes.

"Yep. I guess so. How do I look?"

I stand up and twirl around, dressed in a skimpy spaghetti-strap black top and tight jeans. "Wait," I say, putting up my finger. I slip my feet down into my new sleek black calf-high boots and zip them up the sides. Then I retwirl and do my pose again, overdramatizing it a bit.

"Unbearably sexy as always," he says, grinning, and then he steps up to me and runs my braid through his hand.

Tonight I may be performing solo "Edge of Seventeen" by Stevie Nicks, but for two hours before I go on I'm going to waitress and Andrew will be busing tables. Score! I get the cool job.

It's a packed house when we arrive at seven. I love the atmosphere of this place. The stage is decent sized, but the table and dance floor are enormous. And it's full, which makes me that much more nervous. I walk through to the back, my hand clasped in Andrew's as we weave our way through the crowd. We got lucky with this temp job to be able to work together for a few nights. Every other side job along the trip since Virginia has been sporadic. I'd work cleaning rooms here and there while Andrew would bartend or even fill in as a bouncer. He may not be steroid-big (and I'm glad because that's gross), but his muscles are big enough that they hired him easily. Thankfully he didn't have to drag anyone out by their shirts or get into any fights.

Our boss for the next few days, German—it's his name, definitely not his nationality, because the guy is as redneck as they come—hands Andrew a white apron and a pin-on name tag that says Andy.

I hold in my laughter, but Andrew sees the amused look on my face.

German rubs his chunky sausagelike hand across his nose, wipes it on his jeans and says, "A'soon as someone leaves a table an' takes ther' shit wit'em you get o'er ther' an' get that table ready fer anodder customer." He shakes his finger at Andy, er,

I mean Andrew. "An' don' touch tha tips. Dems' de waitress's, y'hear me?"

"Yes, sir," Andrew says. When German looks down at his order slip book for a second, Andrew mouths the words *What the fuck?* and I try to straighten my lips into a hard line to keep from smiling when German looks back up at us.

German looks at me, I mean really *looks* at me, totally unlike he was looking at Andrew just now. He smiles a yellowed smile and says, "An' you jus' need ta look 'zactly like you do now. Put on dat sweet smile an' rake in dem tips."

I can only imagine what the other waitresses who work here full-time have to go through with this guy.

I bat my baby blues at him and say with a sweet, seductive country twang in my voice, "I sure will, Mr. German. And lata when my shift is ova' I'm sure you will unda'stand that I'll need to go in tha back an' freshen up before I perform t'night."

I notice Andrew's eyes get bigger and more intrigued, but I keep my attention on German, who I already have so tightly wrapped around my finger that if I told him to lick the floor he would ask *Fer how long?*

Andrew

That Southern belle accent that came out of nowhere really turned me on. She and I are gonna have to talk about that later.

I pin on my name tag, tie my apron at the back, and grab the plastic tublike thing German points to when I look over. Hell, I don't mind this kind of work, but German is a redneck dickhead who I hope stays out of my way for the next two hours. And he could use a stick of deodorant. I mean the whole fucking stick. He really doesn't go with the place. He's like a rebel flag hanging in the window of a $400,000 house. The bar-slash-restaurant is actually decked out pretty nice. On the inside, at least.

I head out onto the floor with my tub fixed underneath my arm and go to the first empty table I see. I clear away all of the trash and dirty dishes covered with uneaten fries and hush puppies, and toss everything into the tub. Then I wipe the table down with the rag in my apron pocket, and straighten the ketchup and steak sauce bottles. It's all pretty straightforward, unlike waitressing, which I guess is why only Camryn had to get an hour's worth of training yesterday before she could start today. She may have the tip job where she can work that sexy charm of hers, but she has to put up with the creepy perverted boss. And I'm lovin' the shit out of it. It's what she gets for making fun of me getting the busing job. She joked around by calling me the bar's "bottom feeder." Well, I hope she doesn't expect me to save her skinny butt from German's advances. She's on her own with that one.

I bus a couple more tables, leaving the five-dollar tip on one table and the twenty on another. When I start to head into the back to drop off the load, I'm stopped by four girls at a booth near the bar wall.

"Hey baby doll," one of the older women says, gesturing me with the curl of her finger. "Can you take our drink order?"

"I'm sorry, ma'am, but I just bus the tables."

I try to walk away, but a prettier one stops me.

"I bet if we requested that you be our waiter, you'd get promoted." Her eyes are glassy and her head sways a little. I notice—because it's hard not to—her huge boobs busting out of her tight tank top. She pushes them further into view.

"Well, you could ask," I say, putting on my own charm, lifting one side of my mouth into a grin. "And if the boss man says so, then I'm all yours for the evening."

All four of them look at one another, having some kind of inside conversation. I've got them eating out of the palm of my hand.

Camryn comes up behind me bearing a drink tray lined with shots of whiskey and a glass already stuffed full of bills. I wonder if that's the tip jar or the money she collects from the alcohol. It's making me anxious.

She smirks at me, looks down at the table of women, and then back at me again briefly. "Is he bothering you ladies?" she asks.

I know she's not jealous; it's all about competition tonight, between her and me. And she's going to do whatever she can to keep me from winning the little bet we made in the car on the ride over here:

"You don't think I can rake in tips as a busboy?"

"No," she said. "Busboys don't collect tips."

"Think about it," I said, looking at her from the driver's seat. "It's a bar full of women and alcohol. I bet you I can get tips."

"Oh really?" she asked, pursing her lips.

"Yeah," I said and then took it up a notch because I was feeling bold: "Actually, I bet I can rake in more tips than you."

Camryn laughed. "Seriously? You want to bet on that?" She crossed her arms and shook her head at me like I was being ridiculous.

"Yes," I said when I knew I should've said, No, I'm just kidding.

But I didn't say no, and now I'm stuck in this bet where if Camryn wins, I have to give her an hour-long massage for three straight nights. An hour is a long time for a massage. I can already feel my arms going limp just thinking about it.

The older woman answers Camryn, "No, he's not bothering us at all, sweetie." She looks me up and down like she wants to strip me naked and lick me, propping her chin on her enclosed, upright hands. "He can stay here for as long as he likes. Where is your boss?"

"He's somewhere around here," Camryn says. "Just look for the big guy in the company shirt. His name is German."

"Thank you, doll," the woman says and looks back at me.

That one, I admit, kind of scares me. And since she seems to be the leader of their pack, I decide I need to move on before she really thinks I'm that into her and *I'm* the one needing *Camryn's* help to get me out of the mess I started.

"Have a great night, ladies," I say with an inviting smile and then I turn to walk away.

I feel a hand slide into my apron pocket. I stop and look down as the woman's hand moves away. She's gazing up at me with that famous horny look.

"You too, sugar," she says.

I wink at her and smile at the other three as I casually walk away. When I make it into the kitchen, I empty my tub and then reach into my pocket and pull out three twenty-dollar bills.

Hell yeah, maybe that bet wasn't so ridiculous, after all.

Two hours later...

Yeah, the bet was ridiculous.

"Two forty, forty-one, forty-six, fifty-six." Camryn keeps counting her tips now that our short shift is over. She smirks and adds, "And how much did you get?"

I'm trying to keep a straight face to make my disappointment seem somewhat genuine, but she's not making it easy. So I pull out my money, count it again, and answer, "Eighty-two dollars."

"Well, that's not bad for a busboy, I have to give it to you," she says, pocketing her cash.

"Give it to me how?" I ask as I untie the apron and take it off. "You're letting me out of the bet?"

"Pfft! No way," she says.

German comes up behind us.

"You two betta be good," he says. "An' none o'that rap stuff or dem fancy new-age songs." He snaps his fingers rapidly as if he's trying to name an example, but then he just gives up. "This ain't no 'Merican Idol."

"Understood," Camryn says with that sweet smile of hers.

German, with a big dopey grin on his face, snaps out of her spell, and as he walks away he snarls at me as he passes. It's better than him looking at me the way he looks at Camryn, so I'm not complaining.

I turn to Camryn. "Don't be nervous." I take her hands into mine. "Like I said, you're going to kick ass out there."

She nods nervously. Then she lets a quick burst of air move through her little rounded lips and inhales a deep breath.

"I'll run out and get the guitar while you get ready," I say.

"All right," she says.

I kiss her on the lips and head outside to the car where the electric guitar she bought me for my birthday is hiding in the trunk. "Edge of Seventeen" may be her solo, but the guitar riff itself is so well-known that I'm almost as nervous as she is about performing it. OK, maybe not so much as nervous—it's a fairly easy song to play. What has me a little on edge is screwing it up for her. She's the only reason I feel any kind of pressure about tonight's performance.

I walk up onto the stage to find the drummer, Leif, who we met yesterday, getting set up. "Thanks for doing this, man," I say to him.

"Hey, no problem," Leif says. "I've played this song a number of times at a bar in Georgia I used to work at a few years ago."

Camryn was happy to find a drummer who knows the song. She was prepared for it to be just the two of us, knowing it wouldn't sound the same without the drums, too. But when we met Leif yesterday during her waitress training and he agreed to play with us tonight, I think Camryn's confidence level shot up a few notches.

I slip the guitar strap over my shoulder just as Camryn steps onto the stage.

She walks right up to me, and I lean in toward her ear and say, "You look hot."

She blushes and looks down at her clothes. She changed out of that cute black top she was wearing and replaced it with another black silky top that hangs low in the back, exposing her skin almost to her waist. The necklace I bought for her dangles in the front, shining against the black. And she let her hair down. I love the braid she always wears, but I have to say, she's a whole other level of sexy with that long, soft blonde hair falling all about her shoulders.

The voices in the bar carry through the large space, loud even over Leif messing around with the bass drum behind us. All of the tables on the floor are full, as well as the booths lining the back wall. My four "girlfriends" are still here and have migrated from their booth to a table closer to the stage. They seem intrigued that I went from busboy to guitar player. Normally, I would be scanning the audience for my "victim" of the night by now, but tonight is different and there won't be any of that from either one of us. Camryn's too nervous and focused to try pulling off our usual.

After we finally get set up and are ready to begin, Camryn holds her breath for a moment and looks over at me.

I wait for her to give me the go, and when I see her nod I start to play, and all eyes in the room turn to us. That guitar riff always manages to turn heads in a crowded room. And Camryn, the second she starts to sing, she does like I always do and becomes someone completely different, so much so that it stuns me. She owns it. It's so unlike how she has been during every one of our practices together. Confidence and sexiness exude from every line in the song and every movement she makes and my entire body reacts to it.

"Ooo, baby, ooo, ooo!" I join in with the chorus.

But everybody's looking at her, even my four girlfriends, who I know at first moved closer to check me out. No, they now belong to Camryn for the most part, and it makes me proud.

Before the first verse is even over, the dance floor is packed with bodies. The power and sex in Camryn's voice mixed with the fascination everyone has for her performance sends me over the edge, and I hammer out that riff with more devotion than before.

"Ooo, baby, ooo, ooo!"

Every few seconds I hear a voice scream in the background: "Wooooo!" and again, each time Camryn hits a moving note.

And I can't get enough.

I sing my heart out along with her to the next two choruses, and I know the fourth verse that she always got tripped up on is next. I look over, still moving my pick fast over the strings, my back arched, and I don't see a nervous muscle in her face. She's got this; I can tell by looking at her that there's no way she's going to screw it up.

And then the words come and go so fast and flawlessly from her lips that I feel my face stretched to its limits with a smile as I follow loudly into the next chorus line with her.

Damn, my baby *owns* this song. Look out, Stevie Nicks!

Passing the middle of the song, Camryn sings: *Oooo!* And her voice fades in that ominous part of the song which allows her voice a short rest.

But the guitar riff goes on and on. It's exhausting, but my fingers never stop, never miss a beat.

Camryn and I look at each other and share a moment. Then she starts singing again, and I join in where I'm supposed to.

She sings on, both of her hands come up to grip the microphone stand, her eyes shut as she belts out with so much emotion, *"Yeah! Yeah!"*

Then she looks right at me again and keeps her eyes trained on mine while she belts out the next verse as if she's singing solely for me.

Shivers run up my spine. I grin and fall back into the guitar until the song is over.

The audience erupts with shouts and screams. Camryn takes a bow first, and then I follow. She's smiling so hugely as she looks out at the crowd, and it kind of chokes me up a little inside.

Keeping the guitar strapped around my body, I push it behind my back and walk right over to her, then lift her off the floor and into my arms. There are whistles and shouts all around us, but all I really notice is Camryn looking back at me. I kiss her deeply, and the crowd whistles and shouts even louder.

Before the night is over, we end up playing a full ten-song gig to a growing crowd as the hours wear on. We go back to sing some of our favorites: "Barton Hollow," "Hotel California," and "Birds of a Feather," among others, and each song seems to please the audience as much as the previous one. I don't do a solo tonight, even though at one point Camryn asks me to. This was her night and *only* her night. I refused to be the center of attention even for one song.

We make it back to our hotel by two in the morning, and I'm gladly paying up on the bet I lost.

Camryn

TWENTY-SEVEN

$\mathcal{G}$erman seems to think we're going to be here for a while," I say with the right side of my face pressed into the mattress. "I told him it was only temporary."

Andrew's magical hands knead both sides of my back from my shoulders down to my waist, and I'm putty in his hands. I just lay here and soak up this massage as if I've never had one before. I can hardly open my eyes. He sits on top of my nearly naked body, straddling my waist.

"Yeah, he pulled me off to the side once and asked me what time we were going to play tomorrow night." Andrew chuckles and presses the tips of all ten fingers deeply into my flesh and moves his hands in a solid circular motion.

I moan underneath him.

"We can stay for a few more days," he says, "but I think we should move on soon."

"I agree. Besides, the mosquitos in Mobile are horrendous! Did you see the apocalyptic swarm around the light poles after we left tonight?"

Andrew ignores the question and says, "You really did awesome tonight. I knew you'd do great, but I have to say, I didn't expect *that*."

I finally open my eyes and peer off toward the window. "What exactly?" I ask.

His hands never stop kneading my back. "You got up on that stage and just owned it. You have a natural-born talent."

"I don't know about that," I say. "But I am proud of myself. I don't know what came over me, really. I just shed the nervous feeling in my gut and went with it."

"Well, it worked," he says.

"Only because you were there with me," I say.

We remain silent for several minutes, my eyes closed again as his massage gradually threatens to send me into dreamland. The blood around my eyes feels light; my entire head tingles, and the back of my neck shivers when he works his fingertips into my scalp.

Before his full hour is over with, I start to feel bad for making him do it so long that I open my eyes and say, "If you're tired, you can stop."

And when he doesn't stop, I make him stop by turning around and lying on my back. He lies on top of me and kisses me lightly on the lips. And we stare at each other for a moment, searching each other's eyes, studying each other's lips. I feel him pressing into my body below, and his mouth closes over mine in a passionate kiss as he begins to make love to me.

Andrew

TWENTY-EIGHT

*W*e're on the road again, somewhere on a highway between Gulfport, Mississippi, and New Orleans. The day is perfect, with clear blue skies and just the right amount of heat so that we can still ride with the windows down and not feel the need to turn on the AC in the car. Camryn is driving and I'm kicked back on the passenger's side, a lot like she usually is, with one foot hanging out the window.

We stayed in Mobile for a week and paid for our hotel room, all of our food, and the gas in the car with just a fraction of the cash we scored performing and Camryn's tips from waitressing. My busboy tips were just a drop in the bucket compared to hers.

My cell phone buzzes around in the pocket of my black cargo shorts, and I answer it. "Hey, Mom, what's up?"

She tells me how much she misses me and goes right into questions about my check-ups.

"No, I've been getting checked out," I say. "Yeah, I got a scan not long ago at a hospital in— No, they just called in to Dr. Marsters for my info and— Yes, Mom. I know. I'm being careful." I glance over at Camryn, who is smiling back at me. "Camryn won't let me get away with not going. Yeah. Well, right now we're on our way to

New Orleans. I don't know how long we're staying there, but after we leave we'll swing by home for a visit, all right?"

After I hang up with her, Camryn asks, "Texas?"

Instantly, I get the feeling she's having the same thoughts she did during our first road trip, but she proves me wrong when she says, "Not that I have any problem with it. Just curious about the destination." She smiles, and I can tell right away that she's not hiding anything.

"Texas doesn't worry you?" I ask.

She looks back at the road as we go around a curve, then she glances over at me again. "Not at all. Not like it used to."

"What changed your mind?" I pull my foot from the window and turn to better face her, intrigued by her change of heart.

"Because things are different now," she says. "But in a good way. Andrew, last July was tough. For both of us. I don't know how I know, but I think I knew all along that something bad was going to happen when we got to Texas. For a while I thought it was all just me worried about it being the last stop on our road trip. But I'm not so sure about that anymore. I feel like I knew..."

I smile slimly. "I think I understand," I say. "So then that leads me to one question."

She looks at me, waiting.

"Will we ever settle down?"

Her reaction isn't what I expected it to be. I expected her smile to fade and the moment to be lost, but instead her eyes brighten, and I feel a sense of calm emanating from her.

"Eventually," she says. "But not yet." She looks back at the road and continues, "Y'know, Andrew, I want to see Italy one day. Rome. Sorrento. Maybe not right now or even in the next five years, but I hope to see it. France, too. London. I would even love to go to Jamaica and Mexico and Brazil."

"Really? It would take a long time to see those places," I say, but not in a way to deter her from wanting to do it. I would love to do it, too.

The wind from the open window brushes through her hair, pulling more loose strands from her braid as they dance around her bright face.

"I feel free with you," she says. "I feel like I can do anything. Go anywhere. Be anything that I want." Her eyes fall on me once more and she says, "We'll settle down soon, but I never want to settle down forever. Does that make sense?"

"Definitely," I answer. "I couldn't have said it better."

We make it over the Louisiana state line just after dark, and Camryn pulls over to the side of the highway.

"I don't think I can drive anymore," she says, stretching her arms behind her and yawning.

"I told you an hour ago you needed to let me drive."

"Yeah, well I'm letting you now." She gets cranky when she's tired.

We both get out of the car to switch sides but stop when we meet each other at the hood.

"Do you see where we are?" I ask.

Camryn looks around on both sides of the desolate highway. She shrugs. "Ummm, the middle of nowhere?"

I laugh lightly under my breath and then point to the field. Then I point up at the stars. "Last time didn't count, remember?"

Her eyes light up, but then I sense she's conflicted. It doesn't take me long to figure out why.

"It's a flat, clear field. And there are no cows as far as I can tell," I say.

I know that absolutely nothing I just said makes her feel any better about the possibility of snakes, but I was going for subtle and stupid, hoping she'd overlook it.

"What about snakes?" she asks, *not* overlooking it.

"Don't let your fear of snakes ruin a perfectly good opportunity to finally get to sleep underneath the stars."

She narrows her eyes at me.

I break out the big guns and just beg. "Please? Preeeety please?" I wonder if my attempt at puppy-dog eyes is as effective on her as hers always are on me. My first instinct was to throw her ass over my shoulder and carry her out there, but I'm curious about the effectiveness of my begging technique, just the same.

She mulls it over for a minute and finally caves to my charm. "All right," she says a little exasperatedly.

I grab the blanket from the trunk, and we walk together through the ditch and over the low fence and then through the enormous field until we find a good spot several yards out. It feels like déjà vu. I lay the blanket on the dried grass and do a quick snake-check of the surrounding area just to make her feel better. We lay down next to each other on our backs, legs straight out and flat against the blanket, our ankles crossed below. And we look up at the dark and endless expanse of sky filled with stars. Camryn points out various constellations and planets, explaining each one to me in detail, and I'm impressed by how much she knows and how she can tell them apart from one another.

"I never imagined you'd be so..." I struggle to find the way to word it.

"So knowledgeable?" I can sense her smiling briefly next to me.

"Well, I . . . I didn't mean that I think you're—"

"A brainless, superficial girl who doesn't know that the Milky Way is something bigger than a candy bar or that the big bang theory isn't just a television show?"

"Yeah, something like that," I say, just to play her at her own game. "No, but really, where'd all this come from? I guess I just never took you for the scientific type."

"I wanted to be an astrophysicist. Decided that when I was twelve, I think."

I'm completely shocked by her admission, but I continue to stare up at the stars with her, my smile growing.

"Well, really I wanted to be that *plus* a theoretical physicist *and* an astronaut *and* I wanted to work for NASA, but I was a little delusional back then. Obviously."

"Camryn," I say, still so surprised that I barely know *what* to say. "Why didn't you ever tell me this before?"

She shrugs. "I don't know," she says. "It just never came up. Didn't you ever dream of being something other than what you are?"

"Yeah, I guess so," I say. "But baby, why didn't you pursue it?" I lift away from the blanket and sit upright. This calls for my full attention.

She looks at me like I'm overreacting. "Probably for the same reason you didn't pursue whatever it was that *you* wanted to be." She draws her knees upward and rests her hands over her stomach, her fingers interlocked. "What did you want to be?"

I don't want to talk about me right now, but I guess I better answer her, since she's brought it up twice.

I bring my knees up, too, and prop my forearms on top of them. "Well, aside from the clichéd rock-star dream *everybody* has, I wanted to be an architect."

"Really?"

"Yeah," I say with a nod.

"Is that what you were studying in college before you dropped out?"

I shake my head. "No," I say and laugh lightly at the absurdity of my answer. "I was in college for accounting and business."

Camryn's eyebrows draw inward. "*Accounting?* Are you *serious?*" She's almost laughing.

"I know, right?" I say, laughing it off myself. "Aiden offered me part ownership of his bar. Back then I just had dollar signs in my eyes, and I thought that owning a bar would be an awesome opportunity. I could play my music there and . . . I don't know what I was thinking, but I jumped at my brother's offer. Then he started talking about how I'd need to understand the business aspects of it and all that shit. I enrolled in college, and that was pretty much where the idea ended. I didn't give a shit about accounting, or running a bar or having to deal with all of the negative that comes with owning a business." I pause for a moment and then say, "I guess, like you said, I was delusional, wanted all the positives but none of the negatives. When I realized it didn't work that way, I said fuck it."

She lifts to sit upright with me. "So, then why didn't you pursue the architect thing?"

I smirk. "Probably for the same reason you didn't pursue the astrophysicist thing."

She just smiles, having no real rebuttal to that one.

I gaze beyond Camryn's blonde hair and out at the field. "I guess we're just two lost souls swimming in a fish bowl," I say.

Her eyes narrow. "I've heard that somewhere before."

I smile and point at her briefly. "Pink Floyd. But it's the truth."

"You think we're lost?"

I tilt my head back a little and look up at the stars behind her and say, "In society, maybe. But together, no. I think we're right where we need to be."

Neither of us say anything more for quite some time.

We lie back down next to each other and do what we came out here to do. As I gaze up at the infinite blackness of that sky, I'm in complete awe of the moment. I think I find some of myself up in those stars. For a long time I forget about music, being on the road, about the tumor that almost killed me last year, and the moment of weakness that almost killed Camryn's spirit. I forget about losing Lily, and about the fact that I know Camryn stopped taking her birth control pills and didn't tell me. And I forget about the fact that I stopped pulling out for a reason and didn't tell her.

I really do forget about everything. Because that's what a moment like this does to you. It makes you feel like something so small inside of something so massive that it's beyond comprehension. It strips away all of your problems, all of your hardships, all of your worldly needs and wants and desires, forcing you to realize just how insignificant all of it really is. It's like the Earth becomes completely silent and still, and all that your mind can understand or feel is the vastness of the Universe and you gasp thinking about your place within it.

Who needs psychiatrists? Who needs grief counselors and life coaches and motivational speakers? Fuck all that. Just stare at the night sky and let yourself get lost in it every now and then.

———

Something unpleasant wakes me the next morning. I sniff the air with my eyes still closed, my mind not fully awake but my body and sense of smell working ahead of me. There's a mild chill in the air and my skin feels moist, as if covered by early morning dew. Rolling over onto my other side, I sniff the air again and it's even fouler than before. I hear something rustling nearby, and finally my eyes open a slit. Camryn's passed out next to me. I can just barely see her blonde braid lying on the blanket in between us. She seems to be curled in the fetal position.

What is that smell?!

I cover my mouth with my hand and start to raise myself from the blanket. Camryn begins to move at the same time, rolling over onto her back and rubbing her face and eyes with both hands. She yawns. As I sit upright and open my eyes the rest of the way, Camryn asks, "What the hell is that smell?" and her face contorts.

I'm just about to say that it's probably her breath when her blue eyes grow scary-wide as she looks behind me.

Instinctively, I turn around fast.

A herd of cows stands just feet from us, and when they sense us moving around, they spook.

"Oh my God!" Camryn jumps up faster than she did that night the snake slithered over our blanket, causing me to do the same.

Two cows moo and moan and grunt, backing into the other cows behind them, stirring the herd that much more.

"I think we better get outta here," I say, grabbing her hand and running with her.

We don't wait long enough to stop and grab the blanket at first, but I stop and double back seconds later to snatch it up. Camryn shrieks and I start laughing as we dash away from the cows and toward the car.

"Awww, *shiiiit!*" I yell when I step in a huge pile of it.

Camryn cackles with laughter, and we both practically stumble the rest of the way through the field, me trying to scrape the shit off the bottom of my shoe while running at the same time, and Camryn's flip-flops getting caught on the ground as they try to keep up with her feet.

"I can't believe that just happened!" Camryn laughs, as we finally make it back to the car. She arches her body forward and props her hands on her knees, trying to catch her breath.

I'm out of breath, too, but I still relentlessly scrape the bottom of my shoe on the asphalt. "Dammit!" I say, rubbing my foot back and forth.

Camryn jumps up on the hood of the car, letting her legs hang over the front. "*Now* can we say that we did it?" she asks with laughter in her voice.

I stand still and catch my breath. I look at her, at how beautiful and bright that smile of hers is, and say, "Yeah, I think we can safely mark it off our list."

"Good!" she says. Then she points behind me. "Do it on the grass," she says with one side of her mouth pinched into a hard line. "You're just spreading it around doing it like that."

I hop over into the grass and start rubbing my foot back and forth again. "Since when did you become an expert on shit?"

"Better watch your mouth," she warns, getting into the driver's seat.

"What are you going to do?" I taunt her.

She starts the Chevelle and revs the engine a few times. There's a cruel gleam in her eyes. She props her left arm across the top of the open window and next thing I know she's driving slowly past me.

I give her the warning eye, but her grin just gets bigger.

"I know you won't leave me here!" I shout as she goes past me. *Surely she wouldn't...*

She gets farther away and at first I call her bluff and just stand here, watching her get smaller and smaller...

Finally, I take off running after the car.

Camryn

TWENTY-NINE

*T*he first thing that comes to mind when we make it to New Orleans is *home sweet home.* I get a rush when the sights become familiar: the great oak trees and beautiful historic homes, Lake Pontchartrain and the Superdome, the red and yellow streetcars that always reminded me of toys. And, of course, the French Quarter. There's even a man playing a saxophone on a street corner, and I feel like we've driven directly into a New Orleans postcard.

I look over at Andrew, and he smiles across at me briefly. He flips on his blinker and we turn right onto Royal Street. My heart flutters and pounds at the same time when I see the Holiday Inn. So much happened here ten months ago. This place...a hotel, of all places...it's so much more than that to me, to both of us.

"I figured you'd want to stay here while we're in town," Andrew says, beaming.

Because the memories are still figuratively taking my breath away, I can't answer him, so I just nod and match his smile.

We grab our stuff from the car and head into the lobby. Everything looks exactly the same, except maybe for the two women behind the front desk when we approach. I don't remember seeing them before.

Vaguely I hear Andrew ask about the availability of our old rooms while I'm looking around at everything, trying to soak it all in.

God, I missed this place.

"Yes, looks like both of those rooms are vacant," I hear one of the front desk clerks say. "Would you like both?"

That gets my attention.

Andrew turns to me. I guess he wants to know what I think.

I switch my bag to the opposite shoulder and hesitate for a moment, pondering the question. I never anticipated this, or that it would be such a hard decision.

"Ummm, well…" I look to Andrew and then the clerk, still undecided. "I don't know. OK, maybe we should just get the one we…" I stop myself, not wanting to make us look like two immature sixteen-year-olds this time, and then I eye Andrew with that knowing look. "The one where the *deal was sealed*."

Andrew's lips struggle to remain straight, but I clearly see the smile in his eyes as he reaches out his hand to the clerk and hands her his credit card.

We leave the lobby shortly after and ride the elevator up to our floor. On the way down the hall I'm still absorbing everything around me, right down to the color of paint on the walls, because it's all part of a memory no matter how big or small or seemingly insignificant. The feeling of being here again…I almost feel like I'm going to break out in happy tears. But I'm excited, too, and that saves me from becoming a blubbering mess.

Andrew stops in between the two doors of our old rooms, two bags and the electric guitar I bought him hanging over his shoulders. He's been meaning to buy a case for the guitar, but he hasn't gotten around to it yet.

"Strange being here again, huh?" he asks, glancing over at me.

"Strange, but in a good way," I say.

We stay like this for a minute, looking at each other and then at the two doors, until finally Andrew steps up to the one we paid for and slides the key card through the lock.

It really is like stepping into the past. The door swings open slowly, and it's as if all the emotions that we experienced in this room were left behind and are now greeting us as we enter. As we step inside, I remember every night we slept here, apart and together, as if it happened yesterday. I look at the spot near the bed where I stood when Andrew broke me down and made me his. I glance toward the window overlooking the busy streets of the French Quarter. I envision the day Andrew sat on that windowsill playing his acoustic, and even when I was the one over there, dancing and singing to "Barton Hollow" when I thought I was alone. I turn to see the bathroom, and as Andrew flips on the light in there my gaze falls to the floor first and I recall the night, although vaguely, when he slept next to me.

I guess sometimes the greatest memories are made in the most unlikely of places, further proof that spontaneity is more rewarding than a meticulously planned life. A meticulously planned *anything*.

I turn to Andrew. "I don't know why, but I feel... well, I feel like all these months on the road since December were to get to *this* place. This city. This hotel." I can't believe what I'm saying, and immediately I start questioning my reasons. It could mean so many different things, but the one I think it means most is that we *needed* to come back here.

Yes, that's exactly it, or at least it's what *I* needed. As this revelation hits me, I find myself standing in this room surrounded by thoughts rather than material objects. I look into Andrew's eyes, but I don't really see him. I see him in the past instead. Same magnetic green eyes, different year.

Why am I feeling this way?

"Maybe you're right," he says, and then his tone shifts to something more mysterious. "Camryn, what are you thinking right now?"

"That we left too soon the first time." It was the first thing that came to mind, and only now that I've said it do I start to understand just how true it might be.

"Why do you think that is?" he asks, stepping closer to me.

I don't feel like he's asking me questions he already knows the answers to this time. It's like we're both thinking along the same lines, both trying to make sense of it all and seeking answers from each other.

We sit down on the foot of the bed together, my hands wedged between my thighs, just as his are, and we're quiet for several long seconds. Finally, I turn my head to see him on my right and say, "I never wanted to leave when we did, Andrew. I knew our next stop after New Orleans would be Galveston. I wasn't ready to leave this place . . . but I don't know why."

And this truth makes me anxious.

Why? Other than fearing that Texas meant the end of the road for us, or that I later felt like I knew something bad would happen there, why else would I want to stay here? I didn't necessarily want to stay here forever, just that simply we left too soon.

"I dunno," he says with a mild shrug. "Maybe it's just because this is where we finally *sealed the deal*." He elbows me playfully.

I can't help but smile. "Yeah, maybe, but I think it's more than that, Andrew. I think it's because we found ourselves here." I stare off toward the wall in thought. "I just don't know."

I feel the bed move as Andrew stands up.

"Well, I say that this time we make the most of it before we leave." He reaches out his hand to me and I take it. "Maybe we'll figure it out."

I stand up and say, "Or…maybe it's a do-over."

Honestly, I have no idea what made me say that.

"To do what over exactly?" he asks.

I pause, thinking about it, and then answer, "I don't know that, either…."

Andrew

THIRTY

I cup her face in the palms of my hands. "We don't have to figure that out right now," I say and kiss her lips. "I smell like cow shit and I need a shower. Hopefully, you're not so turned off by that and will join me."

Camryn's thoughtful expression dissolves into that grin I was shooting for.

I pick her up, cradling her ass in my hands, and she wraps her legs around my waist, hangs her arms over my shoulders. The second I taste her warm tongue in my mouth, I'm carrying her off to the shower with me, both of our shirts falling onto the floor before we make it past the bathroom door.

———

The very first place we hit after sundown is Old Point Bar. When we walk through the front door, we're welcomed by an excited Carla who practically pushes two big guys out of the way to get to me, her arms wide out at her sides. We collapse into a hug.

"It's so great to see you again!" Carla says over the loud music. "Let me look at you!" She takes a step back and examines me from my shoes to my head. "Still as handsome as ever."

She turns to Camryn now. Then she glances at me and then

back to Camryn again. "Uh-huh, I knew he wouldn't let *you* go." She pulls Camryn into a hug and squeezes her tight.

"I told Eddie after you two left," she goes on, looking back and forth between us, "that she was a keeper. Eddie agreed, of course. He said the next time you came around here that Camryn would be with you. He tried to bet me money on it." She points at me and winks. "You know how Eddie was."

In two seconds I feel my heart sink into the soles of my feet. "'Was'?" I ask warily, afraid of her answer.

Carla doesn't lose her smile, maybe just a little, but for the most part she doesn't lose it. "I'm sorry, Andrew, but Eddie died in March. A stroke, they say."

My breath hitches, and I take a seat on a bar stool next to me. I sense Camryn step up beside me. All I can see is the floor.

"Oh don't you do that now, you hear me?" Carla says. "You knew Eddie better than just about anyone. He didn't even cry when his own son died. You remember? He played his guitar all night long in Robert's honor."

Camryn's hand interlocks with one of mine. I don't look up until Carla walks around the bar and grabs two shot glasses and a bottle of whiskey from the glass shelf behind her. She sets the glasses down in front of me and starts pouring.

"He always said," Carla continues, "that if he died before any of us did that he'd rather be woken up on the Other Side to people dancin' on his grave than cryin' on it. Now drink up. His favorite whiskey. He wouldn't have it any other way."

Carla's right. Even though she is, and I know Eddie would hate it that anyone grieved over him, I still can't let go of the bottomless hole I feel in my heart right now. I look at Camryn next to me and see that she's trying not to cry, her eyes coated with tears. But she smiles, and I feel her hand gently squeezing mine. Camryn reaches out for the whiskey that Carla poured and waits for me to take the other. I slide my hand across the bar top and grasp it in my fingers.

"To Eddie," I say.

"To Eddie," Camryn repeats.

We touch our glasses, smile at each other and drink it down.

Our serious moment is quickly over when Camryn brings her hand down, slamming the glass upside-down on the bar. She makes the most disgusted, kick-in-the-teeth face I've ever seen a girl make and lets out a sound like her breath is on fire.

Carla laughs and takes her shot glass away, wiping the area underneath it with a rag. "Didn't say it was good, just that it was Eddie's."

Even I have to admit the shit is nasty. Rotgut nasty shit. I don't know how Eddie drank this all those years.

"Are you two still playin' together?" Carla asks.

Camryn climbs up onto the empty bar stool next to me and answers first, "Yeah, we've been doing a lot of that."

Carla looks at us both suspiciously, taking my shot glass and putting it away underneath the bar somewhere now.

"Been playin' a lot for how long? And why haven't I seen you here sooner?"

I sigh heavily and fold both hands on the bar, leaning more comfortably against it. "Well, after we left here we went to Galveston and I sort of ended up in the hospital with that tumor."

"You *sort of* ended up in the hospital?" Carla says, and I wonder if her smart ass is related to that cop back in Florida somehow. She points sternly at me but her words are for Camryn. "We told him to go to the doctor, but he wouldn't listen."

"You knew, too?" Camryn asks.

Carla nods. "Yeah, we knew. But your boy here is as stubborn as a mule."

"I agree with you there," Camryn says with a hint of laughter in her voice.

I shake my head and lean away from the bar again. "Well, before you two gang up on me," I say, "anyway, obviously I'm alive. Later, Camryn and I went through some really messed up things along the way, but we both made it through OK." I smile warmly over at her.

"Looks like you came full circle," Carla says, and it invokes our attention at the same time. "I hope you're going to play tonight. Eddie would've loved to be up there with you one last time."

Camryn and I lock eyes briefly.

"I'm up for it," she says.

"So am I."

Carla smacks her hands together. "Well, all right then! You can go on whenever you want. The only band we had scheduled tonight cancelled."

We hang out at the bar with Carla for an hour before we finally make it to the stage. And even though the bar is only half-full tonight, we play to an excited crowd. We start off with our trade-mark duet, "Barton Hollow"; it seems only fitting that it be the first one, since Old Point is where we performed it together the first time. We go through several songs before finally getting to "Laugh, I Nearly Died," in which I make an announcement on stage before-hand that it's in honor of Eddie Johnson. I play it without Cam-ryn and with an Eddie replacement, some nice Creole man named Alfred.

A little after midnight, Camryn and I say good-bye to Carla

and Old Point Bar. But in true New Orleans style, we don't go to bed early, we stay out and party with the best of them. We hit d.b.a. first, then head over to the bar where Camryn schooled me in a game of pool that night. It's been almost a year since we were here last and were kicked out on our asses after a bar fight; I hope they don't remember me. By two in the morning, after several games of pool and several drinks, just like last time I'm helping Camryn into the hotel elevator because she can barely hold herself up.

"You all right, babe?" I laugh lightly, repositioning my arm around the back of her waist.

Her head sways side to side. "No. I'm not all right. And you *would* laugh."

"Aww, I'm sorry," I say, but it's only partly true. "I'm not laughing at you, just wondering if we're going to be sleeping next to the toilet this time."

She moans, though I think it was her way of arguing with me instead of expressing her discomfort. I get a better grip on her as the elevator opens, and I walk with her out into the hall and back to our room. I lead her to the bed, strip off everything but her panties, and help her into one of her tank tops. She lies down against the pillow, and I start to cover her with the sheet. But I remember that being this drunk, anything other than her panties and top will just make her sweat profusely, ultimately causing her to lose all of the alcohol she drank tonight.

Just in case, I grab the small wastebasket near the TV and place it next to the bed on the floor. Then I go into the bathroom, wet a washcloth with the cold water, and wring it out over the sink. But by the time I make it back to the bed to swab Camryn's face and forehead, she's already passed out.

———

When I wake up the next morning, I'm surprised to see that she's awake before me.

"Mornin', baby," she says so softly it's almost a whisper.

I open my eyes to see her lying on her side, facing me, her face pressed against her pillow. Her blue eyes are warm and vibrant, not the tired, hangover kind that I expected.

"What are you doing up so early?" I ask, reaching out to brush her cheek with the backs of my fingers.

"I'm not sure," she says. "I was a little surprised myself."

"How do you feel?"

"I feel fine."

I drape my arm over her waist and pull her body next to mine, our bare legs tangling together. She traces the tip of her finger around the definition of my chest muscles. Her touch breaks my skin out in chill bumps.

I study her eyes and her mouth and let my fingertips follow every path that my eyes take. She is so beautiful to me. So goddamn beautiful. She reaches up and caresses my fingers underneath her own and then she kisses them, one by one, and pulls her body even closer. Something is different about her.

"Are you sure you're all right?" I ask.

A gentle smile warms her eyes and she nods. Then she touches her lips to mine, pressing her breasts firmly against my chest. Her nipples are hard. *I'm* hard long before I feel her hand grip my erection. She licks the tip of my tongue before closing her mouth around mine and I wrap my arms around her body possessively. She presses herself against me below, the softness of her skin, her wetness that I feel so easily through her thin, cotton panties. Without breaking the hungry kiss, I reach down with one hand, slipping my fingers behind each side of her panties and take them off. I thrust my hips toward her, pressing my swollen cock against her warmth.

I roll over on top of her and look down into her eyes. But I don't say a word. I don't tell her how wet she is, or force her to look at me. I don't dominate her with words or gestures or demands. I just gaze into her eyes and know that this is a moment where words are not needed.

I kiss her lips again softly, the corners of her mouth, the outline of her cheekbone. Parting her lips with my tongue, I very softly kiss her and reach down and take my cock into my hand, rubbing it against her. I feel her hips shift toward me, letting me know how bad she wants me inside of her. I don't want to tease her this time, or deny her what she needs, so I push myself in just barely and watch her lose control of her gaze, her eyes fluttering, her lips parting. Forcing my cock in further, I feel her legs tremble around me. She moans softly, biting down on her bottom lip. I kiss her again and finally push myself deep inside of her, as far as I can go. I hold it there, basking in the shaking of her thighs, the trembling of her hands as they hold onto me, her fingers digging into my back.

I rock harder against her, gyrating my hips. A thin layer of sweat begins to bead off our bodies. I want to lick it off her, but I don't stop. I can't stop…

I raise my body up enough that our chests are no longer touching and I grab one of her legs from around me, gripping under the bend of her knee, pushing it back so I can thrust deeper. I pound her harder, pushing her thigh down against the bed. She calls out my name, both of her hands clutching my waist, but she pulls them back and curls her fingers around the top of the mattress above her head. I watch hungrily as her breasts bounce up and down against her chest and I thrust even harder, leaning over to take her nipples into my mouth and then into my teeth.

My vision gets hazy. She moans loudly and then begins to whimper. The whimpering makes me crazy. I let go of her thigh and feel my body closing in on hers again, her breasts smashed into my chest, her arms wrapped tightly around my back. I feel her fingernails press painfully into my flesh. She rocks her hips against mine, and my mouth crashes over hers. As I start to come, my kiss becomes more ravenous. Tremors move through my body and I moan against her mouth and my hard thrusts are reduced to gentle rocking. Camryn takes my bottom lip between her teeth and I kiss her gently, still rocking my hips against her until I'm finished.

I collapse onto her chest. My erratic heartbeat trying to find its rhythm again, I feel the pumping of blood in my fingers and in my toes and aggravating the vein near my temple. I lay the side of my face against her bare breasts, my mouth parted, the breath expelling unevenly from my lips. Her fingers move through my moist hair.

We lie here together just like this, all morning, without saying a word.

THIRTY-ONE

I don't remember falling asleep. When I open my eyes, the clock beside the bed says that it's eleven ten. And I realize that I don't feel naked because I have no clothes on, but I feel naked because Camryn isn't in the bed with me.

She's sitting on the windowsill, dressed in a pair of shorts and a T-shirt without a bra. She's gazing out the window.

"I think we should go," she says without taking her eyes off the bright New Orleans landscape.

I sit up on the bed with the sheet draped over my lower half. "You want to leave New Orleans?" I ask, confused. "But I thought you said we left too soon the first time."

"Yeah," she says, but still doesn't turn around. "The first time we left too soon, but we can't stay here longer now just to make up for that."

"But why do you want to leave? We've only been here one day."

She turns to face me. There's something like sentiment or resolve in her eyes, but I can't make out which, or if it's both.

After a long hesitation, she says, "Andrew, I know this might sound stupid, but I think if we stay here...I..."

I stand up from the bed and step inside my boxers I find on the floor. "What's going on?" I ask, approaching her.

She looks at me. "I just think that…well, when we first got here yesterday all I could think about is what this place meant to us last July. I realized that I kept picturing the times before, trying to relive them—"

"But they're just not the same," I add, having an idea.

It takes her a second, but finally she says, after a subtle nod, "Yeah. I guess it's just that this place is such a significant memory— Shit, Andrew, I don't even know what I'm saying!" Her thoughtful expression dissolves into frustration.

I pull out a chair at the table in front of the window and sit down, leaning forward and draping my folded hands between my knees, and I gaze up at her. I begin to say something to add to her explanation, but she beats me to it.

"Maybe we should never come back here."

I didn't expect her to say *that*. "Why?"

She presses the palms of her hands on the windowsill to hold up her body, her shoulders rigid, her back slouching. Confusion and uncertainty start to fade from her face as the seconds pass and she begins to understand.

"It's like, you know, it doesn't matter what you do, even if you try to replicate an experience down to every last detail, it'll never be the way it was when it happened naturally the first time." She looks out at the room in thought. "I remember when I was a kid. Cole and I would always play in the woods behind our old house. Some of my best memories. We built a tree house back there." She glances at me and laughs lightly under her breath. "Well, it wasn't so much a tree house as it was a few boards fixed between two branches. But it was *our* tree house and we were proud of it. And we played in it and in those woods every day after school." Her face is lit up as she recalls this moment of her childhood. But then her smile begins to fade. "We moved away from there and into the house my mom lives in now, and I always thought of those woods and our tree house and the fun times we had together there. I used to sit alone in my room, or be driving somewhere, and get so lost in those memories that I could actually *feel* those feelings just like I felt them years ago." She places her hand on her chest, her fingers outstretched.

"I went back there one day," she goes on. "I got so addicted to the nostalgia that I thought I could intensify the feeling if I went, stood in the spot where our tree house used to be, sit down on the ground where I used to sit and drag a stick through the dirt to leave secret messages for Cole to read if I got there before him. But it wasn't the same, Andrew."

I watch and listen to her intently.

"It wasn't the same," she repeats distantly. "I was so disappointed. And I left that day with an even bigger hole in my heart than I had when I went there looking to fill it. And every day after that, whenever I'd try to envision it like I used to, I couldn't. I shattered that memory by going back there. Without realizing it until it was too late, I *replaced* that memory with the emptiness of that day."

I know exactly that feeling of nostalgia. I think everybody experiences it at some point in their lives, but I don't elaborate or go into my own experience with it. Instead, I just continue to listen.

"All morning, I've been tricking my brain into believing that we're not really in this room. That the bar we went to last night wasn't Old Point. That the sad news about Eddie was just in a dream I had." She looks me straight in the eyes. "I want to leave before I destroy this memory, too."

She's right. She's absolutely right.

But I'm beginning to wonder if...

"Camryn, why were you trying to relive it?" I hate it that I'm about to say this. "Are you not happy with how things are? How *we* are?"

Her head snaps upward, her eyes filled with disbelief. But then her features soften and she says, "God, no, Andrew." She moves off the windowsill and stands in between my parted legs. "That's not it at all. I think it's just that because we came here I subconsciously started trying to re-create one of the most memorable experiences of my life." She rests both hands on my shoulders, and I reach out and hold both sides of her waist, looking up at her. I couldn't be any more relieved by her answer.

I smile and stand up with her and say, "Well, I say we get the hell out of here before that brain of yours knows you're full of shit."

She chuckles.

I move away from her and immediately start tossing our stuff in our bags. Then I point to the bathroom. "Don't forget anything." Her smile widens and she rushes immediately past me into the bathroom. In just a couple of hectic minutes, everything is packed. We each have a bag and a guitar, and without looking back, we leave the room. Neither one of us even glances at the door of the room next door that we didn't rent this time. When we make it downstairs and into the lobby, I step up the counter and request a refund for the week in advance that I paid for. The clerk takes my credit card and refunds it back as I slip our card keys across the counter to her.

Camryn waits impatiently next to me.

"Stop looking at shit," I demand, knowing she's risking the memory.

She laughs lightly and squeezes her eyes shut for a moment.

"Thank you for staying at the Holiday Inn New Orleans," the

clerk says as we leave the counter. "We look forward to seeing you again."

"Holiday Inn?" I pretend. "No, this is the...Embassy Suites in...Gulfport. Yeah, this is Mississippi. What's wrong with you, ma'am?"

The clerk's features crumple and she raises a baffled brow, but doesn't say anything back and we exit the building.

Camryn plays along once we get outside and start loading everything in the Chevelle: "I say we drive straight past New Orleans when we get to Louisiana."

It's not really as hard as I thought it would be to pretend we're someplace we're not.

"Sounds like a plan," I say, shutting my door. "We can drive straight past Galveston, too, if you want."

"No, we have to visit your mom," she says. "After that we can go wherever."

I put the car into gear and say just before backing out, "Doesn't mean we can't stop somewhere on the way to Galveston, though."

She purses her lips, nodding in agreement. "That's true." Then she looks at me as if to say, *Now let's get out of here.*

———

We take the long way out of New Orleans and make our way northwest through Baton Rouge and Shreveport, and eventually over the Texas state line and then into Longview. We stop for gas in Tyler and drive from there to Dallas, where Camryn insists we drop in West Village for a "gen-you-ine cowgirl hat" (her words, not mine).

"Cain't road-trip through Texus without dressin' like ah Texun!" she said just before I agreed to take her.

Personally, I don't do cowboy hats or boots, but I have to say it looks good on *her*.

And we stop off for a night at La Grange, where we have a few drinks and watch a great country-rock band play. And the next night we hang out at Gilley's, where Camryn rides El Torro the mechanical bull, of course, with that sexy cowgirl hat on. And later, when we go back to our hotel, being the horny bastard that I am, I pretend I'm the mechanical bull and let her ride *me*. Wearing the cowgirl hat, naturally.

Two days later, we find ourselves about an hour from Lubbock, broke down on the side of the highway with a blown tire. I guess I should've checked out all four of the tires back at that gas station in Tyler.

"This is fucked up, babe," I say, squatting down next to the shredded rubber. "I don't have another spare."

Camryn leans against the side of the car, crossing her arms over her chest. Sweat glistens on her face and the skin above her breasts. It's hot as hell out here. There's not a tree or a structure of any kind for miles. We're surrounded by an almost completely flat, barren landscape of dirt. It's been a long time since I was this far west in Texas, and I'm starting to remember why.

I stand up straight and hop on the hood of the car. "Let me see your phone," I say.

"Gonna call a tow truck?" she asks after reaching in the front seat to get it and placing it in my hand.

I run my finger over the touch screen, flipping two pages to find her Yellow Pages app. "It's the only thing we *can* do." I type in "tow trucks" and scroll the results before choosing one.

"I hope this one actually shows up this time," she says.

The tow service answers, and while I'm talking to the guy, telling him what size tire I need, I notice Camryn lean into the back-seat through the open window and emerge with that sexy cowgirl hat on, likely to help keep the beating sun off of her.

She moves around to the hood and jumps up on it next to me.

"OK, thanks, man," I say into the phone and hang up. "He said it'll be at least an hour before he can get here." I set the phone on the hood and grin over at her. "Y'know, all you'd have to do is cut that pair of jeans in your bag into a pair of Daisy Dukes, take off your bra and just wear the tank top, and you could—"

She puts her finger on my lips. "No way," she says. "Don't even think about it."

We sit quietly for a moment, looking out at the nothingness that surrounds us. It feels like it's getting hotter, but I think it's more due to sitting directly in the sun on the hood of a black car that's soaking up the heat like a sponge. Every now and then a nice breeze brushes our faces.

"Andrew?" She takes her hat off and places it on my head, then lies down with her back against the windshield. She fixes her hands behind her head and draws her knees up. "Number five on our list of promises: if I die before you, make sure I'm buried in that dress we bought at the flea market and without shoes. Oh, and none of that eighties blue eye shadow stuff or drawn-on eyebrows." Her head falls to the side and she looks at me.

"But I thought that was the dress you wanted to marry me in."

She squints, turning her eyes away from the sun. "Yeah, it is, but I want to be buried in it, too. Some believe that when you die, your afterlife is reliving the happiest moments of your life. One of mine will be the day I marry you. Might as well take the dress with me."

I smile down at her.

I take the hat off and lie next to her, pressing my head close enough to hers that I can prop the hat over both of our heads to help keep the sun off. After I get it balanced I say, "Number six: if I die before you, make sure they play 'Dust in the Wind' at my funeral."

She glances over carefully so the hat doesn't fall away. "Are we back to that again? You're starting to make me hate a perfectly good classic, Andrew."

I laugh lightly. "I know, but I saw an episode of *Highlander* when his wife Tessa died. They played that song in the background. I've never been able to get it out of my head since."

She smiles and reaches up to wipe sweat from her brow.

"I promise," she says. "But since we're on the topic, I'd like to add number seven. Have you ever seen *Ghost*?"

I glance over briefly. "Well, yeah. I guess everybody's seen that movie. Unless you're sixteen. Shit, I'm surprised *you've* seen it." I nudge her with my elbow.

She laughs. "That was my mom's doing," she admits. "*Ghost* and *Dirty Dancing* I've seen about a hundred times. She had a thing for Patrick Swayze, and I was the only girl around growing up she could talk to about how handsome he was. Anyway, so you've seen it. Number seven: if anyone ever kills you, you better come back like Sam and help me find your killer."

I laugh and shake my head, accidently knocking the hat off momentarily. "What is it with you and movies? Never mind. Yeah, I promise I'll come back and haunt your ass."

"You better!" She laughs out loud. "Besides, I know I'll be like those people who think their loved ones are still around after they've died. Might as well give me more reason to believe it."

Not sure how I'll pull that off, but whatever. Hell, I'll try.

"I'll promise, if *you* will," I say.

"As always," she says.

"Number eight," I go on, "don't bury me where it's cold."

"Fully agreed. Me either!"

She wipes more sweat from her face and I lift away from the hood, reaching out my hand to her. "Let's sit inside, out of the sun."

She takes my hand and I help her down.

Two hours later, the tow truck still hasn't showed up and it's starting to get dark. Looks like we'll get to watch the sunset together over the barren Texas landscape.

"I knew it," Camryn says. "What the hell is it with the tow trucks?"

And just when she says that, a set of blinding headlights comes down the highway toward us. Overly relieved, we get out to meet him and the first thing I notice is the same thing Camryn notices. The guy could be Billy Frank's doppelgänger. She and I glance at each other, but we don't comment out loud.

"You need a tow or a tire?" he asks, thumbing the straps of his denim overalls.

"Just the tire," I say as I follow him around to the back of his truck.

"Well, I don' have much time to stay here while ya change it," he says and then spits chewing tobacco on the road. "You two'll be all right?"

"Yeah, we'll be fine," I say. "But wait one second." I hold up my finger and lean into the car to turn the key. When the engine starts without a problem, I shut it off and walk back over to him. "Just wanted to make sure it started."

I pay the doppelgänger and watch his truck's brake lights fade into the darkening horizon as he drives away. When I walk back to the car where I left the tire, I'm shocked as hell to see Camryn already lifting the car up with the jack.

"Hell yeah, that's my girl!"

She smiles up at me, but keeps on working at it, that blonde braid draped over one shoulder.

"It's not so difficult," she says, now rolling the new tire over after managing to get the lug nuts off the old one by herself. I think I'm getting a hard-on. No, wait, I've definitely got a hard-on.

"No, it really isn't," I finally reply, my smile getting bigger.

Several minutes later, she's letting the car back down and tossing the jack into the trunk. I lift the old tire for her and throw it back there, too.

We get inside and just sit here.

It's so quiet. Enormous streaks of pinkish-purple and blue cirrus clouds are cluttered together in the sky, stretching far over the horizon. As the heat of the day wears off, the mild breeze of approaching nightfall funnels through the opened car windows. The sunset is beautiful. Honestly, I've never paid much attention to one before. Maybe it's the company.

And I'm not sure what's happening right now between us, but whatever it is, we're so synced with each other that we both share it. I look at her. She looks at me.

"Are you ready to go back?" I ask.

"Yeah." She pauses, looking toward the windshield, lost in thought. Then she turns back to me, more sure now than she was just seconds ago. "Yeah, I think I'm ready to go home." She smiles.

And for the first time since I left Galveston on my own that day, or when Camryn boarded that bus in Raleigh that night, we finally feel...fulfilled.

Camryn

THIRTY-TWO

I guess we really did come full circle. But I have to say, now that we're finally back in Galveston after seven months, it feels different this time. I'm not worried about being here, or afraid that mine and Andrew's time together is going to end. I'm not waiting for a medical tragedy to rear its ugly head at any given moment. It feels *good* to be here. And as we pull into the parking area of his apartment complex, I feel a sense of satisfaction. I can even picture myself living here. But then again, I can also picture myself living in Raleigh, too. I guess what this means is that maybe we *are* ready to settle down. Just for a little while. Never forever, like I told Andrew before, but long enough that we can recuperate from being on the road.

Andrew agrees. "Yeah," he says grabbing our bags from the backseat. "Y'know what?" He drops the bags back in the same place and looks over the top of the roof at me.

"What?" I ask curiously.

His eyes are smiling. "You're right about not wanting to be on the road so long that we get tired of it, or staying fixed in one place for too long for the same reason." He pauses and stretches his arms over the roof of the car. "Maybe if we only travel in the spring or summer, leave the fall and winter for living at home and doing the family thing during the holidays—my mom was pretty upset that we didn't spend Christmas or Thanksgiving with her."

I nod. "That's a good idea. And since it sucks traveling when it's cold, that makes total sense."

We just stare at each other over the roof of the car for a long moment until I interrupt all of the gear-churning inside our heads and say, "Well, get the bags. We can talk about it inside. You need to check on Georgia."

"Ah, Georgia's fine," he says, leaning over inside the backseat again. "My mom's been watering her."

I grab the guitars and my purse. When we enter Andrew's apartment, it smells exactly like it did the first time I ever came here: vacant. And just like Andrew said, Georgia is alive and well.

I practically fall onto the couch, exhausted, hanging my legs over the arm at the knees.

"But the next place we go," Andrew says as he passes the back of the couch, "will be far away from here." I hear his keys hit the top of the counter in the kitchen.

I rise up and call out, "*How* far?"

"Europe, South America," he says with a big grin as he reenters the living room. "You said you'd like to see Italy and Brazil and all of those places. I say we pick one and go there next."

A shot of energy zips through my body. I stand up and look at him, so excited right now about the prospect that I can hardly contain it. "Seriously?"

He nods with a giant, close-lipped smile. "Hell, staying true to tradition, we could even write down all of the places we want to see on little strips of paper, drop them in a hat and pick one at random."

I squeal. I actually *squeal*! My hands come up vertically against my chest. "That's perfect, Andrew!"

He sits down on the couch now, propping both feet up on the coffee table, his knees bent. I can't sit down. I stay right where I'm at and just stare down at his smiling face.

"Of course, we've got to keep the money flowing," he says. "We've still got plenty in the bank, but traveling out of the country will definitely drain it quicker."

"I can't wait to get a job," I say, and that comment stimulates my memory. "Andrew, you told me before to be completely honest with you about where I'd rather live."

That gets his attention. "Where do you want to live?"

I contemplate it for a moment and answer, "For now, I think Raleigh, but only because I'd like to be where Natalie and my mom are, and because I know I can easily get a job where Natalie works. Her boss really seemed to like me and told me to fill out an application and—"

Andrew stops me. "You don't have to explain your reasons." He reaches out for me and I sit on his lap, facing him. I didn't realize I was babbling nervously. I just don't want him to feel obligated.

He smiles at me and locks his fingers together behind my waist. "My question," he says, "is what exactly do you mean by 'for now'?"

"Well . . . that's the hard part," I say.

He tilts his head slightly to one side, looking at me curiously, his dimples barely visible in his cheeks.

Eventually, I just come out with it. "I don't think we should spend all of the money on a house because I don't want to stay there forever. And besides, if we do that, we won't have as much money to fall back on when we want to go to Europe or wherever, and working minimum-wage jobs won't help us save much."

He gives me a sidelong glance. "Wait. I hope you don't want us to live in your mom's house. We need our privacy. I want to be able to bend your sweet little ass over the coffee table whenever I want."

I laugh and squeeze my thighs around his playfully. "You are so bad!" I say. "But no, I definitely don't want to live with my mom."

"Well, if you don't want to buy a house and you don't want to live with your mom, the only thing left is renting, and that drains a lot of money, too."

I feel embarrassed, because it's to the point where I have to talk about Andrew's money as though it's mine also, which I doubt I'll ever get used to.

I look away from his eyes. "Remember when you said we could get a *little* house somewhere?"

"Yeah," he says, and his eyes are getting brighter, as though he knows what I'm going to say already.

"Well, we could maybe pay cash for a very small house or a condo, just big enough for us...I don't know, something cheap but decent, and still have a lot left over to keep in the bank for our trips. We won't have rent, and all we'll have to pay every month are utilities and things like that, which we can do from working and from playing gigs but never take from our savings."

Why is he smiling like the Cheshire cat?!

I feel my head fall in between my shoulders, my face getting hot. "What's so funny?!" I ask, pressing my palms against his chest and trying not to laugh.

"Nothing's funny. I just like it that you've finally realized that what's mine is yours." He tightens his fingers around my waist.

"Whatever," I say, trying to conceal the blush in my cheeks, pretending to be offended.

"Hey," he says, shaking my hips, "don't do that—just finish what you were saying."

After a long pause, I say, "And when we leave to go wherever that piece of paper in the hat tells us to, we can get Natalie to house-sit. Or!" I point upward. "When we finally find that peaceful place on the beach that you dreamed about and want to live there, we can either sell our house in Raleigh or rent it out to draw in extra income. Maybe even rent it to Natalie and Blake!"

I can tell there's something going on inside his mind. His smile is still soft and he never takes his eyes off me. But he's so quiet until finally he breaks the silence and says, "It sounds like you've put a lot of thought into this. How long did it take you to figure all of that out?"

Only right now do I realize that it's been long enough. I think back to the day when I started trying to piece together our future, when I officially had it in my head that I did want to settle down and that I was tired of being on the road.

Andrew waits patiently for me to answer, always with soft and thoughtful eyes, his way of constantly reminding me that nothing I can say to him is going to create any negativity between us.

"It was on the highway after we left Mobile," I say. "When I first told you that I wanted to see Italy and France and Brazil one day. When I said I never wanted to settle down forever. From that night on, I was determined to figure it out. How we would pull everything off." My gaze strays. "I broke the rules and planned it all out."

He leans forward and kisses my lips.

"Sometimes planning is necessary," he says. "You did a good job. I think the whole plan is perfect." And then he crushes me against him, kissing me passionately.

When the kiss breaks, I gaze at him for a moment, his face in my hands. "But I want to marry you here," I say, and his eyes brighten. "I don't want your mom to feel left out, y'know? She's really the only reason I feel bad about wanting to move to Raleigh. And I feel even worse that she was planning that baby shower and we never got—"

"She'll like that," he says, stopping me before I start babbling again. "I definitely do."

He kisses me again.

Andrew

THIRTY-THREE

I couldn't have asked for a more perfect day. The weather is perfect. The plans to get married that we *didn't* make all fell perfectly into place. I called my mom up yesterday and told her to meet us on the beach on Galveston Island. She made it on time, without having any idea why we asked her to be here.

I raise my hand above me when I see her, waving her toward us, and the second she sees us, she knows. Her face breaks out into the biggest smile, and it's easily contagious.

"Oh, you two," my mom says, stepping up to us, "I can't believe you're finally doing this. I'm just... I'm so..." Tears roll down her face and she reaches up to wipe them away, laughing and crying at the same time.

Camryn, barefoot and dressed in that ivory vintage gown she found at the flea market, wraps her arms around my mom and hugs her.

"Oh, Marna, please don't cry," she says, though I think it's more of a plea because seeing my mom cry is choking Camryn up.

"Is anyone else coming?" my mom asks when she pulls away.

"You're our exclusive guest of honor," I say proudly.

"Yeah," Camryn adds, "it's just you and the reverend here."

My mom moves around us to give Reverend Reed a hug, too.

She has been attending his church for nine years—tried to get me to go a hundred times, but I'm just not the church type. But I thought who better to ask to marry us?

And while Reverend Reed is standing in front of us on the beach, holding his worn Bible in his hands and saying a few words, all I can see or hear is Camryn standing in front of me with her hands in mine. The breeze combs through her loose strands of hair, free from that golden braid over her shoulder that I love so much. I love her smile, her blue eyes, and her soft skin. I want to kiss her now and get it over with. I press my fingers gently against the tops of her hands and pull her a little closer. The wind whips through the long fabric of her dress, pushing it against her hourglass form. I hold in my smile when I notice a piece of hair fly into her mouth. She tries to covertly work it out with her tongue without drawing attention to herself.

Knowing she doesn't want to create any kind of interruption, even for something as simple as this, I reach up and move the hair away for her.

I feel like we're the only two people in the world.

When it's time to say our vows, I know that neither one of us wrote anything down or had much time to think about what we wanted to say. And so pretty much the same way we tend to do everything, we just do it.

I grip her hands tighter between us and say, "Camryn, you are the other half of my soul, and I will love you today and every day for the rest of our lives. I promise that if you ever forget me, I'll read to you like Noah read to Allie. I promise that when we get old and our bones hurt, that we'll never sleep in separate rooms, and that if you die before me, I'll make sure you're buried in that dress. I promise to haunt you like Sam haunted Molly." Her eyes are beginning to water. I caress the insides of her palms with my thumbs. "I promise that we'll never wake up one day years from now wondering why we wasted our lives away by doing nothing, and that no matter what hardships befall us, I'll always, *always*, be right here with you. I promise to be spontaneous, to always turn down the music when you're asleep, and to sing about raisins when you're sad. I promise to always love you no matter where we are in the world, or in our lives. Because you're the other half of me that I know I can never live without."

Tears pour from her eyes. It takes her a second to gather her composure.

And then she says, "Andrew, I promise never to leave you on life support and let you suffer when I know in my heart that your life is spent. I promise that if you're ever lost or missing that I will…never stop looking for you. *Ever.*" This just makes me smile. "I promise that when you die, I'll make sure that 'Dust in the Wind' is played at your funeral and to never bury you where it's cold. I promise to always tell you everything no matter how ashamed or guilty I feel, and to trust you when you ask me to do something because I know that everything you do has a purpose. I promise to be by your side always and to never let you face anything alone. I promise to love you forever in this life and wherever we go in the afterlife, because I know I can't go on in *any* life unless you're in it too."

Pastor Reed says to me, "Do you, Andrew Parrish, take Camryn Bennett to be your wedded wife, to have and to hold, for better or worse, for richer or poorer, to love and to cherish, from this day forward?"

"I do," I say and place the wedding ring I bought in Chicago on her finger. She gasps quietly.

Then he turns to Camryn and says, "Do you, Camryn Bennett,

take Andrew Parrish to be your wedded husband, to have and to hold, for better or worse, for richer or poorer, to love and to cherish, from this day forward?"

"I do."

Finally, I hand her my ring, because I've been hiding them both from her until this very moment, and she slides it on my finger. Pastor Reed finishes up, including those anticipated seven words—"I now pronounce you husband and wife"—and then he gives me permission to kiss my bride. It's all we've wanted to do since the ceremony started, and now that we can, we find ourselves just staring at one another, lost in each other's eyes, seeing each other in a different light, one so much brighter than we've seen it since the day we met in Kansas on that bus. I feel my eyes beginning to sting, and I scoop her up into my arms and crush my mouth over hers. She sobs into our kiss and I squeeze her around her back, lifting her bare feet completely from the sand and I spin her around. My mom is bawling like a baby. I feel like I might never stop smiling.

Camryn is my wife.

Camryn

I just became Camryn Parrish. I can't wrap my head around the emotions that I feel. I'm crying, but kind of laughing inside at the same time. I feel excited, yet I feel anxious. I look down again at this ring he just slid on my finger, and I know he spent a lot of money on it. Then I glance at his ring, almost identical to mine though it's a masculine version, and I just can't be mad at him for them. I just can't. I hear Marna sobbing behind me, and I can't help but walk over and hug her again.

"Welcome to the family," she says, her voice shuddering.

"Thank you." I smile and wipe my tears away.

Andrew slips his arm around my waist, and the pastor joins us. Once he and Marna start talking and catching up, Andrew and I slip a few feet away from them, and he can't stop looking at me. It makes me blush.

"What is it?" I ask.

He shakes his head, his smile glowing. "I love you," he says, and it just makes me want to cry again, but I manage to keep it together.

"I love you, too."

We spend our honeymoon at our apartment, very untraditionally. Because we want to wait until our first out-of-the-country trip to do a real honeymoon.

"Where do you think it'll be?" he asks.

We're sitting outside in two lawn chairs, having a beer and listening to the live music playing on the beach or in the park, in the distance somewhere.

"I don't know," I say and take a drink from the bottle. "Want to make a bet on it?"

Andrew rubs his bottom lip with the pad of his thumb. "Hmmm." He contemplates it, takes another swig of his beer, and then says, "I think the first one we pull out of that hat will be..." he purses his lips "...Brazil."

"Brazil, huh? Nice one. But I don't know—I have this weird feeling it'll be something more like Italy."

"Really?"

"Yep."

We both take a swig at the same time.

"Maybe we should make some kind of bet," he says, the dimple on the right side of his cheek deepening.

"A bet, huh? Sure, I'm in."

"All right, if it's Brazil, then you have to go with me to the beach, true Rio de Janeiro style." His grin is wicked.

It takes me a minute to realize what he's talking about, and when it dawns on me, I feel the night air hit my teeth as my mouth falls open. "No. Way!"

Andrew laughs.

"I'm not prancing around on a public beach topless!"

He throws his head back and laughs louder. "No, I don't think they really do that over there, babe," he says. "But I mean you have to wear one of those Brazilian bikinis. None of that I'm-self-conscious shit and cover up like you did in Florida. You've got a bangin' body." He takes another swig and sets the bottle down on the table in front of us.

I ponder it for a moment, chewing on the inside of my mouth. "Deal," I say.

Looking a little surprised that I agreed to it so easily, he nods.

"And if it's Italy," I say with a smirk of my own, "you have to serenade me on the Spanish Steps . . . in the native language." I cross one leg over the other. I knew that last part would trip his sexy ass up.

"You can't be serious," he argues. "How the hell am I gonna pull that off?"

"I dunno," I say. "I guess if I win, you'll have to figure it out."

He shakes his head and presses one side of his mouth into a hard line. "Fine. It's a deal."

THIRTY-FOUR

Raleigh, North Carolina—June

Surprise!" several voices shout when I walk into my and Andrew's new house.

Actually surprised, I gasp and my hand flies to my chest. Natalie is front and center, with Blake beside her. My friends from my favorite Starbucks and Blake's sister, Sarah, who I met two weeks ago when Andrew and I arrived back in town, are all here.

"Wow, what's the occasion?" I ask, still trying to catch my breath a little because they scared the crap out of me. I turn my head to look at Andrew. He's grinning, so it's obvious he had something to do with it.

Natalie, now with auburn highlights in her hair, pulls me into a hug. "It's your *official* welcome-home party." She smirks at me and glances at Andrew. "Why do you think I've been acting so who-the-hell-cares-she's-back the past few days?"

"You haven't been acting like that," I say.

"OK, maybe not that noticeably," she says, "but come on, Cam, couldn't you tell I was holding something in?"

I guess she does have a point, now that I think about it. She has seemed happy that I'm home, but she hasn't been overjoyed like she would normally be. I guess I've been assuming that maybe Blake had finally tamed her some.

I turn to Andrew again. "But we don't even have any furniture."

"Oh yes you do!" Natalie says, grabbing my wrist.

She drags me into the living room, where eight beanbag chairs are placed randomly on the floor. In the center of the room are four red milk crates pressed together with a flat piece of lumber on top, which I'm assuming is the coffee table. The electricity isn't even on yet, but the "coffee table" holds three unlit candles sitting inside the lids from cookie tins, ready and waiting for when night falls several hours from now.

I just laugh. "I love this!" I say to Andrew. "I say we forget about the furniture altogether and stick with the retro beanbag theme!" I'm totally kidding, and Andrew knows it.

He plops down on the nearest beanbag and splays his legs out onto the floor, leaning back into the cushioning vinyl. "I can manage with these, but we'll definitely need our bed." I sit down in the one next to him and get comfortable. Everybody else follows suit as Natalie and Blake head into the kitchen area.

Andrew and I found this small house five days after we got here. Wanting out of my mom's house as soon as humanly possible, he spent hours on the Internet and looked at real estate magazines even while I was slacking off and just relaxing after the long drive from Galveston. I pretty much just let Andrew take the house-hunting thing and run with it. He'd show me pictures, and I'd give my opinion. But this house was perfect. It was the third one we looked at physically (and I really don't think his love for it had anything to do with accidently seeing my mom half-naked when she thought we'd left for the day). It was priced great because the sellers, who already moved out four months ago, wanted to sell it and get it over with. We ended up buying it for twenty thousand less than what it's worth, and we agreed that the sellers didn't need to make any repairs before closing. Since we were cash buyers, everything happened really fast.

Today is officially our first day as its new owners.

We brought a lot of things with us from Galveston, rented a small U-Haul trailer to tow behind us, which we stuffed full of whatever we could fit. But we'll have to go back soon for the furniture. Unfortunately, Andrew is still adamant about keeping his dad's old, smelly chair, but he promised to get it cleaned. And he'd better!

Natalie and Blake walk back into the room, each holding three beer bottles, which they start to pass out.

"Thanks, but none for me," I say.

Natalie looks heartbroken, sticking out her bottom lip as she stares down at me. She's wearing a tight white shirt that makes her boobs stand out.

"I'm played out on beer for at least a week, Nat," I say.

She wrinkles her nose but then shrugs and says, "More for me!"

After Blake hands Andrew his beer, he goes to sit down on the only beanbag left, but Natalie races and beats him to it. So, he sits on top of her. While they're playing around, Natalie lets out this weird peal of laughter, and I glance over to see the look on Andrew's face.

"*Shenzi,*" he whispers and shakes his head with the beer bottle at his lips.

I laugh under my breath, knowing now what Andrew meant the first time he called her that. I googled the name shortly after and found out it refers to the mouthy hyena in *The Lion King*.

"Now, you promised to tell me about your road trip," Natalie says, now sitting between Blake's legs on the beanbag.

Everybody looks over at me and Andrew.

"I've told you stuff already, Nat."

"Yeah, but you haven't told *us* anything," says Lea, my friend who works at Starbucks.

Alicia, who works with her, adds, "I went on a road trip with my mom and my brother once, but I'm sure it wasn't anything like yours."

"And you still haven't filled me in on what happened in Florida," Natalie says. She takes a drink of her beer and then sets it down beside her on the floor, afterward resting her arms over Blake's legs. Blake kisses the side of her neck.

I cringe inside, just thinking about Florida, but I realize it's because Andrew would really be the one of us who might be embarrassed about what happened. For a second, I can't even make eye contact with him because I feel guilty for bringing it up to Natalie at all. I didn't give her any details, just mentioned that something really messed up happened while we were there.

When I do meet Andrew's eyes, I can tell he's not mad at me. He winks and sets his beer on the floor beside him, too.

"Florida," he says, to my surprise. "That was probably the worst part of our trip, if not also the strangest—and yet, somehow parts of it I didn't mind so much."

I have no idea where he's going with this.

Everyone is looking right at Andrew now, especially Natalie, whose eyes are bugged out with anticipation.

"We met this group of people who offered us to drive out and party with them on a hard-to-find area of the beach. So we did. And we had a good time. But then shit got weird."

"Weird how?" Natalie interrupts.

"Like LSD or who-the-hell-knows weird," he says.

Natalie's eyes get bigger and grow fierce as she looks back at me. "You did LSD? What the fuck is wrong with you, Cam?"

I shake my head. "No, no way did I do it willingly. They *drugged* us!"

Everyone's eyes match Natalie's now.

"Yeah," Andrew goes on. "We're not even sure what they gave us, but we were both trippin' out of our minds."

"I was roofied once," Blake's sister, Sarah, says.

She looks about eighteen.

Blake's body jerks forward to sit straight up, causing Natalie to hit her front teeth on her beer bottle. "*What?*" he asks with fire shooting from his eyes.

"Oh, you didn't know about that?" Sarah says sweetly, acting like she had simply forgotten to tell him at some point.

Obviously, it was better that he hadn't known.

"*Owww!*" Natalie whines, holding her mouth.

"I'm sorry," Blake says. He kisses her cheek and turns back to his sister. "Who the fuck roofied you, Sarah? Don't shit me, either. You better tell me...Did anything happen?" There's dread in his face.

Sarah rolls her eyes. "No. Nothing happened because Kayla was there and she drove me home. And no, I don't know who did it, Blake, so please just chill out." Then she turns back us. "You were saying?"

"I'll go with you, man," Andrew says to Blake. "You ever find out who did it, just let me know. That's bullshit."

I elbow Andrew softly. He takes the hint and says, "Anyway, Florida was an experience, I have to say, but I never wanna do it again."

Andrew doesn't tell them anything about that skanky bitch

who tried giving him a blow job. I'm glad he doesn't, because that would be an awkward conversation. Not to mention, Natalie would have a field day with information like that. We hang out in the beanbag chairs and talk to our friends for a few hours until around eight o'clock, when Blake has to drive Sarah home. Shortly after the three of them leave, everybody else follows, and Andrew and I are alone in our first official home together as newlyweds.

He comes back in from the kitchen with a candle in his hand after lighting it on the stove. The gas was turned on early. Then he uses that flame to light the others on the table.

"Are we going to sleep on the floor?" I ask, watching him.

"Nope," he says as he moves away from the candles. He drags all the beanbags into the center of the room and fits them closely together, creating a makeshift bed, then pats one of them with the palm of his hand. "This'll have to do for now. I'm not sleeping on the floor. Talk about waking up with a stiff back."

I smile. "This is strange, isn't it?" I say, looking around at the bare walls of our house, envisioning what kind of pictures or paintings might look good on them.

"What, having no furniture or electricity? You should be used to that by now." He chuckles.

I get up from my beanbag by the wall and sit down on the bed he made. I reach out toward the table and poke my finger around in the hot wax of a candle, letting it sting and then cool and conform to the tip of my finger.

"No, I mean this house. Us. Everything, really."

"Strange in a good way, I hope."

"Of course," I say, smiling up at him.

Silence fills the house. The light from the candles cast large dancing shadows on the walls. It smells like bleach and Pine-Sol and other various cleaners, although it's faint.

"Andrew," I say, "thank you for moving here."

Finally, he sits down beside me and we both stare into the flames for a moment.

"Where else would I be other than wherever you are?" he says.

"You know what I mean," I say. I reach out and move the palm of my hand over the top of one flame, just to feel the heat on my skin and to see how close I can get before it's too much.

"I know," he says, "but just the same."

I pull my hand away and look at him; his face looks soft in the orangish glow of the candlelight, even with the stubble he's started letting grow again.

"Camryn, I need to tell you something," he says.

Instantly, my heart locks up in my chest at the way he said it.

"What . . . I mean, what do you mean you have to tell me something?" I'm so nervous. I don't know why.

Andrew draws his knees upward and props his forearms on top of them. He looks back at the flame once, only for a few seconds, but even a few seconds is too long.

"Andrew?" I turn around fully to face him.

I notice his throat moves as he swallows. He looks me in the eyes.

"I've been having headaches," he begins, and my heart falls into my stomach. I think I'm going to throw up. "Just since Monday, but I set up an appointment with a doctor here. Your mom recommended him."

I hate her right now for keeping this from me. My hands are shaking.

"I asked your mom not to say anything because I wanted this house stuff to go smoothly—"

"You should've told me."

He tries to reach out for my hand but I inadvertently push it away and rise to my feet. "Why'd you *keep* this from me?!" I feel dizzy.

Andrew stands up, too, but he keeps his distance. "I told you," he says. "I didn't want—"

"I don't care! You should've *told* me!"

I fold my arms over my stomach and arch over forward a little. I'm surprised I haven't already puked. My nerves are so frayed it feels like they're really coming apart inside me. "This can't be happening…" Finally, I bury my face in my hands and rupture into sobs. "Why the fuck is this *happening*?!"

Andrew is next to me in seconds. I feel his arms wrap around me. He pulls my trembling body into his chest and holds me. Tight.

"It doesn't mean anything," he says. "I honestly don't feel like I did before, Camryn. I'm having headaches, yes, but they feel different."

When I tame my sobs enough that I feel like I can speak without choking, I raise my head to see him.

He encloses my face in his hands and smiles faintly at me. "I knew you would react this way, baby," he says in a quiet voice. "I don't want you to stress out for the next four days until my appointment on Monday." He holds my gaze still. "It *doesn't feel the same*. Just focus on that, because I'm telling you the truth."

"*Are* you?" I ask. "Or, are you saying that to keep me from worrying?" I already have it set in my mind that the latter is exactly what he's doing. I pull away from him and start pacing the floor, my arms crossed, one hand resting on my lips. I can't stop shaking.

"I'm not lying to you," he says. "I'm going to be fine. I feel like I'm going to be fine, and you have to believe that."

I whirl around to face him again. "I can't do this anymore, Andrew. I won't."

He tilts his head slightly to one side; his gaze is thoughtful, curious, concerned.

I know he wants me to elaborate on what I said, but I can't. I can't because the things I want to say would only upset and hurt him. And they would just be words. Words born from pain and anger and a part of me that wants to look God, or whoever, or whatever, in the face and tell It to go to Hell.

I need to calm myself. I need to take a step back and breathe.

I do just that.

"Camryn?"

"You're going to be fine," I say to him matter-of-factly. "I know you're going to be fine."

He steps back up to me, kisses me on the forehead, and says, "I will be."

Andrew

THIRTY-FIVE

The past four days have been stressful. Although Camryn said she'd remain positive and not let it get to her, she hasn't been herself. Her nerves are shot all to hell. Twice I've heard her crying in the bathroom and throwing up. Ever since I told her about the headaches last Tuesday night, she's been acting a lot like she was before we left to visit Aidan and Michelle in Chicago: faking her smiles and pretending to laugh when something is supposed to be funny. She's just not herself. Worried about her and remembering what happened after her miscarriage with the painkillers, I flat out asked her if she's found that "moment of weakness" at all again.

She says she hasn't and I believe her.

But nothing is going to fix her this time except us leaving this hospital today and me having a clean bill of health.

If I don't ... well, I don't want to think about that.

I'm more worried about her than I am about myself.

Camryn was asked to wait in another room while the scan is being done. I can tell she wanted to argue with the nurse, but she did as she was asked. And just like the last time, I feel like I've been in here for hours, feeling slightly claustrophobic in the tunnel of this huge, noisy machine. *Be very still,* the technician had asked me. *Try not to move or we'll have to do it over.* Needless to say, I practically didn't breathe for fifteen minutes.

When the scan was over, I pulled the earplugs from my ears and tossed them in the nearby trash.

Camryn just about lost it when the nurse who came to discharge me said that it would be Wednesday before we'd know anything.

"You've got to be kidding me!" Camryn's eyes were feral. She looked between me and the nurse, back and forth, hoping that one of us could *do something.*

I looked at the nurse. "Is there any way we can find out the results today?"

Knowing just by looking at Camryn's expression that she wasn't going to budge, the nurse sighed and said, "Go sit out in the waiting room and I'll see if I can get Dr. Adams to come look now."

Four hours later, we were sitting in Dr. Adams's office.

"I don't see any abnormalities," he said, and I felt Camryn's hand release its death grip on mine. "But given your history, I think it will be in your best interest to see me once a month for the next several months and for you to make note of any changes you feel need noting."

"But you said you didn't see anything," Camryn said, squeezing my hand again.

"No, but I still think it would be in Andrew's best interest. Just to be on the safe side. That way, if anything does start to show up, we'll catch it very early on."

"You're saying you think something's going to show up?"

I wanted to laugh at the look of mild frustration on that doctor's face, but instead I looked at Camryn to my left and said, "No, that's not what he's saying. Just calm down. Everything's fine. See, I told you everything would be fine."

And all I could do from that day onward was hope I was telling her the truth.

Camryn

THIRTY-SIX

Many months later...

*A*ndrew wrote me another letter sometime during our first month in our new house. I think I've read it a hundred times. Usually, I cry, but I find myself smiling a lot, too. He told me that he wanted me to read it once a week to mark another week gone by and nothing happened, that everything was still fine. And I did. I usually read it on Sunday night after he had already fallen asleep next to me in our bed. But sometimes, when I'd fall asleep before him, I'd reach over the next morning and take the letter out of the book beside the bed and read it before he woke up. And just like every other time before it, I would look over at him sleeping when I was done and hope for another week.

Andrew has always amazed me. He amazed me with the way his mind worked. The way he could look at me without saying anything and make me feel like the most important person in the world. He amazed me with how he could always be so positive even when life was falling apart around him. And how he could make a light shine in the darkest recesses of my mind when I thought that I'd never see another light there again.

Sure, he had his bad days, his "moments of weakness," but by far I've never known anyone else like him. And I know I never will.

Maybe I really am a weak person at heart. Maybe if it wasn't for Andrew, I wouldn't be the person I am today. Sometimes I wonder what would've become of me if I never met him, if he wasn't there to save me from that dangerous, reckless bus ride I decided to take on my own. I wonder what would've happened to me if he didn't care about me enough to help me through *my* moment of weakness. I hate to think of myself this way, but sometimes you just have to face the reality of what is, of how things are and how they might've been based on your actions. I know in my heart that if it wasn't for Andrew, I might not be here today at all.

These last several months have been very hard for us, but at the same time, they've been full of life and excitement and love and hope.

Life is a mysterious, often unfair, thing. But I think I've learned in my time with Andrew that it can also be a wonderful thing, and that usually when something happens that seems unfair, it's just Life's way of making room for better things to come. I like to think that. It gives me strength when I need it most.

And right now I need it.

I try to look up at the clock high on the sterile-white wall of the room, but I can barely make out the little black hands through the blur in my eyes. I want to know how long I've been here. I'm exhausted and weak, mentally and physically and can't take it anymore. I swallow down a lump in my throat and my mouth feels as dry as sandpaper. I reach up to wipe a tear from my eye. But only one. I haven't really cried much at all. Because the pain had been so unbearable before that it practically dried up all of my tears.

I can't do this. I feel like at any moment I want to just give up. I want to tell everyone in the room to go away, to just leave me alone, and stop looking at me as if my soul needs mending. It does! It fucking does! But no one here can do it.

Mostly I'm just numb. I can't feel anything anymore. But the hospital walls are starting to close in around me, making me somewhat claustrophobic. But as far as pain and heartache, I can't feel *anything*. I wonder if I'll be numb forever.

"You have to try to push," Andrew says next to me, holding onto my hand.

I whip my head to the side to see him and argue, "But I can't feel my waist! How can I push if I can't *feel* myself *pushing*!" The only pushing I think I've managed to do were those words through my gritted teeth.

He smiles down at me and kisses my sweating forehead.

"You can do it," Dr. Ball says from in between my legs.

I close my eyes tight, grip Andrew's hand, and push. I think. I open my eyes and allow myself to breathe.

"Did I push? Is it working?"

God, I hope I don't fart! Oh my God, that would be so fucking embarrassing!

"You're doing great, baby."

Andrew looks at the doctor now, waiting.

"A few more times and that should do it," the doctor says.

Not liking her words, I let out a frustrated breath through my lips and throw my head back against the pillow harshly.

"Try again, baby," Andrew says softly, never losing his cool, even though every time I notice him look at the doctor I sense a hidden level of worry in his face.

I raise my back from the pillow again and try to push, but like usual I can't really tell if I'm actually pushing or I just think I am.

Andrew adjusts one arm behind my back to help me to stay upright, and I bear down and push again, shutting my eyes so tight that I feel like they're being shoved into the back of my skull. My teeth are gritted and bared. Sweat beads off my forehead.

I yell out something inaudible as I stop pushing and am able to breathe again.

And I feel something. Whoa...it's not pain—the epidural cured me of that—but the pressure of the baby I *definitely* feel. If I didn't know better, I'd think someone just stuck something unnaturally large into my vagina. My eyes get bigger and bigger.

"The baby's head is out," I hear the doctor say and then I hear a gross sucking sound as she cleans the baby's throat out with a suction bulb.

Andrew wants to look; I see his neck stretch out like a turtle, trying to get a better view, but he doesn't want to leave my side.

"Just a couple more, Camryn," the doctor says.

I push again, putting even more effort into it now that I know it's actually working.

She pulls the baby's shoulders out.

I push one more time and our baby is born.

"You did great," the doctor says while clearing the baby's throat some more.

Andrew kisses my cheek and my forehead, and he wipes my sweat-soaked hair away from my face and the sides of my neck. A few seconds later, the baby's cries fill the room with smiles and excitement. I burst into tears, sobbing so hard that my entire body trembles uncontrollably with emotion.

And then the doctor announces, "It's a girl."

Andrew and I can hardly take our eyes off of her until he's asked to cut the cord. He leaves my side, but smiles proudly as he makes his way over and does the honors. He can't seem to decide who he wants to look at more, me or our daughter. I smile and lay my head back down against the pillow, utterly exhausted. I can finally make out the clock on the wall. It tells me I've been in labor for more than sixteen hours.

I feel more pressure and prodding and tugging between my legs as the doctor does stuff that, quite frankly, I don't want to know about. I just stare up at the ceiling for a moment, lost in my glimpses of the past nine months, until I hear our baby shrieking on the other side of the room and I raise my head again so fast I almost get whiplash.

Andrew stands by as one of the nurses cleans her up and starts to wrap her in blankets. He looks over at me and says, "She definitely has your lungs, babe," and plugs his ears with his fingers. I smile and watch the two of them, trying not to think about that tugging still going on downstairs. And then Andrew comes back around to the side of my bed.

He kisses me on the lips and whispers, "Sweaty. Look like you just ran a marathon. No makeup. Hospital gown. And you still manage to look beautiful."

And despite all of that, just the same, *he* still manages to make me blush.

I reach up, an IV running along my hand, and I cup his face, pulling him back down toward me. "We did it," I whisper onto his lips.

He kisses me softy again, and then the nurse steps up next to us with our daughter in her arms.

"Who would like to hold her first?" she asks.

Andrew and I look at each other, but he goes to move to the side so that the nurse can give her to me.

"No," I say. "You go first."

Only slightly conflicted about it, Andrew finally gives in and reaches out to take her. The nurse places her carefully into his arms and steps away once she sees that he's got a good hold on her. At first, he appears awkward and boyish, afraid he's going to drop her or that he's not holding her right, but he quickly becomes more relaxed.

"Blonde hair," he says next to me, beaming, his green eyes glistening with a thin layer of moisture. "And a lot of it, to boot!"

I'm still so worn out that the most response I can manage is a smile.

Andrew looks down at her, touches her little cheeks with the backs of his fingers, and kisses her forehead. After a few moments, he places her into my arms for the first time. And the second I come face-to-face with my baby girl, I lose it all over again. I can hardly see through the thickness of my tears. "She's so perfect," I say, not taking my eyes off of her. I'm almost afraid to, scared that if I look away for just a second that she'll be gone, or that I'll wake up from a dream. "Perfect," I whisper and kiss her tiny nose.

Andrew

THIRTY-SEVEN

*T*he whole family, mine and Camryn's both, are out in the waiting room—minus Camryn's dad and brother. They still don't know if it's a boy or a girl. Camryn and I didn't know through her whole pregnancy. We decided to let her surprise us. And she did.

Before I let the family in to see them, I sit with Camryn in the private room we were moved to shortly after the delivery. We've been in here for a short while, waiting on the nurses to bring her back after doing whatever it is they do. I take her into my arms after the nurse checks Camryn's hospital bracelet and matches it up with the one "Baby Parrish" is wearing around her tiny ankle. I check it myself too before letting the nurse leave. And I look her over real good. One can never be too careful these days, and I'm gonna make damn sure they bring the same baby back they left with. But there's no mistaking that thick blonde hair and that small yet blood-curdling scream that makes me completely submissive to her. If she could talk, I'd do anything she said without thinking twice about it. *Give me a bottle!* Yes ma'am! *Change my diaper!* You got it! *Step on that nurse's foot for wrapping me up like a frickin' burrito!* All right, babygirl!

Camryn holds her close to her chest, letting her suckle on her breast.

When Camryn first found out that she was pregnant again was the day before we moved into our new house. But she didn't tell me about it until after my doctor's appointment that following Monday. She said she was afraid to, I guess in the same way I was afraid to tell her right away that I was having headaches again. But after that, we talked a lot about how we were going to do things differently this time. One of those things was her decision to breast-feed. With the first pregnancy, Camryn wasn't too thrilled about a baby sucking on her tit, especially when she might need to feed her in public. Back then, I was just agreeing with her wishes and never tried to change her mind. I had no reason to, really.

But this time, when Camryn brought the issue up again, she said, "Y'know what, baby? I've been reading a lot more about pregnancy and the benefits of breast-feeding, and I really don't care what people think. I feel like I want to and I *should*."

And I said, "Then I think you should, too."

I sit down next to her. I was glad she made that decision on her own, without me adding my input. Hey, as long as I don't start that man-lactating stuff and she expects *me* to try it, I'm good with whatever decision she makes.

"I read that most babies are born with blue eyes," Camryn says, looking down at her, "but I think later she'll have your green eyes."

I brush our daughter's head lightly with my fingertips. "Maybe so." I can't stop looking at the two of them, my beautiful wife and my precious little girl. I feel like I've stepped into another world, one brighter than I ever imagined. I really didn't think I could be any happier the way I have been with Camryn. I didn't think that was possible.

I think Camryn is still somewhat in shock.

"What's on your mind?" I ask, never losing my warm smile.

Her tired eyes soften as she looks up at me. "You were right," she says.

The baby makes a little sucking noise, so faint I barely hear it, but I find myself attentive to every noise and move she makes.

Camryn goes on, "You said that I wouldn't miscarry this time. You said that your tumor wasn't going to come back. You said that everything would work out. And it did." She glances at the baby for a moment, brushing her eyebrow with her finger, and then looks back up at me. "Thank you for being right."

I stand up from the chair, take one side of her face and chin into my hand, and I raise her head so I can kiss her lips.

There's a soft knock at the door and it opens slowly. My mom's head peeks around the corner.

"Come on in," I say, gesturing her inside.

The oversized door opens the rest of the way, and so many people walk into the room one after the other that I stop counting after Aidan and Michelle, who is five months pregnant.

There's a lot of hugging going around, everybody wrapping their arms around my back but trying to get a glimpse of the baby at the same time.

"Congratulations, bro," Aidan says, patting my back. "I had a feeling you'd have one before me." He reaches over and rubs Michelle's rounded belly. She playfully brushes his hand away and says something about how he better not stick his finger in her belly button again. Then she hugs me and makes her way to Camryn's bedside.

"We're having a boy," Aidan says.

"Really?" I ask. "Awesome."

The announcement gets Camryn's attention too, but Michelle speaks up first.

"He doesn't know that for sure," she says. "He just *thinks* he knows."

Camryn laughs lightly and says, "Take it from me, if a Parrish brother says he's having a boy or a girl, he's probably right."

"All right, well we'll see," Michelle says, still not convinced.

I look at my brother, and I've seen his confident look before. Yeah, they're definitely having a boy.

"Oh my God," I hear Natalie say quietly from somewhere in the room, "the blanket is pink. Does that mean what I think it means?" She brings both hands up to her face, her ring-adorned fingers touching her lips. I'm actually surprised that she's being so tame. Blake stands next to her, quiet as ever.

Camryn looks at me first and I give her the nod of approval and then she says to everybody, "Yes, this is our daughter."

All of the women immediately migrate the rest of the way through the room and over to the bed. Camryn's mom reaches out, first wanting to hold her, and Camryn covers her breast with her gown and carefully hands her over.

"Oh, she's so beautiful, Camryn," Nancy says harmoniously. Her bleached-blonde hair is fixed into a sloppy bun on the top of her head. Her eyes as blue as Camryn's. They really do favor one another. "She's perfect. My perfect little granddaughter." Camryn's stepdad, Roger, looks terrified standing against the wall by himself. I'm not sure if it's because this kind of thing makes him uncomfortable or because he realizes he's now married to a grandmother. I laugh inside.

Asher hugs me next. "If it would've been a boy, I would've been worried with having another one of *you* running around." He grins and nudges me with his elbow.

"Yeah, well, just wait, little brother," I say, sucking on my tooth, "you're next in line, and another one of you is just as bad as another one of me."

"I don't know about that," he counters.

"No, you're right," I say. "You have to have a girlfriend first to pull it off. I don't think you have much to worry about as far as having any kids anytime soon."

"Dude, I have a girlfriend," he says.

"Who? Lara Croft? Or one of Luis Royo's girls?" I laugh.

"Whatever, man," he says, crossing his arms and shaking his head, but I know it'll take a lot more to get under his skin than that. If I didn't screw with him he'd think something was wrong with me.

"Uncle Asher," I say, to make up for it anyway. "It has a nice ring to it."

He nods contemplatively and says, "Yeah, I think it does, too."

Nancy passes our daughter to my mom next. I've never seen her so proud before. She keeps looking over at me and then back at the baby, back and forth.

"She's got your nose and your lips, Andrew," my mom says.

"And Camryn's hair and her lungs," I point out.

Natalie is at the foot of the bed now and she's fidgeting, her hands down in front of her. My mom notices how anxious she is to hold her, so she kisses her new granddaughter on the head and passes her to Natalie.

"I hope you washed your hands, Nat," Camryn says from the bed.

"I did!" Natalie says, and then ignores Camryn and starts talking to my daughter even though she's asleep, "Oh, you are the cutest thing I've ever seen." Her voice rises a little higher the more excited she gets. Then she looks up straight at Camryn and says with a serious face, "Oh my God, I want one."

Blake's eyes get huge, and I think he's stopped breathing. When I look back at him a few minutes later, he's already made his way to stand next to Roger against the wall.

Camryn's aunt Brenda holds her next, and then one of her cousins. After Michelle holds her for a few minutes and gushes about how beautiful she is, she places her back in Camryn's arms. I take the chair next to Camryn against the bed again.

"So, have you decided on a name?" my mom asks.

Camryn and I look at each other, and we're both thinking the same thing.

"Not yet," Camryn answers, and it's all that she says. I know I'm probably the only one in the room who sees it now that the name issue has been brought up: Camryn can't help but think about Lily. But she lets that moment pass and kisses our baby on the cheek, so obviously proud of what she has despite what she lost.

Most of the family is gone before night falls, but our moms hang around a little longer afterward, getting to know each other. This is the first time they've officially met. And finally they leave, shortly before seven, just as the nurse comes into the room to check on the baby and Camryn.

When the three of us are alone again, I dim the lights in the room so that only the one near the private bathroom is on. Our daughter is sleeping soundly in Camryn's arms. I know Camryn's tired, completely exhausted, but she can't bring herself to lay the baby down so she can get some sleep herself. I offered to take her so she could sleep, but she insisted she stay awake.

I watch the two of them for a moment, such a perfect moment, and then I walk over and sit down on the side of the bed next to them.

Camryn looks over at me, then back down at our sleeping angel.

"Lily," I say simply.

Camryn looks back over at me, confused.

I nod slowly as if to say, *Yes, you heard me right*, and I touch our baby's soft head again.

"Do you remember what I told you? Back in Chicago when I found the pills?"

She shakes her head no.

This time I touch Camryn's face, tracing my fingers down one side and then the other.

"I said that Lily just wasn't ready then." I pause and then add with a smile, "Same soul, different body."

Something thoughtful sparks in Camryn's eyes. She tilts her head gently to the side, looking at me in wonder. And then she gazes down at the baby again and doesn't look back up for what seems like forever.

When she does, tears are trailing down her cheeks. "You think so?" she asks, hopeful.

"Yeah. I do."

She starts to cry harder and gently presses baby Lily against her breasts, rocking her. Then she looks up at me and nods several times. "Lily," she whispers quietly and kisses the top of her head.

The next morning, I stir awake in the chair beside Camryn's bed where I fell asleep the night before. I hear Camryn's voice speaking quietly in the room, and like every other time before, I pretend to be asleep while she reads that letter I wrote her months ago.

Camryn

THIRTY-EIGHT

Dear Camryn,

I know you're scared. I'd be lying if I said I wasn't a little scared, too, but I have to believe that this time around everything will be fine. And it will be.

We've been through so much together. More than most people in such a short time. But no matter what, the one thing that has never changed is that we're still together. Death couldn't take me away from you. Weakness couldn't make me look at you in a bad light. Drugs and the shit that comes with them couldn't take you away from me, or turn you against me. I think it's more than safe to say that we're indestructible.

Maybe all of this has been a test. Yeah, I think about that a lot and I've convinced myself of it. A lot of people take Fate for granted. Some have everything they've ever wanted or needed right at their fingertips, but they abuse it. Others walk right past their only opportunity because they never open their eyes long enough to see that it's there. But you and I, even before we met, took all the risks, made our own decisions without listening to everybody around us telling us, in so many ways, that what we're doing is wrong. Hell no, we did it our way, no matter how reckless, or crazy or unconventional. It's like the more we pushed and the more we fought, the harder the obstacles. Because we had to prove we were the real deal.

And I know we've done just that.

Camryn, I want you to read this letter to yourself once a week. It doesn't matter what day or what time, just read it. Every time you open it, I want you to see that another week has passed and you're still pregnant. That I'm still in good health. That we're still together. I want you to think about the three of us, you, me and our son or daughter, traveling Europe and South America. Just picture it. Because we're going to do it. I promise you that.

You're everything to me, and I want you to stay strong and not let your fear of the past taint the path to our future. Everything will work out this time, Camryn, everything will, I swear to you.

Just trust me.

Until next week…

Love,
Andrew

I look up from the letter in my hand, letting it rest on the bed at my side, clasped in my fingertips. Lily is sound asleep next to me in the hospital bassinet. It took some convincing by Andrew before I finally agreed to lay her in it instead of just holding her throughout the night. But I did wake up often to check if she was still breathing. I check again now. I can't help it; I'll probably do that for months.

Finally, I fold Andrew's letter again into the same worn creases. He probably thinks that I'll stop reading it now that Lily has been born. But I won't. I never stopped reading the first letter he ever wrote me, but he doesn't know that. Some things I keep to myself.

"Ready to put those destinations into that hat?" Andrew asks.

I wonder how long he's been awake. I look over at him and smile. "Let's wait a few months."

He nods and rises from the chair.

"How did you sleep like that?" I ask. "You should've gotten on the couch." I glance at the small couch next to the window.

Andrew stretches his arms out at his sides and then pops his back and his neck. He doesn't answer.

"I guess we can finally get all of that stuff from the first baby shower at my mom's and bring it to the house," I say.

Andrew smiles mischievously.

"Wait . . . you already did it, didn't you?"

He stands up and stretches some more. "Technically, not me. Yesterday, Natalie, Blake, and your mom took everything over there after we left for the hospital and they've already set it all up."

I never wanted to do that during the pregnancy. It was just another way of worrying about getting ahead of myself and then miscarry all over again. Same reason I refused to know the sex of the baby before she was born. I didn't want to focus or depend on any of that stuff like I did before. I thought it might jinx it. Andrew didn't really agree with it, but he never said anything or tried to convince me otherwise.

"And, as you can probably imagine," he goes on, "since Michelle and my mom are in town, there's a lot more than just the baby shower gifts waiting for you when you get home."

———

The next day, when Andrew opens the front door of our house and I walk in with Lily in my arms, I see right away that he was right about that, too. The house is immaculate. I never could've cleaned it like this myself. As Andrew walks me through the living room toward the hallway, I glimpse one baby monitor on the kitchen bar as I walk by, one on the living room coffee table, one on the counter in the bathroom, and, finally, one in Lily's room when I step inside.

I gasp with wide eyes. "Oh wow, Andrew, look what they did!"

Lily stirs in my arms, probably from the excitement in my voice, but quickly she becomes still again.

The baby bed is set against one wall with a cute Winnie the Pooh musical mobile hovering over the top. A matching chest of drawers and changing table sits against the wall by the window. Andrew opens the drawers to reveal that each one is full of clothes and receiving blankets and burp cloths and little socks and other various things. He opens the closet and I see dozens of little dresses and outfits. So many packages of diapers are stacked against the wall near the changing table that I feel like we'll never have to buy diapers ourselves. Of course, I know that's just wishful thinking.

Andrew takes me back out into the hall and opens the closet next to the bathroom to show me the brand-new walker and baby swing and some strange play-gym thing, all still in the boxes they came in.

"I'll have to put them together when she's ready for them," he says. "But that'll be a little while."

"Think you can manage that all by yourself?" I joke.

He raises his chin and says, "Without even reading the instructions."

I just laugh inside.

Then he takes me into our room. There's a white bassinet next to the bed on my side.

"I bought that for you," he says, smiling proudly. "I know you won't be ready to put her in the room by herself for a long time, so I figured you'd need it."

He's blushing. I step right up to him and kiss the side of his mouth. "You were right," I say. "Thank you."

Lily starts to stir again, and this time she wakes up. Andrew takes her from me. "I'll change her," he says.

I pass her over and lie down across our bed and watch him. He lays her down on our bed, too, and unwraps her from the receiving blankets. The cutest yet loudest cries come from her tiny lungs. Her little arms and legs move stiffly back and forth. Her whole head turns beet red. But Andrew doesn't flinch. And when he opens her diaper he doesn't gross out at the surprise she left him. I admit I'm surprised at how easily he's already taken to being a daddy.

———

I started back at Bath and Body Works after my maternity leave was over, but now I'm only on a part-time shift. My boss, Janelle, is awesome, and she likes me so much that she gave me a one-dollar raise when I told her I was expecting. Only me and Natalie work there now; Natalie is full-time and she picks up a lot of my slack since I've been off the past six weeks. But she doesn't mind. Says she's saving for a place of her own. She and Blake seem to be really into each other every time I see them together. Truthfully, I've never seen Natalie this happy before. I thought she was happy when she was with Damon, but I'm realizing all that must've been was tolerance and low self-esteem. Blake is different. I think they just might make it.

Andrew has been working for an auto body and mechanic shop since about three weeks after we moved into our house. His knowledge of cars really earned him a great spot on the payroll. He's definitely making way more money than me, but he tries to make me feel better about that by saying: "This ain't shit compared to you pushing my baby girl through your—" I stop him right there each time.

Not necessary, Andrew. But thanks!

Child care is pretty much only for rich people, in my opinion. Honestly, I don't see how anyone working a minimum-wage job can afford child care. They'd be working *just* to pay it, which makes no sense. But aside from that, Andrew and I both agreed that we don't want to leave our daughter in the care of strangers, anyway. So, I worked it out with Janelle that I work only part-time shifts in the evenings when Andrew is home and every other weekend.

We've been living well and pulling everything off as though we've been doing it this way our whole lives. We may have six figures in savings, but we are no strangers to putting back as much as we can from our earnings and spending as little as possible. Other than our day jobs, Andrew and I have been playing gigs pretty consistently, every other Saturday night when I'm not working, at a bar that Blake's brother Rob opened up in town. Something happened with the Underground and Rob had to shut it down. Rumor is that Rob narrowly avoided a jail sentence. I'm guessing it had to do with him not having a bar license, I don't know. But Blake is manager of the new bar now, and on the nights that Andrew and I perform there we get half of the cover charge, which is more than we've ever made playing at any bar other than Aidan's. Last Saturday, we raked in eight hundred bucks.

It's just more cash flow for our savings and our future plans to go wherever that hat tells us to go.

And although Andrew will always put his heart and soul into every performance, like he always has, I can tell now that when we're up on that stage together that he just can't wait to be finished so we can pick Lily up from my mom, or whoever is lucky enough to have her for those few hours at night.

Andrew is so great with Lily. He never ceases to amaze me. He gets up in the middle of the night about as much as I do to change her diapers, and sometimes he even stays awake with me when I feed her. He has his guy moments, too, so he's not entirely Mr. Perfect. Apparently, he's not fully immune to crappy diapers, and just this morning I caught him gagging while trying to change her. I laughed, but I felt so bad for him that I couldn't help but take over. He left the room with the neck of his shirt pulled over his mouth and nose.

And... well, I don't really want to get too ahead of myself with the assumption, but I think Lily may have softened Andrew so much that he might actually like Natalie now. Maybe just a little. I don't know, but whenever Nat is over, holding Lily and making Lily smile by talking to her with that animated personality of hers, Andrew seems OK with it. By the time Lily is three months old, I honestly can't remember the last time Andrew called Natalie a hyena behind her back, or gave me that exasperated look when he knew she wasn't looking.

He still cringes when she refers to herself as Lily's godmother, but... baby steps. He'll come around.

Andrew

THIRTY-NINE

February 9—Lily's first birthday

"idan and Michelle are here!" I hear Camryn say from the living room.

I fasten the last button on the back of Lily's dress and then take her by the hand. But she doesn't like it when I hold her hand and always wiggles it away and grasps my index finger instead.

"Let's go, baby girl," I say looking down at her. "Uncle Aidan and Aunt Michelle are here to see the birthday girl."

I swear she knows what I'm saying.

She squeezes my finger as tight as she can, giggles, and takes one big step forward, as if I'm not fast enough to keep up. With my back arched over, I take fast half steps as we shuffle down the hallway, letting her run on her chunky little baby legs out ahead of me. When she starts to fall as she rounds the corner, I grip her hand, lift her slightly off her feet, and let her get her balance again. She started walking at ten months old. Her first word was "Mama" at six months. At seven months she said "Dada," and I melted when I heard her call me that the first time.

And Camryn was right—she's got my green eyes.

"*Lily!*" Michelle says all dramatic-like, squatting down to

Lily's level and wrapping her up in her wide arms. "Oh my goodness, you're so *big*!" She kisses her cheeks and her forehead and her nose, and Lily cackles uncontrollably. "Nom nom nom!" Michelle adds, pretending to eat her cheeks.

I look over at Aidan, who has my nephew, Avery, attached to his hip. I reach out for him, but he's shy and recoils toward Aidan's chest. I back off, hoping he doesn't start crying. Aidan tries to coax him.

"Is he walking yet?" Camryn asks, standing next to me.

Michelle follows Lily into the living room where a plethora of pink and purple helium balloons are pressed against the ceiling. When Lily realizes she can't reach the balloons, she gives up and goes straight over to her stack of presents on the floor.

Aidan hands two wrapped gifts to Camryn, and we all join Michelle and Lily in the living room. Camryn sets the gifts next to the others.

"He's been trying," Aidan answers about Avery's walking progress. "He holds on to the couch and walks alongside it, but he hasn't quite got the urge to let go yet."

"God, he looks just like you, bro," I say. "Poor kid."

Aidan would punch me in the gut if his arms were free.

"He's adorable," Camryn says as she reaches out to take him.

Of course he is, but I have to mess with my brother.

Avery looks at her like she's crazy at first, but then gets me back for talking crap about his daddy by going straight to Camryn with no problem.

Aidan laughs.

Nancy and Roger, Natalie and Blake, Sarah and her boyfriend, who already has a kid from an ex-girlfriend, all show up practically at the same time. Afterward, our next door neighbors, Mason and Lori, a young married couple with a two-year-old, show up with gifts. Lily, being the little show-off she is, bends over with her hands and head on the carpet, sticking her diaper-covered butt in the air. Then she pretends to fall down and says "Uh-oh," to everyone's laughter.

"Look at that curly blonde hair," Michelle says. "Was Camryn's hair that white when she was a baby?" she asks Camryn's mom, who is sitting next to her.

Nancy nods. "Yeah, it definitely was."

Later, after everyone has arrived, Lily gets to open her presents and, just like her mama, she sings and dances and puts on a show for everybody. And then when she gets to blow out her candle (really, I kind of blew it out for her) she practically bathes herself in cake and purple icing. It's in her hair and hanging off her eyelashes and shoved up both nostrils. Camryn tries, futilely, to keep her from making too big of a mess, but she gives up and lets Lily have her fun.

Lily's passed out cold from all of the excitement long before the last of her guests leave.

"I think the bath did it," Camryn whispers to me as we stand over her bed.

I take Camryn by the hand and pull her along with me, shutting Lily's door but leaving it open just a crack.

We lie on the couch together watching a movie for the next two hours, then Camryn kisses my lips and leaves to take a shower.

I turn off the TV and lift up from the couch and look around the room. I hear the water running in the shower and the cars driving by on the street outside. I think about the conversation I had with my boss yesterday, about how since I've been at my job for nearly two years now, that I have two weeks of vacation time coming up. But I know that two weeks just aren't enough when it comes to Camryn and me doing the things we want to do. The whole job situation is the only thing that we never quite worked out when it comes to what we'll do when we want to leave Raleigh for a month or more. Neither one of us wants to lose our jobs, but we ultimately came to one conclusion at least: it's a sacrifice that we're willing to make and will *have* to make if we're going to fulfill our dreams to travel the world and to avoid being victims of that everyday, monotonous life that scares us shitless.

We know we won't be at these jobs forever. And, well, that's kind of the point.

But I told my boss that, yes, I would need to take those vacation days in the next couple of months. I decided not to give him any kind of notice about leaving, until after I talk to Camryn tonight first.

I get up from the couch and grab a notepad from the drawer at the computer desk and sit down at the kitchen table with it. And I start to write down the various places that Camryn and I have already talked about wanting to see: France, Ireland, Scotland, Brazil, Jamaica…I write until I have a pile of strips of paper in the center of the table. While I'm folding them one by one and dropping them into Camryn's cowgirl hat, I hear the water shut off in the bathroom.

She comes into the kitchen with wet hair plastered against her back.

"What are you doing?" she asks, but realizes it before I have the chance to answer. She sits down next to me. And she smiles. That's a great sign.

"Maybe we should leave in May or June," I suggest.

She drags a comb through her wet hair a few times and seems

to be thinking about it. Then she places the comb on the table. "You think Lily is ready for that?" she asks.

I nod. "Yeah, I think she is. She's walking. We said we'd wait at least until she started walking."

Camryn nods, too, still thinking about it, but she never looks unsure. "Have to get her started early," she says.

We definitely aren't like other families. A lot of parents would completely reject the idea of traveling out of the country with a small child just to be traveling. But not us. I admit that it's not for everybody, but for us it's the only way. Of course, our "travels beyond" won't be like the times Camryn and I spent on the road in the United States. Driving around aimlessly for hours and days and weeks on end with a baby in the car isn't entirely feasible—Lily would hate that. No, these travels will be more staying put in cities we want to explore than going from one city to another without much rest in between. And unfortunately, we won't be taking the Chevelle.

Camryn pulls the cowgirl hat over to her and shuffles her hand around inside. "Did you add all the ones we put on the list?" she asks.

"Of course," I say.

She playfully narrows her eyes at me. "You're lying."

"What? No, really I did."

She nudges me in the shin with her bare foot underneath the table. "You're full of shit, Andrew."

Then she starts pulling out the strips of paper and unfolds them and reads them off.

"Jamaica." She sets it down. "France." She sets it on top of the other one. "Ireland. Brazil. Bahamas. Virgin Islands. Mexico." One by one she stacks them on top of each other.

After several more she pulls out the last one, holds it up folded loosely in her fingertips, and she snarls at me. "Something tells me that this doesn't say 'Italy.'" She's trying so hard not to smile.

I really don't know why I thought I could actually pull this off.

While I'm trying not to laugh and keep a straight face, she unfolds the paper and reads its contents: "Australia." She drops the paper on the top of the pile. "I should penalize you for trying to cheat," she says, rounding her chin and crossing her arms stubbornly over her chest.

"Oh come on," I say, unable to keep a straight face after all. "At least I didn't add a few more that say 'Brazil.'" I laugh.

"You thought about it, though, didn't you?!"

I wince at her loud voice, and we both glance toward the hall where Lily is sleeping in her bedroom.

Camryn leans over the table some and hisses through her teeth, "I'm penalizing you. No sex for a week." She leans away again, pressing her back against the chair and smirks at me.

OK, this isn't funny anymore.

I swallow down my pride, hesitate, and then say, "Come on, you can't be serious. You like it as much as I do."

"Of course I do," she says. "But haven't you ever heard anywhere that women have this magical ability to be able to live without it longer? I'll get *myself* off."

"You're bluffing," I say, not convinced.

She nods subtly with that hell-no-I'm-*not* gleam in her eye, and it's making me nervous. "What are you going to do to make up for it, then?"

One side of my mouth lifts into a grin. "Whatever you want." I pause, holding up my finger and add before it's too late, "Well, as long as it's not degrading, disgusting, or unfair."

Her grin getting bigger, Camryn stands from the chair slowly. I watch every move she makes with the utmost attention, a part of me worried I'm going to miss something. She fits her thumbs behind the elastic of her panties and taunts me with the idea of sliding them off.

Oh my fucking God…seriously? You call this *a punishment?*

I try to retain my composure, pretending as though the few gestures she's made haven't affected me in any way whatsoever when, in truth, it takes practically nothing to make me crazy for her.

She walks away from me.

"Where are you going?" I ask.

"To get myself off."

"Huh?"

"You heard me."

OK, so I did, but…that's not how this was supposed to go down.

"But…what's my punishment?"

She stops just long enough to turn and look back. "You're going to watch."

"Wait…*what?*"

I start to follow. *Evil witch.*

She goes into the living room and lies down on the couch, her head resting upon the arm, one leg propped over the back.

Evil, evil witch!

She looks up at me seductively and that's all it takes; the second her eyes meet mine I move over and on top of her, crushing my mouth over hers. "No fucking way, babe," I whisper hotly onto her mouth, and I kiss her even harder.

Her hands grasp the front of my shirt, her tongue tangled passionately with mine.

And then Lily starts to cry.

I stop. Camryn stops. We look at each other for a moment, both of us frustrated, but we can't help but smile. Lily is a deep sleeper and hardly ever wakes up at night anymore, but somehow her timing tonight doesn't surprise me.

"I'll do it this time," she says, lifting herself from the couch.

I stand up, running my hand over the top of my head.

After she disappears down the hallway, I head back into the kitchen and sit back down at the table to scrawl "Italy" on another strip of paper. I drop it into the hat and refold all of the others and drop them in it, too.

Minutes later, the house is quiet after Camryn gets Lily back to sleep. She sits down in the chair next to me again, pulling her bare legs onto the seat and crossing them. Propping one elbow upon the table, she rests her chin in her hand and looks at me with a warm smile, like something's on her mind.

"Andrew," she says. "Do you really think we can do this?"

"Do what, exactly?"

She rests both arms across the table out in front of her, tangling her fingers.

"Travel with Lily."

I pause and then lean my back against the chair. "Yeah, I do think we can pull it off. Don't you?"

Her smile weakens.

"Camryn, do you not want to travel anymore?"

She shakes her head. "No, that's not it at all. I'm just really scared. I've never known anyone personally who has tried anything like that. It's just scary. What if we're just being delusional? Maybe normal people don't do this sort of thing for a reason."

At first, I was worried. I had this gut feeling that maybe she had changed her mind, and while I'd be OK with whatever she wanted to do, a part of me would've been disappointed for a while.

I lean back up and rest both arms across the table in front of me just like Camryn. My eyes soften as I look at her. "I know we can do this. As long as it's what we both want equally, that neither one of us are only doing it because we think it's what the other wants, then yes, Camryn, I *know* we can pull it off. We have the savings. It'll be a few years before Lily starts school. There's nothing stopping us."

"Is it what *you* really want?" she asks. "You promise there's not some part of you that's only going through with it because of me?"

I shake my head. "No. Even though if I didn't want it as much as you, I *would* do it anyway because it's what you want—but no, I truly want it."

That weak smile of hers strengthens again.

"And you're right," I go on, "it's scary, I admit. It wouldn't be so much if it were just you and me, but—think about this for a second. If we didn't do this, what else would we do?"

Camryn looks away in thought. She shrugs and says, "Work and raise a family here, I guess."

"Exactly," I say. "That fear is the fine line between us and them." I gesture outward to indicate "them," the kind of people in the world we want to avoid becoming. Camryn understands; I can see it in her face. And I'm not saying that people who choose to stay in one place all their life and raise a family are wrong. It's the people who *don't* want to live like that, who dream about being something more, *doing* something more, but never pull it off because they let fear stop them before they get started.

"But what will we do?" she asks.

"Whatever we want," I say. "You know that."

"Yeah, but I mean later on. Five, ten years from now, what will we be doing with our lives, with Lily's life? As much as I love the thought of doing it forever, I really can't imagine it being realistic. We'll run out of money eventually. Lily will have to start school. Then, we'll end up right back here and become one of them anyway."

I shake my head and smile. "Make that fear *and* excuses that make up that fine line. Babe, we'll be OK. Lily will be OK. We will do whatever we want, go wherever we want to go and we'll enjoy our lives, not settle for a life that neither of us really want. Whatever happens, whether we start to run out of money, can't find work to replace it, Lily needs school and we have to make the decision to stay put in one place for a long time, even if that place is back here in this house, then we'll do what we have to do. But right now—" I point sternly at the table "—*right now* those aren't things we have to worry about."

She smiles. "OK. I just wanted to make sure."

I nod and reach across the table, nudging the hat over toward her with my finger.

"You get first pick," I say.

She starts to reach inside, but stops and narrows her gaze on me. "Did you put Italy in there?"

"Yes, I did. I promise."

Knowing I'm telling the truth this time, Camryn reaches the rest of the way into the hat and shuffles the pieces of paper around with her fingers. She pulls one out and holds it in her crushed fist.

"Well, what are you waiting for?" I ask.

She places her hand into mine and says, "I want you to read it."

I nod and take the paper from her and carefully unfold it. I read it to myself first, letting my imagination run wild with visions of the three of us here. I was so fixated on winning that bet with

Brazil that I never thought much about any of the other countries, but now that I've lost, it's easy to imagine.

"*Well?*" She's getting impatient.

I smile and toss the strip of paper onto the table, faceup. "Jamaica," I announce. "Looks like we both lost the bet."

Camryn smiles widely. That tiny strip of paper lying on the table in front of us is something so much more than paper and ink. It has officially set in motion the rest of our lives together.

Camryn

FORTY

*A*nd what an amazing and wonderful life it turned out to be.

I remember it like it was yesterday, the day we left in late spring and set off for Jamaica. Lily wore a yellow dress and two flower barrettes in her hair. She didn't cry or fuss on the plane to Montego Bay. She was the perfect angel. And when we arrived at that first destination, the moment we stepped off the plane and into a new country, it all became real.

That was when Andrew and I became...different.

But I'll get to that in a moment.

This was a long time ago, and I want to start from the beginning.

For two months leading up to the day we boarded that plane, I remained afraid of going through with it. As much as I wanted to do it, as often as I told myself that Andrew was right and that I shouldn't worry, I *always* worried, of course. So much so that two days before we were to leave, I almost backed out.

But I thought back to a time when Andrew and I first met, when he made me shove his clothes into that duffel bag, of all things:

"So, where are we going to go first?" I said, folding a shirt he gave me to pack, on top of the pile.

He was still rummaging through the closet.

"No, no," he said from inside, his voice muffled. "No outlines, Camryn. We're just going to get into the car and drive. No maps or plans or—" He popped his head out of the closet and his voice was clearer. "What are you doing?"

I looked up, the second shirt from the pile already in a half fold.

"I'm folding them for you."

I heard a thump-thump *as he dropped a pair of black running shoes on the floor and emerged from the closet. When he made it over, he looked at me like I'd done something wrong and took the half-folded shirt from my hands.*

"Don't be so perfect, babe; just shove them in the bag."

A seemingly insignificant moment we shared, yet it was ultimately what gave me the courage to get on that plane. I knew that if I stayed, if I continued to put too much thought into it, the only thing I'd accomplish would be to let fear control my, *our*, entire life from that point on.

And every day that I look back on our life now, the only thing that scares me anymore is knowing that we came within an inch of spending the rest of our lives in North Carolina.

We spent three weeks in Jamaica, loved it so much that we didn't really want to leave. But we knew that we had so much more to do, so many places yet to see. And so one night after mingling on the beach with the locals, Andrew reached inside the bag (we swapped out the cowgirl hat for a purple Crown Royal bag, since it was easier to carry around) and pulled out Japan. On the other side of the ocean . . .

This was something we didn't anticipate.

Needless to say, we ditched the bag and the draw-a-country-at-random idea altogether because of this. We started choosing where to go next based on our location: Venezuela, Panama, Peru, and eventually Brazil. We saw them all, spending the longest time, two months, in Temuco, Chile, and avoiding at all costs places known to be more dangerous to travelers, cities and even whole countries in any state of unrest. And everywhere we went, we found ourselves feeling more and more a part of each culture. Eating the food. Participating in the events. Learning the languages. Just a few key phrases here and there was mostly what Andrew and I managed.

And we did go back home to the United States for the holidays. Thanksgiving in Raleigh. Christmas in Galveston. New Year's in Chicago. And, of course, we also spent Lily's second birthday in Raleigh. We took Lily to her doctor to get a checkup and to keep her shots up-to-date. And yes, Andrew got checkups too, and just like his daughter, he was as healthy as a horse.

Just before spring, Andrew agreed to the idea of letting Natalie and Blake rent our house. It was kind of perfect, actually. They were looking for a place, and we could have used the income, plus it eliminated us having to pay any more utility bills. We still had plenty of money in the bank, but traveling like we were was definitely putting a dent in it. But we started learning the ins and outs of spending while abroad by taking advantage of hostels and cheap hotels and even cheaper vacation homes. We didn't need luxury, just a safe and clean place for Lily.

But I think what saved us the most money was that we never traveled anywhere as tourists. We didn't buy souvenirs or anything that we didn't need. We weren't there to join the vacationers

on guided tours or to spend money doing all of the things that people planning a vacation might do. We only bought the necessities
and occasionally splurged on some good food or a new toy for Lily
when she'd get bored with the one she had.

And we did perform every now and then for a little extra money,
but with Lily, we never performed together. Since we wouldn't dare
think of leaving Lily in someone else's care even for a few minutes, I
stopped performing altogether, and Andrew played his acoustic and
sang for a while on his own. But ultimately, he stopped, too. Foreign
countries. Different styles of music. Completely different languages.
It didn't take us long to see that our music wasn't as effective in these
places as it was back home.

A few months after Lily's second birthday, Andrew and I
decided that it was time to move on. We wanted to see as much as
we could before we had to settle down somewhere so that Lily could
start school. And I was ready to see Europe. So as summer drew
nearer, Portugal became our next destination.

Andrew and I "grew up" the day we stepped off that plane in
Jamaica. That was what I meant when I said we became different.
Sure, Lily straightened us up a lot after she was born, but when we
walked off the plane and felt the breeze on our faces, not only did I
finally know that the air really *does* feel different in other countries,
but we knew that it was for real. We were far away from home with
our daughter, and no matter how much fun we might have from
that day forward, we could never let our guard down.

We grew up.

Andrew

FORTY-ONE

I think a lot about my life before, even before Camryn and I met, and I see that it's kind of scary how much I've changed. I was what she calls a "man whore" when I was in high school. And, OK, I was a bit of a man whore *after* high school, too—she knows about every woman I've ever been with. About my partying days. She knows pretty much everything about me. Anyway, I think about my past a lot, but I don't miss it. Except every now and then when reminiscing about growing up with my brothers, I do feel that nostalgia that Camryn was talking about our second time in New Orleans.

I don't regret anything I did in my past, as wild as I was at times, but I wouldn't do it over, either. I managed to get through that life and score a beautiful wife and daughter, which I really don't deserve.

I found out yesterday that Aidan and Michelle, after two kids and years of marriage, are getting a divorce. I hate that for them, but I guess not everybody is meant to be together like Camryn and me. I wonder if they could've made it if they hadn't killed themselves working. That bar consumed my brother, and Michelle was being consumed by her job, too. Camryn and I talked about how they seemed to be drifting apart, even on Camryn's first visit to see them before Lily was born.

"All they do is work," Camryn said one night last year. "Work, take care of Avery and Molly, watch TV, and go to bed."

I nodded contemplatively. "Yeah, I'm glad we didn't end up like that."

"Me, too."

Asher, on the other hand, is with a sweet girl named Lea. And I'm proud to say that they decided one day to spontaneously make the move to Madrid. My little brother has really done well for himself, landing a job as a systems software engineer, which allowed him to relocate. He didn't have to. He could've stayed put in Wyoming, but apparently he's more like me than I knew. Thankfully, Lea shares his interests and determination; otherwise, their relationship would end up more like Aidan and Michelle's than mine and Camryn's. And Lea's income from selling handmade dresses on the Internet is pretty awesome, I hear. Camryn thought about trying something like that out, until she realized she'd have to sew.

With them living in Madrid, it gave us a place to stay while we were there ourselves. Asher insisted that we didn't have to pay rent, but we paid it anyway. Camryn didn't want to be a "moocher," as she put it.

"One dollar," Asher said, just to appease her.

"No," Camryn said. "Six dollars and eighty-four cents a week, and not a penny less."

Asher laughed. "Girl, you are kind of weird. Fine. Six dollars and eighty-four cents a week."

It started out that we were only going to stay with my brother for a couple of weeks, but one night, Camryn and I had a heart-to-heart.

"Andrew, I think maybe we should stay put for a while. Here, in Madrid. Or, maybe we should go back to Raleigh. I don't want to, but…"

I looked at her curiously, yet at the same time it was apparent to me that we have been thinking along the same lines. "I know what's on your mind," I said. "It's not as easy as we wanted it to be, traveling with Lily."

"No, it's not." She looked off in thought, and her expression hardened. "Do you think we did the right thing? By taking her to so many places?"

Finally, she looked at me again. I could tell by the look in her eyes that she hoped I would say that yes, we did the right thing.

"Of course we did," I said, and I meant it. "It was what we *wanted* to do when we set out on that first day. We have no regrets. Sure, we had to do things differently for her safety, bypass a lot of places we wanted to see, stay put in places longer than we wanted to so we didn't give her whiplash, but we did the right thing."

Camryn smiled softly. "And maybe we instilled a love for travel in her." She blushes. "I don't know…"

"No, I think you're right," I said.

"So what do you think we should do?" she asked.

We stayed with Asher and Lea for three months before we set out again. We had one last stop to make before we were to head back to the United States: Italy. Camryn finally admitted to me the reason behind her persistent desire to go to Italy. Her dad took her there once on a business trip when she was fifteen. It was just the two of them. And that trip with her dad was the last time she felt like his little girl. They spent a lot of time together. He spent more time with her than he did on business.

"Are you sure it's a good idea?" I asked before we left for Rome.

"What if you go back there and ruin the memory, like you did that day with the woods behind your childhood house?"

"It's a risk I'm willing to take," she said, packing Lily's clothes into our suitcase. "Besides, I'm not going there to relive those six days with my dad, I'm going to *remember* those six days with my dad. I can't ruin something I can't fully remember."

When we got there I witnessed Camryn remembering everything. She took Lily and sat down with her on the Spanish Steps, I imagine much in the same way her dad did when he brought *her* here.

"We love you very much," Camryn said to Lily. "You know that, right?" She squeezed Lily's hand.

Lily smiled and kissed her momma on the cheek. "I love you, Momma."

Then Lily sat between Camryn's legs while Camryn worked her fingers through her blonde hair, twisting it into a new braid and laying it over her shoulder to look just like her own.

I smiled and watched thinking about a day so long ago:

"It would be a friendship thing, I guess," she said. "Y'know, two people who happen to be sharing a meal together."

"Oh," I said, grinning faintly. "So now we're friends?"

"Sure," she said, obviously caught off guard by my reaction, "I guess we are sort of friends, at least until Wyoming."

I reached over and offered my hand to her, and reluctantly, she took it.

"Friends until Wyoming it is, then," I said, but I knew I had to have her. Longer than Wyoming. Forever would be sufficient.

It still blows my mind how far we have come.

After nearly three years on the road it was finally time to go home.

We went back to Raleigh and back to our humble little house. Natalie and Blake moved out and got a new place on the other side of town. Lily later started school, and for the next several years we were happy, but there was always a part of us that felt empty. I watched my little girl grow up into a beautiful young woman with dreams and goals and aspirations in life that rivaled mine and Camryn's. I like to think that we—Camryn and I—are to take credit for how Lily turned out. But at the same time, Lily is her own person, and I think she might've turned out the way she did even without our help.

I couldn't be prouder.

It seems like so long ago. And, well, I guess it was. But even today, I look back on the day I met Camryn on that Greyhound bus in Kansas, and it's still so vivid and alive in my mind that I feel like I could reach out and touch it. To think, if the two of us hadn't left like we did, told society and its judgments to piss off, we never would've met. If Camryn would've let fear of the unknown get to her too much, we might never have gotten on that plane to Jamaica. We truly lived our lives the way *we* wanted to live them, not the way the world expected us to live. We took risks, we chose the unconventional route, we didn't let what anyone thought about our choices get in the way of our dreams, and we refused to settle doing anything for too long that we didn't enjoy. Sure, we did things all the time that we didn't want to do because we had to—worked in a few fast-food restaurants for a while, for instance—but we never let any of it control our lives. We found a way out eventually instead of letting it win. Because we only have one life. We get one shot at making it worth living. We took our shot and ran like hell with it.

And I think we did pretty damn good.

I honestly don't know what else to say. It's not like our life is over now that our story seems to be. Nah. It's definitely far from being over. Camryn and I still have so much left to do, so many places to see, so many of Life's Rules to defy.

Today is the first day of the rest of our lives. It's a special day, for Lily, for us, for everything the three of us stand for. Our story is over, yes, but our journey isn't, because we'll always live on the edge until the day we die.

EPILOGUE

Fifteen years later

Lily

"Lily Parrish!" Mrs. Morrison calls out my name from the stage in the auditorium. I hear my friends and family shouting from the crowd, followed by whistles and clapping.

I reach up and hold my graduation cap on my head as I ascend the wooden steps. It fits oddly. My dad teased me, said it's because I have an oddly-shaped head, and it's my mom's fault because I couldn't have gotten it from him.

As I walk across the stage more whistles and shouting and clapping fills the auditorium. My heart is beating fast against my ribs. I'm so excited. I think I've been smiling this big for the past twenty minutes.

Principal Hanover holds my diploma out to me, and I take it from her hand. The clapping gets louder. I look down at the front row at my parents, standing next to their seats, bright-eyed and animated with excitement. My mom blows me a few kisses. Dad winks at me and claps. They are both so proud of me that it's choking me up. I wouldn't be here if it weren't for them. I couldn't have asked for better parents.

After the graduation ceremony is over, my boyfriend, Gavin, and I make our way through the crowds to find my mom and dad.

Mom engulfs me in her arms and kisses my head. "You did it, Lily!" She squeezes me. "I'm so proud!" I hear the tears in her voice.

"Mom, don't cry. You'll mess up your mascara."

She rubs her finger underneath both eyes.

Dad hugs me next. "Congratulations, babygirl," he says.

I push up on my toes and kiss him on the cheek. "Thank you, Daddy." Then he pulls me around to his side and fits his hand on my waist protectively.

He gives Gavin the evil eye, looking him up and down, the same way he has every time he's seen him in the two years we've been together. But this time, it's all in good fun. For the most part, anyway. It took my dad a year to cut Gavin some slack and trust him enough to let me go out on a date with him *without* him or Mom going with us. So embarrassing. But the overprotectiveness never managed to run Gavin off, and I think that alone gave my parents more reason to respect him.

He is really a great guy, and deep down I think my parents know that.

"Congratulations, Gavin," my dad says and shakes his hand.

"Thanks." Gavin is still kind of terrified of my dad. I think it's cute.

My parents throw a huge graduation party for me at home and everybody shows up. I mean *every*body. There are people here I haven't seen in a few years: Uncle Asher and Aunt Lea came all the way from Spain! Uncle Aidan is here, too, with my cousins Avery and Molly, and his new wife, Alice. My grams, Marna and Nana Nancy (she doesn't ever want to be called anything with a *GR* in it) are here, too. Nana isn't doing so well. She has multiple sclerosis.

"Oh my God, girl, you're going to leave me!" my best friend, Zoey, says as she comes up to me. We grew up together, just like her mom, Natalie, did with *my* mom here in Raleigh.

"I know! I hate it, but you know I'll visit!" I hug her tight.

"Yeah," she says, "but I'm going to miss the hell out of you."

"I told you," I say, "you could always move to Boston to be closer."

She rolls her eyes, her dark-colored hair falling about her shoulders as she steps away and hops up onto the kitchen bar stool. "Well, not only will I *not* be moving to Boston with you, looks like I won't be staying in North Carolina much longer, either."

"What do you mean?" I ask, surprised.

I sit down on the bar stool next to her. My uncle Cole walks into the kitchen with a few empty beer bottles in his hands. He chucks them in the trash.

Zoey sighs, props her elbow on the bar, and starts twirling a few strands of hair between her fingers. "My mom and dad are moving to San Francisco."

"What? Seriously?" I can hardly believe it.

"Yeah."

I can't tell if she's disappointed or just doesn't know how to feel about it yet. "Well that sounds awesome," I say, hoping to encourage her. "You don't want to move?"

Zoey pulls her arm from the bar and crosses her legs. "I don't know what to think, Lil. That's a long way from home. Not like it's just up the street."

"True," I say, "but it's *San Francisco*! I would love to go there."

She smiles a little.

Uncle Cole, in his tall, brooding glory, takes three more bottles of beer from the fridge and wedges them by the necks between his fingers. He smiles at me as he passes and slips into the living room with the house full of people.

He's awesome. When he arrived, he slipped me a congratulations card with two hundred bucks in it.

"Zoey, I think it's great. And honestly, I can't wait to visit my best friend in California. Yeah. That even sounds good when I say it. *California*." I gesture both hands dramatically.

She laughs. "I really am going to miss you, Lil."

"Me too."

Her mom comes into the kitchen behind her with her dad, Blake, not far behind. "Did you tell Lily the news?" her mom asks as she reaches inside the fridge.

"Yeah, I told her just now."

"What do you think, Lily?" her mom asks.

Her dad kisses Zoey on the head, takes the beer from her mom, and heads outside, probably to smoke a cigarette.

"I'm excited for her," I answer. "I'm moving to Boston for college. She's moving to California. We may not be together like we have been growing up anymore, but there's something about not staying stationary in the same place forever that makes it all feel right."

"You are *definitely* the daughter of Andrew and Camryn Parrish, that's for sure," her mom says, grinning.

I smile proudly and hop down from the bar stool to follow her and Zoey back into the living room.

"A toast!" my dad says in the middle of the room, holding up his beer. He looks across the room at me. We have the same green eyes. "To our little girl, Lily. May you show everybody at college how it's done!"

Everybody takes a drink. "To Lily!"

I spend the entire day, all the way until nightfall with my friends and family and, of course, Gavin, whom I love so much. We are so much alike. We met shortly after he moved here from Arizona. His locker was on the same wall as mine, and he ended up in almost all of the same classes as me. Zoey honed in on him first, which isn't a surprise given her flirty personality. I remember her telling me on his first day of school, "That one *will* be mine. You watch and see." And I never had any intention of interfering, but apparently Zoey was too much for someone like Gavin. I think maybe I can give Zoey the credit for Gavin and me ending up together, though. If it wasn't for her, he might never have had an excuse to force himself to talk to me instead.

Zoey was over him as fast as he made it obvious I was the one he was interested in.

It's really weird, too, because Gavin and I are so eerily alike that it almost feels like fate brought us together. We both had our sights set on the same college. We love the same music and movies and books and television shows. We both love art and history and have, during different points in our lives, thought about what it would be like to travel through Africa. Gavin is interested in archeology. I'm interested in archeological conservation.

Gavin wasn't my first boyfriend, or my first kiss, but he was my first everything else. I can't imagine spending my life with anyone other than him.

I hope we turn out like my parents did. Yeah, I really hope for that.

———

After graduation, I spent the summer with my parents. And I didn't waste a minute of that time with them because I knew it would be short. In the fall, I moved to college, and Mom and Dad—well, their plans were as big as mine. I think they did an awesome job raising me, but I knew that once I moved out on my own and started a life for myself with school and with Gavin, my parents would be setting off to fulfill a life dream of their own.

I'm so happy for them. I miss them every day, but I'm *so* happy.

They never forget to mail me letters—not e-mails, but real handwritten letters. I've saved them all, from the ones stamped in Argentina and Brazil and Costa Rica and Paraguay to the ones that came from Scotland, Ireland, Denmark, and places all over Europe. I love it that my parents are the way they are, so free-spirited and driven and in love with the World. I admire them. From the stories they tell me about when they were a little older than me, I realize that their lives, even before they met, started out rocky, but eventually everything fell into place. My mom told me about her past and how she used to be very depressed. She didn't go into too much detail, and I could always tell that she was holding things back. But she wanted me to know that she and my dad would always be there for me, no matter what happens or what decisions I make.

I think she was worried I might make some of the same wrong decisions that she made when she went through some hard times, but honestly, I can't imagine ever being unhappy.

Mom told me about when she met Dad, too. On a Greyhound bus, of all things. I just laughed. But whenever I think about them and about the things they went through together, I can't help but be awed by it.

According to Mom, my dad was a little wild back then. She said the way he used to be is the number one reason why it took him so long to warm up to Gavin. She didn't go into details about that, either, but . . . dang, my dad must've really been . . . Yuk! Never mind.

But I learned so much from my parents. They taught me how precious life is and never to take a second of it for granted, because any second could be my last. My dad was big on me being myself, standing up for what I believe in, and speaking my mind rather than someone else's. He told me that people will try to make me just like them, but not to fall for it because before I know it, I *will* be. My mom, well, she was big on making sure I knew that there is so much more out there in the world than crappy jobs and paying bills and becoming a slave to society. She made sure I understood that no matter what anyone says, I don't have to live in a way that I don't choose. *I* pick my path. *I* make my life one to remember and not one that will fade into the background of every other uneventful life around me. Ultimately, it's my choice and only my choice. It will be hard at times, I may have to flip burgers and scrub toilets for a while, I will lose people I love, and every day won't be as bright as the one before it. But as long as I never let the struggles pull me completely under, one day I will be doing exactly what I want to do. And no matter what happens, or who I lose, I won't be sad forever.

But what I think I learned the most from my parents is how to love. They love me unconditionally, of course, but I mean the way they love each other. I know a lot of married couples—most of my friends' parents are still married—but I've never quite known two people more devoted to each other than my mom and dad. They've been inseparable all my life. I can only recall a couple of arguments between them, but I've never heard them fight. Ever. I don't know what it is that makes their marriage so strong, but I sure hope that whatever it is, they passed some of that magic onto me.

Gavin walks into my dorm room, shutting the door behind him. He sits down on the edge of my bed. "Another letter from your folks?"

I nod.

"Where are they now?"

"Peru," I say, looking back down into the letter. "They love it on that side of the world."

I feel his hand on my knee to comfort me. "You're worried about them."

I nod again, gently. "Yeah, as always, but I worry about them more when they're over there. Some places are really dangerous. I just don't want them to end up like—"

Gavin reaches out and fits my chin in his fingertips. "They'll be fine, you know they will."

Maybe he's right. My mom and dad have been backpacking across the world for two years now, and the worst danger they've encountered—by what they've told me, anyway—was that my dad was robbed once and another time they had an issue with their passports. But anything could happen, especially being alone like that with only backpacks and the open road.

Apparently, I'm a lot like my mom when it comes to how much I worry.

"Two more years and they'll be just as worried about you," he adds, and then pecks me on the lips.

"I guess so," I say, smiling up at him as he stands from the bed. "My mom will probably be up every night wondering if I got mauled by a lion."

Gavin smiles a crooked smile.

We decided six months ago that we really want to go to Africa after college. When we first met, it wasn't so much an idea as it was something we brought up in casual conversation. But now, it has become our goal. At least for now. A lot can change in two years.

I fold the letter and place it back inside the discolored envelope and set it on my nightstand.

Gavin reaches out his hand to me. "Ready?" he asks, and I take it and stand up from the bed with him.

I go to leave the room to celebrate Gavin's birthday with our friends, and just before I step out into the hall, I look back once at the letter before closing the door softly behind me.

A LETTER FROM THE AUTHOR

Dear Reader,

　　As with just about every book written, there are scenes that just don't make the final cut. What you're about to read is the "baby shower scene" that ultimately didn't make it into the book, but I thought it would be nice to at least let you all read it.

　　The scene introduces you to Anna, a childhood friend of Camryn's who you might recall was mentioned in THE EDGE OF NEVER. When Camryn left home and didn't want her mom to know where she was, she told her mom she was staying with Anna in Virginia. Well, I wanted to introduce her in THE EDGE OF ALWAYS and thought the baby shower was the perfect place to do it. But in the end, not only was Anna's character not vital enough to leave in the book, but the whole scene was cut because I worried that leaving it would've slowed the story down unnecessarily.

　　I think the best part of this particular scene though are Andrew and Blake's reactions to Camryn playfully asking them if they're ready to take part in the baby shower with the rest of the women. I thought it really demonstrated

Andrew's character, and how he's just like any other guy who is repelled by that kind of stuff.

Enjoy watching Andrew squirm! I sure did. ☺

Sincerely,

BONUS MATERIAL

BONUS DELETED SCENE
CAMRYN'S BABY SHOWER

"I'm so glad you're home," my mom says. She grabs me and hugs me. I can smell the hair dye she recently had put on her hair, and it's a hundred times stronger than usual.

"Me too, mom," I say, hugging her back tight and trying not to fall over from the chemical overload.

Just like Natalie had done, my mom puts her hands on my stomach and rubs it, smiling like she just won the lottery. I'm starting to think my belly is going to get more attention than me on this visit! And that's perfectly OK. It just makes me smile.

Natalie and my mom did an awesome job with the baby shower decorations. The living room and kitchen are decorated in pink and purple and white. Dozens of see-through balloons are pressed against the ceiling with glitter and pastel-colored confetti inside of them, long colorful streamers dangle from the bottoms and float amid the room. A cute banner with a stork carrying a pink blanket in its beak reads: WELCOME BABY GIRL! stretched across the wall over the fireplace. Little girly-colored cookies and pink and purple candies are placed on a big round serving tray in a neat formation.

No one has shown up yet, but there's already a nice mound of gifts sitting in the center of the room. No doubt, my mom and Natalie would go all out in the gift-giving area.

Andrew comes into the living room with Blake close behind and he and my mom hug and say their hellos. I notice Andrew doesn't look forced to hug her like he did with Natalie. Could he be any more obvious? This also makes me smile. Well, it makes me laugh inside. He can't stand Natalie, but it's cute how he tries oh so hard to pretend. I admit she's not an easy one to manage unless you've known her for several years and have built up an immunity. Or you're sleeping with her. I should probably feel bad for thinking about my best friend like that, but I don't. Natalie knows the brutal truth as much as I do. And she's proud of it.

"People will start arriving within the hour," my mom says. "Oh, this is so exciting!"

I had a good relationship with my mom growing up and she has always been there for me, but it's kind of weird seeing her this excited about something other than her new husband and the dozens of places he's been taking her since July. But I like it. I kind of miss the mom that used to take me with her to the beauty salon and out shopping on Saturdays.

"Who all did you invite?" I ask, taking a pink cookie from the tray. I nibble on the corner of it.

I glance over to see Andrew and Blake talking near the kitchen entrance. He smiles across the room at me and I get lost in it for a second.

"*Every*-body," Natalie answers. "Gwen and Vivian, Lori Shepherd, who is bringing her sister along—never met her, but I figured so what, just means more free stuff for you. Oh, and Jennifer Matthews said she'd come."

"I thought she was moving to Florida?"

Natalie shrugs and goes on.

"Alicia and Lea from our favorite Starbucks will be here, too."

My mom says, "Your aunts will be here. Your cousin Steph. Bonnie can't make it, she's got the flu."

The two of them go back and forth naming off people. Thirty minutes later and the first of the guests arrive. I go to the door with my mom to let them in, and I'm surprised to see my friend Anna from Virginia in all of her red-haired glory. She walks in with three gift bags dangling from her arms and a huge, glistening smile. We hug and do the ten-second catch up before we make our way back into the living room. More arrive almost immediately after and by this time, Andrew and Blake look like two scared little boys standing in a room full of aunts and sisters and hormones.

"Ummm, is that your fiancé?" Anna whispers to me looking toward Andrew and Blake.

She takes my hand and glances briefly at my engagement ring.

"Yeah, one of them is."

"Let me guess," she says pressing her shoulder into mine, "the blond guy is hot, but something tells me the one with the dimples is yours."

I nod. "Yeah, that's Andrew."

She barely takes her eyes off of him. "Wow. No disrespect, girl, but he is beautiful." Anna is a welcoming change from Natalie's colorful personality.

My face gets red, and I lock eyes with Andrew again. Anna's right, he really is beautiful.

But right now the smile he's wearing isn't one hundred percent real. I need to save him before he doesn't forgive me for it later.

"I'll be right back," I tell Anna and walk through the room toward him.

Slipping my hand around his elbow, I push up a little on my toes and kiss his lips. "So, are you two ready to play the Hot Flash and Morning Sickness game?" I'm making these up as I go along, but they don't know that.

Andrew's and Blake's faces freeze in a sort of spooked display. Andrew swallows nervously and looks just like Blake now with his hands buried in his pockets. I want to laugh out loud, but I keep it low and peck Andrew on the side of his mouth. "I'm kidding. You two can leave and do whatever." Relief deflates their stiff bodies. "Blake, just have him back here before dark."

Blake grins over at Andrew. "You've got a curfew?"

Natalie walks up behind us and says, "So do you. Be back before dark," and then Andrew is the one grinning.

Natalie sticks her tongue out at Blake. They really are cute together.

Sometimes life takes you off course...

To find out how Camryn and Andrew's journey started

See the next page for an excerpt from

The Edge of Never

ONE

*N*atalie has been twirling that same lock of hair for the past ten minutes and it's starting to drive me nuts. I shake my head and pull my iced latte toward me, placing my lips on the straw. Natalie sits across from me with her elbows propped on the little round table, chin in one hand.

"He's gorgeous," she says staring off toward the guy who just got in line. "Seriously, Cam, would you *look* at him?"

I roll my eyes and take another sip. "Nat," I say, placing my drink back on the table, "you have a boyfriend—do I need to constantly remind you?"

Natalie sneers playfully at me. "What are you, my mother?" But she can't keep her eyes on me for long, not while that walking wall of sexy is standing at the register ordering coffee and scones. "Besides, Damon doesn't care if I look—as long as I'm bending over for *him* every night, he's good with it."

I let out a spat of air, blushing.

"See! *Uh huh*," she says, smiling hugely. "I got a laugh out of you." She reaches over and thrusts her hand into her little purple purse. "I have to make note of that," and she pulls out her phone and opens her digital notebook. "Saturday. June 15th." She moves her finger across the screen. "1:54 p.m.—Camryn Bennett laughed at one of my sexual jokes." Then she shoves the phone back inside her purse and looks at me with that thoughtful sort of look she always has when she's about to go into therapy-mode. "Just look once," she says, all joking aside.

Just to appease her, I turn my chin carefully at an angle so that I can get a quick glimpse of the guy. He moves away from the register and toward the end of the counter where he slides his drink off the edge. Tall. Perfectly sculpted cheekbones. Mesmerizing model green eyes and spiked up brown hair.

"Yes," I admit, looking back at Natalie, "he's hot, but so what?"

Natalie has to watch him leave out the double glass doors and glide past the windows before she can look back at me to respond.

"Oh. My. God," she says eyes wide and full of disbelief.

"He's just a guy, Nat." I place my lips on the straw again. "You might as well put a sign that says 'obsessed' on your forehead. You're obsessed short of drooling."

"Are you *kidding* me?" Her expression has twisted into pure shock. "Camryn, you have a serious problem. You know that, right?" She presses her back against her chair. "You need to up your medication. Seriously."

"I stopped taking it in April."

"What? *Why?*"

"Because it's ridiculous," I say matter-of-factly. "I'm not suicidal, so there's no reason for me to be taking it."

She shakes her head at me and crosses her arms over her chest. "You think they prescribe that stuff just for suicidal people? No. They don't." She points a finger at me briefly and hides it back in the fold of her arm. "It's a chemical imbalance thing, or some shit like that."

I smirk at her. "Oh, really? Since when did you become so educated in mental health issues and the medications they use to treat the hundreds of diagnoses?" My brow rises a little, just enough to let her see how much I know she has no idea what she's talking about.

When she wrinkles her nose at me instead of answering, I say, "I'll heal on my own time, and I don't need a pill to fix it for me." My explanation had started out kind, but unexpectedly turned bitter before I could get the last sentence out. That happens a lot.

Natalie sighs and the smile completely drops from her face.

"I'm sorry," I say, feeling bad for snapping at her. "Look, I know you're right. I can't deny that I have some messed-up emotional issues and that I can be a bitch sometimes—."

"*Sometimes?*" she mumbles under her breath, but is grinning again and has already forgiven me.

That happens a lot, too.

I half-smile back at her. "I just want to find answers on my own, y'know?"

"Find *what* answers?" She's annoyed with me. "Cam," she says, cocking her head to one side to appear thoughtful. "I hate to say it, but shit really does happen. You just have to get over it. Beat the hell out of it by doing things that make you happy."

OK, so maybe she isn't so horrible at the therapy thing after all.

"I know, you're right," I say, "but..."

Natalie raises a brow, waiting. "What? Come on, out with it!"

I gaze toward the wall briefly, thinking about it. So often I sit around and think about life and wonder about every possible aspect of it. I wonder what the hell I'm doing here. Even right now. In this coffee shop with this girl I've known practically all my life. Yesterday I thought about why I felt the need to get up at exactly the same time as the day before and do everything like I did the day before. Why? What compels any of us to do the things we do when deep down a part of us just wants to break free from it all?

I look away from the wall and right at my best friend who I know won't understand what I'm about to say, but because of the need to get it out, I say it anyway.

"Have you ever wondered what it would be like to backpack across the world?"

Natalie's face goes slack. "Uh, not really," she says. "That might… suck."

"Well, think about it for a second," I say, leaning against the table and focusing all of my attention on her. "Just you and a backpack with a few necessities. No bills. No getting up at the same time every morning to go to a job you hate. Just you and the world out ahead of you. You never know what the next day is going to bring, who you'll meet, what you'll have for lunch or where you might sleep." I realize I've become so lost in the imagery that I might've seemed a little obsessed for a second, myself.

"You're starting to freak me out," Natalie says, eyeing me across the small table with a look of uncertainty. Her arched brow settles down, and then she says, "And there's also all the walking, the risk of getting raped, murdered, and tossed on the side of a freeway somewhere. Oh, and then there's all the walking…"

Clearly, she thinks I'm borderline crazy.

"What brought this on, anyway?" she asks, taking a quick sip of her drink. "That sounds like some kind of midlife-crisis stuff— you're only twenty." She points again, as if to underline her next words: "And you've hardly paid a bill in your life."

She takes another sip; an obnoxious slurping noise follows.

"Maybe not," I say, thinking quietly to myself, "but I *will* be once I move in with you."

"So true," she says, tapping her fingertips on her cup. "Everything split down the middle—Wait, you're not backing out on me, are you?" She sort of freezes, looking warily across at me.

"No, I'm still on. Next week I'll be out of my mom's house and living with a slut."

"You bitch!" She laughs.

I half-smile and go back to my brooding, the stuff before that she wasn't relating to, but I expected as much. Even before Ian died, I always kind of thought out of the box. Instead of sitting around dreaming up new sex positions, as Natalie often does about Damon, her boyfriend of five years, I dream about things that really matter. At least in my world, they matter. What the air in other countries feels like on my skin, how the ocean smells, why the sound of rain makes me gasp. "*You're one deep chick.*" That's what Damon said to me on more than one occasion.

"Geez!" Natalie says. "You're a freakin' downer, you know that right?" She shakes her head with the straw between her lips.

"Come on," she says suddenly and stands up from the table. "I can't take this philosophical stuff anymore, and quaint little places like this seem to make you worse—we're going to the Underground tonight."

"What?—No, I'm not going to that place."

"Yes. You. Are." She chucks her empty drink into the trash can a few feet away and grabs my wrist. "You're going with me this time because you're supposed to be my best friend and I won't take no *again* for an answer." Her close-lipped smile is spread across the entirety of her slightly tanned face.

I know she means business. She always means business when she has that look in her eyes: the one brimmed with excitement and determination. It'll probably be easiest just to go this once and get it over with, or else she'll never leave me alone about it. Such is a necessary evil when it comes to having a pushy best friend.

I get up and slip my purse strap over my shoulder. "It's only two o'clock," I say. I drink down the last of my latte and toss the empty cup away in the same trash can.

"Yeah, but first we've got to get you a new outfit."

"Uh, no." I say resolutely as she's walking me out the glass doors and into the breezy summer air. "Going to the Underground with you is more than good deed enough. I refuse to go shopping. I've got plenty of clothes."

Natalie slips her arm around mine as we walk down the sidewalk and past a long line of parking meters. She grins and glances over at me. "Fine. Then you'll at least let me dress you from something out of *my* closet."

"What's wrong with my own wardrobe?"

She purses her lips at me and draws her chin in as if to quietly argue why I even asked a question so ridiculous. "It's *the Underground*," she says, as if there is no answer more obvious than that.

OK, she has a point. Natalie and me may be best friends, but with us it's an opposites attract sort of thing. She's a rocker chick who's had a crush on Jared Leto since *Fight Club*. I'm more of a laid-back kind of girl who rarely wears dark-colored clothes unless I'm attending a funeral. Not that Natalie wears all black and has some kind of emo hair thing going on, but she would never be caught dead in anything from *my* closet because, she says, it's all just too plain. I beg to differ. I know how to dress, and guys—when I used to pay attention to the way they eyed my ass in my favorite jeans— have never had a problem with the clothes I choose to wear.

But the Underground was made for people like Natalie, and so I guess I'll have to endure dressing like her for one night just to fit in. I'm not a follower. I never have been. But I'll definitely become someone I'm not for a few hours if it'll make me blend in rather than make me a blatant eyesore and draw attention.

———

Natalie's bedroom is the complete opposite of OCD clean. And this is yet another way she and I are so completely different. I hang my clothes up by color. She leaves hers in the basket at the foot of her bed for weeks before throwing them all back into the laundry to be washed again because of the wrinkles. I dust my room daily. I don't think she has ever actually dusted her room, unless you count wiping off the two inches of dust from her laptop keyboard, cleaning.

"This will look perfect on you," Natalie says holding up a thin, half-sleeve tight white shirt with Scars on Broadway written across the front. "It fits tight and your boobs are perfect." She puts the shirt up against my chest and examines what I might look like in it.

I snarl at her, not satisfied with her first pick.

She rolls her eyes and her shoulders slump over. "Fine," she says, tossing the shirt on the bed. She slides her hand in the closet and takes down another one, holding it up with a big smile that is at the same time a manipulation tactic of hers. Big toothy smiles equal me not wanting to crush her efforts.

"How about something that doesn't have some random band plastered across the front?" I say.

"It's *Brandon Boyd*," she says, her eyes bugging out at me. "How can you not like Brandon Boyd?"

"He's all right," I say. "I'm just not into advertising him on my chest."

"I'd like to actually *have* him on my chest," she says, admiring the tight-fitting V-neck top made much like the first one she tried to show me.

"Well, then *you* wear it."

She looks across at me, nodding as if contemplating the idea. "I think I will." She takes off the top she's already wearing and tosses it in the laundry basket next to the closet, then slips Brandon Boyd's face down over her huge boobs.

"Looks good on you," I say, watching her adjust herself and admiring what she sees in the mirror at several different angles.

"Damn right he does," she says.

"How's Jared Leto going to feel about this?" I joke.

Natalie spats out a laugh and she tosses her long dark hair back and reaches for the hairbrush. "He'll always be my number one."

"What about Damon, y'know, the nonimaginary boyfriend?"

"Stop it," she says, looking at me through the reflection in the mirror. "If you keep raggin' on me about Damon like you do—" She stops the brush midway in her hair and turns at the waist to face me. "Do you have a thing for Damon, or something?"

My head springs back and I feel my eyebrows knot thickly in my forehead.

"No, Nat! What the hell?"

Natalie laughs and goes back to brushing her hair. "We're going to find you a guy tonight. That's what you need. It'll fix everything."

My silence immediately tells her that she went too far. I hate it when she does this. Why does everybody have to be with somebody? It's a stupid delusion and a really pathetic way of thinking.

She places the brush back on the dresser and turns around fully, letting the jest disappear from her face and she sighs heavily. "I know I shouldn't say that—look I swear I won't pull any matchmaking stuff, all right?" She puts both of her hands up in surrender.

"I believe you," I say, giving in to her sincerity. Of course, I know too that a promise never stops her completely. She may not directly try to hook me up with somebody, but all she has to do is bat those dark eyelashes of hers at Damon about any guy in the place and Damon will know right away what she wants him to do.

But I don't need their help. I don't want to hook up with *anyone*.

"Oh!" Natalie says with her head in the closet. "This top is perfect!" She turns around dangling a loose-fitting black top with the fabric in the shoulders missing. Across the front it reads: SINNER.

"Got it at Hot Topic," she says, sliding it off the hanger.

Not wanting to drag this shirt-choosing session out any longer, I slip off my own shirt and then take it from her hand.

"Black bra," she says. "Good choice."

I slip the top on and check myself out in the mirror.

"Yeah? Say it," she says, coming up behind me with a big smile on her face. "You like it, dont'cha?"

I smile slimly back at her and turn to look at how the bottom of the shirt just barely covers the top of my hips.

And then I notice it says SAINT across the back.

"OK," I say, "I do like it." I turn around and point sternly at her. "But not enough to start raiding your closet, so don't get your hopes up. I'm content with my cute button-up tops, thank you very much."

"I never said your clothes weren't cute, Cam." She grins and reaches up and snaps my bra against my back. "You look frickin' sexy on a daily basis, girl—I'd totally do you if I wasn't with Damon."

My mouth falls open. "You're so damn sick, Nat!"

"I know," she says as I turn back to the mirror and I hear the devilish grin in her voice. "But it's the truth. I've told you before and I wasn't joking."

I just shake my head at her, smiling while picking her brush up from the dresser. Natalie had a girlfriend once, during a short breakup with Damon. But she claimed she was "way too cock-crazy" (her words, not mine) to spend her life with a girl. Natalie's not a *real* slut—she'll knock your face off if you ever call her one—but she is any boyfriend's nympho dream, that's for sure.

"Now let me do your makeup," she says, stepping up to the vanity with me.

"No!"

Natalie thrusts her hands on her hourglass hips and looks at me wide-eyed, as if she was my mom and I just mouthed-off to her.

"Do you want it to be painful?" she asks, glaring at me.

I give in and plop down on the vanity chair.

"Whatever," I say, holding up my chin to give her full access to my face, which has just become her blank canvas. "Just no raccoon-eye shit, all right?"

She cups my chin vigorously in her hand. "Now hush," she demands, barely breaking a smile and trying to look all serious. "An ar*teest*," she says with a dramatic accent and the flourish of her free hand, "needs quiet to vork! Vut do you think these ees, a Deetroit beautee parlor?"

By the time she's finished with me, I look exactly like her. Except for the giant boobs and silky brown hair. My hair is the kind of blonde some girls pay a salon a lot of money to have, and it stops just to the middle of my back. I admit I was lucky in the perfect hair department. Natalie said that my hair would look better if I wore it down and so I did. I had no choice. She was very intimidating...

And she didn't make me look like a raccoon, but she didn't go light on the dark eye shadow, either. "Dark eyes with blonde hair," she had said as she went about applying the thick, black mascara.

"It's sexy hot." And apparently my little open-toed sandals just weren't going to do, because she made me toss them and wear a pair of her pointy-heeled boots, which fit snugly over the legs of my skinny jeans.

"You are one sexy bitch," she says, looking me up and down.

"And you owe me big-time for doing this," I say.

"Huh? *I* owe *you?*" She cocks her head to the side. "No, honey, I think not. You'll owe me before this is over with because you're going to have a great time and will be begging me to take you there more often."

I sneer playfully at her with my arms crossed and my hip popped out. "I doubt that," I say. "But I'll give you the benefit of the doubt and hope that I have a good time, at least."

"Good," she says, slipping on her boots. "Now let's get out of here; Damon's waiting for us."

TWO

We make it to the Underground just as night falls, but not before driving around in Damon's souped-up truck to various houses. He would pull into the driveway, get out and stay inside no more than three or four minutes and never say a word when he came back out. At least, not about what he went inside for, or who he talked to—the usual stuff that would make these visits normal. But not much about Damon is usual or normal. I love him to death. I've known him almost as long as I've known Natalie, but I've never been able to accept his drug habits. He grows copious amounts of weed in his basement, but he's not a pothead. In fact, no one but me and a few of his close friends would ever suspect that a hot piece of ass like Damon Winters would be a grower, because most growers look like white trash and often have hairdos that are stuck somewhere between the '70s and '90s. Damon is far from looking like white trash—he could be Alex Pettyfer's younger brother. And Damon says weed just isn't his thing. No, Damon's drug of choice is cocaine, and he only grows and sells weed to pay for his cocaine habit.

Natalie pretends that what Damon does is perfectly harmless. She knows that he doesn't smoke weed and says that weed really isn't that bad and if other people want to smoke it to chill out and relax, that she sees no harm in Damon helping with that.

She refuses to believe, however, that cocaine has seen more action from his face than any part of her body has.

"OK, you're going to have a good time, right?" Natalie bumps my backseat door shut with her butt after I get out and then she looks hopelessly at me. "Just don't fight it and *try* to enjoy yourself."

I roll my eyes. "Nat, I wouldn't deliberately *try* to hate it," I say. "I *do* want to enjoy myself."

Damon comes around to our side of the truck and slips his arms around both of our waists. "I get to go in with two hot chicks on my arms."

Natalie elbows him with a pretend resentful smirk. "Shut up, baby. You'll make me jealous." Already she's grinning impishly up at him.

Damon lets his hand drop from her waist and he grabs a handful of her butt cheek. She makes a sickening moaning sound and reaches up on her toes to kiss him. I want to tell them to get a room, but I'd be wasting my breath.

The Underground is the hottest spot just outside of downtown North Carolina, but you won't find it listed in the phone book. Only people like us know it exists. Some guy named Rob rented out an abandoned warehouse two years ago and spent about one million of his rich daddy's money to convert it into a secret nightclub. Two years and going strong; the place has since become a spot where local rock sex gods can live the rock 'n' roll dream with screaming fans and groupies. But it's not a trashy joint. From the outside it might look like an abandoned building in a partial ghost town, but the inside is like any upscale hard-rock nightclub equipped with colorful strobe lights that shoot continuously across the space, slutty-looking waitresses, and a stage big enough for two bands to play at the same time.

To keep the Underground private, everybody who goes has to park elsewhere in the city and walk to it because a street lined with vehicles outside an "abandoned" warehouse is a dead giveaway.

We park in the back of a nearby Mickey D's and walk about ten minutes through spooky town.

Natalie moves from Damon's right side and gets in between us, but it's just so she can torture me before we go inside.

"OK," she says as if about to run down a list of dos and don'ts for me, "If anybody asks, you're single, all right?" She waves her hand at me. "None of that stuff you pulled like with that guy who was hitting on you at Office Depot."

"What was she doing at Office Depot?" Damon says, laughing.

"Damon, this guy was *on her*," Natalie says, totally ignoring the fact that I'm right here. "I mean, like all she had to do was bat her eyes once and he would've bought her a car—you know what she said to him?"

I roll my eyes and pull my arm out of hers. "Nat, you're so stupid. It wasn't like that."

"Yeah, babe," Damon says. "If the guy works at Office Depot he's not going to be buying anybody any cars."

Natalie smacks him across the shoulder playfully. "I didn't say he worked there—anyway, the guy looked like the lovechild of... Adam Levine and...," she twirls her fingers around above her head to let another famous example materialize on her tongue, "...Jensen Ackles, and Miss *Prudeness* here told him she was a lesbian when he asked for her number."

"Oh shut up, Nat!" I say, irritated at her serious over-exaggeration illness. "He did *not* look like either one of those guys. He was just a regular guy who didn't happen to be fugly."

She waves me away and turns back to Damon. "Whatever. The point is that she'll lie to keep them away. I don't doubt for a second that she'd go as far as to tell a guy she has Chlamydia and an out of control case of crabs."

Damon laughs.

I stop on the dark sidewalk and cross my arms over my chest, chewing on the inside of my bottom lip in agitation.

Natalie, realizing I'm not walking beside her anymore runs back toward me. "OK! OK! Look, I just don't want you to ruin it for yourself, that's all. I'm just asking that if someone—who isn't a total hunchback—hits on you that you not immediately push him away. Nothing wrong with talking and getting to know one another. I'm not asking you to go home with him."

I'm already hating her for this. She swore!

Damon comes up behind her and wraps his hands around her waist, nuzzling his mouth into her squirming neck.

"Maybe you should just let her do what she wants, babe. Stop being so pushy."

"Thank you, Damon," I say with a quick nod.

He winks at me.

Natalie purses her lips and says, "You're right," and then puts up her hands, "I won't say anything else. I swear."

Yeah, I have heard that before . . .

"Good," I say and we all start walking again. Already these boots are killing my feet.

The ogre at the warehouse entrance inspects us at the door with his huge arms crossed in front.

He holds out his hand.

Natalie's face twists into an offended knot. "What? Is Rob charging now?"

Damon reaches into his back pocket and pulls out his wallet, fingering the bills inside.

"Twenty bucks a pop," the ogre says with a grunt.

"Twenty? Are you fucking kidding me?!" Natalie shrieks.

Damon gently pushes her aside and slaps three twenty-dollar bills into the ogre's hand. The ogre shoves the money into his pocket and moves to let us pass. I go first and Damon puts his hand on Natalie's lower back to guide her in front of him.

She sneers at the ogre as she passes by. "Probably going to keep it for himself," she says. "I'm going to ask Rob about this."

"Come on," Damon says, and we slip past the door and down one lengthy, dreary hallway with a single flickering fluorescent light until we make it to the industrial elevator at the end.

The metal jolts as the cage door closes and we're rather noisily riding to the basement floor many feet below. It's just one floor down, but the elevator rattles so much I feel like it's going to snap any second and send us plunging to our deaths. Loud, booming drums and the shouting of drunk college students and probably a lot of drop-outs funnel through the basement floor and into the cage elevator, louder every inch we descend into the bowels of the Underground. The elevator rumbles to a halt, and another ogre opens the cage door to let us out.

Natalie stumbles into me from behind. "Hurry up!" she says, pushing me playfully in the back. "I think that's Four Collision playing!" Her voice rises over the music as we make our way into the main room.

Natalie takes Damon by the hand and then tries to grab mine, but I know what she has in store, and I'm not going into a throng of bouncing, sweaty bodies wearing these stupid boots.

"Oh, come *on!*" she urges, practically begging. Then an aggravated line deepens around her snarling nose and she thrusts my hand into hers and pulls me toward her. "Stop being a baby! If anybody knocks you over, I'll personally kick their ass, all right?"

Damon is grinning at me from the side.

"Fine!" I say and head out with them, Natalie practically pulling my fingers out of the sockets.

We hit the dance floor, and after a while of Natalie doing what any best friend would do by grinding against me to make me feel included, she eases her way into Damon's world only. She might as well be having sex with him right there in front of everybody, but no one notices. I only notice because I'm probably the only girl in the entire place without a date doing the same thing. I take advantage of the opportunity and slip my way off the dance floor and head to the bar.

"What can I get'cha?" the tall blond guy behind the bar says as I push myself up on my toes and take an empty barstool.

"Rum and Coke."

He goes to make my drink. "Hard stuff, huh?" he says, filling the glass with ice. "Going to show me your ID?" He grins.

I purse my lips at him. "Yeah, I'll show you my ID when you show me your liquor license." I grin right back at him and he smiles.

He finishes mixing the drink and slides it over to me.

"I don't really drink much anyway," I say, taking a little sip from the straw.

"Much?"

"Yeah, well, tonight I think I'll need a buzz." I set the glass down and finger the lime on the rim.

"Why's that?" he asks, wiping the bar top down with a paper towel.

"Wait a second." I hold up one finger. "Before you get the wrong idea, I'm not here to spill my guts to you—bartender-customer therapy." Natalie is all the therapy I can handle.

He laughs and tosses the paper towel somewhere behind the bar. "Well that's good to know, because I'm not the advice type."

I take another small sip, leaning over this time instead of lifting the glass from the bar; my loose hair falls all around my face. I rise back up and tuck one side behind my ear. I really hate wearing my hair down; it's more trouble than it's worth.

"Well, if you must know," I say, looking right at him, "I was dragged here by my relentless best friend who would probably do something embarrassing to me in my sleep and take a blackmail pic if I didn't come."

"Ah, one of those," he says, laying his arms across the bar top and folding his hands together. "I had a friend like that once. Six months after my fiancée skipped out on me, he dragged me to a nightclub just outside of Baltimore—I just wanted to sit at home and sulk in my misery, but turns out that night out was exactly what I needed."

Oh great, this guy thinks he knows me already, or at least my "situation." But he doesn't know anything about my situation. Maybe he has the "bad ex" thing down, because we all have that, eventually, but the rest of it—my parents' divorce; my older brother, Cole, going to jail; the death of the love of my life—I'm not about to tell this guy anything. The moment you tell someone else is the moment you become a whiner, and the world's smallest violin starts to play. The truth is, we all have problems; we all go through hardships and pain, and my pain is paradise compared to a lot of people's and I really have no right to whine at all.

"I thought you weren't the advice type." I smile sweetly.

He leans away from the bar and says, "I'm not, but if you're getting something out of my story then be grateful."

I smirk and take a fake sip this time. I don't really want a buzz and I definitely don't want to get drunk, especially since I have a feeling I'm going to be the one driving us home again.

Trying to take the spotlight off me, I prop one elbow on the bar and rest my chin on my knuckles and say, "So then what happened that night?"

The left side of his mouth lifts into a grin and he says, shaking his blond head, "I got laid for the first time since she left me, and I remembered how good it felt to be unchained from one person."

I didn't expect that kind of answer. Most guys I know would've lied about their relationship phobia, especially if they were hitting on me. I kind of like this guy. Just as a guy, of course; I'm not about to, as Natalie might say, bend over for him.

"I see," I say, trying to hold in the true measure of my smile. "Well, at least you're honest."

"No other way to be," he says as he reaches for an empty glass and starts to make a rum and Coke for himself. "I've found that most girls are as much afraid of commitment as guys are these days, and if you're up front in the beginning, you're more likely to come out of the one-nighter unscathed."

I nod, fitting my fingertips around my straw. There's no way I'd openly admit it to him, but I completely agree with him and even find it refreshing. I've never really given it that much thought before, but as much as I don't want a relationship within one hundred feet of me, I am still human and I wouldn't mind a one-night stand.

Just not with him. Or anyone in this place. OK, so maybe I'm too chicken for a one-night stand, and this drink has already started going straight to my head. Truth is, I've never done anything like that before, and even though the thought is kind of exciting, it still scares the shit out of me. I've only ever been with two guys: Ian Walsh, my first love, who took my virginity and died in a car accident three months later, and then Christian Deering, my Ian rebound guy and the jerk who cheated on me with some red-haired slut.

I'm just glad I never said that poisonous three-word phrase that begins with "I" and ends with "you," back to him because I had a feeling, deep down, that when he said it to me, he didn't know what the hell he was talking about.

Then again, maybe he *did* and that's why after five months of dating, he hooked up with someone else: because I never said it back.

I look up at the bartender to notice he's smiling back at me, waiting patiently for me to say something. This guy's good; either that, or he really is just trying to be friendly. I admit, he's cute; can't be older than twenty-five and has soft brown eyes that smile before his lips do. I notice how toned his biceps and chest are underneath that tight-fitting t-shirt. And he's tanned; definitely a guy who has lived most of his life near an ocean somewhere.

I stop looking when I notice my mind wandering, thinking about how he looks in swim shorts and no shirt.

"I'm Blake," he says. "I'm Rob's brother."

Rob? Oh yeah, the guy who owns The Underground.

I reach out my hand and Blake gently shakes it.

"Camryn."

I hear Natalie's voice over the music before I even see her. She makes her way through a cluster of people standing around near the dance floor and pushes her way past to get to me. Immediately, she takes note of Blake and her eyes start glistening, lighting up with her huge, blatant smile. Damon, following behind her with her hand still clasped in his, notices, too, but he just locks emotionless eyes with me. I get the strangest feeling from it, but I brush it off as Natalie presses her shoulder into mine.

"What are you doing over here?" she asks with obvious accusation in her voice. She's grinning from ear to ear and glances between Blake and me several times before giving me all of her attention.

"Having a drink," I say. "Did you come over here to get one for yourself, or to check up on me?"

"Both!" she says, letting Damon's hand fall away from hers and she reaches up and taps her fingers on the bar, smiling at Blake. "Anything with Vodka."

Blake nods and looks at Damon.

"I'll have rum and Coke," Damon says.

Natalie presses her lips against the side of my head and I feel the heat of her breath on my ear when she whispers, "Holy shit, Cam! Do you know who that is?"

I notice Blake's mouth spread subtly into a smile, having heard her.

Feeling my face get hot with embarrassment, I whisper back, "Yeah, his name is Blake."

"That's Rob's *brother*!" she hisses; her gaze falls back on him.

I look up at Damon, hoping he'll get the hint and drag her off somewhere, but this time he pretends not to "get it." Where is the Damon I know, the one who used to have my back when it came to Natalie?

Uh oh, he must be pissed at her again. He only ever acts like this when Natalie has opened her big mouth, or done something that Damon just can't get past. We've only been here for about thirty minutes. What could she have done in such a short time? And then I realize: this is Natalie and if anyone can piss a boyfriend off in under an hour and without knowing it, it's her.

I slip off the barstool and take her by the arm, pulling her away from the bar. Damon, probably knowing what my plan is, stays behind with Blake.

The music seems to have gotten louder as the live band ends one song and starts the next.

"What did you do?" I demand, turning her around to face me.

"What do you mean what did I do?" She's hardly even paying attention to me; her body moves subtly with the music instead.

"Nat, I'm serious."

Finally, she stops and looks right at me, searching my face for answers.

"To piss Damon off?" I say. "He was fine when we came in here."

She looks across the space briefly at Damon standing by the bar, sipping his drink, and then back at me with a confused look on her face. "I didn't do anything…I don't think." She looks up as if in thought, trying to recall what she might have said or done.

She puts her hands on her hips. "What makes you think he's pissed?"

"He's got that look," I say, glancing back at him and Blake, "and I hate it when you two fight, especially when I'm stuck with you for the night and have to listen to you both go back and forth about stupid shit that happened a year ago."

Natalie's confused expression turns into a devious smile. "Well, I think you're paranoid and maybe trying to distract me from saying anything about you and Blake." She's getting that playful look now and I hate it.

I roll my eyes. "There is no 'me and Blake,' we're just talking."

"Talking is the first step. Smiling at him—(her grin deepens) which I totally saw you doing when I walked up—is the next step." She crosses her arms and pops out her hip. "I bet you've already had a conversation with him without him having to pry the answers out of you—Hell, you already know his name."

"For someone who wants me to have a good time and meet a guy, you don't know how to shut up when things already appear to be going your way."

Natalie lets the music dictate her movement again, raising her hands up a little above her and moving her hips around seductively. I just stand here.

"Nothing's going to happen," I say sternly. "You got what you wanted and I'm talking to someone and have no intention of telling him I have Chlamydia, so please, don't make a scene."

She gives in with a long, deep sigh and stops dancing long enough to say, "I guess you're right. I'll leave you to him, but if he takes you up to Rob's floor, I want details." She points her finger at me firmly, one eye slanted and her lips pursed.

"Fine," I say, just to get her off my back, "but don't hold your breath, because it's *not* gonna happen."

Turn the page for a preview of
J. A. Redmerski's next novel

Song of the Fireflies

Available for pre-order now.

ONE

Elias

They say you never forget your first love, and I have to say that they were right. I met the girl of my dreams when we were both still fans of treehouses and dirt cakes—she made the best dirt cakes in Georgia—and today, seventeen years later, I still see her smile in everything good.

But Bray's life has always been...complicated. Mine, well, I guess the same can be said for me, but as much as she and I are alike, there are just as many things that makes us so very different.

I never thought a relationship with her, other than being the best of friends—sometimes with benefits—could ever work. Neither did she. I guess in the beginning, we were both right. But by the end—and damn, the end sure as hell blindsided us—we were proven wrong. Our love for each other, and I admit a few dozen mistakes along the way are what led us here to this moment, holed up in the back of a convenience store with cops surrounding the building.

But wait...let me start from the beginning.

Fourth of July—Seventeen Years Ago...

The kind of crush a nine-year-old boy has on an eight-year-old girl is almost always innocent. And cruel. The first time I saw Brayelle Bates flitting toward me through the wide-open field by Mr. Paron's pond, she was marked my victim. She wore a white sun dress and a pair of flip-flops with little purple flowers made of fabric sewn to the tops. Her long, dark hair had been pulled neatly into ponytails on each side of her head and tied with purple ribbons. I loved her. OK, so I didn't really "love" her, but she sure was pretty.

So, naturally I gave her a hard time.

"What's that on your face?" I asked as she started to walk by.

She stopped and crossed her arms and looked down at me sitting on my blanket beside my mother, pursing her lips at me disapprovingly.

"There's nothing on my face," she said with a smirk.

"Yes there is." I pointed up at her. "Right there. It's really gross."

Instinctively, she reached up and began touching her face all over with her fingertips.

"Well, what is it? What does it look like?"

"It's everywhere. And I told you it's gross, that's what it looks like."

She propped both hands on her hips and chewed on the inside of her mouth.

"You're lying."

"No I'm not. Your whole face, it's really ugly. You should go to the doctor and get that checked out."

The tip of her flip-flop and her big toe jabbed me in the back of my hip.

"*Owww*! What was *that* for?" I reached around and rubbed the spot with my fingertips.

I noticed my mother shake her head at us, but she went back to her conversation with my aunt Janice.

Bray crossed her arms and snarled down at me. "If anyone out here is gross, it's you. Your face looks just like my dog's ass."

My mom's head snapped around hearing that, and she glared at *me* as if I was the one who cursed.

I just shrugged.

Bray turned on her heels and sauntered away with her chin held high, catching up with her parents who were already many feet out ahead of her. I watched her go, the throbbing in my hip a reminder that if I was going to mess with that girl anymore that there would be more pain and abuse where that came from.

Of course, it only made me want to do it again.

As the pasture filled up with Athen's residents come to see the yearly fireworks display, I watched Bray do cartwheels in the grass with her friend. Every now and then I saw her look over at me, showing off and taunting me. She did get the best of me, after all, and it was only natural for her to gloat about it. I got bored fast sitting with my mom, especially since Bray seemed to be having so much fun over there.

"Where are you going, Elias?" my mom asked as I got up from the blanket.

"Just right over there," I said, pointing in Bray's direction.

"OK, but please stay in my sight."

I sighed and rolled my eyes; mom was always worried I would get kidnapped or lost or hurt or wet or dirty or any number of things.

"I will," I said and walked away.

I weaved my way through the few families sitting in the space between us in lawn chairs and on blankets and with ice chests filled with beer and soda next to them, until I came face to face with that abusive girl I couldn't get enough of.

"You really shouldn't do cartwheels in a dress, you know that, right?" I asked.

Bray's mouth fell open. Her blonde-haired friend, Lissa, who I knew from school, smiled up at me. I think she liked me.

"I have shorts on under my dress thank-you-very-much," Bray snapped. "Why were you looking, anyway?"

"I wasn't *looking*, I just…,"

Bray and Lissa burst into laughter.

My face flushed hot.

Bray had only just moved here from Atlanta a week ago, and it didn't take long for her to fit in. Or rather to pretty much own the place as far as the kids went. She was the kind of girl so damn mean and intimidating and pretty that the other girls knew they had better befriend her or else end up her enemy. She wasn't a bully, she just had this way about her that demanded respect.

"Want to go sit by the pond?" I asked. "The fireworks look cool reflected off the water."

Bray shrugged. "I guess so." Then she went to her feet; Lissa was already standing up ready to go before Bray had even made up her mind.

And just like that, as if I'd never called her ugly and she had never kicked me, we walked side by side toward the pond and sat together for the next two hours. My friend, Mitchell, joined us eventually and the four of us laid on our backs on the grass and watched the fireworks explode in an array of colors in the clear black sky. And although Lissa and Mitchell were there with us, Bray and I carried on with each other as if we were alone. We laughed at stupid jokes and made fun of people walking by. It was the best night of my life and it was only just beginning.

Shortly after the fireworks ended and the darkness settled across the pasture again, most of the town had already packed up and gone home.

My mom found me with Bray, Lissa, and Mitchell.

"Time to go," she said standing over me.

Bray was lying next to me, her head pressed against the side of my shoulder. I hadn't really noticed it much, but my mom sure did. I saw a look in her eye—upside-down since she was standing behind us, which made that look all the more scary—that I've never seen before. I raised up from the grass and turned around to face her.

"Can't I stay and hang out a while longer?"

"No, Elias, I have to work in the morning. It's already late."

She gestured with her free hand for me to get up and follow.

Reluctantly, I did as I was told.

"Oh come on, please Ms. Kline," Mitchell said on the other side of me. "I'll walk home with him."

Mitchell was a year older than me, but I did *not* need him to walk me home. This made me mad, probably because it embarrassed me in front of Bray.

I glared at Mitchell and he looked back at me with apologetic eyes. "I'll see you guys later," I said.

I took the ice chest from my mom to relieve her of some of the load she was carrying, and I followed her through the pasture toward our truck parked along the dirt road. Aunt Janice waved us goodbye and sputtered away in her old beat-up Corsica.

My mom went to bed right after we got home. She was the manager at a hotel and rarely got any time off. My dad lived in Savannah. They divorced three years ago. But I had a great relationship with them both, often staying at my dad's in the summer except that this year he had to go to Michigan for his job and so I stayed with my mom all summer for the first time since their divorce.

I think it was fate. Bray never would've ended up outside my bedroom window that night, tapping on the glass with the tip of her finger if my dad hadn't gone to Michigan. I wondered how she knew where I lived but I never asked, figuring Mitchell or Lissa must've told her.

"You're already in bed?" Bray asked with disbelief as she looked up at me.

I raised the window the rest of the way and the humid summer air rushed in past me.

"No. I'm just in my room. What are you doin' out here?"

A sly little grin crept up on the edges of Bray's lips.

"Want to go swimming?" she asked.

"Swimming?"

"Yeah. Swimming." She crossed her arms and cocked her head to one side. "Or, are you too chicken to sneak out?"

"I'm not afraid to sneak out."

Actually, I kind of am. If my mom catches me she'll whip me with the fly swatter.

"Then come on," she said, waving at me. "Prove it."

A challenge. Fly swatter or not, I couldn't back down from a challenge or she'd never let me live it down. She'd go to school and turn my friends against me. The whole town would think I was a chicken afraid of his "mommy" and I'd grow up an outcast and never have a girlfriend. I'd end up homeless and die an old man living underneath a bridge—these are the things my mom told me would happen to me if I ever dropped out of school.

OK, so I was overthinking this whole sneaking out thing.

I bit down on my bottom lip, thought about it for a moment and when I noticed Bray about to start running that mouth of hers again, I tossed one leg over the windowsill and hopped outside, landing in a smooth crouched position, which I was quite proud of.

Bray grinned, grabbed my hand and pulled me along with her away from my house.

Admittedly, I thought of the fly swatter all the way to the pond in the pasture.

TWO

*B*ray was so free-spirited, she didn't seem to have a worry in the world. I noticed this about her the moment we reached the outskirts of the pasture and she broke away from me and ran out toward it. Her arms were raised high above her head as if she was reaching for the stars. Her laughter was infectious, and I found myself laughing right along with her as I ran behind her. We jumped off the end of the little rickety dock and hit the water with a loud splash, not even stopping to take off her flip-flops or my shirt beforehand.

We swam for a while, and I splashed her in the face every chance I got, until I think she finally had enough and swam back to the dock.

"Have you ever kissed a girl before?" Bray asked, taking me by surprise.

I glanced nervously at her to my left; we both moved our feet back and forth in the water.

"No. Have you?"

Her shoulder bumped against mine hard and she giggled and made a horrible face at me.

"No way. I wouldn't kiss a *girl*. Talk about gross."

I laughed, too. Really, I didn't realize what I had said until after she pointed it out; I was too blindsided by the kissing topic to notice. But I played it off smoothly as though I was just being weird.

"I've never kissed a boy," she said.

There was an awkward bout of silence. Mostly the awkwardness was coming from me though, I was sure. I swallowed and looked out at the calm water. Every now and then I heard a random firework pop off in the distance somewhere. And the song of crickets and frogs surrounded us.

Not knowing what to say, or if I was supposed to say anything at all, I finally added, "Why not?"

"Why not, what?"

"Why haven't you kissed a boy before?"

She looked at me suspiciously. "Why haven't you kissed a *girl* before?"

I shrugged. "I dunno. I just haven't."

"Well, maybe you should."

"Why?"

"I dunno."

Silence. We stared out at the water together, both of us with our hands braced against the dock's edge, our bodies slumped between our rigid shoulders, our feet moving steadily in the water pushing poetic ripples outward across the surface.

I leaned over and kissed her on the cheek, right next to the corner of her mouth.

She blushed and smiled. I knew my face must've been bright red, but I didn't care and I didn't regret it.

I wanted to do it again.

Next thing I know, Bray is jumping up from the dock and running back out into the pasture.

"Fireflies!" she shouted.

I stood up and watched her run away from me beneath the dark star-filled sky and she grew smaller and smaller. Hundreds of little green-yellow dots of light blinked off and on out in the wide open space.

"Come on, Elias!" Her voice carried my name on the wind.

I knew I'd never forget this night. I couldn't have understood why back then, but something within me knew. I would never forget it.

I ran out after her.

"We should've brought a jar!" She kept reaching out her hands, trying to catch one of the fireflies, but she was always a second too late.

On my third try, I caught one and held it carefully in the hollow of both hands so that I wouldn't crush it.

"Oh, you got one! Let me see!"

I held my hands out slowly and Bray looked inside the tiny opening between my thumb and index finger. Every few seconds my hand would light up with a dull glow and then fade again.

"So pretty," she said, wide-eyed.

"Just like you," I said, though I had no idea what made me say that. Out loud, anyway.

Bray just smiled at me and looked back down into my hand.

"OK, let it go," she said. "I don't want it to die."

I opened my hands and held them up, but the firefly just stayed there crawling across the ball of my thumb. I leaned in to blow on it and its tiny black wings finally sprang to life and it flew away into the darkness.

Bray and I spent the whole night in the field chasing the fireflies and laying on the grass, staring up at the stars. She told me all about her sister, Rian, and how she was a snob and was always mean to Bray. I told her about my parents because I didn't have any brothers or sisters. She said I was lucky. We talked forever, it seemed. We may have been young, but we connected deeply on that night. I knew we would be great friends, even better friends than Mitchell and I had been and I had known him since first grade when he tried to con me out of my peach cup at lunch.

And before the night was over, we made a pact with each other that would later prove to live through some very troubled times:

"Promise we'll always be best friends," Bray said, lying next to me. "No matter what. Even if you grow up ugly and I grow up mean, you'll always be my best friend, Elias."

I laughed. "You're *already* mean!"

She elbowed me.

"And *you're* already *ugly*," she said with a blush in her cheeks.

"OK, I promise," I gave in, though really I needed no convincing.

We gazed back up at the stars; her fingers were interlaced and her hands rested on her belly.

I had no idea what I was getting into with Brayelle Bates. I didn't know about such things when I was nine. I didn't know. But I would never regret a moment with her. Never.

———

Bray and I were found early the following morning, fast asleep in the grass. We were awoken by three cops, Mr. Parson who owned the land and my frantic mother who thought I had been kidnapped from my room, stuffed in a suitcase and thrown on the side of a highway somewhere.

"Elias! Oh dear God, I thought you were gone!" She scooped me into her arms and squeezed me so tight I thought my eyeballs were going to burst out of the sockets. She pulled away, kissed me on the forehead, embarrassing the crap out of me, and then squeezed me again.

Bray's mom and dad were there, too.

"Have you been out here all night with him?" Bray's dad asked with a sharp edge in his voice.

My mom immediately went into defensive mode. She stood up the rest of the way with me and wrapped one arm around the front of me, pressing my back against her.

"That daughter of yours," my mom said and already I was flinching before she finished, "she has a mouth on her. My son would never have snuck out unless he was influenced."

Oh geez...

I sighed and threw my head back against her.

"Mom, I—"

"Are you blaming this on my *daughter*?" Bray's mother said, stepping up front and center.

"As a matter of fact, I am," my mom said boldly.

Bray started to shrink behind her dad and I felt worse about her being blamed, every second that passed

Before this got too out of hand, I broke away from my mom's arms.

"Dammit, Mom!"

Her eyes grew wide and fierce and I stopped mid-sentence.

"Watch your mouth, Elias!" Then she looked at Bray's mom again and added, "See, Elias never uses language like that."

"Stop it! Please! I made my own decision to sneak out! I know right from wrong! I chose to do wrong and only I can be blamed for that, so leave Bray out of it!"

I hated shouting. I hated it that I had to put my mom in her place like that in front of her "enemy," but I spoke what I felt in my heart and that's something my mom always taught me to do. Take up for the bullied, Elias. Never stand back and watch someone take advantage of someone else, Elias. Always do and say what you know in your heart to be right, no matter what, Elias.

I hoped she would remember those things when we went home.

My mom sighed deeply and I watched the anger deflate with her breath.

"I apologize," she said to Bray's parents. "Really, I am sorry. I was just so scared something had happened to him."

Bray's mom nodded, accepting my mom's apology. "I understand. I'm sorry, too. I'm just glad they're safe."

Bray's dad said nothing. I got the feeling he wasn't as forgiving as her mom had been.

I was grounded for the rest of the summer for that stunt I pulled. And yes, I met the fly swatter that day to which I vowed never to sneak out of the house again. But whenever it came to Bray, from that time up until we graduated high school, I did sneak out. A lot. But I never got caught again after that first time.

I know you must be wondering why after so many years of being best friends, attending the same school, working together at the local Dairy Queen, even often sharing a bed, why we never became something more to each other.

Well, the truth is that we did.